The Broken Spur

A Novel

The Broken Spur

A Novel

Gary Harmon

The Broken Spur
Harmon, Gary

Cover photo: Rob Smith
Cover design: Drinian Press LLC

Drinian Press LLC
PO Box 63
Huron, Ohio 44839

Online at www.DrinianPress.com.

Library of Congress Control Number: 2017956642

ISBN-10: 1-941929-06-0

ISBN-13: 978-1-941929-06-3

Printed in the United States of America

To
Lawrence Harmon

He was a great cowboy who could have been even better if he hadn't been so busy being a daddy. He knew a lot about cows and a lot about boys.

To
Juanita

She always loved her son. Even when he brought the pony into the kitchen.

Authors note: So many people have helped and encouraged me I'm almost sure to forget someone. Some names that come to mind on the spur of the moment are Dona, Lauren, Jenny and Justin. There are others, to be sure, who helped me tell the tale of *The Broken Spur*.

The Broken Spur

Contents

Part One: The Trail

Part Two: Old Robert

Book Three: The Big House 1888

The Broken Spur

A Novel

Part One: The Trail

Chapter One

Raiders at Murphy Flats
1888

The dream lay to the west. How far to the west Pamela could only imagine. Forty-four days on the road were behind her and what was left ahead could have dissuaded all but the strongest and most determined. Pamela Carstin felt no such exhaustion. Certainly, no suggestion of quit. Despite the pitifully slow pace of the oxen, the constant struggle with the string of horses and the debilitating torture of the Kansas summer heat the dream was alive within her as ever. To start a new life in the west with Alex and Justin. To build a horse herd of animals as new as the dream itself. This was enough for her. She felt as though she could go on forever. There had never been quitting in her makeup.

Pamela Carstin's graceful form, viewed through the old brass telescope, was the most disturbing sight Beaver Parker ever remembered encountering. The thought of the soft white flesh that pushed tautly against the light, blue chambray gave him a hollow feeling in the pit of his stomach. It was a feeling not unlike that of hunger, yet somehow, strangely different. He had felt this before when the doing of murder was on his mind.

More of a burn, he thought. *I'm burnin' up inside.* He glanced at the rifle crooked in his arms. *Live or die*, he thought. *Here's the power to live or die.* Beaver thought often of rifles– rifles, women, and knives. The Springfield carbine felt good to the touch. He loved the 45/70. When it hit, it was all over no matter what the target. Though unfired, the barrel was hot to the touch. The broiling Kansas sun beat down upon his prone body as an unrelenting furnace. Somehow this blistering heat that would have tortured other men only served to intensify Beaver's longings. His mind was often cloudy, but here in this bright sun light and intense heat, stimulated by the thoughts of the woman in the cottonwoods, he found his thoughts were somehow sharp and clear. He savored this absolute clarity that he experienced so seldom.

His mouth was hot and dry and tasted of old iron. He was lost deep into the haunts of his favorite thoughts. He kept at it. He liked these dark and terrible images and the passions they brought with them. Relentless now, he swirled the images in his brain, forcing himself to ponder the single sinister notion that he knew would exhilarate him most. *Killing*. It was in killing that one found his true self. He knew that while he may appear small and frail to those who looked upon him, there was no frailty in killing. His rifle changed all the differentials in position that were established by a man's size. It took courage to kill. Mostly he knew it took willingness. Beaver Parker had both. And he had one more thing even more potent: Beaver had desire. He liked killing. He drank in the feeling, savoring it, letting it spread throughout him like the raw fire of green whiskey. He had felt this way as long as he could remember. Beaver was nineteen years old. He believed at least that he was nineteen. There was no way to be exactly sure. As far back as he could recall he had imagined the exhilaration that went hand and hand with robbery and murder.

Beaver could often visualize, in the dim corners of his clouded mind, his fantasy victim's frantic dread. Now here in the blistering Kansas heat, with an actual victim right before him -- the perfect woman --- he could envision the scene even more vividly than ever before. He could feel her terror coursing through his own body. It was a mixed feeling of tingle and passion and shortness of breath. Beaver had never had a woman before. Now here was one, a perfect one, and a robbery, too. The excitement crawled up his back in an exciting tingle. Deadly and dangerous, the feeling persisted. It moved about within his stomach and groin as though he had swallowed a live serpent. He knew the feelings would eventually take control. They always did. His most basic instincts told him this was what he needed. He dug his nails into his sweaty palms until they ached. A woman, a girl, added a whole new dimension to the forthcoming activity. The addition of her presence was what he needed most in the world. The pert blonde figure he beheld within the spy glass brought a shiver to his back and shoulders. She was more perfect than the girl of his imager

The four outlaws lay sweltering in their ambush atop the grassy slope. Well hidden by fallen oaks and decaying cottonwood logs, they were nonetheless totally exposed to the relentless, unforgiving mid-afternoon sun. Tired and hungry, they were mostly just hot. They lay in what little shade they were able to find in prairie country such as this. Their shirts were plastered to their backs with stains of dark sweat. Anxious for their next move, they could feel their tempers shortening. To escape the heat was becoming almost as important as gathering up the horses they had come for. It was only when the rare, slight breeze blew across their prone figures and the moving air touched the fabrics' sweaty dampness that even the slightest cooling occurred. September is not a cool fall month on the Kansas plains The September temperatures of Kansas are some of the year's most torturous. The heat intensifies as one moves south and west across Oklahoma territory and on to Texas.

For three sunbaked and withering days, they had ridden hard with little food and even less rest. They were glad to know they would not have to wait much longer. Awaiting their chance to affect the planned ambush, the quartet watched the little campsite in the cottonwood grove five hundred yards below them intently. How envious were they of the shade the cottonwoods afforded those at the foot of the slope beneath them. Through the trees, they could further see the cooling waters of Caney Creek. Each was dejectedly resigned that there would be no enjoyment of the creek's waters for some time to come. There would be no time for that luxury. They would hit, take the horses they had come for, and ride.

The next days would be as hot and as hard and as dusty as the three past. Additionally, they would have a horse herd on their hands. A small herd of eight head it was true, but a herd never the less. And four of these were stallions. Handling horses was always troublesome, but more so when you had stallions to contend with and especially if you were on the run. This was a long hard raid. It was less than half over by far. Everything was as they had been told: The old Conestoga wagon was the focus of the camp, and as they expected, there were only three people in attendance. None of the three really posed much danger or resistance to the determined bandits.

Those in the camp moved about slowly in the day's heat. They kept to the shade as much as possible.

A small boy of eight or nine moved here and there about the encampment. The man, only average in size, exited the big wagon and went about typical camp chores. He was either fetching water from Caney Creek or gathering wood for the cook fire. Mostly though, the man attended the eight fine horses in the little rope coral. Corralled as they were, the little herd grazed peacefully on the rich buffalo grass. The man fussed over them incessantly.

The smallest outlaw, a sandy haired, bowlegged man with a tobacco-stained chin -- the one the others called Charley, slipped down the back side of the hill from where they were viewing this placid scene. He made a detailed check on their own horses. He tenderly wet their lips with water from a canvass canteen poured into his bandanna. The horses eyed his grizzled appearance suspiciously but the scant water he offered them seemed to overcome their anxieties. These four animals had traveled hard, too. A further more demanding test lay just a few hours ahead of them. Charley was pleased with their solid appearance. The men had brought the saddlers along slowly. The horses were thirsty of course, but they looked as though a good drink was all they would need to get them back into the Indian Territory. The branches and tributaries of Caney Creek would soon provide water for all of them.

Charley just wanted to get on with it. He hated this waiting. He had stood these delays many times before. This lingering that all bandit chiefs seemed to believe was somehow strategic. Were he the leader, he would hit the target now and hit it hard. Yet, he knew that a running escape might be called for. Running a good horse hard in the mid-afternoon heat would probably end up as a disaster. He dismissed his idea of leading this band of raiders and turned back to the horses. He understood that success or failure depended more upon these mounts than on him. In a little while they would be called into action, and he wanted the horses ready and in good shape. Besides his impatience, he had an annoying back ache. He was glad they would be moving soon. He felt the stirring about would be good for him. He rubbed his back and buttocks with both hands trying for relief.

He had grown tired of the hot and boring surveillance. There was not that much to watch. Other than the little amount of activity in the camp, there was mostly just the prairie. It stretched out endless before their watchful eyes, its immeasurable monotony broken only here and there by scant groves of cottonwood or occasional, sparse thickets of locust and sumac.

The prairie lay there before them, the waves of heat casting a shimmering glassy appearance to the overall scene. The cloudless sky above them was a blue canopy that seemed to hold the unrelenting heat low and heavy on the breast of the earth. The sun was a blazing orb that pierced the sky as a searching probing white flame. Caney Creek ambled its way across an endless tract that was western Kansas. Though its water was low this time of year, the willow-lined banks offered at least a hint of coolness.

The outlaws knew that five miles over the hillock to the east was the little settlement of Murphy Flats.

Brooker's store was about the extent of accommodations in Murphy Flats. That and a blacksmith shop and a tiny post office housed in low, flat wooden sheds. It was more than eleven miles back to Dodge City and any form of truly organized law. This spot on the Caney Creek bank was a decent place for a robbery or a horse rustling party. The open spaces, gullies and rock outcroppings could swallow up a horse and rider very quickly. The hot weather would make tracking difficult if one avoided dusty trail crossings and kept away from open ground. It was only three days back to the safety of the territory; maybe less since they could move out faster than they had dared to move in. All in all, this setup was a better one than they had dealt with many other times.

Obviously, the outlaw chieftain was the one called Amos. A larger man than any of the other three, it would have been instantly evident to the most casual observer that he was a considerably brighter personage. His self-appointed superiority and general demeanor quickly marked him in the commanders' role of this shabby little band. Amos Younger was an experienced outlaw. One who had indeed captained much larger and more sophisticated bandit rings... By comparison this was a rather seedy and tattered lot.

"Well, they's all I got", he thought. "No use wishin' for what ain't comin'."

Resigned, he rolled onto his back and lay looking upward at a sultry sky. A lone golden eagle drifted aimlessly in its listless hunt. The bird seemed the only movement in the still of the glassy heat. He glided in tight circles, barely fingering the air as if wing movement was too difficult. The Eagle hung nearly stationary, so high above the earth that he appeared only as a tiny black dot against the shimmering azure. The pillars of hot air lifting from the prairie floor made his flight nearly effortless. Amos had never watched one of these soaring birds without feeling slight pangs of envy.

"Maybe he's a might cooler; bein' so high up. Sure is swelterin' to beat hell down here."

Amos tried to keep watch on the activites in the camp below through an old brass telescope. Tried, that is, because the boyish one of the four kept grasping for the spy glass, insisting on using the viewing apparatus himself. Peering incessantly through the brass tube, the bucktoothed youngster, Beaver Parker, was determined to keep the monocular under his personal command.

As Beaver watched, he found the man, boy, wagon and even the unusually splendid horses to be of only minimal interest. It was, in fact, these very horses that he knew were to be his primary mission. He felt there were other things far more exciting than horse rustling. In fact, Beaver had never cared for the spoils of the outlaw life at all. It was the action and excitement that drove him wild. When there was a woman involved, the intensity was heightened almost to the point of his passing out. Though new at the outlaw game, Beaver knew. it would never be the money. It was the exhilaration of creating fear. Killing, he thought, could not be so pleasurable without first terrifying the victim. If the victim was to be a handsome woman, he felt it could be no better. He was enjoying himself immensely by watching *this* woman. He had never seen a gentlewoman so exquisite in his entire life. Maybe he had, but he couldn't remember.

This one stirred the hot feelings in his lower stomach. Indeed, his aunts -- the only women he'd ever really had anything to do with -- were hags compared to this sleek and haughty vision. He could picture his two aunts. Momma Nell was the one who raised him when his mother had deserted him. He could picture the old aunts in his mind's eye now. They had tried so hard to have Nellie Parker consign him to an orphanage. She had held fast that the boy needed her and she could care for him.

"But he just ain't right," the aunt called Helen chided... "He needs puttin' away. "

"Not to worry a bit," Momma Nell had told them. "He just needs care'n for. He's never had no one to love him or take up for him at all you know."

He recalled as a small boy when the cat calls of "Hey Bucktooth…Hey Beaver! "had made him cry. Even Aunt Minnie had declared that he looked all the world like a beaver. But it was Nellie Parker who held him on her lap and told him that "Beaver" was a good name. After all, the beaver was hard working and an animal all the trappers sought because of his beautiful fur. She told him how the richest folks in the land cherished the beaver for his wonderful fur

"The softest, richest pelt of all. the creatures of the forest," she had told him. "Fine hats, wonderful coats and cloaks. Why them as calls you "Beaver," don't really know much about beavers or about you. Both of you are just fine with me."

After that George Parker preferred the name "Beaver" to the name given him by the mother who had left him alone…Deserted him. It didn't take much for him to hate the two aunts either.

Slimy old bats, Beaver thought. He could still picture them as they had looked that day. Thin, dried up old women with flat chests and tightly pulled back hair. Drawn back lips as thin as wire. Thin white skin that reminded him of the writing paper Momma Nellie sometimes used….

But now his thought returned to Pamela Carstin. Helen and Minnie were nothing like this graceful creature before him now. She was magnificent. Beaver liked everything about her. Her hair was bobbed short and from this distance it appeared the color of the sun. Though he couldn't hear her, he could see by observation, as the scope greatly magnified her pretty face that she laughed a lot. He was captivated by the fact that she seemed so lively and energetic. Even in this heat. She wore men's clothing of course. Trail travel required that. But the thin blue work shirt and tan denim riding pants were just tight enough. The fabric clung to her form in all the exciting places. She appeared rounded and softly generous in form.

He watched the thrust of her shirt front and wished the telescope had been stronger. Once she paused and vigorously brushed and curried one of the horses. This stroking action animated the shirt front. It caused the flesh to oscillate somewhat sensually. Observing this jiggling action, his mouth went suddenly dry. His body felt a rush of the strange and tingly sensation again. He tasted stronger iron in his mouth now. He suddenly realized he had bitten into his lower lip, causing a slight blood flow. He cursed his pronounced overbite. He hated the extended bucked front teeth that had spawned his nickname.

Beaver found himself wondering if his rifle would shoot straight enough to kill her from this distance. It must be three, four or maybe five hundred yards. A hard test for even a .45-70 government cartridge. He could, in his mind's eye, see the .45 caliber bullet hitting her right where her shirt rose in front. She would die and never know what killed her. That was strength. In that kind of control lay the only real authority. In this rifle lay the absolute power of life and death. It wasn't really what he had in mind for her, but it was entertaining him now. He enjoyed allowing that vision to diffuse and mingle among the myriad others that now whirled uncontrollably within his mind.

She bent over now to lift a bucket, and he could clearly see the stretch of the fabric across her womanly buttocks. The sight was more than he could bear. His body seemed to have a life of its own. Lying on his stomach, he ground his pelvis hard against the earth. He somehow had to finally relieve himself from these remarkably bizarre and wonderful sensations. He wasn't sure he could stand the excruciating tensions for very much longer.

Beaver saw that Amos was asleep now. The thin one, Beaver's cousin, Willy slept, too. Sleep brought some relief from the sore muscles and relentless heat though Beaver could never understand how anyone could sleep just before a raid. These were experienced hands. At least, Amos Younger was. They were resting up, waiting for the coolness of evening, and then they would steal the horses. They would want enough remaining sunlight to get them well away from the raid site. Driving horses in total darkness was a poor plan and a good way to be killed. It would be that hour or two before full sunset that was the most important. Steal the horses and get an hour or so head start was the plan outlined by Amos Younger. Beaver knew that was all they would do.

They were so stupid. They would simply steal the horses and run. They would leave the woman behind. They would just take the horses and run. He despised them. More than anything he hated having Amos Younger for his boss. The outlaw, Beaver Parker, wished he were on this raid alone.

When the sun sank low enough to resemble a glowing sliver of reddish-gold in the western sky, the four bandits began to saddle up and check their guns. In the camp below them the woman had just taken up the supper plates from her young son and husband and was sloshing them about in a large sudsy pot. Somewhere, invisible in the last glow of the western sky, a coyote complained of the sun's retreat with short, yipping barks. The bob white quail were calling now, too, their cries intent and plaintive and vital. They sought, desperately, to bring the feeding covey back together for the evening roost. Sunset was underway....

The four riders were mounted now. They ambled toward the wagon. From the high sage there was the call of a whippoorwill's relentless summons. For an instant, the horsemen were silhouetted by a few washes of distant heat lightning raggedly crossing the southern sky. The man in the camp and his young son were seeing to the eight fine horses confined by double strands of lariat rope in a makeshift corral. When the woman had cleansed the plates, she began to feed large pieces of driftwood to the campfire located in the center of their camping complex.

The dry cottonwood branches mad a poor fuel. They would spring to life in colorful blazes and for a short time they gave off blistering heat and firelight of the brightest intensity. All too soon though cottonwood would consume itself and it knew none of the lasting powers of woods like oak or maple. The banks of Caney Creek though were strewn with it, and so it was ready fire fodder for the horse camp.

The man looked up from his chores at the sides of his horses and saw a movement coming down the slope toward them. Through the twilight he had trouble discerning just what the movement was, but as they drew nearer, he identified four riders. The first thing that raced through his mind was the fact the riders were approaching from the direction of the open Kansas plains, not from the direction of the little town of Murphy Flats as one might reasonably expect.

The direction of their arrival was a concern to him. He was not normally. a suspicious man but this was Kansas. Since the Civil War Kansas abounded with outlaws and rustlers. After all, he had these fine horses to guard. He saw. now that the riders were closer, that they were coming on in his direction at a short lope. Men who cantered horses in twilight or near darkness were men in a hurry he knew. A horse could stumble or trip in this fading light so easily. These riders were bearing down on his camp with a purpose.

"Pamela," he called out. "Get the boy. Fetch the boy and get in the wagon."

"Alex?" Her voice was questioning. She had turned now so that he could see her finely featured face in the light of the cottonwood brands.

"Get Justin," he cried out, a little louder now; more commanding, she thought, than his usual tone. "Hide out in the wagon 'till I see what these riders comin' in are about." Now the woman turned her face up the slope and for the first time saw the quartet of horsemen.

"They're coming from the wrong way, I think." By now he had covered several long strides and was nearer her side. "Grab up Justin and get in the wagon, Pamela. It's likely nothing, but let's be sure who these men are."

"Probably just want to see a Kentucky horse," she said.

"I'd expect your right. Hide out in the wagon with the boy though, till we know. Remember what Henry Brooker told us about men who ride in from the west. If they aren't driving cattle, they're probably outlaws. Remember when he told us that?"

Her eyes affirmed his remarks. Now she quickly grabbed up the tow-headed youngster of eight or nine years, and she secluded him along with herself in the darkness of the Conestoga's interior. In only a few seconds she heard the hoof beats of approaching horses. Then came the nearly inaudible sounds of deep male voices. She pulled her son to her and strained her hearing to listen to the conversation. It was a bit too distant. She could only hear a word or two now and then clearly enough to understand.

At last, she found a slit in the wagon's canvas cover and peeked carefully through it. She could see her husband Alex standing before the four mounted men. The raging fire threw off more than adequate light, but the flicker of the blazes gave everything a confusing and eerie look. She wished she could hear better. She could only hear a voice rising in anger now and then. By Alex's gesturing she could see he was ordering the men away from their camp.

"What is it you men want?" Alex's voice betrayed a hint of fear. He stood squarely between the mounted foursome and the brightly leaping campfire.

"We're takin' the horses," the largest of the four said.

"I'm afraid I don't follow your meaning, sir. These animals are not for sale." Alex waved his arm towards the animals in the rope coral. The four riders laughed heartily.

"I didn't say we wanted to buy them. We're just goin' to take 'em."

"The law won't permit that," Alex said. His eyes were strangely drawn away from the big man who was certainly the leader. He found himself, instead, watching the small young man with the exaggerated buck teeth.

Something alerted Alex to the fact this lean youngster was the most volatile and threatening of the four. His wild eyes were constantly moving. He was obviously searching the camp for something. Alex could not imagine what the boy was looking for, but it was clear he wasn't interested in horses. They were right out in the open and easy enough to see.

"What law? What law you talking 'bout dude? Ain't no law hereabouts. Guess you could say we're the law." Three of the riders broke into laughter again. Though not the boy with the dirty blonde hair hanging in loose strands from under his crushed black felt hat. He continued to probe the camp with wild and frantic eyes.

"There's law here a plenty," Alex said. "Henry Brooker right here in Murphy Flats. He's a Ranger, you know. He's a real Texas Ranger."

"Well it's more than five miles up to the Flats from here, now ain't it? Then that Brooker feller? Why hell I knows him. He ain't no Ranger. Was once I hear tell, but now he keeps store. That is unles you know some Henry Brooker I don't."

Alex was just opening his mouth to answer when the wild-eyed boy broke in.

"Where's the woman?" Beaver Parker demanded.

"What?" Alex was so taken back he wasn't sure he had heard correctly. Even the other outlaws seemed surprised by the forthright question from the boy with the buck teeth.

"Where's the Goddamn woman? Trot her out here. To hell with all this horse talk. Let's take a look at the woman."

Alex felt the rage boil up inside him. He could no more imagine someone talking of his wife this way than he believed he could fly. He looked at the faces of the blonde boy's three companions. He was, desperately, seeking support from any one of the three. He saw looks of bewilderment on their faces as they looked one to the other. They seemed as surprised and as baffled as Alex himself. He resigned himself though that he would receive no aid from them.

Alex was facing this problem alone. His fury though, was becoming overwhelming. Alex, who had never really ever lost his temper this completely before, could stand no more. Wildly, and out of control, he suddenly lunged for the bridle of the buck-toothed vagrant's horse. It was the last thing that Alexander Carstin would ever do.

From under his loose shirt, the boy whipped an Army Model Colt .45 pistol and thumbed back the hammer. The first shot took Alex squarely in the face and spun him backwards. In her hiding place in the wagon, Pamela jerked wildly at the astounding report of the heavy pistol. She was as stunned as if the ball had hit her instead of Alex. Panic filled her eyes, and she lurched drunkenly back to her observation point. When Alex's staggering had brought him in a complete turn he was, somehow, still on his feet. Blood flooded his entire face, and against the white of his shirt he made a ghastly vision in the firelight. Pamela watched, terrified and rooted in fear.

She could feel her heart pounding within her ears. Bile rose within her mouth and she blanched at the sour taste. Her voice was stuck deep in her throat and she could not cry out. She saw Alex swaying back and forth like some bloody, intoxicated dancer. He was desperately trying to stay upright, fighting to retain his footing. He staggered side to side within the eerie firelight.

Then the boy blasted at Alex's exposed chest with two more quick shots. Even muffled as they were by the canvas of the wagon cover, the shots were ear splitting to Pamela. Her body jerked uncontrollably at each report. Alex went down hard. From flat on his back, he looked up with dying and questioning eyes. All he could see was the shooter. The boy with the pistol was taking careful aim again. Alex felt the next slug hit his chest and was surprised at how much it felt like a punch from a fist. The gunman was a grey ghost through the thick cloud of black-powder gun smoke. Two more shots were pumped into his chest, but he felt neither. Alex tried to rise, but something pinned his shoulder to the ground. He was uncomprehending now. He understood something was wrong, but the source of his confusion deluded him. He opened his mouth to ask for help in rising and was astonished to see a flow of blood leak from his parted lips.

I've got blood in my mouth, he thought. *Why in the world would I have blood in my mouth? I'll have Pamela check my mouth later. Maybe she can find out why there's blood...* Alex could sense the fire was dying. The flames had been so hot and bright. Now they were dimming, and a chilly wind drew itself across his body. The day had been so hot. Now it was growing cooler...no... colder! He gave way to an uncontrollable shiver. There was so much shouting and horses running to and fro. Alex thought a horse might step on him, and he tried to move again. He was surprised when he could not.

Horses and men were moving in and out of the dying firelight. He sensed this rather than saw it.

I'm stuck on the ground with all this blood, he thought. *When Pamela comes, she can help me up... and look for this blood in my mouth...*

Someone shouted, "Get them all! Damn it, I said get all them horses!" Then Alex thought someone called out, "Too much shootin'... Take what you got and run.! Ride, damn it, ride! Beaver, you crazy sumbitch!"

Alex didn't want to listen anymore. He was tired now. He thought he'd just lie still until Pamela came. She'd have Justin with her. Maybe when she came, there wouldn't be so much yelling... so many horses running around. There were horses everywhere. They were running through the fire.

Then Pamela was at his side. He looked up into her face. What's wrong with her face? Is she crying? She was trying to help him up. He knew she would. He sensed the boy was by the wagon, watching. But were they both crying?. Why were they crying?.... Yes, they were definitely crying. He couldn't cry. He had blood in his mouth. Too much blood.... too much...

Pamela Carstin held the body of her husband in her arms. She sat flat on the dusty ground and slowly rocked him back and forth. Her tears slender, silver rivulets, dropped softly from her cheeks and onto his. In the distance, she could still see the riders through the fading twilight. They were heading back up the slope from the way they had come. Riding hard, they were a larger group now. They were leading four of her eight fine horses away at a hard gallop. As she watched them ride away, she was suddenly aware that one of the riders stopped his horse, turned and looked back at her through the fading light.

It's the smallest one, she thought. The shooter...

For a moment, the way he acted, she believed he might just spur his horse and return. He sat there on his horse staring back at her. She could feel his strange eyes on her even at this distance. Though the others shouted for him to come along, he seemed to defy them. She thought aloud, "He's ignoring their calls. He's coming back." The thought that he might return was a terrible one. She looked toward the wagon where she knew the shotgun rested. But at the last instant the rider turned his back on her and kicked up his mount.

Amos Younger had drawn his own pistol and pointed directly at Beaver Parker's face. "You crazy bastard," he shouted. "You come on now, or I'll kill you right where you are!"

Beaver thought of the woman. She was just probably just right in that wagon, he reasoned. Now she was in the open and in plain view. He could easily take her right now. He gave some thought to defying Amos, but the pistol barrel didn't waver. Beaver knew he had upset the raid with the killing, and Amos would surely shoot if he did not now obey. Grudgingly he pointed his horse up the rise and spurred the animal far harder than was necessary. Pamela believed she could hear his companions shouting at him. She couldn't be sure. They were too far out to really hear anything. After what seemed an eternity the small rider finally wheeled his mount and took his place among the fleeing horsemen. In moments they were out of sight, hidden in the prairie's failing light...

How silent, she thought after a long moment. *The plains are as silent as death.*

Pamela Carstin buried her face into the neck of her dead husband and cried aloud. Her weeping and the soft flutter of a dying fire were the night's only sounds. Now she looked towards the wagon and saw her son standing near the rear wheel. She had never seen Justin look so small and frail. Terrified, he was sobbing aloud uncontrollably. She extended her arms.

"Justin," she called. He ran to her and pinioned himself to her breast. She sat spread legged in the dust cradling both her fallen husband and her terrified son.

"What's this thing that's happened?" she asked herself aloud. "What's this terrible thing that's happened? Oh Justin ... Oh my God, Alex!"

Chapter Two

The Dodge City Stockyards
1888

Colin Trav was in a better mood when he woke in the mornings at trail's end than he was this cock-crow. After all trail's end meant a welcome end to long and tiring twelve-hour shifts of herding the cantankerous longhorn cows. Trail's end held the promise of a few relaxing days of haircuts, steamy hot baths, some whiskey... maybe even a girl or two from the Birdcage. Now at fifty years of age, or somewhere thereabouts, he didn't long for women the way he once had during the trail's endless days. Yet it was something he still enjoyed when the cattle were sold and the money was deposited with the exchange.

This, however, wasn't trail's end.

It was something his drovers expected of him as trail boss and top hand. Out on the trail his position of authority kept him somewhat apart from his crew of drovers. Here in town though it was a long-established tradition that the boss of the gang would drink, gamble and carouse with his men until the cattle were sold and the trip home was started. At that point, the priorities always somewhat mystically returned. Colin loved and trusted his gang and always enjoyed this four- or five-day respite of authority immensely.

"Best in the business," he thought. "The Broken Spur drovers are as good as they come."

From time to time, it bothered Colin that he didn't know his correct age. That fact was made bearable by the realization that, with his miserable past, his disastrous childhood, he was lucky to remember anything at all. He had survived, and just being alive had to be enough.

He stretched his lanky frame out full length, luxuriating in the wonderfully soft feather ticking. The Dodge House kept these splendidly yielding mattresses for just such travelers as Colin. For more than a hundred running nights he had slept on the ground, bedded with cold, stiff tarpaulin and saddle blankets reeking of horse. This downy cloud was something Colin imagined akin to heaven.

He sat up on the edge of his bed and studied the room, while he fished a tobacco sack and papers from his old boots and began to roll a morning smoke. Boots were the place to keep tobacco on the trail unless one preferred dew damp papers and makings. The room hadn't changed much since Colin had slept here at the end of last year's drive. There was still the same flowered paper on the walls, the familiar Chinese throw carpet was still at bedside affording a warm place for the day's first step. The draperies were unchanged, lacy and fine and far too delicate to be described as anything other than feminine.

A water pitcher and basin stood waiting on a stand near the door. Colin pushed his mane of grey- streaked black hair out of his face and thought a bit more about the girls of Front Street. Actually, Front was more an alley than a street. A cobbled narrow passageway that fronted the stockyards exchange building where the Livestock Dealers Bank was housed. The bank and the offices of a dozen commission firms stood on the north side of this winding alley. The south side was given over to a tumble-down collection of tar paper shacks that housed everything from taverns and brothels to the cheapest hotel cribs available in Dodge.

The Livestock Exchange building was a massive brick and stone structure three stories high. Its facade, stately and serene, gave a promise of responsible and sophisticated business. Directly in its rear though were more than two hundred acres of cattle and hog pens and alleyways. These were crisscrossed by a network of overhead catwalks and punctuated by holding pens, scale areas and trading bays. It was a noisy, bustling hub of activity that confused all save those who earned their livings within this cacophony of sights, sounds and smells.

Intense traders stalked the alleys, and colorful drovers on horseback clattered overhead on the high catwalks. Buyers and sellers cried their bids and asks aloud. Bells clanged noisily to announce the openings of trade on one alley or another. All of this activity mingled with the ten thousand voices of confused, nearly panicked hogs and cattle made for an ear shattering unruly din. The exchange would handle hundreds of thousands of dollars each day. Thousands of live animals and hundreds of commission trades. In 1888 Dodge City was the cattle capital of the world.

Strategically located among these countless rows of pens was a score of scale houses. These gave cover to the gigantic scales that could weigh fifty cattle at a time or a hundred hogs. The nation's beef and pork commerce happened here. On the far side of the building lay Front Street and another type of commerce. Dusty in dry weather and a narrow sea of mud in the rain, the north side of Front was a continuous row of low rude wooden structures.

These stood, waiting in their gaudily painted facades of red and blue and yellow, as welcoming beacons to the hundreds of drovers who made their bread by "Drivin' to Dodge." Beyond the fancy lettered glass of the showy windows and the slatted batwing doors, lay the toughest saloons, bordellos and gambling dens in Dodge City. A notable exception, most respectable and resplendent of these, was the Birdcage. Far more successful than all the rest and catering to the hierarchy of trail herding, the Birdcage seemed arrogantly out of place surrounded by its lower class neighbors.

Colin's mind wandered to the opulent interior of the Cage again and of the pretty and accommodating girls who lived there. The rude huts neighboring the high three-story wooden structure housed the lowest of the street's prostitutes, while the Cage was home to the prettiest and youngest of the street's "ladies."

Now that he was getting older, he felt this particular desire should diminish, if for no other reason than propriety. So far, though, it hadn't happened. The fact that it hadn't, caused him, from time to time, to wonder about his own morality. His yearnings while out on the trail were not so intense as when he was a younger man. When he reached Dodge, however, just the proximity of the girls seemed to heighten his libido when he reached Dodge, the Birdcage girls were a lavish treat at the end of a drive that it was just hard to pass up.

The recreational activity of the Birdcage was more to be expected of younger men he felt. He thought he felt about the same as he always had, but he realized that he was no longer young. He only pondered the subject of prostitutes and the Cage for a short time. He decided he would do whatever he felt like in the matter when the time came. He would not to dwell on this annoying subject any longer.

He was looking forward to a new hat. A new pair of boots, too. Maybe black this year. New boots were an annual reward. He loved the feeling of accomplishment that came at trail's end when he knew he'd earned a few days' rest with the stockyards people. They were, after all, his closest friends in the world when he was away from the Broken Spur.

There would be good food. No beef would be tolerated of course; far too much of that fare had been consumed out on the drive. He craved chicken, ham and fish. He yearned for fresh vegetables— cold lettuce, celery, beets and turnips. Dishes he had not tasted for far too long. There would be intense card playing, Kentucky whiskey and Saint Louis beer. He normally woke in a good mood, eager for that wonderful, many faceted flurry of excitement the cowboys called "funnin' in Dodge." This particular morning though his mood was not so cheery.

Colin Trav didn't wake up angry very many mornings, but this was one of the few. Somebody had been beating up on Little Buck, and he intended to find out who it was and put a stop to it. He'd seen Little Buck last evening with a couple of brutal welts across his face and a swollen watery eye. Anger welled up inside him when he replayed the distressing picture in his mind. He had a lot to do today but he thought he'd better take care of the Little Buck business first.

Further, he had three thousand longhorn cattle to market this very morning and that entailed a mountain of work and details. There was to begin with sorting the steers from the cows and heifers. Then sorting the grades, negotiating commissions and sales prices and arranging for the Dodge Exchange to get the money back safely into a Texas bank. Colin Trav loved the old Dodge City Stock Yards. He had been here so many times at the end of so many drives that every inch of its vast maze of pens and alleys were as familiar to him as the back of his own hand. He liked nothing better than waking in the old rundown bunkhouse the stockyards company provided for the drovers, hearing the lowing of cows mixed with the occasional bellow of a confused bull and crowned off by a cacophony of squealing hogs.

Actually Colin had never cared much for hogs– sheep either for that matter– but he was polite enough to the herdsmen who brought them to this enormous railhead market. In the colder or rainier weather, Colin stayed in the Dodge House Hotel or at the Clarion. Both were wonderfully accommodating and even somewhat luxurious by frontier standards. On splendid September mornings like this one, though, he preferred to stay right in the stock pens with his cattle. He had enjoyed the Dodge House mattress but found himself wishing he had slept in the old familiar hay bunker.

After all, the commission firm employed by the Spur used the select cattle pens that were all under roof. That was luxury enough after a hundred days and more of sleeping under the open sky. He departed the Dodge House and strode down Front to his assigned pens. He had to check on his cattle. They would need hay and water if they were to hold their weight. Wild cattle seemed to do nothing but walk and bawl when they were at last brought into a stockyards. For the first time ever, they would be confined in pens and surrounded by hundreds of their kin.

All were bound to be milling about and lowing at the top of their voices. Colin had learned a long time ago that fresh water and some good clover hay would help to settle them. It would greatly reduce the weight loss excited cattle always suffered. Called "shrink" by the drovers, this weight loss could mean the difference of an enormous amount of dollars when spread over three or four thousand head of cattle. Controlling shrink, death loss and excessive bruising was a major part of a cowboy's responsibilities.

The sun was just starting to tint the dawn sky with it's September pink. Front Street was completely deserted at this hour. Colin knew though that by noon, when the first cattle payments had been issued, the street would be bustling again. He usually doted on these noisy early morning wakeups. Pulling on his old worn brown boots, he went strolling down through the alleys. He generally bought either coffee or an early morning beer from the Chinagirl's cart and lazily browsed the maze of pens and alleys. He loved seeing the other herds and visiting with the commission men. They were the ones who would handle the actual selling of the Spur's herd to the cattle buyers from Chicago, Saint Louis and Kansas City.

Now his handmade cigarette coupled with a mug of steaming Arbuckles tasted wonderful in the morning air. All was right with the world in Colin's mind this fine September morning, all except the mistreatment of Little Buck. That issue preyed on Colin's mind. There was no question he was angry. This morning the commission men readily sensed that Colin wasn't his usual friendly self. More than walking the alleys, he seemed to be stalking. It was as though Colin Trav was actually looking for trouble… spoiling for a fight. Not at all his typical demeanor.

The traders in the yards had never seen Colin quite like this. Oh they knew that no one could abuse this trail-hardened cowboy and get away with it. Yet this morning it was Colin who seemed ready to dish out the abuse. The traders and yard men put their backs against their assigned gates and wondered what could have been on Colin's mind that caused him to act so surly. He strode though the alleys in evident anger, as if he were deep in thought and casually swinging a rawhide bridle from his hand.

The Dodge City Livestock Yards Company held about forty commission salesmen, representing about a dozen trading firms. These firms paid pen rent and feed and water charges to the stockyards company that actually owned the physical pens, scales and alleys. The stockyards company also provided the roust-abouts to wrangle horses, drive the cattle and hogs to their penning or weighing destinations, shovel out the manure and scrub the watering troughs.

Within the pecking order of the livestock sector of commerce, these were the lowest; though, without their tireless efforts and backbreaking labor, the whole scheme would've tumbled. They were a hard lot who worked long and hard and were paid far too little. Some aspired to one day become a trader or a commission man themselves, but most were resigned to a lifetime of tending livestock for others.

The traders were the industry's aristocracy. Some were totally independent. Others were referred to as commission men; all were remarkably skilled at sorting cattle up in groups that were as alike as peas in their pods both in quality and weight. This was the way the buyers liked to purchase, and it was the way cattle brought the most dollars in sale. In these loud and boisterous markets and their negotiating with buyers, these frontier salesmen knew no peers.

Dirty tricks were sometimes afoot here, too, and these cattle sharps knew them by the dozens. They knew how for instance to give a pen of cattle extra salt. Every pen was supplied with a block of licking salt but sly traders were apt to add more. It would be finely ground and mixed in with the hay the cattle were being held on. Salted thusly, they would fill up on water just minutes before crossing the scales. Those scales set the weight the buyer was to be charged for. The traders knew water weighed eight pounds for each gallon and a salt-thirsty steer could drink up about eight to ten gallons. They found this an easy way to pick up a seventy- or even an eighty-pound gain. Multiply this by hundreds of heads of cattle, and water has never sold so dear.

They could, sometimes, bury a pregnant cow deep in a pack of more select, higher yielding animals in order to extract a like, and unfair, price for the inferior animal. Once the slunk– as unborn calves were referred to– was removed by the butchers, the cow's yield would be as much as ten or twelve per cent less than a similar unbred or straight cow.

Young bulls with small scrotums could sometimes be passed off as more valuable steers if the buyer was sleepy enough. Poorly castrated bulls– called stags, and worth far less per pound than a well-cut steer– could also slip by the eye of a trusting or careless buyer. This mistake would only be detected far down the chain of events, when someone tried to actually eat the beef involved in the swindle and found it to be totally nonchewable except by wolves, bears, catamounts and their like..

The men who bought these cattle for the meat packers of Chicago, Saint Louis and Kansas City were just as savvy, just as sharp and knew just as much about cattle as did the commission men. Called "buyers" or "order men" as one might expect, the negotiations and bartering that took place between these two highly efficient and cow-smart factors was lively to say the least.

Colin knew a lot about cattle on the range, on the grass or on the trail, but here in the terminal markets he bowed to the expertise of these highly-accomplished barterers. They would, for a slight commission charge, sort a herdsman's cattle, shape them into salable groups and negotiate them to the buyer whose order most nearly fit the finished product. Once the salesmen had shaped the cattle, they would stand by the gates of their assigned pens; and the buyers would ride by on horseback. When a buyer found a pen of cattle that fit his order, spirited trading and negotiating would commence.

Actually, the buyers knew, before daylight, the locations of desirable cattle and would often try to out run other buyers to particularly select pens. That was why the stockyards officials had installed the bell. You could look all you wanted, and you might even discuss price; but nothing could be sold until the bell rang and formally opened the market for that day. Seven o'clock at morning had been selected as the appropriate commencing hour of trade.

It was incredible to Colin that sometimes the yards held as many as fifty thousand head of cattle, especially during the heavy fall run. Within thirty minutes of the bells clanging, every single head would be sold... If a buyer hesitated too long, he went home empty handed that day. Too many empty days, and a buyer would be replaced by his employer with a bolder, faster man.

Colin had seen this marketing process so many times, yet he enjoyed it every time, as though it were a totally new experience. For more than thirty years he'd brought the herds from the Broken Spur to this market, and he had watched it progress from a few holding pens and a watering trough or two into a vast span of pens and alleys covering more that two hundred acres of land. The main trading alley was even under roof now to accommodate the well-heeled meat packers' buyers. There had been many such changes over the three decades. Colin felt as though he, the yards and the Broken Spur had sort of grown up together.

The eighty to a hundred or so days on the trail that it took to bring a herd from the Canadian river to this Union Pacific rail head, was filled with backbreaking work and hardly a diversion. Mostly it was boring work except for those occasionally exciting moments wild cows can sporadically perpetrate. Once his herd was safely boxed in the yards though, there was an opportunity for warm comradeship and relaxation that Colin thoroughly enjoyed.

The cattle traders and handlers of Dodge City were people he would only see once a year. Twice in those rare years the Spur's range buyers could find cattle so plentiful they could put together two annual drives. Yet these scantily renewed relationships were close ones indeed. He wished he were in more of a mood to enjoy his present market days more, but the more he thought of Little Buck the blacker his disposition became.

Trent Markely had been Colin's commission man of choice for about the past twelve or thirteen years, and Colin actually thought of him as family. Colin admired things that stayed the same. He found change upsetting to his general nature. The Chinagirl with her wagon of food, beer and coffee was a different girl every year or two, but the wagon was the same. Trent Markley was the same.

There were, surely, flashier salesmen on the alley. Some with hand-tooled boots or large white hats. One cattle salesman, Burt Martin, even carried a Colt's pistol strapped to his hip in a hand-tooled Mexican holster…a reminder of wilder days when serious, sometimes deadly, trouble over cattle prices was a more common occurrence.

Trent Markley wore overalls, either indigo or tan, high-top flat shoes laced well above his ankles, and a dust-covered black derby. Colin liked the plain little fat man for his honesty and the gentle way he had of handling livestock. It was obvious to Colin that Trenton Markley simply knew more about cattle than any man he'd ever met. Colin recalled that one of his principle mentors, Juan Garcia, had once observed that Markley was more stirred by cows than by cowboys. Colin had learned over the years that Garcia's counsel was wise indeed.

Most of the drovers used whips or canes to move cattle, and some could be quite cruel in beating a cow or steer into going where the drover wanted. Trent Markley carried a cane but seldom used it. It seemed to Colin that he more often coaxed the animals into minding him that anything else. His handling methods were a series of audible clucks and whistles and a bit of cooing. The animals seemed to do exactly what he wanted them to do and when he wanted it. Old Robert had told Colin when he was a boy that men who were gentle with animals were generally good men. Old Robert's sage advice was even more revered than that of Garcia.

As Colin neared, Trent spied his tall and lanky frame approaching and called to Chinagirl for two Arbuckles coffees. Colin was angry now that he was letting his mood upset him so much. He always looked forward to this part of his trip, too. He, for years had drank the Chinagirl's beer and ate the German sausages she sold. She kept the sausage piping hot with a little pan of charcoal in the floor of the wagon. When someone would ask what the sausage was made from she gleefully replied, "Doggies… I keep 'em plenty hot you bet." It was a different girl over the years, but the remark changed precious little. That reply kept the traders laughing, and the delicious food kept them from leaving the alleys. Colin always wondered just how much Chinagirl was worth to the stockyards company. He liked her just fine. Just as all the other cowboys present, he joked with her and laughed about the "doggies". All the drovers enjoyed the good natured teasing and cajoling of the Chinagirl.

Colin knew she was popular with these rough men, and if someone had made a move to hurt her... Well, the thought made Colin shudder. Chinagirl liked all the cowboys and Colin especially. She thought his salt-and-pepper hair was a mark of maturity and therefore dignity. She liked his blue eyes made narrow by days in the sun. His teeth were even and white in his sun-browned face. Most people would not have called Colin handsome– his face was a little craggy, a little too sharp-featured for that– but Chinagirl thought he was noble. A hawk, she thought. He is a hawk... Or a wolf.

"Trent," said Colin, "I want to talk with you about Little Buck." Markley knew at a glance there was something serious on Colin's mind. He took the two tin cups from the smiling Chinagirl and handed her a coin.

"What is it, Colin? What can I do for you this morning? That is, besides sell your herd to that old German bastard, George Swift, so dear as to make you rich?"

"Hell, just sell 'em to the Armour Company, Trent. We'll both be rich," Colin laughed.

Trent Markley had made thousands of dollars in commissions over the years from negotiating sales of the Broken Spur cattle. That, however, wasn't the reason he was always ready to serve Colin. He and Colin were friends. They shared a common bond in their love of cattle and the cattle industry. In addition, they were alike in a lot of ways as men. Certainly, not in their looks.

Round and short, Markley was the only commission man who had ever been invited to visit the Broken Spur ranch, and indeed had spent a very pleasant spring there a few years back. He genuinely liked Colin and Juan Garcia. Of course, the most colorful figure and the most interesting on the Spur was Old Robert.

He was the founder and owner of what was arguably the biggest cattle operation in the state of Texas. Not the biggest in land holdings. That distinction was divided among no less than ten enormously vast spreads. But when size was expressed in sheer numbers of cattle, it was the Broken Spur that traders called the mother lode.

It was the strategy of old Robert and Juan Garcia that the Spur hands would round up and capture wild cattle. They would additionally raise a calf crop of their own from an ever-growing cow herd. Further, the Broken spur would become a buying station serving all the smaller spreads along the Canadian and Red Rivers.

Many settlers and small ranchers in that area had never dreamed of trailing beef to the railheads. They simply popped the wild cattle out of the thickets, slapped them with a hair brand and sold them for gold to Old Robert Trav and his roving traders. As an afterthought, Trent suddenly remembered the letter.

"Here, Collie. A letter came to the office for you. I told 'em I'd see you right away and give it to you."

Colin took the brown paper envelope from Trent and, without much regard, folded it and slipped it into the rear pocket of his Levi riding pants. Letters at trail's end were nothing new. It was probably from Old Robert or maybe Garcia. There were usually such letters waiting, mostly containing encouragement on the selling end of a trail drive or instructions for scarce items to be purchased before returning home. Colin was not in the mood for a letter. He was sharply agitated, and Trent Markley could see it.

Trent was a short, overweight man with a florid face and a big roaring laugh when he was tickled. Colin, on the other hand, was lean and nearly as brown as an Indian from his long hours in the saddle. They were about the same age though and shared the bond that neither had ever married.

"You know, Colin, I'll be fifty-three next birthday, 'n I'm still a-batchin' over on Pump Creek," Markley had said to him last night in the Dodge House bar.

"I reckon you just can't find the right gal, Trent," Colin said.

"That ain't the problem, Collie. Problem is I loves 'em all. I been in love with every one of these gals around the Dodge House here, Collie. I love all them women up the street at the Birdcage, too. Even them old rough whores on Front Street. I tell you, Collie, I just loves every one 'o them'. Why, I think the prettiest thing in the world is a gal, Collie. And I don't care if she's fat 'er skinny 'er short or tall 'er what by God. I think they is just the most beautifullest things in the world. Tell me true now, Collie, ain't they the prettiest ever?"

"Well, yeah, they are I guess," Colin said. "'Bout the only thing prettier I know of would be a three-year old cow with twin calves." Both men howled.

"Trent," Colin began," Last night when we came home from the bar, I went out to the wrangler pens to check that little buckskin horse I rode in here on. I told the wrangler's boy to feed him a few oats and keep him away from the other horses. He's still a stud you know and apt to fight a bit, but he's the sweetest little stallion you ever saw. I rode him as a shift horse 'bout every day, and I tell you Trent he never acted up even once." Colin had Trent's attention now.

"Anyway," Colin went on," I found him down there in a pen without no water nor grain neither. 'Sides that he'd been whipped in the face. Had a couple o' quirt lashes clean across his face and some blood in his nose. Worst though is his eye, all puffy and swollen up, just leakin' to beat hell. Got him a big old red spot in the white of that eye. I walked up on him and he wheeled on me, just ready to fight you know. I just want to know what kind of a stockyard company shithead's been whippin' my horse."

"Damn, Collie, I never seen you take on so about a horse. He's just a cut out of the Spur remuda, ain't he?" Markley used the Tex-Mex word for horse herd.

"That's right. He's just a herd horse, but I like this little feller a lot. You know how it is. Mostly when you ride a stallion you spend a lot of time on your ass. This buckskin though is sweeter'n a sugar loaf. If you pen him in a stall away from mares, I believe you could trust him."

"Well, Collie, I tell you I'd hate to see you go 'round trustin' stud horses. That's a sure way to keep from gettin' any older. But hell, Collie, I'm sure the stockyard company will pay you for any damage to your horse. I can get you a vet if you want one. You know, a horse doctor. The company'll pay for it. That is, once they get over the shock of knowin' a cowboy can care that much about a damned old horse. Your big business here in Dodge, Collie. I can collect for your stud."

"That ain't the point, Trent. Matter o' fact I think the horse'll be just fine anyhow. And he ain't old. 'Bout a three-year old I'd guess. Caught him last year up north of the big ditch. He's just a grade horse, but he's a cut above what you normally catch. Anyway, I'm figuring on ridin' him back to Texas. It's just that I'm damn mad that some lowlife peckerwood thinks he can get away with whippin' a Broken Spur horse in the face. 'Specially a sweet little cow handler like Little Buck."

"Well Gawddamn, Collie, don't tell me you gave the horse a name? Damn, Collie, I never know'd you to be on speakin' terms with no horse. You sure it ain't a fancy little mare you met in some tavern ?" Trent was surprised at Colins' interest in this particular horse. He knew the Broken Spur had hundreds of such horses. Mostly they were caught on the open range as wild mustangs. A few of these horses would have been selected for breeding at the Spur based on size and strength.

Most of the better horses were usually coaly bay or sorrel in color. Pinto and buckskin was a totally wild horse color, and these were usually the least appreciated by the cowboys who had to ride them. Color phases such as buckskin, strawberry or blue roan, pie-bald, paint or pinto generally meant wild mustangs and a very hard time for the riders. For a horseman as experienced as Colin Trav to display this much interest in a range horse was mystifying to Trent Markley.

"Anyway, Collie," Markley went on, "…the man you want to talk to is probably Chester Crawford. He's the wrangler pullin' last night's shift, and I can tell you for sure he was as drunk as an owl last night on his shift 'cause I saw him. I had to go down to the horse pens for some hay bills that got sent down there by mistake, and I saw him in the hay sheds tryin' to sleep it off. If I was to check out who caused any devilment in the wrangler pens, I most likely would start with Chet Crawford. I cant figure why he's around here anyway; I can't abide that man."

"Why's that?" Colin wanted to know.

"Well, he's dirty for one thing. I know this stockyard work is dusty and muddy and o' course there's always manure around; but damn it, Collie, a man can clean up a bit on Sunday anyhow. Most everybody on the yards cleans up a bit after work. Hell, not Chester. He shows up at the Alley Restaurant or the Dodge House smellin' like the floor of a cattle car. Even goes to the Bird Cage lookin' for a woman he does." Trent stuffed his pudgy hands deep into his overall pockets for emphasis.

"Most the girls," Trent continued, "…just won't take his business anymore, and I got to say I'm damn glad. I mean, just think about it, Collie. Hell, you or me might get one o' them girls after she's been with old, dirty Chet. Damn if I can see any good in that. I'll tell you somethin' else, too, Colin. You ought to see the way he looks at the Chinagirl. I tell you, Collie, just the look on his face when she comes by makes me feel all squirmy inside. I can't put words to it, but it ain't like a man lookin' at a woman… more like a rattler watchin' a bird. Mostly though, he's just plain mean, dirty and drunk."

"I think I want to talk to this Chester Crawford, Trent. Point him out to me."

"You wont have to wait long, Collie. He's gonna show up here in a minute or two and buy coffee. I don't think he even drinks it. He just comes around cause Chinagirl's here. You'll know who he is right off. Got a big black beard, and he's a big fellow, too. Maybe some fat, but the wranglers say he can knock a horse down with his fist." Trent offered Colin tobacco and papers and he began to build a smoke.

" I tell you, Collie, I wouldn't just walk up and yank on him unless you know just what you're gonna do with him. He's likely to be harder to turn loose than he is to grab. He's probably pretty tough, and I don't think your gonna make no mustang lover out of him by just talkin' to him. Maybe, Collie, you ought to just let this pass."

"I want to talk with him."

"Well if you're sure... That's him right over there by the scale house. See the big fellow with the black hat? That's Chester Crawford."

Colin looked down the alley to an area by the scale house where the morning trades were tallied and printed on a large chalk board. No trades had been recorded yet this morning, but the various herds that were in the mammoth yards were listed in roster fashion here. Many buyers had favorite herds that they were loyal to, and they came to the board to see which outfits were at trail's end. Colin picked out Crawford right away. Even from this distance, Colin could see he was a bull of a man with an unkempt black beard, a barrel chest and a face red from the drinking of too much whiskey. He stood laughing and smoking with a tough looking group of wranglers. Colin started in his direction.

"You want some help, Colin?" Trent Markley didn't look as though he could be much help, but then one never really knew about these quiet men.

"My horse, my show," Colin said.

"Just be careful then," Markley said to Colins' back as he strode towards the scale house. Then he called, "You'll recognize him right off Colin... He'll be the one smells like he shit 'n his overalls."

Chapter Three

Waiting for the Texan
Summer/Fall 1888

"Pamela Hartford Carstin," she said aloud to herself. She pronounced each word with a feigned regal elegance, as though she was announcing her own majestic entrance at some imagined fancy dress ball back in Oswego or perhaps Chicago.

"Such a noble name for the shape I'm in."

Her voice, a bit crestfallen now, held a suggestion of irony. Pamela Carstin would have been a beautiful woman had she not appeared so bedraggled. She was young and had a sunny disposition even in trying times. She was at once sensually feminine and yet strong and self reliant. Exhaustion, frustration, and deep sorrow had sharply etched her normally handsome appearance.

She sat on the empty nail keg which was, nearly, her last piece of furniture. She toiled half heartedly in front of the little campfire, preparing a meal for herself and the boy. listlessly she stirred the hominy and bacon chips into a thick porridge. Nearly all her possessions were gone now. She had sold the two rockers, the clocks, the deacon's bench and even Great Grandma Enid's walnut bedstead.

"Well, I've still got a frying pan and a plate or two," she said, still speaking aloud; but this time she addressed the emptiness around her. "The oxen are gone, but the wagon's still in fine shape. We just got to hold on. We just have to wait for the Texan. Mister Brooker said late September, maybe October. We'll wait. We'll be alright."

She was talking to herself of Henry Brooker and his recommendation to her predicament. Brooker was the hardware store owner who had been so kind to her family ever since the day they had arrived at Murphy Flats. The Flats, as the tiny settlement was known, was in truth a primitive gathering of four or five faded wooden buildings.

Austere and lonely and flanking a single dirt street; more sheds than buildings, they lay about three miles south of Dodge City. Here sat the small outpost on the flat bank of a wide shallow stream called Caney

Creek. Named for the profusion of ten-foot tall wild cane that grew upon its banks in jungle-like wildness. Some of the wild cane gardens were minimal in size but others might easily have filled out to half-mile width. Often they would run along the creek bank for several miles.

Henry Brooker had befriended Pamela's husband, Alexander Carstin, practically from the day they first arrived in Murphy Flats. Since the shooting, Brooker had been such a good friend to her and little Justin she could not calculate her indebtedness to him. She remembered the day Alex had shown him the map of the land her father had purchased and was giving to them in Texas, and Mister Brooker had been very excited by the idea and had even offered to invest money in the Texas horse venture.

He had also been the one who made the arrangements for Alex's burial and, since the shooting, had not mentioned investing again. Currently she and little Justin were living off credit at Brooker's General Store. She had been paying the bill from time to time by selling off her belongings; but nonetheless, the amount owed was steadily rising.

Brooker and his stout wife, Mattie, were also the only friends she had to talk to. Horse traders and curiosity seekers had come into their camp in abundant numbers. They were only there, however, for the novelty of seeing the Kentucky thoroughbred horses. They had simply rode in, expressed their opinions good or bad of the merits of Kentucky horses and, curiosity settled, rode out again.

The Brookers had been the ones that she and Alex had spent time and shared meals with. Now, with Alex dead, they had even drawn themselves closer to Pamela and the boy. It was as though the Brookers were determined to protect her from further harm at the Flats.

Mostly they had pleaded for her to take her son and return home. When she had told, them she was still determined to get to Texas, they were astonished. For the longest time they could not believe that she was still, solidly, committed to the horse plan. When at last they saw their recommendations were falling on stone deaf ears, Henry had said the strangest thing to her:

"If you'll wait a while, I have a Texan friend who may be able to help you, Pamela. He'll be passing through here and going to Texas in September or October. If you're not going home and if you must go to Texas, then you must wait for him. Mattie and I think you should go home to Illinois. We will help you if you wish." Pamela shook her head. "I know. You're not going home. You are bent on Texas. But you must not try that trip alone. Wait here at the Flats. Mattie and I will help you all we can, but you must wait. He is a good man and might help you. If he is with you, you just might get to the Red River."

Pamela tried diligently to question Henry in more detail about this Texas friend. She wanted to know who he was and why he would be going to Texas in September or October. Henry Brooker simply refused to say more. It was as though he was afraid to commit to much information too her. Perhaps the friend would not come at all. Or, if he did arrive, maybe he would not help her. She tried hard and often to ferret out details of the matter, but Henry simply said, "Wait."

Now, in front of her cooking fire, stirring up grits and bits, she repeated, "Wait.... We just have to wait for the Texan that's all. We've just got to. Things aren't too bad yet. I still have Grandma Hartford's silver and I've still got the four-horse string." Her demeanor was not as confident as were her words. Considering what she had been through though, she was holding up remarkably well.

Many other women would've never been able to bear up to Pamela's loss. However, if the truth were known, there was little doubt that Pamela Carstin was scared. She was as scared as she was ever likely to be. It seemed that every hour of every day she was asking herself if she could really handle this situation. Did she really have the courage? Then too, there was the constant temptation of the wires.

Almost daily since the shooting, her father had wired her care of Dodge City, Kansas, General Delivery. They were telegrams of imploring, entreating her to give up and come home at once. She knew her father had her welfare at heart. But the daily telegrams entreating her abandonment of the project that had brought her here were becoming a sore spot. She had started out with Alex to accomplish something. Now Alex had given his life pursuing that vision. She had vowed to hold on as long as she could. She wanted the dream to be a reality. She saw in her mind's eye a special kind of horse. It would be such a horse as the world has never seen before. And it would be good and fine. She couldn't give up, not even for her father. This horse— this special horse— had become her Grail.

"Damn it," she shouted at the gathering darkness. "I'm not quitting. Not yet, I'm not quitting. I'm going to Texas." She seldom used vulgarity in her speech, but this time it felt very good.

Adding to her dismay though was the gnawing fact that somewhere out there on the prairie, in the evening's darkness, was a kill-crazy drunken horse thief with a loaded pistol. There might even be four such savage villains. There had been four. Maybe they were still together. She had never dreamed men such as these even existed. They had killed Alex over the horses as easily as one might swat a fly.

As they fled into the night, they loudly threatened to come back and kill her, too. They would've anyway, she believed, if they had been allotted a little more time. Had the outlaw chieftain not ordered his men to take what horses they could and ride, she dreaded to think of the consequences.

Sheriff Traylor, the thickset and mustached lawman from Dodge, had assured her there was nothing to worry about. According to him, men like these made empty threats all the time. He assured her she was in no danger and that he would personally watch over her.

"I'm pretty sure I know these men, Missus Carstin," the Sheriff said. "I'm right sure it's the work of Amos Younger. He claims he's a cousin to Cole Younger and his brothers. Claims he was at the Lawrence, Kansas, raid with his cousin Cole and Jesse James." Pamela blanched at the mention of one of the west's most notorious massacres.

"Most of us just think Amos is a bald-faced liar," Sheriff Traylor went on. "The way he looks, he must've been about ten years old when that attack took place– Sixty-six I think that was. But whether he's a cousin or ain't, he's dangerous as a rattlesnake. 'Specially drunk. He ain't near as bad a outlaw as he wants to be. I'd reckon he was pretty drunk here alright. This just ain't his usual style. Oh, he'll steal right enough and shoot, too; but I been lookin' everywhere, and I don't think your husband had a gun."

"Alex? No, Alex didn't have a gun. He had a rifle in the wagon, A shotgun, too, but he gave that to me for protection."

"Surely strange, Younger shootin' an unarmed man down that way. Then to empty his gun, too. I can see where he might of got spooked and let off a round. When men empty guns though, it's 'cause they in a killin' mood. It just don't sound like Amos. The description you gave is sure enough old Amos though. I guess this time he was just drunker'n usual."

Pamela could see the sheriff was genuinely concerned. The outlaws hadn't acted in a predictable manner.

"Most likely, the men with him were Charley Stone and Willy Parker. I cain't rightly say who the third man might be," the lawman said. "Probably some drifter old Amos picked up in the Nation somewhere. Anyway, they got the mares, and that's what they wanted. I'm sure they headed for the Nation. It's all Indian territory out there, and can't no law 'cept federal go in. I'm wiring Fort Smith for a Marshall.

Maybe they'll send Heck Thomas or another one of them hard ones. They's the ones that bring their prisoners home tied over their saddles, don't you know? They could shoot old Amos, and it wouldn't bother me none. Not since he's gone and killed an unarmed man like he did.

Anyhow, I think you're safe enough. Stay close to your wagon or better yet stay close to Henry Brooker. You ought to make out alright if you have to stay out here."

The phrase he used, "Shoot old Amos," gave her some concern. The outlaw chieftain she remembered from that night was certainly not old. Quite matter-of-factly, he had appeared somewhat handsome. Pamela was disgusted with herself at this inappropriate thought.

She recalled now that Westerners used the adjective "old," often and sometimes incorrectly by her eastern definition of the word. They called each other "old friend" when they had only just met. They referred to "old" saddles and "old" horses that certainly didn't qualify based on age alone. Often they used a more comical oxymoron such as "old" colt or "old" calf. One cowboy she and Alex knew had become a recent father. He had told her his "old" baby surely cried an awful lot.

She resigned herself to the fact the word "old" didn't properly apply to the killer of her husband. The utterance "old" was simply an overused phrase of hyperbole in constant use by most Southerners but never with the constant alacrity of the Texans.

Her recollections were of four men. One, so authorative and vocal that he was obviously in charge. Then there were the two men who sat silently on their horses with rifles across their pommels. They could only be described as smallish. Neither seemed to have much bearing. Their faces were obscure beneath slouch hat brims. It was as though they were of somewhat less importance than the horses they rode. Far less important than the guns they carried.

Clearest in her mind was the fourth rider. He was the one who had removed his hat and wiped sweat from his brow. For just a moment he was hatless. His hair was long and blonde she remembered. Unruly, too. She recalled a blue bandana tied about his brow. And his mouth. There was something wrong with his mouth. It seemed to stand out way from his face, as though he was holding something under his upper lip.

Food maybe, she thought. Maybe he was eating something…. His eyes had been terrifying. Even at that distance, in the firelight his eyes had appeared wild. His expression was that of a feral dog gone mad or gone crazy. She could swear that he saw right through the slit in the wagon cover and looked directly into her eyes. It had been that night's most terrifying moment.

The actual shooting had, of course, shocked her nearly to the point of sheer panic. Somehow though even the popping gunfire was not the frightening equivalent of the blonde boy's stare. When she recalled it, she could still feel the slow spreading terror invading her body. It happened that electrifying moment when she believed the emaciated light-haired rider had discovered her staring through the peep hole of her hiding place.

She had wanted to run to Alex. To stand by him and to help him, but she was too rooted in fear to do anything. Her body simply would not respond. Paralyzed, she could only watch through the slit. The fear was not all for herself. What about Justin ? She had to protect her son. It stunned her when she realized the wild- eyed raider had to be someone's son, too.

He seemed only to be a boy, she thought. He looked to be little more than a child. Maybe not though... Firelight can be deceiving. Why would a band of outlaws' ride with a child in tow?

Sheriff Traylor broke into her thoughts as he shifted his conversation to another area of his concern.

"Course I ain't never been in favor of you folks campin' out here in these cottonwoods anyway. Murphy Flats, Kansas, ain't New York City, Missus. 'Bout anythin' could happen out here. Least ways you ought to be up in town so's we could watch you better. That is if you're still gonna stay on.

One glance from Pamela and he saw her resolve.

He resigned himself to her determination. "You're likely to run into more trouble way out here, but I don't think it'll come from Amos and the boys. They ain't likely to come out of the Indian Territory after a shootin' like this one. This is a hangin' shootin' if I ever saw one. Then o' course, most outlaws are plenty careful about comin' this close to Dodge."

Pamela had to agree that Dodge City had a reputation of employing skilled and deadly lawmen. They were hired to keep the town safe– safe enough to insure the economic wealth brought in by the cattle herdsmen would continue. Other trail towns had let the lawless element go too far, and the ranchers had turned their herds to other, more hospitable, destinations. No one wanted to drive a herd overland for a hundred days just to end up robbed or, worse, shot. The deserted towns had simply dried up and blown away and were no more now than prairie dust. They lay scattered about the plains now, skeletons of once thriving giants.

The city fathers of Dodge had meant to protect their monetary investments in their town at all costs, they had hired lawmen to keep the peace who, in many cases, were more dangerous by far than the element they were to clean up. Pamela knew these facts from news reports heralding the brave and violent acts of these men. News papers across the nation doted on violence and bloodletting. It made great reading, sold a lot of papers, and, in some cases, made dirty cowardly killers into mounted knights of the plains.

Like all Americans, Pamela knew the names of Wyatt Earp, Bat Masterson and Billy Tilgham. These men were mean, dangerous and extremely opportunistic. Newsmen may have called them heroes, but Pamela Carstin knew they were cold-blooded killers.

Earp for example insisted that a generous table cut of all city gambling in Dodge City be used to embellish his lawman's salary. Therefore, the gambling he had been hired to regulate was allowed to flourish in a wide open manner simply to fatten his personal financial cut. Those who disagreed with his reasoning were shot or had their skulls cracked with the barrel of his heavy pistol.

When he had simply become too tough, too demanding and had ruptured too many skulls, the city fathers had called a town meeting. As terrified as they must have been they banished Wyatt from Dodge. More than twenty years ago, Earp had sought the wilder climate of Tombstone, Arizona.

There were no silly restrictions against skull busting in Tombstone. Wyatt was right at home. Silver and gambling may have been the major sources of wealth in Tombstone, but it was strongly opinioned that Wyatt earned most of his share elsewhere. He was, of course, well paid as a lawman; but his real money came from a seamier side of Tombstone's economy.

True enough, his family owned gambling concessions of their own. The Earp's held this trade out to the public as their principal income source. They were especially proud of their major interest in the Faro table at the lavish Oriental saloon. This occupation though they enhanced nightly by assisting in the operation of the highly profitable red-light district on bawdy old Deadline Street. A thousand miles of lonely cow trails made these brothels the visiting cowboys' first priority. When a big herd hit town, the red-light whorehouses were genuine gold mines. The gold though was in the form of human flesh. The girls could offer the cowboys an ample share of their worldly delights.

It would be men like Wyatt though who could offer the girls protection from abusive customers. A drunken cowboy with a hundred days on the trail under his belt could become explosive. A few nights in and among the cribs, and the most naive or newest girl soon saw the value of having someone around who could put a quick ending to any form of abuse. Most of the girls didn't really mind a split lip or a black eye so much. Usually, they had suffered worse. Often they had become prostitutes in order to escape such abuse. The bruised eye didn't hurt nearly as bad as did the fact no one wanted to employ a whore with a shiner. They learned quickly that if they became disfigured, their earning power would be sharply curtailed. Protection that carried the reputation of an Earp was a cherished thing indeed.

The customers, too, felt more comfortable when they had been steered to a particular brothel by Wyatt himself. It was as though they had legal backing for their pursuits; and, indeed, they did. All in all, it was a mutually beneficial arrangement. Tombstone furnished women and gambling and whiskey. Wyatt kept these pursuits from being interfered with. It took a lot of strong backed and vigorous cowboys to handle the three hundred thousand cattle that trailed annually through Dodge. The only tougher men anywhere could have been the silver miners of Tombstone.

Wyatt prowled these establishments nightly armed with his famous Buntline Colt. It's unknown if he ever really shot anyone with this forty .45 gracing a ten -inch barrel, but few doubted that he would. Most thought he might even enjoy it. Most often he had used his pistol as bludgeon. With only the slightest provocation, he had clubbed overly exuberant celebrants senseless on any number of occasions. Survival was usual but not guaranteed. Rather than to court risk with a dangerous killer like Earp, most outlaws would just rather give Dodge a wide berth. Drunken cowboys were one thing. A sober Earp was another....

However, the sheriff dealing with Pamela now was not Earp. Instead he was but a round-faced, nervous and fat little man. He had a nearly bald head and a curly moustache. Around fifty years ago someone had named him Winstead Traylor. Pamela had never heard of him.

He looked like anything other than a killer or a dangerous man. Yet Pamela knew that all who survived in his chosen profession must have, somewhere in his heart, the spirit of the tiger. Still she accepted his promise of personal protection with some reservation. By now, the attack had taken place nearly five weeks ago. It was true enough, the horse thieves hadn't been back; but then neither had Sheriff Traylor.

It was foolish of Alex to attempt to fight those men, Pamela thought.

These bandits had stolen horses before. They knew exactly what they were doing. Poor Alex had his whole heart tied into this little string of mares and stallions. With his gentle ways, he had attempted to reason with the drunken bandits; and the leader had shot him. The blond-haired one had shown no more remorse than he would have over a crushed spider. He had not simply shot him once but had emptied his heavy pistol into the body of the fallen Alex Carstin. Sheriff Traylor had said it: It was a purposeful killing.

Was it the one called Amos who shot? she asked herself. In all the excitement she couldn't be sure. He was the leader though. That was clear enough. He had led his band to steal the horses, hadn't he? He probably had done the shooting, too.

They had ridden away with Alex's mares but had left on the gallop without the four stud horse string. Pamela reasoned the men feared the noise of the shooting might bring someone to investigate. She had watched most of the bloody little drama from the bed she usually shared with Alex through a slit in the wagon cover. When she could stand no more, she buried her head in her hands and cried aloud.

At last she had flung herself from the wagon and rushed to the side of the dying Alex. She saw the riders herding the mares up the slope and into the darkness. With his dying breath, Alex had asked her why she was crying. Then she sensed that he believed Justin was near. When in her mind's eye she saw him standing by the wagon so small and frightened, her heart broke over and over again.

The men had hardly turned their horses before she was at Alex's side. Pamela had never seen a dying man before but she knew, somehow, that her husband was all but gone. When she was sure he had gone and she could no longer help him, she stood suddenly and ran. Grabbing little Justin by his hand she literally ran the entire distance to the sparse lights of Murphy Flats, dragging her weeping and confused son with her. When she returned with the sheriff in his buckboard, she knew her life was changed forever. Alex was dead. Her husband was dead. Justin's father was dead.....

She felt that she and Justin must surely be still alive because of some special reason. Perhaps it was the dream. The horse dream they had called it. She and Alex dreamed constantly of horses— of special horses thundering over the plains with manes and tails flying wild in the wind. They were horses that looked like no other horses on earth. *Poor Alex*, she thought. *He'll not dream of horses again.* She would though. Now the dream would be all hers. Scared or not, she was as determined as ever she had been.

She ate her meager supper and fed her son. She tucked him into his bedroll and then took her place in her own. She stretched herself out under the Kansas night and drifted off with a tear still visible in the corner of her eye. Her sleep that night would've been fitful were it not for the soothing dreams of galloping horses.

The night was a long one, but dawn's light came at last. As always, the minute she woke she turned to look at her son. Little Justin was fast asleep in his bed roll under the Conestoga. Pamela was alone with her thoughts of him as the first streaks of rose and silver grew out of the Kansas Prairie off to the east. She loved to look at her sleeping son. The boy was nine now and the picture of his father.

A bit sturdier, she thought. *He'll be some thicker than Alex*. His lashes and brows were chestnut, and his hair was a shock of yellow straw that framed a small round face one might call pretty if he were not a boy. He slept soundly. His mother found herself wishing times could always be so peaceful for him. Lately things had not been so perfect.

She salted the hominy gruel lightly after deciding it would still make a suitable breakfast. Now she sat as it heated on her morning fire and reflected on the sleeping boy. His reaction to the shooting of his father had worried Pamela intensely. She wondered if it was something he could overcome, or would it forever be a specter somewhere deep in his soul.

He's so young, she thought. *So small and helpless.*

Justin had been first terrified. Then confusion had set in, and at last he was deeply saddened. The little boy had surely loved his father. For three days after the shooting, Justin had scarcely spoken. Restless, he only picked at his food, and Pamela saw that his eyes were often filled with unspent tears.

At the graveside, Pamela's heart was wrenched when she saw him so racked by sobbing that his small body quaked with grief. Then gradually he had begun to come around. He refused to talk about the incident or even mention his father for that matter. But, day by day, his bearing began to return. In his uncertainty though he clung to his mother with an exaggerated sense of desperation. Pamela tried to swarm him with love and attention. She talked to him incessantly. She told him stories and cuddled him in her arms. She also cooked a lot of the stewed apples Justin liked so much. Pamela Carstin watched her son and wondered if she would ever have him back. She wondered how long it would take.

Dear, sweet Alex, she thought.

His death grieved her so. In his absence, she felt all hollow and sometimes afraid. She wished desperately that he was here to advise her. She hadn't always heeded his advice. No one had. Alex had seldom looked at things very realistically; rather he tended to assess the world as a perfect place filled with perfect people. People who knew Alex thought of him as rather a dreamer. Pamela's mother had called him a "puddin' head." In spite of this, Pamela had always felt that Alex was not only her husband but her friend as well, a dear one.

"If you must make a choice from your head or your heart," he had told her "...go with your heart. You'll almost always be right." She had known she loved him the day he told her that.

She had married Alexander Carstin more than ten years ago. That seemed impossible to her now. Ten years? Where could the time have gone? Alex was the father of her fine son, Justin. And now he'd been taken away from her as swiftly as a lightning flash splits the Kansas sky. She thought about Alex so much these last days. She regretted, sometimes, that she hadn't thought of him more when he was alive.

She missed him so much that, often, she felt a great empty hole in her very heart. Oh, she admitted to herself she had never really loved Alex. Well, anyhow, not in the way authors and poets loved. Or at least the way she imagined they might love. Alex had never "swept her off her feet." He had been funny and caring. He had been thoughtful and kind. He was her friend. It wasn't so much that she so fervently loved Alex; it was that she couldn't imagine being without him.

She had never minded being a wife to Alex though. In fact, she had liked that very much. He was gentle and sweet if not thrilling. Her mother had told her before she and Alex married that the intimate part of marriage was greatly overrated. Pamela believed all the things her mother said. Alex was certainly sweet enough; he just wasn't very intent. Or at least she didn't think so. When she learned she was pregnant with Justin her first feelings were of surprise. It seemed impossible. She hadn't really thought their lovemaking was that serious. Her next emotions, though, were waves of joy. She remembered kissing Alex and telling him she thought he'd be the grandest father.

There wasn't really much else to say, she thought. Alex was a decent man and that was all. A bit of a dreamer perhaps, and maybe not always as shrewd as he might have been. But he cared for her and Justin. He tried hard to make good, too. One thing was for certain: he didn't deserve to die that way.

Stupid, she thought. *Shameful and stupid. Damn men with guns. Ever since we got to Kansas all I've seen are men with guns. Damn stupid men !*

She must have loved Alex, hadn't she? Of course she loved him . She was sure of that. She had married him, hadn't she? She loved him. Just not with... well... passion. She loved him more like... with respect. Well not really respect.. They were far too close for it to be only that. More like appreciation. That was it– appreciation for the way he was constantly trying to make a success of himself and provide a life away from Hartford Place.

Anyway, he was gone now, and she and the boy were alone. He had been a good husband. A good husband and a good man, and she missed him so much she thought her heart might break. She wished the Texan would come. She wanted to go to Texas. She was weary of the wait. When she thought of Alex being gone forever, she began to cry. She had cried everyday since that filthy thief had shot Alex down. It had been so useless. So useless and stupid. Forever... She wasn't used to the word "forever" yet. She was alone, very nearly out of money and still at least three or maybe even four hundred miles from the place in Texas she needed to be. Maybe even farther. She just couldn't be sure.

She stifled her sobs so not to wake the still sleeping child. Through the falling tears she looked over to the little makeshift corral. The four horses looked back at her over their fence of rope with their keen, intelligent faces.

They're so fine, she thought. *So very fine. I still have the stallion string.* She was amazed that as bad as things had gone she had not turned loose her horses. Not yet. It made her proud of her courage and determination. She had kept her horses, and she had stayed in Kansas. Papa... stern, hard Papa who'd never given in to anything, kept telegraphing her to come home to Hartford Place on the next train. Hartford place, the tiny wealthy Hamlet skirting Oswego, Illinois, seemed to Pamela to be more than just a world away. Indeed, it was. There were no parallels between the pristine farms and quaint villages of Illinois and the wide open, wind-tortured plains of Kansas.

Could Texas be even more desolate? she asked herself. Some said "Yes." It didn't matter. She was determined to get to Texas. She still had the horses, and she still had the dream. She still waited for the Texan. Henry Brooker had said the Texan would come.

Alex gave the dream to me and I still have it. Maybe Alex couldn't sell hardware like Papa, but he knew a stallion when he saw one.

It made so much sense when Alex talked about it. Alex had many dreams, and most were not so sensible. Papa had referred to most of Alex's ideas not as dreams but, rather, as "schemes." He also used the words 'far fetched' a lot when discussing Alex's propositions.

But then Alex had begun to talk of "good" horses. He made a lot of sense when he spoke of taking "good" horses to the place where horses were used the most and blooded stock was at the same time most rare. That was Texas. Even Papa had agreed that Texans would love good horses if they only had them.

There were horses in Texas of course. Not, however, the fine spirited animals of Kentucky and Tennessee. The thoroughbred was a far cry from the mustang. Men who loved horses had to love Kentucky horses. They were the world's finest. Also, there lived in Alex's heart the concept of crossing blooded horses with the wild mustang. Many felt that combination held a lot of promise. The great speed of the thoroughbred coupled with the endurance and survival instincts of the range horse excited more than a few imaginations.

Alex had ridden all over Kentucky to find the string she held on to so tightly now. They were her last connection with Alex. They were the end of the dream. Alex had selected these four stallions from dozens he had sought out and viewed. There was no question, they were the best of the lot. The four mares were exquisite. They were gone now... In the hands of the outlaws. She would have to face that fact and move ahead.

God never made a man who knew horses as well as Alex, she thought.

She couldn't say the same for the local horsemen. A lot of riders, cowboys and horse traders had ridden out from Dodge to her little camp at Murphy Flats. They had come to see the pretty girl with the four Kentucky horses. These were westerners who had never seen the Virginia Hunter breeds or the Kentucky thoroughbred before. The Tennessee Walking horse was only a myth this far west. Pamela had found the remarks of these ignorant and insulting.

How, she wondered, could these dolts have been around horses every day for all of their lives and have learned so little?

"Looks like four giraffes to me, little lady," one had said.

"Never seen a horse with legs longer a brass bar rail," said another.

"These studs 're so tall they gonna have to get on their knees to service a mare," another laughed.

"Either that 'er stand the mare on a box."

They hooted in unison at this remark. Pamela dismissed them as stupid prairie trash who wouldn't know a good horse if it ran over them. She vowed to have no association or business dealings with anyone who called her "little lady."

There were others who came, not to see the horses, but for a look at the beautiful young widow camped alone in the cottonwoods. Pamela had never thought of herself as beautiful. Too boyish, was her own self assessment.

The men who rode out from Dodge to see the horses or her never thought her boyish. It was true the trail had been a little rough on Pamela, and she was not as polished as she had been back in Oswego. She was a bit thinner now and of course, her travels with the wagon demanded she dress in pants, boots and mannish shirts. With all this, Pamela Carstin was still a striking woman. She wore her light brown hair shoulder length, and days in the prairie sun had added interesting blonde streaks to it. Her small face was lovely and had been described by at least one of her suitors in Illinois as "exquisite." From hard work on the trail and countless hours in the saddle, her body was trim and maybe a little too hard. But even dressed as a drover, there was no denying the striking femininity so poorly concealed by the rough dress.

Her tan canvass pants and blue chambray shirt did little to conceal the sense of roundness and the promise of a delightful softness that was entirely womanly. There was no hint of "boyishness" here. No one would've called Pamela a girl either. She was, indeed, a woman.

She looked up from her cooking now at her four charges. They stood quietly looking back at her. It was as though they were awaiting some command. She kept them hobbled and in the little rope corral very near the rear of the wagon. She wanted them close. She thought, too, a hobbled horse might be harder to steal.

It was still dark enough in the pre-dawn that her cookfire's light reflected on the horses' intelligent faces. There was light enough for her to see the wide eyes and slightly flared nostrils. One of the horses whinnied softly from deep in his chest. There were two chestnuts, a sorrel and a grey. She found their wonderful faces entrancing. Alex had told her often that highly bred horses had a facial expression that made the horse appear as though he were asking you a question. It was that look of alertness and curiosity that separated them from dull range horses and those that were inbred. Equine judges considered this ingredient a major one in the grading of dressage horses, hunters and thoroughbreds. It was equally substantial in making breeding selections of both sire and dam. Alex had held that, of dozens of important grading points, this look was the primary factor. Without this trait, he thought, there was no use to go further in critical assessment. Even the draft breeds, like Clydesdale and Belgian, had this quality when they had been correctly husbanded. These four, with their ears thrust forward and wide alert eyes looked, for all the world, as though they had just asked her for some bit of vital information. And now they were waiting, anticipating Pamela's answer. By anyone's standards, they were as fine as any string of stallion horses in Kentucky, the land of their origin.

"Alex was right," she said. "You four studs are going to put us in the horse business, and we'll do just fine. "She blushed at her use of the word "studs". "All I have to do now is get us to Texas. I just have to wait for the Texan."

Pamela knew that in a crisis she could always count on her father. Maybe, she reasoned, it was the safety net of her father that gave her the boldness to persist in her Texas plan. Whatever the reason, Alex had lost his life in making the plan work; and she vowed that she would hold on just as long as she could. She only hoped this Texan– whoever he was–

would arrive soon. She hoped he would show before she had to use the safety net.

Chapter Four

The Amos Younger Bunch

Outlaw Amos Younger stirred himself and moved closer to the little campfire. The bandit gang had made a camp high on a grassy flat just inside the Nation. He ladled himself another generous helping of the delicious beans into his tin plate. He had to admit that the new fangled canned beans were the most mouth-watering food he had ever eaten in his life.

It was true they were a bit of a problem to carry as supplies. When traveling cross country on horseback, the cans were a cumbersome burden; they were so delicious, though, they were well worth the effort. They were truly more of a problem to carry on horseback than were the loose variety of pintos and reds. He had depended on these as his staple trail rations for years. He had to admit though, the canned vanities were delectable indeed. He was sure that he had never prepared a bean in his life as tasty as these. There were big chunks of white-pork fat swimming in a spicy red gravy. The mixture of spices and salt made his mouth water even before he lifted his battered old spoon.

Someone had told him the red sauce was made from tomatoes, but he was sure that was a lie. Everyone knew the true name for a tomato was love apple, and they were as poison as a cottonmouth. It seemed that every time he found something that he really enjoyed eating, someone would tell him something bad about it.

"Candy'll rot your teeth," they would say. Or "Too much whiskey will drive you crazy."

Amos wondered where these critics learned all these stifling and detrimental side effects that accompanied good eating and drinking.

"To hell with 'em," he said aloud. "Poison 'er not, by God I'm eatin' 'em anyway."

His three companions stared blankly at him. They were first startled and then bewildered by his sudden outburst.

Actually, Amos Younger had more serious problems on his mind tonight than just the quality of a trail meal. For some time now Amos had steadily become more disgruntled by the diminishing quality of his gang. After all, there had been a time when Amos had rode the river with his cousin Cole. He had robbed the Osceola bank with Grat Dalton. He had shared his trail beans with the likes of an old Pat Garret. Garret, in truth, when he had been a younger man, was a pretty fair hand at outlawing himself. At least he was when he wasn't playing at being a sheriff or a marshal or something just as ludicrous.

Looking at this band now, Amos was truly dismayed. Charley Stone was a five-foot, two inch runt with weak and watery eyes. He had a badly pock-marked face and spent every hour in the saddle complaining about his health. He forever had a headache or the ague or the grip or the flux or the pox or one scourge or another. This continued day upon day.

Not only was he a perpetual complainer, but other riders of the type that a man like Amos would likely come in contact with, ridiculed Charley Stone as often as his name would come up. It occurred to Amos that Charley would forever be a laughing stock. That was, of course, because of what was known in the Nation as the "famous foot-shooting." The shooting was already famous by now. Yet every time the story was told it grew in length, detail and hilarity.

What happened was that Charley had decided to show Bob Dalton how well he could handle a pistol. He jerked a big Merwin Hulbert, .45 caliber revolver out of his belt and promptly dropped it. The cocked revolver hit the ground, fired and shot Charley through the left ankle. Embarrassed, Charley refused to let Dalton cut away his boot in order to treat the wound. He dismissed Dalton's offer of aid by simply declaring the shot didn't hurt very much. After walking around on it for a day or two, Charley finally passed out from blood poisoning.

Bob Dalton finally brought Charley into the little town of Washita in search of a doctor. Since Charley could no longer walk nor ride, Dalton hauled him into town in a wagon they had stolen and left him there for treatment. Dalton promptly left town of course. When your name is Bob Dalton, it's not a good idea to hang about any town too long; and Dalton had given Washita an abundance of trouble in the past.

The doctor turned out to be the town constable as well as the brother-in-law to the man who owned the stolen wagon. After he doctored Charley up, just enough to assure a thin chance at survival, he slapped him in the Washita jail for a month for wagon stealing. At every poker table or at every bar in the Nation, you could hear the tale of the desperado who shot himself in the foot and got caught with the jailer's wagon. The story was growing in detail and embellishment every time Amos heard it. And he heard it far too often.

Humiliatin', Amos thought.

And then there was his henchman, Willy Parker. Amos was embarrassed by Willy even more than by Charley if that were possible. Willy Parker was a wiry little man that reminded everyone who saw him of a weasel. Amos knew this to be a fact because on a number of occasions he had asked friends, acquaintances and even total strangers what they thought of when they looked at Willy Parker.

"Weasel," was the answer every time.

Willy claimed to be a Texas bad man, but no one knew for sure whether he had really ever been in Texas or not. Willy also claimed relationship with Hanging Judge Isaac Parker. It was this judge who was the only real law and was the real boss of the territory known as "The Nation." Judge Parker had confronted Willy once inside the courtroom at Fort Smith. He vowed to hang Willy on the spot if he ever encountered him a second time. That was simply because Willy had used the name Parker.

"But it's my name, your honor! It's my genuine name." Willy had told the judge in that brief encounter in the Fort Smith court over a stolen hog.

"Call yourself something else," the judge bellowed. "Damned if I care what. Just so it ain't 'Parker.' Thirty days for hog stealin' in the local calaboose. Now someone get this varmint, whose name ain't Parker, out o' my court."

Amos Younger, an accomplished cattle rustler of cattle and horses, just could never bring himself to tell anyone that Willy had pulled thirty jailhouse days because he had stolen a hog.

"How the hell does a man steal a full grown hog anyway?" Amos pondered.

Most prominent was the fact that Willy had a large livid white scar across his forehead. It was an ugly blemish as wide as two fingers and seemed to be so deep that only a thin, pale layer of skin covered the skull itself.

The scar was the result of a pistol ball fired directly into his face by a Baptist Minister. The wounding had occurred while Willy, drunk as a bat, was attempting to hold up the first Baptist Church of Crawfordsville, Kansas, during Sunday services. Willy had weaved drunkenly down the aisle of the little church during the collection hymn. Brandishing a rusty old cap-and-ball Colt, he had ordered the preacher to "Stand and deliver."

He did just that. Only it wasn't the delivery Willy had expected. Willy's gun had faltered for a second when the organist hit an unintended foul and piercing note. It came about accidentally when she suddenly became aware of what was happening– that a robbery was taking place right in her church. And on a Sunday morning, too.

The raucous sound interrupted the drunken Willy's train of thought, and he glanced her way for a split second. During this opportune instant, the muzzle of his pistol strayed carelessly from its fixed point on the minister's chest. Having previously been a traveling clergyman in Arkansas territory, the pastor knew quite a bit about self-defense. The back roads he had ridden often were the havens of the area's most disreputable....

Without hesitation, the preacher snatched his own gun from its hiding place in his waist band and attempted to shoot Willy squarely between the eyes. The bullet though somehow snapped Willy's head to the left, and the lead ball had plowed the deep furrow across his forehead so evident yet today .

"Vengeance is mine, sayeth the Lord," the minister roared as he fired point blank into Willy's face.

"Hallelujah!" shouted the congregation in response. The organist gave out with a settling, "Amen."

Willy heard none of this, however, as he was semi-conscious, covered in his own blood, and being carted away to yet another jail. He would stay in this one for five years.

The Preacher, it turned out, was an ex-Texas Ranger who had sustained so many wounds fighting the Kiowa that he had decided a safer endeavor was to find God and become a pastor. His years in Arkansas proved nearly as dangerous as Kiowa hunting. He had, at last, gravitated to the Kansas plains. Peace was the mission of his ministry, but after the lessons he had learned during his many years of strife, he figured he could preach just as well if he were discreetly armed. The peace and quiet of the Crawfordsville Baptist Church had enforced his decision as a wise one. Until he had met with Willy Parker, his ministry had seemed a sheltered and uneventful career.

.About the only danger, he faced as a preacher was from over eating as he lunched with his various parishioners each Sunday after services. The sturdy farm wives of this Kansas community were cooks of the highest order and believed the two rules of a proper table were "good" and "plenty". The last thing the Pastor had thought he would encounter was an inept drunken robber in his own church. When he learned that Willy would live after he had fired what he surely thought was a killing shot, the old Ranger dismissed it, saying:

"The Lord moves in mysterious ways... Surely He does."

Holdin' up a church, Amos mused dejectedly. He grew sadder as he pondered on this saga. Some Texas badman. Stickin' up a church on a Sunday morning. Damn that's poor.

On top of all this confusion, there was still the matter of Beaver Parker. The buck-toothed third member of the gang and first cousin to weasel, Willy. Amos would never forget the arrival of Beaver if he lived to be a hundred. Willy had just rode into their camp one day with Beaver in tow and announced that he had to stay with them from now on. This declaration came one day before the band was scheduled to launch a horse rustling raid.

"I got to take care o' him now," Willy had said. "My aunt Nellie is dead now, and there jus' ain't no one else, so he's got to come with us. I got to look after him cause he just ain't quite right. You know what I'm talkin' 'bout?"

"What the hell are you talkin' 'bout?" Amos fairly yelled. Amos could see that this skinny blonde youngster was simply not all together. Anyone who looked could see it. It was as though he were distant, not in the same place as others around him. His body seemed separated from his mind. His eyes held a vacant stare and, at times, he seemed unaware of anything near him. He was given to staring off blankly into space. Amos, correctly, supposed the two immense and protruding front teeth accounted for the nickname.

"You got to be crazy, Willy," Amos said. "Were goin' horse stealin'. From there I figured we'd stick up a bank or two. We can't have this 'idjit' with us. He's liable to get hisself killed. Fires o' hell, Willy, he might get us all killed."

"It cain't be helped. My aunt Nellie's dead now, and there ain't no one to look after him. He's family, Amos. I got to do it. 'Sides that, he can ride real good. He knows what's goin' on. Most o' the time. I just cain't turn him out, Amos. Hell, the wolves'll get him. 'Sides that, he needs watchin' on account o' his problem."

"Problem? What problem?" Amos wanted to know.

"Well... sometimes he... Well, some times he... He kills things."

"He kills things? God Damn you, Willy, are you tellin' me he kills... folks? People?" Amos could hardly say the words.

"No, not folks. He ain't kilt no folks. He kills dogs and cats and pigs and stuff like that... But if I watch him, I think he'll be alright." Amos noted Willy was avoiding eye contact. Amos was familiar with this ploy. Willy was lying about something.

"Willy, you lying son of a bitch. You tell me right now. Has this idjit ever kilt any one?"

"I don't think so." But Willy's words were halting. "There was a little neighbor boy got his sef' drownded in Osceola Pond. Some folks said Beaver did it... but I never did think so."

"You never did think so?" Willy was looking away again. "Listen you little weasel, there's something you're not tellin'. Who else has this scary son of a bitch killed?"

"Well I ain't never gonna believe he did nothing' wrong at all. But when I found him with his momma, my aunt Nellie, she was dead. And he was just watchin' her. Aunt Nellie was just there on the floor, and I.."...." Amos didn't wait for Willy to finish.

"Sweet Jesus and jumpin' hop toads," Amos exploded. "You mean to tell me this bastard went and killed his own mother?"

"I ain't believin' a word of it, Amos... I ain't believing a word. Why, Beaver loved his Momma Nell more'n the angels. Anyway, she weren't his real momma at all. Ain't no one can be makin' me believe nothin' like that. They ain't a lick of proof to nothin' like that. Amos. Don't matter anyhow. I figure if he did or not, they's them that'll come a-lookin' for him. They just know he ain't right all the time, and they like to pick on him. I'll never believe he did nothin' to old Nellie. No sir. Not a-tall."

Amos could see this conversation was going in a circle. He wondered if Willy was trying to convince him of Beaver's innocence or himself. Though Beaver Parker was intently listening to these comments he appeared not in the least interested.

How stupid these sum'bitches are, the boy said to himself. I could never hurt Momma Nellie. They don' even know she waren't my Momma. Well, Willy...he knows I reckon. But nobody here but him knows nothin'."

Nellie Parker had for a very long time lved with her two sisters. The sisters were often asked if they were kin folks of the hanging judge Isaac Parker. The thinnest one called Minnie had always said, "Maybe so. Maybe that wild Comanche Quanah Parker, too." It was her stock answer. No one would ever know for sure. There's just a lot of Parkers in Texas.

"Spinsters three," the neighbors had christened them. After a while of the three living together, Nellie had just grown tired of the constant arguing over such trivial matters as the saving of bacon grease or which hog to butcher in the fall. At last she moved into a small sod home a settler had deserted long ago. With brush and broom and a lot of diligent effort, she had shortly turned the little two-roomed hovel into a presentable, if small, home.

Located near the old Osceola Pond, the overall scene was an attractive one. If Nellie was happy there, she had to admit from time to time she grew a bit lonely. She was feeling especially lonely the day the girl called Dulcy showed up at her door with the little buck-toothed boy in tow. Dulcy lived with an old couple about a half mile over the next ridge on the far side of the pond. No one ever took much notice of Dulcy. She was just there.

She could be seen often in the little yard where she stayed or drawing water from the big spring that fed Osceola Pond.

"Miss Nellie," she asked this day, "Kin I leave little Georgie here fer a bit? I'm supposed to meet someone at the crossroads, and Georgie's such a little'n, the walk is too much fer him. I'll be back afore dark, and that's for sure."

Nellie agreed to the arrangement. She thought the little boy might bring a bit of merriment about on this, one of her bluest days. She watched as the girl with the long thin blonde hair made her way down the wagon road. She looked small and pale to Nellie, dressed in only a grey onasberg shift and with her bare feet kicking up little puffs of dust as she made her way.

The boy did not provide the entertainment Nellie had thought he might. Rather he sat on the stoop most of the day looking off in the direction his mother had traveled. He sat there untill dark, and by now Nellie was beginning to sense the girl was not coming back. At least not this day. She took the little boy inside and washed him up, fed him well and tucked him into a small palette on the floor near the dying fire. That's the way it would be for a long time to come.

There was as much speculation in the neighborhood as to what had happened to the girl called Dulcy as there was about who was the father of the little buck-toothed boy. No one ever seemed to have an acceptable answer. As the boy became more familiar with Nellie, it seemed that both of them grew to enjoy their mutual friendship more and more all the time. The boy had been deserted. Nellie knew it was evil of her, but she was glad. The boy was hers now.

Beaver, when he was old enough to understand, knew it was true that his real mother had just left him as a small boy of four- or five-years old one day with Nellie Parker and was never heard of again. He wondered often what had happened to her. Nellie had told him to just forget about her. Nellie had said to him that she was his Momma now, and she would always love him and look after him. As was to be expected, because of his unusual appearance, he would be the butt of many local jokes and torment. When the cat calls of "Hey, Bucktooth" or "Hey, Beaver Boy" from the neighbor children became more than he could bear and caused him to cry, it was Nellie who could soothe and comfort him.

"Who can be crueler to a child than other children?" Nellie asked herself. Then she would call him inside for the comfort she knew he craved.

"Why 'Beaver's' a sure good nick name," she would say. "Beavers are the finest critters in the forest. Don't you know? Richest folks anywhere loves the fine pelt of the beaver. Fine hats, coats and cloaks. Them boys callin' you beaver don't know much about you or beavers either for that matter. Them boys ain't got no value at all compared to a beaver. But you do. You're the dearest thing there is to me." Holding the small boy on her lap, she would rock him in the old chair and coo to him, "Yo're just my little beaver boy, my little baby beaver boy. "Now he came to like being called "Beaver." It reminded him of Momma Nell. He was glad his mother was gone. Momma Nell was a better Momma by far. He knew this as sure as he knew anything.

Sometimes when he thought about his real mother, he dreamed up wild scenarios that might have happened to her. Maybe she was off living in some other place and happy and content. Maybe she had another son, one that folks didn't say he wasn't "quite right" about. Maybe she was dead. Perhaps killed by the Kiowa. He hoped so. He often wished he had the chance to kill her himself.

No good bitch, he would muse. Left me just like I weren't no more than a coyote pup. I hope them Injuns got her hair and killed her dead. I hope they burned her with fire. I would if I could.

He could not have ever hurt Nellie Parker, though. She was the only friend he'd ever had. She made sweet tea for him. And the buttered biscuits with stewed apples she served him were his favorite food in the world. At night, when his mind was restless and ill at ease, she spoke comforting words to him and sometimes sang a little bit of "Gather at the River." Then the day came while she was shelling some beans that an unsettling dizzy spell over came her.

What'n the world's a matter with me? she asked herself. She tried to stand and felt a sharp pain in her right arm. I got to straighten out here, she told herself. "I can't be sick...I got to see to Beaver..."

Slowly she slumped to the floor.

It was late in the day when Beaver had come home to find her on the floor of her little kitchen. He was thunderstruck. He sat next to her body all that day and through the next night. He called to her from time to time to see if he could wake her, but it was just no use. He was still seated on the floor when his cousin Willy found him there. Willy, knowing Beaver exceedingly well, reasoned that Beaver may have had something to do with the old woman's death.

"Come on George." He said excitedly. "We got to get you away from here right now."

"Ain't George. I'm Beaver. I cain't leave Momma like this. I gotta stay."

"Come on, you crazy bastard. Folks're gonna think you killed her. They gonna hang you sure as rain."

It took a lot of coaxing, but at last he got Beaver on his feet. As they fled the kitchen, Beaver, almost as an after thought, grabbed the large butcher knife from the pantry shelf. Secured in its buckskin sheath, he secured its thongs to his belt and followed Willy to the little shed that served as their barn. Now he remembered Momma Nell's gun" An old army Colt .45 she kept buried in barrel of grain that she kept for the lone horse and the few chickens.

Beaver plunged his hand in to the grain and came up with it. He had never known how Nellie had come to own it. She had told him that at one time she had had a soldier for a beau, and he had left it behind. But he had never seen a soldier about. In Beaver's small hand, the big Colt with its seven-inch barrel looked formidable.

"Put that thing away, "Willy called. "We got to leave right now! "

Beaver jammed the long barrel into his waist band. Together they saddled Nellie Parker's old Blackie and caught Willy's bay. Hurriedly the two mounted and rode away leaving Nellie Parker on the floor of her kitchen and forever in the shadowy mind of Beaver Parker.

I never coulda' killed my momma Nell, he said over and over to himself. Why would any body think that? I know there's a lot of women needs killin' bad, but not Momma Nellie. My real Momma …I could kill her just like a dog or a cat. That'd be alright. Not Momma Nell though…" He allowed himself now to think of the biscuits.

Amos walked over to the young man of eighteen or so who was still sitting on the poor black horse. He decided he might as well try to get the story from the boy himself. He thought if he were gentle enough to get the boy's confidence, he might learn more.

"What's your name, son?" Amos asked. There was no response at all. As a matter of fact, the boy seemed to be looking at something wonderfully curious, suspended somewhere in the air above Amos' head.

"Can't you tell me your name, boy?" Again, there was an intent stare at the mystery of the air, no other response. Amos was giving it up now and turned to walk away.

"George," the boy said. "My name is George. I want you call me 'Beaver' though. I'm Beaver."

"Well, I'm Amos. How do you do, Beaver?"

"Amos?" the boy asked. At last his eyes found those of Amos and locked in a steady stare.

"Yes, Beaver?" Amos replied. He tried to put all the kindness and understanding in his voice and expression that he could muster.

"Amos, I think I peed'n my pants."

Since that unsettling first meeting, Amos Younger had to admit his outlaw experiences had been plagued with one misadventure after another. It seemed that everything he had touched had gone wrong.

Now It's gonna look like I've gone and shot a horse trader over a couple of horses. Damn!" he thought. I've never shot any one, but now I'm goin' get blamed. It's gonna look like I've gone and killed a man over four mares, and I don't even know if the buyer will still take 'em. When Lloyd Starrett hears there's, shooting attached to these horses, he might just cut and run. Hell, he might do worse than that.

Thinking of Starrett gave Amos new concerns to ponder. Starrett was a dangerous man to say the least. Now that he had so much more to lose than he had in the past only increased this liability, Amos thought.

He fools so many, Amos thought. With all that church goin' and all that good neighbor stuff he puts out, I wonder what the folks around here would think if they really knew Lloyd Starrett the way I knows him.

Amos felt for certain he would have a problem with Starrett. Starrett had promised Amos two hundred dollars to steal the horses and bring them from Murphy Flats across the Nation and then here– Oklahoma territory. When Starrett learned about the shooting, though, Amos was sure there would be trouble.

It was still another problem that Amos only had half the horses he had been sent to steal. Starrett had hired him to bring in all eight head. When the shooting started and Beaver had so brutally killed Alex Carstin, Amos and his gang took what they could and fled into the night. Amos knew Starrett pretty well all right. He'd ridden with Starrett some ten or twelve years ago and knew Starrett as a hard man. When they had first ridden into the territory, they had done about everything one could imagine to just survive. But they had, indeed, survived.

They had robbed a number of Kansas banks; but as an outlaw vocation, that was senseless. Since the Civil War had displaced so many in the late sixties, Kansas was filled with would be bank robbers. Adding to the problem, was a lack of money in those banks the robbers took. Often the bandit had more money than the bank. Lack of success in their robbing endeavors only served to intensify their vicious attitudes

These were desperate, dangerous men who really didn't have much to lose. Further, they had become acclimated to violence from their time in the war. This greatly increased their capacity for violence. Kansas bankers learned this soon enough and just stopped carrying any substantial amounts of cash on hand. That is, when and if they had it to carry in the first place. If the cash did exist, it was likely in a time lock vault. As many as five or six armed guards might be on hand to protect it.

Amos and Lloyd Starrett had fared better by stealing horses. The problem with horse rustling of course was Judge Isaac Parker. Bank robbery in his court carried a ten- to twenty-year sentence provided no violence had been done; but horse thieves were hung. The gallows attendance by horse bandits in the Central Park of Fort Smith was higher, by three to one, than that of murderers. The Judge had said often, "Anybody can get mad enough to kill, but only a low-down rattler would set a man afoot out here in the Nation." Isaac Parker simply hated horse thieves and was convinced that by hanging a horse thief today, you prevented a more heinous crime tomorrow.

Amos and Starrett had ridden together for more than a year. Suddenly one morning, over their campfire coffee, Starrett had announced he had enough. He had saddled his horse and rode west towards the Texas panhandle country, and Amos didn't see him again for about four years. The next time Amos heard of him was while passing through the little town of Amorada, Oklahoma. The sign in front of the town's hardware store clearly said "Starrett Mercantile". A few questions later, and Amos learned that the store was indeed owned by Lloyd Starrett but was managed and operated by a clever old half breed named John Two Seasons.

Starrett, Amos was told, spent his time on the Starrett ranch north of town raising cattle and, especially, breeding horses.

"How the hell can anyone ranch in this country?" Amos wanted to know. "This is rustler heaven. All the damn stock rustlers in the west steal Okie stock and hide it out in the border territory where there ain't no law. I'd say a man would have a real hard time keepin' his stock at home in this country."

"Not Mister Lloyd," Amos was told by John Two Seasons. "Mister Lloyd's got thirty guns on his grounds. Hundred if he needs 'em. Outlaws here abouts cuts a big trail to keep clear of the Starrett range. Mister Lloyd don't need no lawmen to handle things for him. Rustlers go out to the Starrett; ain't nobody never sees 'em anymore. They just disappear like."

It was a sight Amos meant to see for himself. He rode the eight or nine miles north along a trail that appeared to be well traveled. Mid-afternoon he was stopped by a young man on a good horse carrying a Winchester rifle.

"Headed where?" the young man asked flatly.

"I'm Amos Younger... Come out to see an old friend. Maybe you know him... Lloyd Starrett?"

"Got business with Mister Lloyd?"

"No... No Business... We's just old friends is all. I rode a long way to see him." Amos thought the youngster with the rifle might be dangerous, but the Colt .44 in his own belt gave him some comfort.

In tight together like this," he thought, ...and a good man with a pistol 's 'bout as good as a boy with a rifle.

After some thought, the young man said, "Up the trail... Stay ahead of me. When you get to the fork, go left up over that hog back."

The reunion turned out to be a delightful one. The old saddle pals were equally pleased to see one another again. Amos was duly impressed by Starrett's obvious success. His old partner had put together a quality outfit with a decent ranch house, a couple of barns and a two-story long building Amos guessed was a bunk house. It was large to say the least. Resembling the army barracks he'd encountered in the past, this building could house as many as twenty or thirty men. His old partner looked like the epitome of success, and Amos felt shabby by comparison. Starrett was a big broad man. The passing years had left him slightly paunchy but unmistakably powerful.

Amos recognized right away that Lloyd Starrett was still quick and apt to be dangerous. His hair was coal black and lightly shot through with silver. Now he wore a carefully trimmed full moustache. Starrett looked resplendent in twill trousers and a black bib-front shirt. Amos saw that his boots were soft black calf with red leather, hand-tooled inserts. Indian and negro servants seemed to be constantly at hand and Amos could smell enticing and delectable odors wafting in from a kitchen somewhere about. His mouth watered at the delectable odors.

The two compadres had a night to remember. They ate heartily of good hickory-cured ham. Additionally, as expected, there were the slices of beef steak, pounded tender with a stone hammer, dredged in a seasoned flour and fried up in smoked bacon drippings until they were crisp and flavorful. Brought to the table, smoking hot, these savory morsels of steak were then wonderfully drowned in a sea of rich, cream gravy. Big steaming bowls of collards mixed with hominy and sided by ham-flavored black- eyed peas further burdened the massive table.

As always, there was a large bowl of fried fresh okra. The people of Texas and the Nations have always loved this seedy little pod fried golden brown. Once properly prepared, the coin-like slices would be hit with a sultry Indian sauce made from green chiles and red peppers. These were big and fiery spices that did little to conceal their presence. Raging hot and wonderfully delicious, the dish brought swift beads of perspiration to the upper lip. Forehead and temple sweat was not all that uncommon. There were thin tortillas and cornbread, too, and a green apple pie. All was served on the big oaken table by Indian servants who seemed to delight in pleasing "Mister Lloyd."

After the meal, Lloyd showed Amos a corral filled with good horses and a few closed pens. Here, hogs and a few cattle were fattened for the table of the Starrett place. Amos recognized quickly that his old bandito compadre had reached a level of success that had, only a short time ago, seemed beyond dreams.

Later that night while reliving their past adventures, they drank copious amounts of good Kentucky bourbon. This sour mash "sippin' "whiskey was an authentic treasure here in Oklahoma and the Nations. When the time for sleep came, Starrett summoned forth two young and pretty Indian girls who were obviously in the house for more reasons than serving as house maids.

"Fetch a bottle or two for us," he said to the prettiest girl, the one he called "Willow.". Noticing Amos had really taken an interest in these two comely girls, he added, "They's Kickapoo. Ain't from around here you know. Fur trader from Fort Smith brought 'em here some time ago. Said they was for sale and was I interested. They been here ever since. Right handsome, ain't they? I cain't imagine where in the world they come from."

Amos had a bit of trouble keeping his eyes off the Indian maids. These two were so different from the local Indians Amos was so used to seeing. The girls were lively and animated and given to much giggling. Amos judged them to be in their teen age years. He noticed that they were groomed and dressed as young white women might have been. Little of the Kickapoo heritage was to be found here. Lloyd Starrett had obviously transformed the two girls into what he wanted them to be.

Unlike the stouter and more solid women of the southwestern plains bands, both of these Kickapoo girls were lithe and willowy. Both were endowed with statuesque and graceful bodies. The girls had a scrubbed look about them and, as they brushed past him, Amos detected their hair smelled of some sweet, soap.

Amos had only encountered the Kickapoo occasionally for they were rare in Texas. Having migrated from their north woods home territories as recently as the 1850's, it was estimated, that perhaps five hundred of these northern forest people had, for some mystical reason, migrated from the Upper Michigan Peninsula territory. They had drifted deep, down through Missouri and then south all the way to Mexico. Long migrations seemed to be typical Kickapoo behavior. Somehow, these forest people had thrived on the plains and even in the deserts.

The early French fur traders had named this Algonquin-speaking tribe, Kickapoo or "great pedestrians. Long Walkers." How mysterious this tribe had been through the centuries. Seeming to originate in the northern reaches of the tributaries that were Lake Michigan's icy fingers, they spoke a dialect that could only tie them to the Hudson River Valley, the land of the Iroquois. These two locations were nearly a thousand miles apart.

In the late 1700's, they joined forces with the Shawnee warrior chieftain, Tecumseh, to keep white men from entering the Ohio territory. They had fought alongside their Shawnee allies from the shores of Lake Erie, south to the Ohio River. Gradually, though, the whites prevailed. The spread of the white tide never failed.

The Shawnee and all their allies were driven west from the Pennsylvania border across Ohio. A short time later men like Daniel Boone and Ebeneezer Zane pushed them further west— across Indiana territory and at last to the west bank of the Wabash and beyond. It was here the Kickapoo vanished for more than a hundred years. Kickapoo would forever be one of the most baffling of the native American people.

Reappearing in the late 1880's, this mysterious band joined forces with the previously hated whites and helped to put down the Seminole tribes of old Florida. Given to traveling great distances simply for the pleasure of moving about, this fine-looking Kickapoo nation had blended well with the southwestern plains tribes. Here long distance travel was a simple matter of necessity. The Kickapoo were historically famous for turning up in the most unexpected and most distant of places.

Amos Younger was glad they had turned up here. He found the girls to be strikingly handsome and most desirable. Somehow, they reminded him of the wild mustang colts that came to the high meadows in search of early spring grass when the snows were melting.

The girls' features, it seemed to him, were softer and more delicate than other Indian women he had known. To Amos their faces appeared rather heart-shaped and quite unlike the round moon face of the typical Kiowa. Their noses were thin and aquiline, and their almond-shaped eyes were dark, piercing and spirited with a clever intelligence. He was beginning to hunger for what he anticipated was yet to come.

Amos was fully relaxed and filled with good food and drink. It had been a long time since he had all of his clothes off at once and was able to lounge about in a big wooden tub filled with steamy, soapy water. In fact, it had been a long time since he had slept under a real roof; an even longer time since he had slept with a woman in his arms.

When he stretched out beside the one Starrett had called Willow, on the wide cool down-filled ticking, he admitted that he had known no finer moments. Kickapoo, Amos decided, made fine dining and sleeping companions.

The food had been fine and homey, and the whiskey was exceptionally mellow. Willow, his seemingly assigned companion, had taken all the edge off his nerves, and he felt better than he remembered feeling for a very long time. With the treatment he was currently enjoying, there was precious little that Amos Younger would not do for his old friend and present benefactor, Lloyd Starrett. A little drunk, and very tired now, he slept soundly.

It was in the morning over a breakfast of strong coffee and a rich persimmon pudding that Starrett told Amos about the Kentucky horses he'd seen just south of Dodge at the place called Murphy Flats.

"I offered that little squirt a whorehouse price for them horses, Amos, but he just wasn't sellin'. Might be you and me can get together on somethin'." Amos instinctively sensed Starrett's meaning.

"I figure you pick up a couple o' boys and go and fetch them horses for me, Amos. Ain't nobody likely to chase you into the Nations, and I can guarantee that little fart from Illinois ain't gonna give you no trouble."

"Why don't you just go your ownself?" Amos asked

"Look at what's goin' on here, Amos. I got things pretty good here, and I'm being a pretty good citizen. I built the school here and the church, and we're doing pretty good. Amos, I want those horses… But I cain't stand no trouble. I'm hopin' you can get you a couple of boys and ride up there and fetch them horses back for me. You could handle the pilgrim by yourself, but you'll need the help to drive the string back. Reckon you can find a couple of men?"

"Maybe Charley Stone and Willy Parker," Amos allowed.

"They any 'count?" Starrett wanted to know.

"No, not really. Matter of fact they ain't worth much— just saddle trash— but their 'bout all I know anymore. All the hands we rode with in the old days are either dead or in jail."

"Well, use them then, but be careful. Any trouble crop up, you pull right out. I don't figure anybody'll come into the territory for a few horses. At least till I've had a chance to hide 'em real good; but if there's any other trouble… Well, I just don't want it, Amos. I wont have it 'cause there's too much at stake here.. Just get the horses and come straight here.

You can make the ride in about two or maybe three days. What do you say, Amos?"

"Reckon I can try. I think five or six days though is more likely. I'll see if I can scare up the boys and we'll go have a look. Tell you though, Lloyd, I'm busted out, and I'll need a little cash.

"We can take care of that alright, Amos. One more thing: Can you trust these boys all the way?"

"Hell, Lloyd, I never even trusted you all the way," Amos grinned.

"Reason I'm askin' is this Illinois feller's got his wife with him. And a little boy' too. I'm tellin' you' Amos– this woman's a real looker. You keep a tight rein on your boys, and don't let nothin' get out of hand. Hell, for that matter you keep a tight rein on yourself. She's a sight compared to the Kickapoo, and I saw you went right after that."

"I can take it or leave it alone, Lloyd. Don t worry; I guarantee no trouble."

How could I have made that guarantee? Amos thought. Now here I am with more trouble than I ever been in. Hell, I didn't shoot that feller. I just shot at the ground when all the guns started poppin'. Maybe I did hit him in the leg... or foot maybe. Ain't likely I could miss the ground, but maybe I did... No, I didn't. It was that Beaver. Goddamn that Beaver! Just wasn't no way o' stoppin' him. Here I'm tryin' to scare this pilgrim off, and Beaver lets him have six right in the cookstove. I swear this gang o' mine's gonna be the death o' me....

Amos looked at his little gang sprawled now about the small fire. Charley Stone was fast asleep and snoring softly. Willy Parker, too, was sleeping. He had buried himself deep into his blankets, and only his small weasel face protruded.

As usual, it was Beaver that gave Amos cause for concern. Just the appearance alone of Beaver was most unsettling. His scrawny blonde beard did a poor job of hiding the livid red-and-yellow pustules of advanced acne. With his yellowed buck teeth and dirty blonde hair protruding in unmanageable shocks from under his battered slouch hat, Amos couldn't decide if he looked awful or just pitiful.

Unlike the others, he was wide awake. He stared into the fire with eyes so widely opened Amos could clearly see their whites. In place of his usual barren expression, he grinned wildly now. The smirk was a maniacal one, displaying Beaver's spoiled teeth. Amos found the whole scene before him most disturbing.

What could he be thinking of that would produce such a grin? Amos wondered. What could it be makin' the idjit smile like that?

He tried to think of something that he thought Beaver might have such an unusual reaction to.

Must be thinkin' o' home, he mused. Or maybe somethin' sweet, like pie or candy. But try as he could, Amos could find no excuse for such a grin from the generally expressionless Beaver. He tried to think of a word that would describe it. Just for a second he thought it could be described as terrifying. Then he waved the idea aside as ridiculous and went back to fire-gazing.

Had Amos been able to see inside the mind of Beaver Parker, he would likely have been a great deal more unsettled than he already was. Beaver's mind was being invaded that night by two thoughts he couldn't seem to dispel. Indeed, he didn't want to let these thoughts go. He was enjoying them to the fullest.

First was the thought of the man he had killed. He liked picturing his stricken face over and over in his mind's eye. Beaver cherished the look of astonishment on the man's face as he shot him over and over. He particularly liked the part where the man's eyes suddenly went glassy as the very life ran out of him. It made him feel good, somehow, to see it repeated again and again...

He had killed before. Dogs, cats. And once a range calf. Butt never a man and never with a gun. That was a new and wonderful power. He would always remember the noise, the shock as the recoil of the heavy pistol ran up his arm. And there was the smoke and fire belching from the muzzle... And there was the smell, the charcoal sulphur smell of the white gun smoke.

Breathing deeply now through his nose he found he could recreate that acrid odor of burning gun powder. It came back to him with a rush such as good whiskey produces on an empty stomach. He thought it delectable. He would like to smell it again for real at that moment. The thoughts of the shooting were an entertainment indeed, to Beaver. As pleasant as they were, though, they were far behind the most prominent thought on his mind this night: The woman. He could remember how she moved across the little campsite as he watched her through the telescope.

Her movements were swift and sure. He was captivated by the recollection of the sun-streaked hair. He thought of that confident stride and wondered if she could be so proud if he had her alone somewhere and under his control. He could still visualize the thrust of her shirt front, and the thought made his mouth dry. When he remembered the tight canvass across her shapely buttocks, he felt himself nearly swoon.

Killing the man had been exhilarating, but the things he had in mind for the woman brought actual physical shivers to the pit of his stomach. He worried his protruding front teeth with a busy tongue as he day dreamed on the matter. He would go to her again. There was nothing that could stop him. This time he would go without Amos, and there would be no leaving just when the good part was about to start.

To hell with them horses, he said to himself. I don't care nothin' 'bout no Goddamn horses...

He hated Amos for dragging him away so suddenly. He had wanted to go to the wagon for the woman. And for the boy, too. He would have liked shooting the boy. He knew full well that they were in the wagon, too. He had wanted them badly, but Amos had grabbed his horse's bridle and yelled at him to hold on. They had raced off in the darkness and left so much behind undone.

Amos had kept his horse at a dead run for a long time, and when the horse began to tire, he kept him at a fast canter even longer. Finally Beaver had twisted the reins from Amos' hand and stopped his horse. He wheeled the animal back in the direction of the horse camp. That was when he saw her. She was in the firelight. She was running from the wagon to kneel by the dying man.

That's when I should have gone back, he said almost aloud. Goddamn old Amos. He wouldn' let me stop. Just kept a-hollerin' and yellin'. By God, next time I'm goin' back! Goddamn old Amos Younger. He wouldn't let me stop when I really wanted to. It was Amos made me pee on myself again.

Beaver Parker decided, from these loosely joined thoughts, that he hated Amos Younger. He didn't want Amos to be in control any longer. The problem then was how to get to the woman without interference from Amos. The answer was easy enough. His grin widened even farther when he realized the really good idea had come to him so easily. Kill Amos. It made him happy when he was able to arrive at such good answers to such important problems.

The beans were very good that night, but Amos Younger could find little else to feel good about. After a long time he finally fell into a restless sleep propped on his saddle. Even in a uncertain sleep he couldn't dismiss that absurd grin.

Chapter Five

Leaving Dodge

Colin had, in all the excitement of the fist fight in the stockyards with Chester Crawford, completely forgotten the letter given to him by Trent Markley. He came across it in his pocket just as the waiter seated him at the big round table in the Dodge House dining room. He was to meet Markley here for a final evening of entertainment. Tomorrow he would start his long ride back to the Broken Spur.

He had bathed, shaved and changed into his only suit., then realized he had somehow changed the letter from the hip pocket of his riding pants into the inside breast pocket of the cutaway coat without noticing. Of course, he was hurting a bit. His bruised eye was troubling him some. Perhaps that accounted for him overlooking it. He was finally reading it when Trent Markley appeared and seated himself at the table.

"Colin, I'd say with an eye that big you ought to be able to see all the way to Texas. That is, if you could get it open a little wider."

Colin grinned at his friend's remark, but he felt a pang of embarrassment at having lost the fist fight with Chester Crawford.

"I'd guess I grabbed too much man," Colin said.

"I would think, maybe, that's true Collie; but you gave him a hell of a fight. I'm bettin' he don't want no more of you. When you hit him with the bridle, I thought it was over for him right there. Who would've thought the bastard could get up after that? Anyway, Collie, ten years ago you'd of cleaned his clock good for him." Colin winced a bit as the salt on his celery stick stung his split lip.

"I think that's the problem," Colin said. "I don't know exactly, but I'm fifty years old or so I'd guess. I guess I don't hit like I used to."

"Collie, you hit just as hard as ever you did," Trent grinned. "You just don't hit as often." Both men showed slow grins that spread and widened until they were each laughing uproariously. Colin winced as his own laughter pained his split lip. The waiter had by now brought crystal flagons of cooled wine, and they drank deeply. As the warmth of the ruby liquid spread through their bodies, the cares of the day were washed away, the stockyards brawl forgotten; and both men became visibly serene.

The two friends were at ease that evening. With the herd sold, Colin and Trent alike relaxed in luxury that would've rivaled that found in Chicago or Kansas City. They sat back in their comfortable chairs and ordered up the finest food and wine the Dodge House had to offer. First the white-coated waiter had brought a plate of greens with sweet onions and mushrooms, wilted with the hot drippings from fried smoked ham. Then there were the oysters. Straight from the Chesapeake Bay, they had come overland on the Union Pacific. Packed deep in icy brine, they were as fresh and plump as if gathered just that morning.

At last came the course that had brought fame to the Dodge House dining room: Before each man was set a large platter of roasted quail. The tasty little birds had been prepared to perfection. Each had been basted in pure butter and was a wonderful deep, crusty brown. Each platter held six of the fine little birds surrounded by a ring of tiny roasted new potatoes with their red skins left intact. For flavoring the quail, silver dipping bowls of exotic sauces sat table center. One sauce was a blend of mustard and apricot. Another was of plump raisins and brandy, and there were others that Colin couldn't identify. He thought they may have contained pears and rare bananas.

At the end of this sumptuous repast, came the blackberry cobbler smothered in whipped cream and laced with good Kentucky bourbon. All of this had been served with assorted pans of cornbread and pretty little dinner rolls. Complimenting the breads, there was an assortment of nut-flavored butter and jellies and jams of all flavors. Lastly big pots of steamy black coffee, brewed and perked. This had indeed been brewed and perked and not just boiled in the customary trail manner. Trent had declared it was 'strong enough to float a silver spoon.'

"Ten years ago," Trent told Colin. "…the quail for this hotel were hunted up and shot by Annie Oakley. She shot 'em all in the heads you know, and you didn't have to be so careful about bitin' down on a bird shot. She's a big-time entertainer now, what with her trick shootin' and all. I reckon the hotel got themselves a different hunter now. Annie sure could shoot though."

"I've heard tell of Annie Oakley," Colin said. "Is she from around here?"

"No," Trent answered around a mouthful of savory quail breast. "She's from Ohio as I remember. Shot most of her game though in Illinois and Missouri I'd reckon. Quail's about like the oysters. Come in here on the train. Anyhow, I've eaten some of Annies' quail. That was a long time ago, though."

"Seems like everything we talk about tonight was better ten years ago," Colin said. "Includin' my fist fightin'."

"Well, Collie, the one thing you can count on is gettin' older. That's if you live long enough. And you just might live 'some' longer anyhow, if you quit fightin' young toughs over stud horses. That could keep you from gettin' older, I'd think."

"Well, it ain't just tonight." Colin was lighting a large Cuban cigar." Last week I was passin' through a little trail town just north of Freedom. I stopped of at this little store to get some rifle shells. See, Trent, I got this Henry rifle Old Robert bought for me when I was just old enough to have a gun. I've carried it on my saddle ever since. You know them old Henry's are .44 rim fire which I guess ain't much of a shell, but I think it's stout enough.

Trouble is them old rim fire shells are gettin' hard to find. I asked the man at the hardware store for some shells for my Henry, and he say's they don't sell antique cartridges. Antique, mind you. Well, that makes me pretty hot, and I ride off back to herd. But then I gets to thinkin' I've had that rifle about forty years. That hardware man was right– that damn rifle is an antique. And then I start to wonderin' what that makes me?" He dragged hard on the Cuban. It's round end glowed like a red moon.

"Well, hell, Collie, I guess you're a little seasoned maybe; but I wouldn't call you no antique."

"Yeah, I know you wouldn't, but maybe that's what I am. I've been makin' this drive to Dodge more than thirty years now. I came here the first time with Juan Garcia when there was nothin' here but the train tracks. Them tracks and a couple of old stores. Garcia's been too old to make the trail for more than twenty years now.

"O' course Old Robert ain't never made the trip. Can't nobody hardly get him off the Spur. Garcia and Old Robert both are seventy somethin' now. Neither one knows for sure seventy 'what'. Anyway, not one man who came here with me the first time is still alive except for Garcia."

"I'd say, Collie, that a man as old as you are is entitled to another drink." Trent motioned, and the waiter was instantly at his side.

"I got to tell you, Trent, it's makin' me think some. I just look around and there's old Robert and Juan Garcia... They both showin' age considerably now. And then here's some damn store clerk tellin' me my rifle's an antique. I think the whole thing about it is that I don't mind gettin' old. I just hate to see the things I love get old, too." Colin leaned back in his chair in a reflective mood.

"And, Trent, I'll tell you the truth– I don't want to get too old for the trail. I don't want it to end. I've never had a wife nor no family 'cept old Robert and Garcia. And the truth is, I never wanted anything 'cept that. Hell, Trent, I guess I just want to cowboy forever."

"I don't think your age is about to change things all that much, Collie, but there's a heap of changin' comin' due, with us or without us."

"What kind o' changes do you mean, Trent?"

"Collie, everybody's workin' toward fatter beef that's softer to chew on. When I first started sellin' your cattle, they was all longhorn and that was that. Those old longhorns were buck colored and black-and-brindle. Now everywhere I look I see the roan. Even in the Spur herd I see that red and blue roan." Trent stuffed a linen napkin into his shirtfront and held his knife and fork pointed aloft.

"You got shorthorn bulls out there on the plain somewhere, and so does everyone else. This new white- faced Hereford is comin' on strong, too. Was a time all we had were wild longhorns; Them wild cattle days are 'bout over. Ain't hardly a cow in Texas that ain't wearin' a brand."

"We still get some wild cows at the Spur," Colin protested. "Big wild horse herd too."

"Sure, you do," Trent agreed. "But that's because Old Robert started that cattle-buying business years ago. The Broken Spur has cattle buyers all over Texas, but those little outfits– the ones that used to live by poppin' wild cows out of the big thicket– they're all broke and gone now. Nowadays it takes all the cattle buyers the Spur can hire to fetch in as many head as Old Robert and Juan Garcia used to do alone. I'd say that today there's more cattle bein" raised' in Texas than there is bein' caught. That's good, 'cause they're better cattle. Sad though to see the old mossy horn leave. I tell you, Collie, one of these days these grass cattle are goin' to give way to corn fed cattle for sure. We'll be doing business in a different way when that comes."

"Good Lord, Trent, there ain't that much corn in Texas."

"No but there is in Iowa. I see it comin' to the point where you Texans grass your calf crop to five or six hundred pounds, then rail 'em off to Iowa or Illinois or maybe Indiana. It wont be cattlemen, Collie, who fatten and finish those cattle. It'll be farmers what fattens 'em up. Farmers with corn. The corn yield is gettin' so high with all this new cultivatin', that the hogs cain't eat it all like they have in the past. And besides everybody wants high flavor and tender beef. Corn 'll do that, Collie."

"Dirt farmers handling cows?" Colin was appalled.

"Not cows, Collie. There wont be a market for cows and bulls no more. Well, at least not the beef market we have now. These farmers are gonna want steers and heifers. They'll want cattle that can think about eatin' instead of breedin'. They'll cut the horns off 'em, too, so they can't ventilate each other so easy. The Spur will keep her cows at home and breed 'em to big old fat-assed bulls to make more feeder stock. I think, Colin, the day is comin' when the farmer'll sell his corn by runnin' it through the beef. The rancher's gonna sell him the calves. The farmer's gonna sell us the fat cattle. Old George Swift's meat packing' houses is gonna sell us the beef."

Colin shook his head in disagreement.

"Can't no body drive fat cattle no great distance, Trent. Hell, they'll all die on the drive. They get too fat they just drop dead on the trail. Lean cattle are a sight easier to move. We have to be careful now 'cause some of our Buffalo grass got a heap of red clover mixed in it. That's a fattenin' grass. It gets so rich when there's a lot of rain that sometimes I'd swear it looks downright greasy. If we let a steer get too much of that and fatten too much, he dies on the trail every time. I don't think farmers can move 'em anyway. There's a hell of a lot to know about trailin' cows."

"Railroads, Collie." Trent leaned forward in his chair. He was intent on making his point. "Railroads makin' new trails. Trail drives wont be long and hard like now. Trains'll come and get your cattle someday, take 'em to Iowa, and from there they'll likely end up in Chicago. The big meat packers are seeming to locate there. They're buildin' meat plants there so big they cover up to a hundred acres, I hear tell. When they turn the cattle into meat, it'll probably be trains what brings beef roasts back to Texas. I think railroads and barbed wire're gonna make some real big changes in our lives, Collie. Them, and English bulls."

"Damn, Trent, that don't hardly make no sense at all." Colin was preparing to launch another defense of the present condition of the cattle industry. He raised the wine glass to his lips but stopped suddenly when he saw Trent's eyes widen abruptly.

"We got company Colin." Colin looked up and saw the big man walking toward their table. He braced himself for a continuation of that morning's fist fight he thought was sure to come. The man was Chester Crawford. It was Trent, though, who stopped Crawford as he approached.

"There'll be no trouble here, Crawford. You start somethin' here, and you'll be talkin' to Sheriff Traylor soon enough."

"I ain't wantin' no trouble. Mister Trav, I come to apologize to you and tell you I'm sorry for mistreatin' your horse." Colin was surprised but still a good deal wary of these unlikely events. He saw that Chester

Crawford was clean, too. He looked pretty good in clean overalls and what may have been a new calico shirt.

His beard was trimmed, and Colin noticed that even his grimy nails had been scraped clean. A bit to Colins' chagrin was the fact that, other than an angry purple bruise on his left cheekbone, Crawford seemed to show no signs of their earlier altercation. The big man held his hat before him in his hands and kept his eyes on the floor.

"I lost my job over that fight, and at first I was kind of mad about it, Mister Trav. But then I got to thinkin'.: All I was doing on that damn job was drinkin' whiskey and just gettin' more low down ever day. I ain't never whipped no horse in the face before in my life, and that's a fact. My Daddy would be awful sad if he thought I'd come that far down."

Colin, still alert for trickery, was moved by the large man's apology. His humble demeanor seemed somehow tragic and sincere. He had gotten the best of the fist fight without question. Yet, here he stood, contrite and looking for forgiveness.

"So, I'm glad, Mister Trav. I'm glad I lost that job. This trail town is been hurtin' me, and I been too lonely here. I been thinkin' bad thoughts and drinkin' too much, too. Tell you true, Mister Trav, I'm goin' back to Texas. Well, that's all I got to say. I'm right sorry I upset your supper, but I just had to say I'm sorry to you. You're a decent man, Mister Trav, and I wronged you and your horse, too." The man turned on his heel and started to leave.

"Wait," Colin said " I got this here letter from the man that runs the mercantile out at Murphy Flats. You know how to get to Murphy Flats, Chester?" The big man nodded, puzzlement now on his face.

"Well, I got to go out there in the morning. If you ain't got no job and if you want to trail back to Texas, why don't you meet me there; and we'll trip it together? Would you like to work for the Broken Spur for a while?"

A sudden grin burst forth on Crawford's face, and for the first time Colin saw a front tooth was missing. He wondered if the tooth had always been absent or if perhaps he had taken it out in the fight.

"Oh, yessir, Mister Trav. I'd love a job ridin' for the Spur." Chester Crawford seemed absolutely overwhelmed.

"Then let's do this. You fetch the Spur's buckboard from the stockyards and hitch it up with a couple o' good horses from the remuda pens. You'll know our buckboard when you see it. It's a green Studebaker with red spokes. Lord, be sure you get the right one." Colin was emphatic when discussing this special wagon.

"Old Robert sets a lot of store in that rig. He sent me and Juan Garcia clear back east to South Bend, Indiana, and we bought that outfit from old Clement Studebaker himself. What I'm sayin' is you better handle Old Robert's wagon with care, or he'll likely have your ass and mine, too." The men laughed aloud. This bawdy remark seemed to bind them together as comrades somehow.

Old Robert's Studebaker was, indeed, a wonderful affair. For the most part it was painted deep Lincoln green with a glistening enamel. It's dark verdant sides had then been finely traced with exquisite ivory-colored pin striping. Most notable of all were the wheels. Their spokes were colored a bright orange-red. There was a distinct oriental flavor to the high gloss lacquer finish.

The catalogue that offered this "Wonder of the American Road" for sale had promised that the wagon could be delivered with the wheels colored in "Chinese Red" or "Bright Buttercup Yellow." Colin and Garcia had found it so amusing that Old Robert. could be so confounded by this simple choice. Here was a man who could, in the blink of an eye, come to decisions where cattle or land were involved that might involve thousands of dollars. Yet over this weighty problem, Old Robert had pondered greatly for several days. When it appeared to Garcia and Colin that he would never decide, he had abruptly announced that China Red was, indeed, to be the selection of wheel color for his new wagon. Colin now remembered Old Robert's ear-to-ear grin, so proud he was that he had, at last, arrived at this superior determination.

The wheels, mounted on ball bearings as they were, made it possible for a single horse fitted with shafts to easily draw it about. But Old Robert preferred the double tree arrangement and used the rig normally with a two-horse team. To further add to the elegance and comfort of the buckboard, each of the wheel's rims had been mounted with a hard rubber ring. These were affixed with incredible tightness. Because of them, the wagon glided smoothly and silently over the toughest of terrain. With it's coiled seat springs, the whole affair rode high, smooth and handsome. It was one of Old Robert's favorite possessions. To Colin it was a ranch wagon, and he often relegated its use to standard assignments.

Colin went on with his instructions to Chester Crawford. "Then I guess you better tie about two or three more horses for ridin' and spellin' to the buckboard tailgate and throw the Spur's saddles and tack in the wagon. The boys left 'em all in the store room by the office. You know that store room' Chester?"

"Yes sir, mister Trav; and I know the Spur equipment, too. I helped load some of that gear into the store room myself."

"Well, that's good, Chester. You load up everything that looks like it belongs to the Spur, and meet me 'bout nine o'clock out at Murphy Flats in front of the hardware store. I got some business with Henry Brooker, and then we'll be off."

Chester was enthusiastic and delighted at the prospect of going home to Texas.

"I know Mister Brooker. I know right where that store is, and I'll sure meet you there, Mister Trav. The horses I'm bringin' ? I guess you'll want the little buckskin?"

"Yeah, I guess I'm crazy for travelin' clean back to Texas with a stallion. Almost bound to be trouble. Well, I guess I just like that little horse a lot. Bring him along."

Colin and Trent watched Chester Crawford's back as the big man left the dining room. There seemed to be new spring in his step.

"Damn, I thought we were gonna have another fight," Trent said. "Collie, are you sure you can trust that feller to travel clean back to Texas with?"

"Well, old Robert always says when a bad man says he's sorry, a good man's either got to give him the benefit of the doubt or shoot him dead for bein' a liar. Anyhow, all the other Spur riders have scattered, and I was just gonna ride back alone. With him along, at least I can get the Studebaker and some of the Spur's gear back home."

"Did you say you got business with Henry Brooker, Collie?"

"You know Henry?"

"Sure, I know him. He sells my company livestock supplies and veterinarian medicine and such."

"Well, he's the man who sent me the letter you gave me. Said he needed to see me before I went home. I don't know what he wants, but sometimes Juan Garcia takes a notion for some gee jaw or a new gun or somethin' and orders it through Henry. I always have to fetch it in to him. Mostly he orders a keg of nails or the like, but sometimes it gets strange. Once I had to carry him a sewing machine."

Trent smiled widely as he imagined this preposterous sight.

"I'd guess I'm haulin' somethin' back to Texas, Trent, but I just ain't sure what. Anyway, Trent, It's my last night in Dodge and, although I'm feelin' somewhat ancient, I'm lookin' to have a little fun before that God awful ride home."

"Well, Collie, my boy, I've got a little goin' away present for you all picked out over at the Bird Cage. I guess you're up to a little trip to the Bird Cage?" Trent winked wickedly.

"Well, I used to make several trips over there on the Street when I'd come into Dodge. I guess I'd hate to go home without goin' at least once. Hell, I wouldn't have any stories to tell Juan Garcia. That could get me whipped all over again. You know it was Garcia took me to the Cage for the first time. Lord, that was so long ago I hate to even think about it. Anyhow, I can still remember him tellin' me, 'Don't chisel on the price, Colin. If you don't want to pay it, don't go with the girl to the room; but don't haggle or bargain with her. Remember she's selling you all she has in the world, and it's a disgrace to bargain or chisel when it's for everything. I can almost hear him yet. He said it's a thing of privilege to dicker with a trader who has a barn filled with goods. But when a man has fallen so low that he has to sell you his only horse, honor demands that you must pay his price or walk away."

"You know, Collie, that even sounds like old Garcia. I liked him, Colin. I'd like to see him again sometime."

"The Mexicans call him Mucho Hombre," Colin said. "I guess that about says it all."

Trent was thoughtful but only for a moment. "They got a new little lady of the evening at the Bird Cage right now that's gettin' downright famous," he said. "Tell me, Collie, have you Texas boys ever heard tell of Squirrel Tooth Alice?"

"Squirrel Tooth Alice? Hell, yes, I've heard of her clear back on the Canadian River. I guess she's bout the most famous soiled dove in the whole west. Maybe the whole world. I sure didn't know she was here though. I hear tell she's beautiful."

"She is that. She is that, Colin, and a great deal more."

"Why the name?" Colin wanted to know.

"Well, it ain't got nothin' to do with her looks 'cause she's a sure enough looker. Thing is, she's got a cage in her room and keeps a pet squirrel or two. Now don't ask me why 'cause I've told you all about that name I know."

"Squirrel Tooth Alice. Right here in Dodge. Ain't that a howl?"

"She's here, and she's all yours, Colin. She's yours for the whole entire night, right up to and includin' breakfast in bed. All bought and paid for by a gentleman who wants you to know how much he appreciates the cattle you been lettin' him sell for you and the commission dollars you've been payin' him. We made a lot of money, Collie. Your herd was in good shape, and I got the top of the market for you. It's time for us to howl a little. I think you're gonna have a great time tonight, Collie. I ain't sure, however, that you'll be in Murphy Flat by nine in the morning though. 'Course, when Alice is all done with you, you just may not care where in the hell you are. Bad as you look already I don't think she can hurt you none, but she might give you somethin' to think about when your winterin' back on the Spur, say 'bout January." Trent gave a mighty laugh.

"Well, Trent," Colin said, let's go see this mighty mare, and I'll catch me a little ride. Need to do somethin' to work off all this food."

"Colin," Trent said.

"Yes."

"Try not to act too old for her."

Chapter Six

Ranger, Henry Brooker

It was nearly noon when Colin reached The Henry Brooker Hardware and Mercantile Emporium at the settlement known as Murphy Flats, Kansas. After Colin had left Trent Markley, he had walked down Front Street right up to the door of the Birdcage. He stopped here for a while and studied the grey two-story house. Lighted lamps were in most of the windows, and Colin had to admit to himself the whole idea of the most comfortable brothel in Kansas and the prepaid visit to Squirrel Tooth Alice seemed pretty good to say the least. But then suddenly Colin turned on his heel and walked away. As he continued down Front Street he thought to himself: *Not tonight...It just ain't somethin' I want right now.* He couldn't explain it, but he just felt tired and trail-weary. For the first time he could ever remember the feather bed at the hotel sounded better than the romp at the Birdcage. It was true he was late the next morning for the meeting with Henry Brooker, but the Birdcage had nothing to do with it. Colin had simply overslept.

Mattie Brooker was somewhat famous for the table she set in the local area, and today was no exception. When she had learned that Colin Trav was to sit at early dinner, the name they gave their mid day meal, with them that day, she had thrown herself into a frenzy of pots and pans to prepare her best for one of her dearest friends.

Her luncheon table fairly groaned with a selection of fine, smoked ham sided with vinegared collards and bacon-laced butterbeans. This was served up with big, stone mugs of cool homemade beer. On the sideboard rested a steaming pan of cornbread easily four inches thick. Colin had thought he would never be hungry again after last night's Dodge House feast, but Mattie's cooking was more than he could resist. Besides with no breakfast, because of his tardy rising, he was glad to see Mattie's heavy table and joined right in with little prompting. Looking around outside the store he determined that Chester Crawford had not arrived.

Well he's either three hours late or he ain't comin' at all, Colin thought. He actually felt a little saddened by this turn of events. He had thought he might grow to like Crawford.

Henry Brooker was thinner by far than Colin. He seemed to be one of those men who can, regularly, dine on great amounts of food without ever gaining so much as an ounce. Alas, the same could not be said for poor Mattie. She grew plumper each day and wider with each new baby. Her size though didn't bother Henry in the least. Henry Brooker loved Mattie with all his heart. Colin had noticed that affection on his previous visits. It was good to see it again. The love had not declined.

As Mattie scurried around the table seeing that they had the desired servings of her sumptuous food, Henry couldn't keep his hands off her. He was forever patting her hand or touching her arm. If she were across the room, Colin saw, he touched her with his eyes.

Once, when she had leaned over the table to reach for a serving bowl, Colin caught notice that Henry had placed his cheek against her upper arm. That probably went a long way towards explaining the five plump, blonde and happy children who were remarkably visible around the Brooker residence. Their noisy laughter and unruly behavior seemed to delight Henry and Mattie alike.

Through mouthfuls of the delicious food, Henry began to tell Colin the story of the pretty woman and the boy camped in the cottonwood grove with the stallions. Colin listened carefully but found it difficult not to keep thinking of the Henry Brooker he had known so long ago. The story of Pamela Carstin was indeed greatly interesting, but so were the memories of a Henry Brooker from a long time ago. It was hard for Colin to place Brooker in this present setting as a store keeper.

Colin saw that the two older boys were out in the corral playing with a spotted pony called Junebug. The gentle little mare brought squeals of delight from the boys. Their boisterous antics brought approving smiles from their parents. The children were happy, and Mattie was happy, and that made Henry Brooker happy.

Henry loved to hold Mattie in his thin but muscular arms late at night. She was warm and soft and round and somehow the 'plenty' of her made him feel good. There was a time when Mattie had been many pounds trimmer and could have even been described as lithe. There was never a time, though, that Mattie was more loved than right now. Mattie, the children and the store. Those were the things that made up the man who was Henry Brooker.

Colin was still having hard time believing his own eyes when he was with Henry and Mattie. Henry looked so peculiar now compared to the old days. Today, Henry was thin and nearly bald. His glasses were small and round and looked a bit absurd riding on the lower tip of his nose. He wore a celluloid collar with a red leather bow tie buttoned into place. He had covered his wiry frame with a striped denim shop apron. It was difficult for Colin to believe that his old friend of more than thirty years had become such a model of domesticity. Brooker, in an apron, was a riddle to be reckoned with.

Colin remembered another Henry Brooker; One who had ridden with the Palo Duro Canyon gang under the leadership of Charley Goodnight. They had called themselves Texas Rangers, but no one knew for sure whether they were formally Rangers or not. What was indisputably known was that the twenty armed men who made up the Goodnight bunch had endeavored to chase every Comanche and Kiowa brave out of Texas.

That had been more than twenty years ago. It was a time both Comanche and Kiowa were united under the command of the notorious half breed, Quanah Parker. That bloody chapter of Texas history had begun even before there were Rangers. In 1836 while Travis, Crockett and Bowie were defending the Alamo, there was a great deal of strife pressing other Texans too. Not nearly so publicized, as Alamo the Comanche had launched a reign of terror such as the west had never seen.

The saga really began when nine-year old Cynthia Parker was taken as a Comanche captive in one of these vicious raids. Her father killed, she was led away bound in rawhide thongs to become a Comanche slave. This terrible sentence though never came to pass. Unlike most women who had suffered this same fate, Cynthia Parker thrived. She learned all the ways of the Comanche. Still young enough to adapt, she took to them all. Soon, darkened by the sun, only her blue eyes distinguished her from the other tribal women. Cynthia Parker was a fully recognized tribal member.

When she reached eighteen, she was taken as the bride of a fierce old war chief called Peta Nocona. Two sons were the fruit of this union. The older boy, named Pecos, history would dismiss. It was the second son who was destined to become the Comanches' greatest war chief, Quanha. This blue-eyed Indian warrior would be the last of the great war chiefs to "give up the way." The peace, though, could not come before Quanha had led his band on a hundred raids. Each was bent on murder, insurmountable cruelty and vast destruction.

The half-breed combatant had vowed to kill all whites except for his own mother. In a cavalry raid on the Peace River in 1860, his mother had been recaptured by the whites. Along with Quanha's baby sister, she was taken forever from the Comanche life. The leadership of the Kwahadi band of Comanche, the most warlike of the several clans, became his only family.

His young fighting companions adopted fierce-sounding names as they took to the warpath. They called themselves Big Horse, Fighting Wolf and Wild Bear. At the same time they ridiculed the man called Quanha, the Comanche epithet for "fragrant." Out of love and respect for his mother, he kept the name that meant "pleasant smell' which she had given him. Further, he had assumed his Mothers' last name, 'Parker'.

When his light cavalry braves had soundly thrashed the soldiers led by Colonel MacKenzie at Big Bend country that all the other clans found a new respect for Quanha Parker. The fierce scream of Qua—nha ! would, in fact, become the dreaded war cry of the Kwahadi. It was this battle scream that would freeze the blood of the Kwahadi enemy.

It was this band, and a few more insignificant ones that Charles Goodnight had sworn to rout. It would indeed be at the Palo Duro Canyon site that the Comanche would finally fall. Colonel MacKenzie's troops, along with the Goodnight riders, succeeded in a night raid of capturing the Comanche horse herd.

They drove fourteen hundred head of horses to the head of the canyon that night. There they shot them dead one by one. For days on end the prairie was poisoned by the bloated bodies of the once magnificent herd. It was this great horse massacre that ended the Comanche reign. Some said that to put that majestic horse army afoot had been the end. Others, who knew the Comanche better, had believed the tribe's heart was simply broken beyond repair when they saw the horrible horse slaughter. How could they hope to defeat a people so terrible in battle that they could commit this dreadful atrocity ?

The Comanche looked upon this single act as far more devastating than their own run at human suffering and torture. After all, horses were the religion of the Comanche. They danced the horse dance and would hunt no buffalo without the cayuse. They made babies with their women in the same position used by stallions and mares. To the Kwahadi the horse was the very symbol of life and worshipped as a deity.

Now to look upon the vast acres of carnage was to look upon their own dead children. Or their dead Gods. The whites, they decided, were far too dreadful to continue fighting against. The horses they had loved so much for nearly three hundred years were gone now; with the horses went the Comanche spirit.

Henry Brooker had shot his share of those horses. He never talked about it. He couldn't bring himself even to believe that he was a part of that inhumane slaughter. But Colin knew he was there. Colin had

Rangered with Brooker and Goodnight for a short time as many young Texas men would in those years. Unlike Colin, Henry Brooker thrived on the action and rode the trail of the avengers for several years. It was after the horse extermination that he had drawn himself to Mattie Wilcox, daughter of a small cattle rancher, and put aside the Ranger rides forever.

Brooker had always been thin, but in those days Colin remembered he had hair in abundance. He also wore a beard and large full moustache. Mostly though Colin recalled that Brooker had once owned a spectacular brace of Colt revolvers. They were .44-caliber, single actions, garishly plated with fine nickel and stocked with bright mother-of-pearl. He had carried them butt forward in his waist band. There could be no mistake of the intent of this obvious display. It was the defiant exhibition of the pistolero. "Butt forward" may have been the gun carrying style made famous by Wild Bill Hickiock, but no one looked more natural or at ease with it than had Henry. Henry had called this pair of Colts his "town guns". They were indeed too fancy for the trail. They made precisely the statement that Ranger Henry Brooker intended when he entered a town or settlement that he reasoned might be peopled by dangerous men.

The Palo Duro Canyon Riders swept across the panhandle and into the Oklahoma territory as a great purge of holy fire. They shot it out with Indian bands and rustlers and outlaws alike. Hardly anyone was ever arrested by them but were most often killed. Occasionally, when there were a few arrested survivors, the riders held kangaroo courts right on the prairie. It was Charley Goodnight's particular brand of justice that gave celebrity to the famous "neck-tie party."

All in all, it had been too much for Colin. He had believed it was good for Texas to clean it up lawfully, but he thought these self-appointed, avenging bands went too far. His final decision was made one day when a Ranger Captain called Squib Bodeen could not determine which of three men was responsible for stagecoach robbery had simply hanged them all. He had determined this was the only way to be certain he had punished the right one. When one of the men's wives had complained that he had to be hanging two who were innocent he simply said, "Well that's what they get for bein' 'round here. 'Sides that I'm sure they's guilty of somthin'." The next day Colin had left Rangering for good.

Colin looked now at his old friend, Henry Brooker, in quiet astonishment. He had been the toughest of the tough. Brooker would kill without hesitation. He had been shot, stabbed, and had taken the best that determined adversaries could serve up on him. His enemies were always stunned to find him still fighting them with even more ferocity and a renewed vigor. Brooker had refused to be beaten. He had spent days surviving in the saddle while riding the wildest country any land could offer. Now he was loving a plump wife and doting over five tow-headed children. Of all the changes Colin had seen happen during his tenure in the west, none was more noteworthy than the saga of Henry Brooker.

The meal finished, Colin continued to hear from Brooker the tale of Pamela Carstin and the blooded horses. It was when Brooker showed him a rude copy of Alexander Carstin's map that Colin first understood Henry's concern.

"Right here is the claim that the Carstin woman says her Daddy bought and paid for and signed over to her and her husband." The map was rudely drawn on butchers' roll paper; but it was clear enough. Colin also respected the map because it had been drawn by Henry Brooker, an expert in the lay of all Texas and Oklahoma land.

"They claim there's two sections full and part of another." Colin looked at the spot on the map indicated by Brooker's bony finger. It was easy to see that he was indicating a spot on the south bank of the Canadian that had heretofore been identified as the north east range of the Broken Spur.

"I think I see your reason for concern," said Colin.

"I haven't said a word to them about the Spur, Collie. I didn't tell her much about you either. I just told her a Texas cowman was comin' here and might be willin' to guide her and her horses to Texas. To tell the truth, Collie, I think the horse crossbreeding idea is a good one. Before her husband was killed, I thought I might partner with them a little bit. That was sure before I knew the land they intended to take up belongs to you. Her losin' her husband and campin' there for so long and all... I guess I wasn't very honest with her, Col, but I just didn't want to see her hurt anymore than she already has been."

"I suppose I understand that. Maybe I'll go down to the creek and see if I can talk her into goin' back home."

"Your wastin' your breath Col. She's a-goin to the Canadian River. I just thought it would be better maybe if she went with you. I'm sure I'd hate to start claimin' Broken Spur ground with the likes of old Garcia around."

"Garcia is only a part of the problem. Matter of fact, I think Garcia would kill over a woman quicker than anything. But when it comes to protectin' the land, it's old Robert that you gotta watch. Over the years he's used that old Hawken rifle pretty often."

"Collie, how can things like this happen? Why Old Robert took up that land more'n forty years ago. I'll bet if the truth were only known he had to fight for every square inch of that land. How can there be another claim?"

"Well I expect the first person to blame just might be Old Robert himself. Garcia and others too have told him that his stone monuments that he built around the Spur might not be enough notice. Course up till now they have been just fine. The other person I'd blame is that damned fool in our white house. Old Benjamin Harrison can't be expected to know anything about land in the west. Hell, he's from Niles, Ohio, where ten acres is considered a major land holdin'."

"I guess you're right," Brooker said. "Washington ain't never helped no Westerner yet. Just look at the Indians as a case. It's Washington what riles 'em up and breaks all the treaties with 'em and then we end up havin' to shoot 'em to keep our hair which would've been safe enough if the politicians would keep their asses east of the Mississippi."

Colin nodded his agreement. "Well, I suppose I'd better go and talk to her. Maybe you're right. Maybe the best thing is just to get her to Texas and let Old Robert work things out with her. One thing's sure, he's the fairest man any of us knows. But I tell you Henry. I'm gonna try to get her on an east-bound train, and that's a fact."

"You can try Collie... You can try."

Colin and Brooker were now on the porch of the Mercantile looking the half mile down the slope to the place the covered wagon camp lay nestled in the cottonwood grove.

"Damn." Colin said. "I wish my man had shown up. I guess I'll have to get back to Dodge to get my gear before ridin' out."

"Your man?" Henry asked. "My God Colin are you talkin' about Chester Crawford?"

"I sure am... Have you seen Chester?"

"Course I seen him. Damn, Collie, I just clean forgot to tell you. He was here early this morning. He was drivin' that Indiana wagon. The green one. He said he was goin' on down the trail so you'd have a camp to ride into later this evening. I guess you slept in a little and Chester, why he was ready to move. I've never seen him act like such a go-getter before. And he was all clean, too. I wasn't sure it was him at first. He's been here, Colin, and he's settin' up a camp for you. Left your buckskin horse in my barn, too, right along with your saddle and rifle. He said they would have a good meal for you about sundown if you just follow the bend in the creek and keep a-headin' south. Me and Mattie could see right off they weren't in the mood for waitin' around. Mattie thought they might be tryin' to have a little time alone together, you know?"

"Henry," Colin said curiously, "...you keep sayin' *they*. Who the hell is *they*?"

"Why, Chester Crawford of course. Chester, and the Chinagirl."

Chapter Seven

Taking to the Trail

Colin sat on Pamelas' nail keg now, spooning the good stewed apples to his mouth. They served as a bit of a desert following Pamela Carstin's exceptional wild turkey stew.

Colin had eaten many wild turkeys in his life, but always on the trail he had found them to be rather poor fare. Over an open fire, a bird as big as a turkey was very liable to be burned on the outside and still quite rare in the center. Even raw. A condition Colin associated with fine beef but loathed in fowl.

Colin had shot the bird with the old Henry rifle along the trail and when he entered the camp with it slung over his saddle, Pamela had instantly began to give out orders to her son Justin, and anyone else within earshot. She called for firewood, water and the few vegetables still stored in the wagon. Pamela Carstin busied herself as she prepared to build a mighty stew for the evening meal.

Colin had never heard of a turkey stew, but she assured him it was a table favorite in Illinois. He had to admit over his steaming plate it was delicious. He thought he'd just eat a bit of the turkey to be polite; but when he discovered how good it was, he was heartily taking on a full meal. Over the past ten or so days Colin had come to terms with a lot of facts about Pamela Carstin.

To begin with, Henry Brooker had been dead on target when he had told Colin that this woman was not to be dissuaded nor taken lightly. She was indeed bound for Texas with her stud string. Colin had thought if he refused to accompany her she just might take her boy by the hand and walk. He had also come to grips with the fact that he was only accompanying her.

He might have thought, originally, that he was to serve as her guide. She quickly established that they would be traveling to the Canadian River country together as equal partners. Pamela lost no time in assuring Colin that she was more than capable of handling her end of the labors of this proposed journey. By Colins' assessment she did this just fine.

Not only was she a competent trail traveler but she was a fine mother to the boy, Justin, Colin thought. After some coaxing he got her to call him Colin instead of Mister Trav. From time to time she slipped. though. and said Mister. It made Colin feel ancient. Somehow he seemed to care more about what she called him than he usually did with others. For some reason he didn't feel as confident around her as he would've liked to. It was disconcerting, and he wasn't sure he understood his own feelings.

From time to time though, Colin could sense a deep sadness in her. He realized these were the times she must have been thinking of the night of the shooting. Thinking of her husband, Alex. It saddened Colin, too. He found he grew angry when he realized fear of men like Amos Younger still held great expanses of western land and countless souls hostage.

These bandits thrived on terror and murder. It was harboring thoughts like this one that reminded Colin of the old Rangering days. There had been very few arrests but a plentitude of necktie parties. Where there were Rangers with ropes, there was safety for women and children. It had worked in the pan handle country. Iron men like Charles Goodnight and Henry Brooker had seen to it.

In days past, the Kiowa had been a brutal enemy. That was the Indian's struggle to protect his way of life, indeed himself and his entire race from the very brink of extinction. In this fight, Colin found a kind of honor. Younger though, was an outlaw who plundered and killed only for personal gain. There was no honorable distinction in this.

The outlaws of Kansas and the Nations Territory had grown so bold that respectable people were no longer safe anywhere in the area. Judge Isaac Parker it was true was trying to hang the lawless one by one. They simply were too abundant. Colin wondered how long it might take the law to come to Kansas. Goodnight he was sure could hasten its arrival if he were only there. In these years, Kansas and the Nation were far more dangerous than Texas.

It had taken a few days to get the trip organized, but Pamela and the boy had been stalwart in this effort. Over the several day period things had begun to shape up. Colin may have had his misgivings in the beginning, but now he threw himself into preparations for the trail with a renewed vigor. His enthusiasm surprised even himself It had been a long time since Colin had felt so excited by any endeavor.

He thought Pamela Carstin conducted herself just splendidly. She was exuberant but not silly. She was serious about the project but not without an uncommonly vivacious sense of humor. Lastly, she was beautiful. Colin found her pert face and tousled hair more appealing than anything he had encountered in a long while. Then he remembered her age and was perplexed.

How old could she be? he thought to himself. There's hardly anyway she could be more than twenty- five or -six. Surely, she ain't thirty yet. He felt contrite and somewhat foolish when he realized he might be more than twice her age. He could easily have been her father. Better put those thoughts away right this minute, he thought and turned back to the work at hand.

His face was flushed with humiliation and embarrassment. He resolved to put her and these unsettling thoughts from his mind. Yet, somewhere deep in his inner self, he knew he wasn't finished with these extraordinary feelings she stirred within him. Not yet.

Chapter Eight

Herding Horses to Texas

There were a lot of details and preparations to accomplish before starting the four-hundred-mile journey to the Broken Spur. When Colin had told Pamela the distance of the trip and she quickly calculated that an oxen- drawn wagon was doing well to average ten or twelve miles each day, she was stunned. She knew that there would be days they made only five or six miles. Or even none at all. These were distances she had not considered. She had to steel herself momentarily to recapture her positive disposition.

"Fifty or maybe sixty days on the trail," she bravely declared, "...are precisely what we need to adapt ourselves to Texas." She was resolute and determined, but Colin noted she was never grim

"September's bout over." Colin declared to her. "Time we hit the land between the Canadian and the Red it'll be late fall 'er early winter." I'm hopin' you brought along. The kinds of clothes you and the boy'll need."

"Were all set." She replied cheerily "Good Great Lakes wool and Illinois canvas. It gets cold in Illinois too don't you know?" As Colin walked away he could only think to himself, I hope she knows what a Texas blue norther is all about.

It took three days to get Chester Crawford and the Chinagirl back with the Studebaker buckboard, along with the Broken Spur's equipment and the six-horse string Chester had selected. Henry Brooker had sent a rider down the creek bank to find the errant travelers and return them to Murphy Flats so that they might more properly prepare for the forthcoming journey. Upon their return, Colin had taken Chester aside and asked about the Chinagirl.

"Her name is May, Mister Trav. I hope you'll honor us by callin' her that. I don't want folks to call her 'Chinagirl' no more... Not never."

"I can call her May if you like, Chester. Tell me her last name too."

"Why, it's Crawford of course Mister Trav." Chester had to check himself to keep from exploding at his new employer. "We's 'married,'

Mister Trav... I wouldn't dishonor her in no way in the world. She's with me now, and we're goin" to Texas... I got me a wife in Dodge and found me a good job ridin' with the Spur...

Mister Trav... I'm hopin' it'll be alright to take my wife back to the Spur. That's alright, ain't it.?" Colin was studious for a moment.

"I think it'll be just fine, Chester. I think when May meets Old Robert and Juan Garcia she just might fit in real fine. They're just about as different as she is." Chester Crawford extended his hand, and Colin wasted no time taking it. The Broken Spur was in for something new.

Pamela had never been this close to an Oriental before, and she studied May Crawford carefully. She liked the things she discovered. The girl's appearance was one of delicate beauty as though she were made of exquisite porcelain. Her hair was fine and black as a raven's wing. So black, in fact, it glinted in the sun as the glossy ebony reflected the sun's light. Her almond-shaped eyes were eternally deep pools of livid darkness.

If the one thing that was most appealing had to be selected, though, it would've surely been her jovial, personality. Her laughter was loud and boisterous. She was filled with mischief and teased Chester continually. The combination of her exotic looks and lighthearted behavior combined to form a striking impression. It may have been May's far eastern type of beauty; or perhaps it was her engaging smile. Whatever it might have been, Pamela sensed the existence of something strongly feminine.

Here was a woman, Pamela sensed, that would follow her man wherever he went. She was not just a porcelain doll but a woman easy to picture in the role of wife and mother and equal partner to her man. She may have earned a living selling sausages, beer and coffee; but Pamela instinctively knew she could do so much more.

Everyone, though, came to appreciate the Chinese May Crawford's sense of humor and general good nature. She filled the air around the little camp with shrieks of delight and hearty laughter. She was always willing to help out with any chore no matter how unpleasant. When Colin saw her using an axe like a man to chop firewood, he knew she would be a fine companion on the trail.

"What we need now is eight or ten good draft horses to drag that monster wagon of Miss Carstin's back to the Canadian." Colin told Chester.

"I think pulling horses' may be a problem to find. There's lots o' crops out here in Kansas and the harvest starts next month. I think we may have to do with oxen till we get down the trail a ways, and then maybe we can hook up with horses."

"Well it'll make travel a lot faster. Ox always gets there but they're uncommonly slow. Is the trail open enough for horses?" Chester asked.

"We'll take the cattle trail back. It's open enough for anything to travel it. Must've had a hundred thousand cattle driven over it this summer. When the old timers crossed the prairies, the horses just couldn't make it. They had to find passable trail and then bust it open. The herds have got it all opened up now. One thing different from us and those old settlers, Chester; we know the country and the trails and they didn't. I can show you all the grass, water and beer joints from here to Mexico.

Those old pioneers had to find it as they went along. When they didn't find it, their horses died. That's why they used oxen. A horse's a delicate thing compared to oxen. The ox can survive on about nothin'. 'Specially if he's got a little longhorn in his breeding. We'd be just fine with horses now that the trails are open and marked but I guess we'll have to use oxen. You're right, Chester. Harvest comin' on the way it is, good work horses are just not going to be for sale."

Colin had Chester scour the countryside around Murphy Flats, and with a little luck he had soon turned up ten nice oxen. There were no work horses for sale as they had predicted although the Kansas countryside was well populated with Belgian, Clydesdale and the big, grey Percheron. They were magnificent as they worked the huge wheat expanse. These dray animals would be used to make the Kansas harvest in the next months and could not be bought, even at extravagant prices. Colin hadn't very much experience with handling oxen in the yoke, but Chester claimed to have driven oxen many times and knew precisely how to hook their tug lines to the Conestoga.

"Lucky we got such a fine wagon." Chester allowed. "Pennsylvania boys make these wagons at a place called Conestoga Creek. They been makin' wagons since ever I can remember. They soaks the oaken wheels in the creek. Makes them wood wheels swell up tight against the steel rims. Gives you a wagon can roll a long way with the wheels all swole up like that you know? We'll stop at water holes and creeks and soak them wheels again ever chance we get. They'll hold true, Mister Trav." Chester went on talking of the Conestoga's virtues. Colin had never been too interested in the production of wagons, but he had to admit Chester had his attention.

"These is the best wagons ever made. See how they belly down in the middle? That keeps the load from shiftin' as you go up and down hills. I figure we'll keep six ox in the yoke and four or six in the drag. We'll change 'em everyday... or twice a day in this September heat maybe. Dependin' on how they fare. Maybe we'll get a chance for fresh oxen along the trail and, if so, I'd say buy 'em. Or else trade these for fresh.

Thirty or forty days on the trail and most ox ain't got much left. Ten 'er twelve extra ox ain't too much for four hundred miles 'er more."

"In two days we'll hit a lot of Buffalo grass." Colin said. "That and Gramma too. Some of it's so good it's down right greasy, even in this heat."

"Well, that'll be a sure 'nuff help, mister Trav. Good grass and decent water, and you can stretch your oxen out ten days or so I'd say. We ought to get along just fine."

"Chester, how come you know so much about oxen and wagons?" Colin wanted to know.

"My Grandpa, Mister Trav... He was one of them old timers you was talkin' 'bout. He and my Mamaw Ellen came all the way from up by Lake Erie in north Ohio to Texas in a rig like this. He learned me about ox and wagons." It seemed to Colin that all things in Texas were somehow linked to the past. A product left behind by the 'old timers.'

Pamela insisted she pay for the oxen and the supplies, but Colin said Brooker was to keep all expenses on the Broken Spur account books. They agreed they would settle up when they knew the final tally. Pamela reluctantly agreed to this, but petulantly insisted that she would keep her own financial records and square up as soon as she was able. It was the day before the trail that Pamela amazed Colin with her infinite knowledge of horses.

"This is horse-fighting day," she announced after a robust breakfast of stewed apples, coffee and red beans. "May and I will clean up this breakfast and then we'll work on the horses."

"I beg your pardon, Miss Pamela?" Colin questioned her with his voice and eyes...

"Well..." she began, ..." I've got four stallions to take to Texas and you're riding a stallion of your own. Mine have already been thrown together, but with yours along it's got to be done all over again."

Chester Crawford was as confused as Colin. "Miss Pamela, I ain't sure I know just what you're talkin' about."

"Well," she began, "you Texans sure use horses a lot to know so little about them. We've got five stallions here, gentlemen. I can assure you they will fight every step of the way from here to the Canadian. You should know that when studs get together they have to form a pecking order all their own, or they're just not biddable. You can't tell them which one is to be the dominant horse, so you put them together and let them sort it out themselves."

"You mean a horse fight?" Wide eyed, May Crawford was aghast.

"That's it." Pamela responded.

"Well, I ain't sure I want to see these good horses all cut up and kicked apart. I kind o' like little Buck just the way he looks." Colin said.

"Mister Trav, I'd be a fool to let one of these horses get hurt. Little Justin and I have paid a dear price for these stallions. While I'd not give stable room to your yellow broom tail, I'm glad to know you like him as he looks. The idea is to let them fight it out but at the same time keep them from hurting each other.

Oh, there'll be a few bumps and bruises for sure. But it's got to be done, or the injuries will be a whole lot worse. My Alex showed us how to live in peace with stud horses without shooting them."

"Tell us how you do that, Miss Pamela." Colin was willing to listen. This was a woman who knew about things from a man's world. "I've been kinda' dreadin' to hit the trail with five of these four-legged fightin' machines. That bald-faced one of your'n tried to bite me just last night. Pro'ly likes to eat me alive, could he get a-hold on me."

"Well, first we hobble them. Not front legs but front to back. Then we'll cross the hobble in the stride. Hobble left front to right hind and the like. Then over there in the wagon, we've got leather muzzles, all padded with wooly, sheep skin. That'll stop the biting.

"We slip a blinder halter on them so they can only see straight ahead. The blinder flap helps protect their eyes too. Then we let them out on the plain together. They can't kick or run away because of the hobbles, and they can't bite with the muzzles on. The blinders will keep them milling so close together they can't hurt each other. Not very much anyhow.

"Two hours from now each horse will know his place and pretty well stay in it. There might be a spot of trouble now and again; and if it happens, we stop and do it all again. Horse men call that 'reinforcing a behavior.' Alex did it all the time. 'Course he wasn't a cowboy like you two... But he was a horseman... One of the best. The best... I ever knew." Colin looked to Chester who simply shrugged.

"You're the boss, miss Pamela." Colin said finally. "Let's throw 'em together."

The horse fight went just as Pamela had predicted. The five stallions had put on a fierce show of bravado. Their wheeling, kicking and biting efforts were greatly curtailed by the hobbles and muzzles. It was easy to see that without these precautions, one or more of the horses could have been easily severely injured or perhaps killed. They mostly fought their restraints and only attempted to fight each other.

At last, exhausted, they began to settle. The futility of the struggle was becoming evident. After thirty minutes or so of laborious effort, the stallions began to tolerate each other. After an hour and a half the horses were actually nuzzling, rubbing sides and even drinking the creek water side by side.

They kept their suspicions of each other and they were, indeed, wary; but the fight was gone, at least for now. The five stallions appeared ready for some well behaved travel. The blooded horses were spirited but somewhat pampered. They were the ones that settled into the new docile role first. The tough relentless little prairie stallion proved his dominance by fighting a lot longer. Inwardly, Colin could not help but feel a bit proud. Although Colin had kept his curiosity to himself until now he could hold back his questions no longer.

"Miss Pamela." He said. "I just gotta ask you. Why would you bring horses to Texas? We got a passel of 'em you know. Seems to me you've put with more than a little to make this work out and I just had to ask you why."

"It's a long story Mister Trav. Judging by the Texans who've come here to see these horses I don't believe I could ever explain it to them…or you. Maybe it'll give us something to talk about on the trail. Right now though I've got to liniment treat a couple of horses." She turned and walked away. Colin stared after her retreat. He fished out his tobacco sack and began to roll a smoke. Her answer hadn't helped him at all. He was still more than a little curious about the need for more horses in Texas.

On the eve before the departure was to occur, Henry Brooker had appeared in the camp bearing an enormous beef stew. Mattie had prepared the wonderful smelling dish and sent it to the travelers as a farewell present. While the others dipped robust chunks of sourdough bread into the rich and savory dish, Brooker called Colin aside.

"Colin, this Amos Younger is still out there on the plain somewhere, and you just might need to deal with him."

"If he comes, we'll deal." Said Colin.

"Well and good, Colin, and well spoken… But I'm wonderin' if you got any guns?"

"I have my Henry… I saw a double barrel shotgun in the Conestoga… Oh yes I have a Colt-.45 in the saddle bags. At least I think it's still there. I haven't seen it for a while."

"Collie, I'm bringin' you four rifles. I've already put them in the covered wagon. They're all Winchesters and they're .44-40 caliber. There's five boxes of shells in the wagon too. Colin, you arm Chester and the Chinagirl. Give Miss Carstin a rifle too and even the boy. I got a feelin' if he needs to, he'll shoot right enough. And I brought this along for you."

Brooker reached under his coat and produced a nickel-plated Smith and Wesson-.44. It was the American model so revered by the Texas

Rangers. Its ivory grips were yellow with age and honest wear, and the satin gleam of its nickel finish was tempered to a dull luster by holster wear.

It was the Colt single action army revolver that garnered lasting popularity. This celebrated six shooter was even occasionally referred to as the gun that won the west. The Colt's striking appearance and butter-smooth action assured its rightful place in the history of arms. Men who had to depend on guns every day though had often shunned it as being somewhat fragile. More rugged revolvers such as the Remington single-action or the Smith and Wesson Schofield or the American had proven their rugged reliability time and again.

"This was my Rangerin' gun, Collie, and it shoots like hell. I packed this Smith along when I was chasin' old Quanha up in the Palo Duro. I had the barrel shortened to about five inches so you can carry it in your belt on horseback a lot easier. I was clear over in Laredo with the Goodnight bunch once. Me and Charles went into this hardware store and they had two of these guns. Goodnight bought one and I bought the other. "

"He always fetched his along in a hip holster. I can't abide a holster when I'm tryin' to ride. It's the best shootin' piece I've ever owned, Collie, and it's never quit on me once. I hope I can persuade you to arm Chester with your Colt and you tuck this iron into your own belt. Keep it right at hand all the time. Don't put it in your saddle bag or tuck it in your bed roll and forget about it. Just remember, Col– If the time comes when you actually need a gun, you're probably gonna need it in a hurry."

"I ain't carried a gun on my person in the last ten years, Henry. 'Sides that I hate to take your pistol, what with you havin' it so long and all."

"Don't worry about takin' the pistol. Mattie's been after me for years to do away with it. She thinks it might, somehow draw me back to Rangerin' I guess. Anyway, she don't like our sons to fool around with it, and I can't blame her none. I know you ain't gone around armed since we put down the Commanch' at Palo Duro, but this is different.

"I can't figure out what the hell old Amos is up to. It ain't like him to shoot things up this way…. do a killin' over a horse or two. Even if they're as valuable as the Carstin string. Anyway, Collie, I think he's slipped his buckle, and I want you to promise me you'll keep this gun at hand."

"Well, Henry, I guess the least I can do for a good friend like you is to promise that. I'll carry the Smith if you say so… But I'm tellin' you, Brooker, I'm going to give your gun back to you some day… That is, if your boss Mattie says you can have it." The two friends laughed heartily now.

"One more thing, Colin. Yesterday I sent a telegraph to the Broken Spur. I told Juan Garcia to get some men together and come up the cattle trail to meet you. I figure they'll travel a lot faster'n you and you might meet up with 'em in twenty or twenty-five days. You know you could just stay right here and wait for them. That, of course, makes too much sense for you I'm sure."

"Henry, you're a good friend. f anyone else had sent a wire like that I guess I could've been angry, but I can't get mad at you, Brooker. The other thing I can't do is allow Amos Younger to stop me from goin' home when I damn well please. But I expect we could use Garcia's help. Anyway your telegraphing him ain't gonna hurt nothin' and that's for sure."

"I thought you'd see it that way Collie. I shouldn't go with you. Mattie's in a family way again and not doin' too well at that."

"Mattie's havin' another baby?" Colin Whooped. "Damn it, Henry your older'n me. Just how old does a fellow have to be before he loses interest in all that baby makin'?"

"Blamed If I know, Collie, but if you're gonna find out you'll have to ask somebody a heap older'n me." Both men shared another good laugh. "Anyway, I'm carin' for her and the store and the other children too." The September heat was causing Henry's balding pate to sweat, and he wiped it with a blue bandana. "Altogether it's keepin' me hoppin' Colin. But if you tell me to quit them, and ride with you... I think you know I will."

"That can't happen, Henry... Kiss Mattie for me and thanks for the guns. Especially this here pistol. After all those years it still looks real fine." He turned the pewter-colored pistol in his hands. "Probably still shoots good enough to part old Quanha's top knot too." Colin broke open the Smith and satisfied it was fully loaded, except for the traditionally empty chamber under the hammer, then he tucked it into his waist band. He shook the hand of one of his oldest friends, and he and Henry walked back to the campfire to join the others in the beef stew feast.

It was just at daybreak the next morning when the travelers lined themselves for the start of the long-awaited journey. Colin couldn't help but be amused by the unlikely appearance they affected. It was an unusual formation to say the least.

In the lead, at the head of their column, rode Colin astride the little buckskin. He would be the point rider. His job would be to ferret out the easiest route of travel for the great wagon.

Behind him came the string of oxen pulling the Conestoga. Chester Crawford walked alongside the lead oxen's head on the left. May Crawford rode on the Conestoga's seat sometimes, but more often she acted as a header by walking on the right side of the lead Oxen. Hitched by ropes to the rear of the wagon came the four fine stallions and walking unfettered along with them was the little mixed herd of extra oxen and horses.

Colin had put the boy, Justin, on the back of a gentle roan mare, and his job was to keep this little herd from straying. It was the first duty the boy had ever been assigned, and it filled him with pride. He greatly admired Colin and made no secret of it.

Last in the column came Pamela Carstin driving the Studebaker. The high sideboards had been mounted onto the buckboard now, and so it was a cargo wagon. Her greatest challenge was to keep all participants an appropriate distance from each other within the procession in relation to the slow moving oxen.

As she sat perched on the high seat of the Studebaker with the sun haloing her straw-streaked hair, Colin couldn't help but admire this beautiful and determined woman. Mounted atop the high spring seat, she appeared almost Amazonian…. like an ancient CelticPrincess with the sultry sun as her backlight. When at last the ranks were formed the way Colin thought they should be, he pierced the air with a resounding whistle. With a starting lurch, the unlikely caravan settled in and moved slowly forward to the south west.

At last, Pamela Carstin thought. *I'm taking Alex's horses to Texas.*

Chapter Nine

Dishonor Among Thieves

The meeting of the horse rustlers and Lloyd Starrett was an explosive one. Amos Younger and Starrett had arranged to meet in a little canyon just north of the Starrett spread. They had elected to rendezvous on the twenty-first of September after full moon rise.

That span of time was elected as a proper one for Younger to affect the plunder of the coveted horses. It further allowed him time to escort them seventy miles east across the plain to their new home in the Nations.

Further, the night of the twenty-first promised a full moon. Moving horses around in pitch blackness was a risky proposition. There was the danger of rock, chuck and prairie-dog holes. Stumps and fallen logs were a tripping hazard to a horse in the night.

And of course, because they are night predators, there was always a chance of stepping on one of the big diamondback rattlesnakes that abundantly populated the rugged country. Moonlight would greatly help the horse transfer. The large eye of the horse with its amazing light-gathering properties allowed the animals to see better than the men. Some moonlight though was some comfort to man and horse alike.

Lloyd Starrett showed up at the outlaw camp around the middle of the night as they had arranged. He needed to collect his horses from the Younger gang and move them to his own territory. That meant driving the horses between ten and twelve miles under the cloak of darkness. His original goal was to arrive on Starrett land before sun up. The bandits couldn't know the killing of Alex Carstin had changed the plans considerably. Amos felt the midnight rendezvous with Starrett made this timing just about perfect.

Starrett rode into the glow of the rustlers' small campfire. He was accompanied by another rider Amos recognized as Leonard Peach. Amos knew Peach slightly from his previous visit to the Starrett ranch. Younger innocently believed that Starrett had brought this young cowboy along to assist in driving the horse string farther east to Starrett lands.

The story of the shooting had already crossed the prairie. Starrett knew of the Carstin killing before Amos had arrived with the horses. Amos almost at once detected a change in the demeanor of his old business partner. Starrett was steaming with anger and made no move to conceal that fact. Now Amos caught a better look at the young rider he thought had been brought along to assist Starrett in a moonlight horse drive.

He was a typical young trail hand, or seemed so, in the evening gloom. The flicker of the campfire though revealed the young man was wearing a hip holster. It was too dark to recognize the type of gun he carried, but Amos was aware of what kind of men wore open-topped holsters. Men who wore guns on the outside of their coats in plain view, were either trouble or they were looking for trouble. Lawmen, armed robbers and pistoleros carried guns in this fashion. Not cowboys. Amos decided that Leonard Peach might not just be there in order to assist in a horse drive. He determined to keep himself alert.

Peach had always thought himself a gun hand. He had practiced long and hard at whipping out the big revolver and firing it at tree stumps or man-sized boulders. He liked riding around with Lloyd Starrett in the role of bodyguard. He was certain that Starrett had made the right choice by selecting him as a protector. Men like Wes Hardin and Bill Hickock were of the very type he believed himself to be. Though he had never shot at anyone, he was certain that in a gunfight he would prevail based on his talent and the hours of hard and constant pistol practice. As he was armed with a .45 and a quick-draw holster, he felt infallible.

When Starrett spoke, his voice was so hard that Amos was completely taken off guard.

"You get this saddle trash off Starrett lands tonight Amos." Starrett's voice trembled in rage. "I want you gone before daylight. Take those horses with you. I got no use in the world for horses like them now... Tell you the truth Amos, I ought to kill you for bringin' 'em here."

"Now hold on, Lloyd..." Amos tried to speak but was cut off mid-sentence.

"God damn you, Amos. I told you I had a lot of good things happening here for me. I wanted you to 'slip' these horses away and I was willing to pay and pay well. Then you had to go and shoot down an unarmed eastern horse trader. Now you've got every damned federal policeman in the Nation out to find you." Lloyd Starrett was growing more furious as he spoke.

"I didn't shoot nobody, Lloyd." Amos attempted to explain. "It was the idjit... I..."

"He's your lookout, Amos... They all are. Where in the hell did you find such trash? Now we got big trouble, and I sure can't afford to be any part of it... Can't afford to have these horses found around here either."

"Oh hell, Lloyd." Amos was trying now to calm Starrett. "We're in the territory now. I don't like that fellow gettin' shot and all either. But it's already done. I'd say the territory's the best place to be. I don't think there'll be any trouble. Not clear out here in the Nation."

"Then you're stupid, Amos. You're stupid, and these saddle bums your ridin' with are worse than stupid... If you think you can shoot an unarmed traveler over a few horses... I mean, to shoot him down right in front of his wife and kid... If you think old Judge Parker ain't already tyin' your neck knot, then you must've been feedin' on loco weed. Now get these tramps on their feet, kick out that fire, and be clear of Starrett land by sun up."

Beaver Parker was watching this discussion with a lively interest that belied his usual unconcerned attitude. His eyes had fixed on the holstered pistol on the hip of the quiet young man to the left of Lloyd Starrett. The gun was in the shadows from Amos' angle of view.

But by the light of the fire, Beaver could see it plainly. He could see that the pistol was a shiny one. It was nickel plated. The firelight danced on the shiny surface of the part protruding from the low cut, 'speed' holster. The grip was of some white material Beaver imagined must be ivory or pearl glowing in the firelight. It was true enough Beaver had a pistol of his own. But not a shiny one like this.

He imagined himself with such an exotic firearm. It was true he shot his rifle well enough, but this gun held a new promise. The rifle was after all unwieldy for close work. With a pistol like this, he imagined he could impress any woman. He could ony think of the woman with the stud horses. He would never stop until he found her again. Oh, he hadn't forgotten the woman. Not in the least. He loathed these stupid horse thieves. He was after bigger and more important prey. He would never stop until he had her. This he knew this for sure.

The thought caused a shiver to course his spine. He would find the woman again, and he knew it. If he had this pistol when he found her... His imagination was running full gallop now. Why were these men talking about police and horses? Those things were so unimportant he could barely listen. Nearly oblivious to the heated discussion taking place before him. Beaver silently slipped a shell into the Springfield's chamber.

"I want you out of here tonight..." Starrett's words were lost in the sudden explosion of Beaver Parker's rifle. Everyone jumped in total surprise. Each was totally stunned by the shock from the unexpected thunder clap. Everyone except Leonard Peach.

Beaver's bullet was supposed to make for his forehead, but Beaver had calculated poorly and shot low. The bulled had ruined Peach's mouth and ripped though the back of his head. The big slug had pitched him headlong from his horse. It was only a short fall from the saddle to the ground. Somewhere during that drop, Leonard Peach, who had loved his fancy pistol and Mexican holster, died in flight. Someday he might have been destined to be another Wes Hardin, but he would never have the chance now.

Charley Stone and Willy Parker were simply rooted in place by shock and fear. Ears a-ring from the unexpected detonation, their eyes widened, they stared slack -awed at the falling cowboy. Both Charley and Willy felt as though their muscles were made of frozen stone. Lloyd Starrett tried to react, but the surprise had caught him too far off base as well. It took him that split second to assess what had happened, and that was too long.

Amos Younger was as surprised as anyone. The last thing he had expected was for Beaver to fire a shot with no warning. The difference between Amos and Starrett was conditioning. Starrett took a second to figure out what was happening and what to do next. Amos Younger had been in this situation before and, without a thought, did precisely the right thing but arguably to the wrong target.

With lightning reflexes he snatched his short-barreled Colt's revolver from the leather-lined front pocket of his saddle pants and shot Lloyd Starrett twice. The first bullet hit Starrett somewhere in the neck he thought, and he centered his chest with the second shot. Instinctively he sensed where danger was laying in wait next and, without hesitation, he wheeled and stretched his shooting hand toward Beaver.

He was too late. The surprise and the second shot he had needed for Starrett had given Beaver time enough to slide another round into his rifle's chamber, and he fired at Amos with deadly calculation. He knew if he missed, Amos would kill him in an instant.

His shot was a true one. The heavy bullet drove Amos backward, and he was dead before he hit the ground. Beaver, fearful that Amos might have a flicker of life, might still pose a danger, was over his dead body in a flash. He centered a safety round into the fallen outlaw.

Charley and Willy slowly came to life now, some minutes after the shooting had stopped but before the gun smoke had cleared. The air was reeking with the smell of charcoal and sulphur. Their ears ached and rang incessantly.

The shootings had taken less than ten or twenty seconds. Three men now lay dead in the moonlight. The outlaws, Willy and Charley, looked one to the other. Baffled and terrified, they wondered if Beaver was about to open fire on them. Beaver looked at them and giggled nervously.

"We the bosses now, Willy."

Willy Parker had never expected this. The remark physically drove him backward a step.

"Yeah, Beaver... I guess we are... That is... You can be boss, Beaver... Me and Charley ain't in no mood... We ain't... You be the boss." Willy was in no frame of mind to antagonize his cousin.

Beaver was already stripping the carved holster and nickled pistol from the body of Leonard Peach.

"This here pistol's a Remington.... Ain't it a purty? Lookit how it just shines." Beaver was twisting the gun in his hand and marveling how the firelight was reflected on the gleaming surface. Charley Stone spoke now.

"Did you kill him just for that gun, Beaver?" The thick, heavy gun smoke clung to the ground like a morning mist. The firelight gave the fog a rosy glow, and the smell of sulphur was dense and oppressive in the still night air. Charley Stone wondered if this was what Hell would smell like....

"Yeah... I have a need for this here gun.... That, and I think he was here to kill us, too." Charley and Willy looked at each other. They sensed there was a kind of wisdom in this last bit of madness. Now that they considered it, there was a better than even chance that Peach was along for exactly that reason.

"How come you shot Amos?" The weasel was asking, his eyes bright with excitement.

"Don't like Amos no more. He can't be boss no more neither. 'Sides don't be so stupid. He was gonna shoot me next. Come on Charley. Get your saddle. Willy you bring them horses too. We can trade 'em for somethin'. We got to go now. This Starrett's prob'ly got lot's o' riders. We goin' right now."

"But where in the hell we goin', Beaver?" It was another question from Charley.

"We go south and east. We see if we can cut Caney Creek and go down to find the rest of the horses. That woman... She goin' south on the creek bank as long as she can. Till the trail goes west."

"Beaver," Charley complained, "...what we gonna do with more horses?' Sides that, they gonna have guards and all now... I don't think we ought to go nowhere near Caney Creek or Murphy Flats. I think we better go to Arkansas or Missouri maybe."

"Charley... You be still now.... You can go with me and Willy to the Creek or we can leave you here with this Starrett and Amos."

Charley Stone saw something in Beaver's face he had never seen before. He realized that his vote was invalid, as was Willy's. If they intended to live they would obey the 'idjit'. Maybe another day would hold escape or some other answer. One thing was for sure: Today, they were heading south to Caney Creek.

"Thirty miles to the creek." Beaver seemed to be talking to himself. "Farmer down there named Primble. Got him a wife and two daughters. Them daughters are just jolly and fat and pretty. Wife's a skinny old bat though. You come with me Willy... You too Charley... We go down the creek and call on them Primble girls. We gonna find that wagon too... Huh? I'm the boss now, ain't I, Willy?" He handed Nellie Parker's old colt pistol over to Willy and tucked his new found nickel-plated treasure into his belt. It was time to move on. To head out for the Primble place.

Chapter Ten

The Silver Harp

The first long days of travel passed slowly and uneventfully for the little Texas-bound caravan. The oxen plodded, the Conestoga creaked, and the September sun was a bit too warm. The days became a monotonous progression of striking camp in the morning and moving along the creek trail till about five in the afternoon. Then, the making of a new camp.

As the days wore on and the first five weeks passed, Pamela found the near boredom somewhat comforting. At first she could think of nothing but Alex. How devastated was she by his loss. Being on the trail, at last, and away from the scene of the shooting seemed to give her a kind of peace and solace she sorely needed. For the first time in weeks she found herself watching and appreciating other people around her; this, instead of dwelling in the constant concern for her own predicament. It felt good to be concerned with others for a change.

Chester's Chinese wife, May, had proven to be a great friend to Pamela. As unlikely as it seemed, considering their greatly varied backgrounds, they spent many campfire hours in the evenings. When the evening meal was put away, the two engaged in lady-like conversation.

It was talk, Pamela thought, as pleasant and as demure as any had ever been back in Illinois. May was lively and spirited. It delighted Pamela to learn they were mutually interested in so many similar homemaking and child rearing particulars.

May wanted to know Pamela's favorite cooking recipes. She wanted to know where she might obtain sewing patterns. She asked what cloths she should select so that she could make herself some western clothing. Pamela found her Oriental styles delightful. The clothing May wore so gracefully looked both cool and comfortable and resembled ornate pajamas. The Chinese girl though felt a need to be less conspicuous. She wanted to dress as Pamela dressed.

May was also interested in Christianity. She seemed to like the idea of a God who would send His Son to look over His subjects with eternal vigilance. She plagued Pamela to tell her more and more about this strange God who was everywhere at once. When Pamela had told her that, "as important as God is he even takes time to look after the sparrows," May had been simply enchanted. The concept of a God stooping to help a tiny sparrow stole her heart away. She promised herself that when she and Chester had a proper home, she would seek more learning of this western God, this God of the sparrows.

It was one night at mealtime when she had astounded the camp. She had brought about this amazement by announcing that she would, from that day forth, call the oxen that pulled the Conestoga, birds. She further announced that she would call her husband Chester by some other name too; she hadn't yet made a selection but thought 'horse' might do...

"Why in the world would you do that, May?" Chester asked. "The right name for an ox is an ox. I don't want to be called 'horse' or anything else, May. I am Chester."

"And I am 'Chinagirl'." She answered. "I am the girl who sold coffee to the cowboys in the stockyards. It is an honorable thing to sell coffee. My Mother before me sold coffee in the stockyards and she was' Chinagirl'. Now my young sister pushes my cart and she is 'Chinagirl'. Chester, you call me May. It is because you think it is wrong or dishonorable to be 'Chinagirl'. It is a mistake, Chester. I have shown no dishonor. I am not a Birdcage girl. "

"May, you don't need to say these things." Chester tried to interrupt.

"They are the things that I must say for my heart is injured. I am low when you feel' Chinagirl' is a bad thing. Cowboys may have thought that I might shame my mother and father and have offered me money to do so. For all their money, I have not shamed my honorable family or myself. I will not shame my husband. You are my husband and you are 'Chester.' I am your wife and I am' Chinagirl'. You are much changed now, husband. You are clean and you do not drink all of the whiskey, but you are still 'Chester.' I think that is good. I change, too. I don't sell the coffee, and I am now a wife of a good American. I am changed but I am 'Chinagirl'."

Pamela sensed her cue and chimed in at once. "I think you'd just prefer to be called 'Chinagirl.' I think it's a wonderful name don't you, Chester?" Pamela asked, hoping Chester would take the cue.

"I think it's the bestest, dangdest name ever I heard." Chester was all smiles now on the outside. Inside, his heart was greatly moved.

"Your God, someday to be mine," May went on, " ...looks after the sparrow you have said... I think he wants the sparrow to be a sparrow. How silly if the sparrow called himself a horse. Would God call this sparrow a pig? And if the sparrow took other names, how could God find him if he wanted to give him a blessing?"

From that night, the travelers called Mrs. May Crawford by her preferred autograph. She was, henceforth, 'Chinagirl'. True, it rankled Chester some. But when he saw that May was happy with the arrangement, it made him happy, too. 'Chinagirl' it is to be., he resolved...

Pamela was impressed with the developments between Chester and Chinagirl. Never had she seen two people who cared more for each other than these unlikely lovers. This hulking powerful man and the fragile china doll who had proven she was not so fragile after all. More remarkable though were the things happening with her son, Justin, and Colin Trav. Yes, and with herself and Colin Trav when she allowed herself to think about it. She rued having any thoughts of Colin in a romantic way with Alex's death so fresh on her mind. Never the less...

It was easy to see that the boy, Justin, was enthralled with the lanky cowboy. His blue eyes fairly glistened with admiration when Colin approached. Pamela saw that the boy did everything in his power to please Colin. He cared for his horse and helped in the camp. He was forever asking Colin if there was anything else that needed doing. He seemed to be losing some of his boyishness. Pamela grudgingly admitted to herself that his relationship with Colin was turning him into a man.

Even more phenomenal was Colin's reactions to Justin. He seemed equally engrossed with the youngster. Colin seemed ever at the boy's side showing him how to tie a cinch or hitch a team. Colin took the boy on hunting forays and showed him how to shoot the Henry. He never "played" with Justin but treated him as he would have another man. A partner.

The closeness between the two was becoming more apparent every day, and it seemed totally mutual. Pamela liked the things happening between Justin and Colin, but she was less sure of the things happening between Colin and her inner thoughts.

How could I think that that? She chastised herself. I love Alex...I'll always love Alex.

She caught herself on several occasions watching Colin as he rode along at the head of their little column. She liked the way he rode with a lazy informality that was so unlike Alex's strictly, regimented form of sitting his horse. She was of course smart enough to know that Alex's dressage style was true and classic horsemanship. The western cowboy form of riding was "just staying on top." But somehow, she thought Colin looked so natural and at home on horseback.

If western riding was informally crude, Colin managed to give the style a sort of rustic dignity. She liked the way his hard, angular body sat in the saddle. There were other things she liked too. They were little things that she couldn't explain, but they were real. So were her feelings. When he rolled a cigarette and lit it ,she felt a stirring. She was moved when she saw him showing Justin how to strap spurs onto his boots. The warm feelings she encountered at times like this were impossible to describe. She had never experienced them before, but they were as real as the sunrise. There was the day he had brushed against her as he helped her hang a heavy water bucket from the wagon spike.

Their bodies had touched for only the briefest of instants. Yet each had recoiled as if from fire. Their eyes had met for a fleeting moment. Then each had quickly turned away. Their movements were so simultaneous, they had appeared comic. A thought of Alex flashed through the two minds at exactly the same time. Pamela felt her face flush hot, and an unsettling feeling gripped her low in the stomach. It was a feeling not unlike the one experienced at the same moment by Colin.

There were other, less emotional but still unsettling moments shared between the two. She passed him a coffee cup and his hand covered hers. They held this posture for only a second. Their eyes locked for an instant. Then followed the embarrassed and inevitable looking away, pretending interest elsewhere and breaking of the touch. It had started very slowly, this thinking of Colin, but it was fast becoming a fixation.

Pamela often questioned the morality of these thoughts. She would have to admit some were not quite decent. After all, she was so recently widowed. There were standards of mourning to be observed. Yet, when she really thought about it, all things prim and proper seemed so out of place here in the west. Illinois was so far away. The customs she had believed to be law back there seemed so out of touch with the reality of this life on the open plains. Here, life moved and ended at a hellish pace. Illinois was so insignificant compared to these Great Plains and skies that ran on forever.

How, oh how can I live with these thoughts? She was tortured by her loyalty to a man who was gone forever and her confusion of what may lie ahead out there in the vast open spaces.

She couldn't explain it but life here seemed somehow so much more vital. There was a primitive quality about everything here. The male-female relationship was no exception. The formalities of courtship she had once deemed as so important now seemed silly and childish. More importantly, they seemed so wasteful of time.

Not needed between stallions and mares, she thought aloud. *And not between men and women.*

It was further disconcerting to see the way Chester and Chinagirl sat up their little camp each evening. They had their meals with Pamela,

Justin and Colin; but when the meal had ended, they went to their own area. Each night they selected a place far from the Conestoga where Pamela and Justin slept. They would park the Studebaker buckboard two or three hundred yards away, and their privacy came under the cover of darkness.

Often Pamela would stare out the back gate of the Conestoga into the night in the direction of the Studebaker. She would try and imagine what was taking place out there in the night. She was usually embarrassed by her own behavior. Sometimes she thought herself to be lewd. But mostly, she hugged herself and wondered what the future might bring... If it might, somehow, involve Colin Trav.

It was the night she found Justin crying that made all the difference. Supper had been over and the camp was shut down for the night. Chester and Chinagirl had retired to the Studebaker, and Colin had taken a late evening stroll. Pamela had been cleaning up the supper dishes and no one had really paid much attention to the boy.

He had seemed to be in high spirits all day, but now Pamela spotted him sitting in front of the small evening fire. Even though she was at some distance, she sensed he was sobbing. She knew her son well, and there was something about his posture, his head supported by his hands, she understood he was crying.

She had just started to walk toward him when she noticed Colin was stepping into the firelight. Without really knowing why, she stepped backward into the darkness. Hidden there in the shadows, she watched and listened as Colin approached Justin.

"Long day, wouldn't you say, Justin?"

"Yes sir." The boy was trying to choke back his tears now. He would rather anyone in the world see him cry than Colin.

"Some days I get that old trail dust in my eyes so bad it makes 'em water 'bout all night." Colin said. "That ever happen to you, Justin?"

"Sometimes."

"Then there's times when I'm on the trail a long time I start to realize how big everything is. It makes me feel so little. It just kind of scares me. I guess a fellow don't ever know how big the world is until he tries to cross it on a horse. Does it ever scare you a little, Justin?"

"Well,... sometimes a little, I guess."

"Well, that makes me feel better, Justin. See sometimes I think I'm the only one that gets afraid... But I guess you and me are a lot alike, ain't we?"

"Yes sir, I was thinkin'..." The boy trailed off, his sentence unfinished. Colin knew the boy was stifling a sob.

"Other times I get real fretful is when I let myself think of sad things too long. Just the other day I was thinkin' of a huntin' dog my stepfather got for me. It was an old blue-tick hound called 'Bugle.' I got to tell you, Justin, I sure liked that old dog. Why he'd fight javelinas and rock chucks just for the plain fun of it. Rattlers, too."

Justin recoiled at the mention of rattlesnakes.

"Most dogs are just natural shy about snakes, but old Bugle would just give them rattlers what for every time he'd catch one." The boy was snuffling a bit but he was all ears now. All boys like to hear about dogs and snakes

"Anyway, a couple o' Wichita braves came along to the ranch one day, and they admired the dog. Tried to buy him. They even offered a little mustang colt for him. Old Robert, my stepdad said no. Cain't buy the boy's dog. Well, you know what happened already, don't you?" Justin's eyes were wide now. This story had Indians in it too.

"Next day," Colin said, "The Wichita's were gone, and so was old Bugle. Well, Old Robert and this Mexican Uncle I got called Garcia, took right after them Indians in a minute. But Wichita's are hard to catch. They don't fight much you know, so they really know how to run and hide. Anyway, I lost my dog."

The boy nodded, sadly understanding.

"Well I's thinking' 'bout that there dog...." Colin paused here and spoke to the boy with a deep sincerity. "You know, Justin, I wouldn't tell any other man in the world this, but you and I are close enough friends. I reckon you won't hurrah me too much about it. Anyway, thinkin' about that old dog like I was, I got all saddened up and I... well, I guess I cried a little. Justin, I sure hope you don't tell anybody about that. You know cowboys don't cry. Well, at least not very much."

"Colin... What's a step dad?" Justin's wide, blue eyes fixed on Colin's face.

"Well, you see, pal... my Momma and Daddy are dead. Well, I think they are. Don't know for sure. But I was alone. And I had this sister who was sick and dyin' too. I was in pretty sad shape to tell the truth. I can't remember who I really am or where I came from or anything." Justin found this to be amazing at first. Then horrifying.

"It was like I had a lame horse and was too far from the train I guess," Colin went on. "Anyway, this old Scotsman and a Mexican just about as old took me in. They looked after me and taught me to work. They showed me how to laugh and sing. Taught me all about cattle. That's a step dad...Sort of a replacement father. They learned me about horses too. I thought I knew a lot about horses 'till I met your Momma.

She knows more, I reckon. She knows more 'bout horses than anyone I know. I hope you won't tell her I said that." The boy affirmed he would protect the secret by a nod of his small blonde head.

"Anyway, that old Scot and Garcia told me I always had to be brave. Even when things made me sad and hurt me. They learned me I had to be a man. See, there ain't no other choice. They were there when I needed them, Justin, and they taught me to be the best man I can be. Why old Garcia asked me if I knew why my dog was gone. Did I understand? I told him, no, I didn't understand! I told him I'd never understand. You know what he said, Justin? He said, 'cause that's how it is. That's all he said. That's just how it is. I think we grow up a heap, Justin, when we figure out some things cain't be explained. It's just the way it is, that's all."

"I miss my Daddy, Colin. Why did those men have to shoot my Daddy? He never bothered no body... Just stayed around horses all the time... I bet he'd taught me those things, Colin. Why did they have to kill him?"

"I don't reckon I can tell you that partner. Old Robert, that's my step dad's name, says there's men about that just ain't fit to live. I guess we got to look out for them. Matter of fact, Justin, we got to look out for each other."

"Colin...could you be my step dad? Just for a little while?"

"Well, it don't always work like that, Justin... See your Momma's still alive, and she's lookin' after you. She's lookin' after you real good, too. See, the only way I could be your step dad with your Momma alive and all would be if I were to marry up with her. Your Momma I mean."

"Would you ever do that, Colin? Marry my Momma?" The boy wanted to know.

"Look son, your Momma's as pretty as a picture and young, too. Hell, Justin, I look like an old boot... Your Momma'll find a good, young man to marry and probably pretty soon. If you all are lucky, he'll be from Texas, too. Anyway,, Justin, I want you to always know I'll be around. When you need a buddy, you just whistle up old Collie. But now don't you go and tell nobody I was cryin' over that old, blue tick dog, Bugle."

Pamela's heart was as heavy as stone as she listened. Her eyes glistened wetly.

"I think Momma would marry you, Colin... She watches you sometimes."

"Men and women always watch each other, Justin. It don't mean they're getting married."

"It ought to."

"Well, maybe it should... But listen, Justin, let's talk about somethin' else for a while. I need a favor from you... Do you know much about music?" Colin needed a subject change in the worst way.

"I can sing 'Jesus Loves Me' and 'The Farmer in the Dell'."

"Well here then, you'd better take this."

Pamela could see by the firelight that Colin had handed the boy a small silver harmonica.

"That's the prettiest, thing I've ever had, Colin. Am I to keep it?"

"Oh sure. I want you to keep it; And to learn to play it, too. Nothin' settles a herd down late at night like a mouth harp played real low."

"Play it for me, Colin... I want to hear it."

"Reckon that's why I'm givin' it to you. I cant play it at all. I been carryin' that thing in my pockets for more'n thirty years and can't play a note on it. You keep it and see can you come up with that 'Farmer in the Dell' tune...That sounds real pretty."

"Colin, couldn't you take my Dad's place? I like you an awful lot, Colin...I was just thinkin'...." Justin's chin trembled. He felt to ask this question was somehow wrong, but he was terribly alone now. His great sad eyes were swimming.

"Look, Justin." Colin took the boy's hand now. "No one can ever take your father's place... I never met him, but I know he was a good man. I know that because your mother loved him, and she would only love a good man. I know that because you're his son. You could only be the son of a good man."

"I can't take his place, Justin, and you wouldn't want me to. I'll always be your partner though. I'll help your Mom see to you if she'll let me. Or until she marries again and fetches you a real daddy. I think, right now, you ought to just take your mouth harp and go off to bed on account of It's late. Tomorrow we'll reach the Primble farm about dark. Now old Mr. Primble can show you how to make music on the harp. He can sing and whistle right pretty too. He can sound like any bird you want him too. You're goin' to like him and his wife and two girls a lot."

"Girls? Do I have to like girls, Colin?" Justin wrinkled his nose disapprovingly.

"Well it'll be of a help if you can... Off to bed with you now, Justin. Tomorrow's a long day and that's a fact."

Pamela stood in the darkness and felt the hot tears streak her face. She would never forget the thing she had just witnessed. Her son was in deep trouble and had been offered the strong hands of a good man. She stood alone in the darkness and watched Justin climb into the Conestoga and into his bedroll. She watched silently as Colin rolled a last smoke. He lit up with a flaming twig, stretched himself sleepily and lolled a few minutes alone before the fire.

At last, he dropped the spent butt into the dying embers and stood up. Colin retreated to his own little private camp far back into a copse of stately pecan trees. It took Pamela a long time to decide. But after a while she left her secluded and shadowy spot. She didn't go to the Conestoga this night. She silently slipped into the pecan grove.

It was late, and the moon was high. Coyotes railed at the lunar brightness. They called out, rather mournfully she thought, from several directions at once. She easily found Colin asleep on the ground. His long body was stretched and comfortably nestled in his blankets. She stood silent, looking at the sleeping man before her for a long time.

In the moonlight, she could make out his square jaw line. It was easy, by moon glow, to see the black comma of hair that spilled over the right of his forehead, nearly covering one eye. He was breathing slow and deep. There was something about the rise and fall of his chest that Pamela found enticing, yet disturbing. Something stirred, low and hot in her stomach.

At last, her decision made, fully clothed in the day's dusty outfit, she slipped into the bedroll beside him. It momentarily surprised her to discover he was not asleep at all but decidedly awake. Without comment, he moved his body sideways to make room for her inside the blanket pack. For an instant, Pamela was as embarrassed as she had ever been.

What must he think of me? She wondered. Her face felt hot. She was glad he couldn't see her expression in the dark.

"I heard you coming through the grove," he said. "I wasn't sure it was you... I'm glad it was."

"I'm glad too, Colin. I heard you talking to Justin this evening... It was nice... The way you handled it... Thank you..."

"Is this visit a 'thank you?'"

"I think not, Colin... I think this is for me." The coyotes were howling again.

"I can't help but feel strange about it," he said. "You know I'm old enough to be your...."

"Just stop it, Colin... Stop it right now." Her voice had an edge to it. "Don't think it... Don't say it... Just don't say anything. I'm tired of all the talk and the guns and the horses... I'm tired of being a man, Colin... I want to know what it's like to be a woman again... It's been a long time... I don't want to hear any more... I don't want to hear about 'Old' Robert or 'old' Juan or, especially, 'old' Colin.... I don't want to know that you're old enough to be my 'whatever'. And please don't tell me that you've got boots that's older than me... I'm a little worn out with that old chestnut, too.

As a matter of fact, Colin, why don't you just shut up for a while? You've talked quite a lot for one evening... Why don't you just put your arms around me... and just stop talking... If you can? Why don't you just kiss me and be quiet? I'm going to need some time, Col. Alex is on my mind every day. It's going to take time, but I'm sure I know what I want." The weathered cowboy nodded his unspoken agreement. It was a deal, as the stockyard traders would say. It was a deal and it was solid...solid for a long time to come with no more doubts.

"I've never been in a bed before with a woman who kept her boots on." He said playfully

"I suppose now you see what you've been missing," was the reply.

"At least you're not wearin' spurs ...Are you?"

They held each other long into the night. No longer were they two separate persons but now, ever so slowly, they were becoming one. Each had been with others in this way in the past; it was true. Regardless, they both sensed that, somehow, this time was different. Very different and very rare. There was something happening here in the long, shadows of the pecan grove that was unique... and urgent... and somehow as forever as the prairie.

Pamela had never felt this way before. It was as though her heart and mind were melding together around the lean, hard, physical presence of Colin. Colin would never replace Alex in her heart. He wouldn't have to. This was a feeling all of its own.

He's like an oak tree, she thought. She felt good about oak trees. They were strong and honest. Oak trees were to be trusted. If she had earlier experienced doubts about her true feelings for Colin they were gone now; washed away in the floodtide of a sweet and gentle holding...

As for Colin, he knew this was no Birdcage girl from the Dodge City bordellos. He felt himself being swept along in the hot prairie wind of a mutually uncontrollable passion. Yet, he knew these kisses and caresses he shared with Pamela were real. They were not just the touching of lips or the pressing of bodies. These were the rawhide bindings that tied souls. He made himself be calm. He understood he only knew a little about Pamela Carstin but he would know more...a lot more. Not in moments or even days. This thing that was happening here had eons of time in front of it. Somehow, he just knew it.

It surprised him how clearly he understood this difference. This understanding revealed to him, a sensitivity about himself that he had long wondered about. He wasn't sure these feelings truly existed within him.

Now, here they were. The flames that stirred within him were unlike any he had ever known. They washed over him as a sheet of fire.

The fact that he was taking Pamela Carstin into his bedroll, he knew, meant he was making a real and bonding commitment to a woman, not 'just' a woman but a whole person. One who would still be here tomorrow in the light of day. Now he was giving himself over completely to her by an unspoken but eternal pledge. It was for the first time in his life. He had always believed that when this moment came, if it ever did, that he would probably experience some doubt, some uncertainty as to his actual feelings. There were none. There was no doubt at all; and if there ever had been, it had vanished now. He knew memories of Alex Carstin would always be there, and it was somehow alright. He and Pamela were on a different level. They were in a place where memories could be kept and even revered, but it would not interfere with the sharing of these new and splendid feelings

In the place of disbelief there was instead the very real body and soul that made up Pamela Carstin. Her sexuality was taking Colins' breath away. Yet there were deeper feelings here, too. Feelings crazily mixed of searing, desire and respect and admiration.

"She's as honest and open as Old Robert." He marveled. "She's as daring as Juan Garcia."

Scant clouds drifted across the face of the ebbing moon. Somewhere in the darkness a whippoorwill belabored his redundant plaintive song. In the pecan grove, a ritual as old as the earth herself was taking place. Pamela and Colin thought the feeling that what was happening between them was unique; it was not. These events had happened a million times before between men and women. Indeed, they would occur a million times more. The setting would be different and the time perhaps. But the happening would always be. It would, at the same time be exactly alike and totally different. Here was the bonding. This time it was the joining of a beautiful, young horsewoman from Illinois and a somewhat older Texas cowboy from the Canadian River.

Chapter Eleven

The Primbles
1862 / 1889

William Hearndon was not usually such an early riser. Quite the opposite he often slept until eight o'clock and then lingered over a long leisurely breakfast before finally arriving at his law offices around ten each morning. One reason he often slept late was his use of alcoholic drink. He occasionally imbibed until late at night and did not make a morning appearance until he was sure he presented a stolid appearance. It would be this trait seemingly so harmless at this early age that would prove to be a burden in his later years. Hearndon was a fastidious dresser and other than the rather bushy beard he wore his appearance was generally one of the very successful attorney that he was indeed. This particular day was different though. He had wanted to speak privately to his law firm partner without the interference of the daily business. As of late though they had been so covered up with legal business neither had the time for personal meetings. During the hours of business there was only time for them to briefly discuss the most pressing of the more than twenty cases now pending upon their desks. Their commerce was brisk and both were relentless workers.

Both partners loved to immerse themselves within the legal problems of their clients and equally loved the earnings of fees. Hearndon knew his partner was an early riser and thought this morning he would arrive at the office ahead of his associate and be waiting for him when he arrived. It surprised him when he entered the offices at seven A.M. and discovered Lincoln was already there. He sat in his swivel chair staring out a window at the streets of Springfield Illinois watching his town awaken and ready itself for the bustling day a state capitol could expect.

"Good morning Will." He offered. "Isn't this just a rousin' good day?"

"Abe," Hearndon responded. "I think we just need to have a talk. A really serious talk this time. I've told you my thoughts before and now I hope to make it stronger. Abe I think you've just got to look into the formation of this new party. These Republicans.

Long and lanky, thin and needing a morning shave Lincoln replied, "I know Will. I've been expecting to have this come up again. That's what makes you such a good attorney Will. You just never give up." He grew thoughtful now," Will, you've just got to try to understand. When I was lawyerin' up in New Salem the fees I earned were just pitiful. I was practicing law out of a buggy…I was never home and was pretty often paid off with a pig or two…"

"I know but…"

"Let me finish Will. Last year I made one thousand and five hundred dollars and a little more. That's the same as we pay the governor of this state and twice what we pay a circuit judge. I just collected a fee from the Illinois Central Railway of five thousand dollars. Did you know Will that I never have even seen that much money at one time before?" He paused and with finger tips he brushed some of the unruly hair from his forehead. "Now the river freighters have petioned to tear down the Rock Island Bridge. Will that's the first bridge to cross the Mississippi. I'm going to win that case and save that bridge as sure as you're born. I don't know what I'll make for a fee on that case but it might even top the five thousand. Mary and the young'uns are just doing' so much better than we ever were before.' He turned his thin body in the chair and stared out at the street again.

"Are you saying that Mary doesn't want you to run for president Abe?"

"Aw shucks Will. You know Mary. She'd rather be in the white house than to be an angel in heaven. But what makes you think I can win anyhow. After all the campaigning I did for Taylor he dropped me flat and I guess that pretty much leaves me in the cold with the Whig party. These Republicans you talk of…Why Will they're so brand new. What makes you think they could win? Squeezing in between the Whigs and the Democrats is a pretty tight fit Will. Even if they could make that work what makes you think they'd want me?" Hearndon took a few minutes to answer.

"Zachary Taylor was a fool to drop you as a friend Abe. He was a war hero true enough and that's always tough to beat… But just look what a mess he made of his political friendship with you. He all but promised you that you would head up the federal land office when he was in office. Everyone knew it too. After he just out and out betrayed you no one would trust him anymore. His promises just didn't hold up. But he's been dead more than ten years now any way. He was pro slavery. He never made any bones about that. I don't think you can give up your entire political career based on what he did to you ten years ago. He was right in the middle of that fugitive slave law bill and I guess he figured with your views on slavery you weren't likely to be much help to have around.

Since him there's been Fillmore with his re-enforcement of the fugitive act. Another pro slavery move. Here comes Frank Pierce next. He's probably the original instigator of the Kansas and Nebraska act. That's about as pro slave as you can get. President Buchanan is trying right now to right some of those wrongs but he's no match for this up and coming Steven Douglas. He's the one we need to watch.

But put that aside for the moment. It's true our law practice is flourishing. Together we've just about topped our profession...Put that aside too. You can't let Douglas win the seat Abe. You just can't. "Lincoln swiveled his chair back now and faced his friend. Hearndon continued. "You're the last hope the people of colour in this nation have. Steven Douglas has already proposed that all the territory in the Louisiana Purchase be open to slavery. Damn it Abe, he's already got it down on paper and ready for a congressional vote. Maybe you haven't heard the latest one but he also wants to let Kansas and Minnesota use state powers to decide if they are a free or slave state. He wants that done with no federal say so at all. He sounds just like Frank Pierce when he talks. You know that's just to get votes from those two states and has nothing to do with right or wrong." Hearndon paused now and realized he was perhaps getting overly excited... "The Republicans may have a few weak planks in the platform." He continued," but the absolute foundation of they're existence is total abolition!" He slapped the desk top with his open palm. Now he took a different tone of voice and went on.

"I can't say I even understand it Abraham but you walk around town quoting things from the Bible...and Shakespeare...I sometimes get to thinking I have a nice but rather windy fellow for a partner. It amazes me Abe but everyone you meet likes you. If I were to quote those old sayings the way you do I believe they'd lock me up. When you do it though they swoon. Abe you've got to try to stop Douglas and you've got the popularity to do it! You've served twice in the legislature and did well in your two-year congressional term. You know the ropes as well as anyone and you just need to make the move.

Darn it Abe, the country needs you to make the move. I'll be losing the best law partner anyone ever had but those people out there are in trouble. They need you Abe." Then he added, "Did it ever occur to you Abraham that this nation has had fifteen presidents and not a one of them has done any thing to raise Negro race even one step on the ladder?

They're people Abe. They're men and women and children. We use them like commodities. Like raw materials for industry. It's got to change…It's just got to."

Lincoln thought long and hard. With nervous hands he fumbled with a few papers on his desk. He picked up a quill pen and studied its point intently. The silence in the room was thunderous. Will Hearndon was putting a voice to thoughts he'd had himself for a long time. Slavery was evil to him He despised it so. But he constantly had asked himself if he had the grit it would take to fight it. He knew it would take a total commitment if it worked out at all. Could he walk away from the only financial success he had ever known? What of Mary and the children? At this very moment he wished that William Hearndon had kept his thoughts to himself and minded his own business. He felt the room was hot and he was immensely uncomfortable at the moment. He felt this was a moment of truth. And indeed it was. It was exactly that. At last he tossed the quill onto the desk top and asked,

Even if I am elected…How I get rid of slavery? It's a lot older than the Republicans. How do I just do away with it even if I win the office?

"You just proclaim it Abe!"

"What?"

"You proclaim it! You know…You issue a proclamation. If you get elected over Douglas it'll mean you have the backing to do that. Even a slavery soft congress will side with you if the voters do away with Douglas…They'll be afraid not to if you carry the popular vote. They'll want to keep their jobs you know. You just proclaim it!"

It wasn't quite as easy as Will Hearndon had predicted. The campaign debates between Douglas and Lincoln were legendary as both men were skilled orators of the highest order. But at last in 1861 it came to pass that Abraham Lincoln rode the Republican ticket to become the sixteenth president of the United States of America. It would further come to pass that he would issue that emancipation proclamation that Will Hearndon had spoken of. That proclamation abolished slavery in America forever. The after math was bloody and horrendous.

First came four long years of a bloody civil war that nearly tore the nation asunder. America was in the middle of the great industrial revolution. Advanced industry brought about greater and deadlier weaponry. That fact in turn accelerated the carnage to unbelievable proportions. Gettysburgh…Twenty-three thousand dead. Fredricksburgh…Twelve thousand. Chancelorville, site of twenty-three thousand lost. And the list of names of battles went on like an endless roll call of death. In the end, it would be the south that surrendered...but no one won.

The Great War was followed by the assassination of that good man Lincoln. He was shot from behind by an actor who was himself hunted down and shot to death within ten days. When it was discovered that there were other conspirators in on the assassination plot they were hunted down, tried for treason and punished accordingly. Because of the great love the people had for Lincoln the public clamored for the severest of punishment for the conspirators. Then it was discovered that one of the ring leaders was forty-five-year-old Mary Surratt. She had owned and operated the boarding house where the murderous conspirators had met to plot the killing of Lincoln. If she played more of an active part in the plotting of the assassination than just being there history has shrouded it. None the less she was tried and convicted of treason of the highest order. It's true that the American citizenry all wanted the sternest of justice. Still most Americans felt a pang of embarrassment and discomfort both at home and abroad when Surratt became the first woman ever to be hanged in America. Three of the condemned conspirators made loud announcements that Surratt was innocent and did not deserve to be hanged. But their voices were unheeded and all four were hanged together On July 7th 1865 at about one, fifteen in the afternoon

In the following years those who believed the American Constitution really meant all men and not just whites would propose and pass three constitutional amendments. All of that and the lives of most people of African decent in America had changed very little. Prejudice still held sway over the land. Even in the most emancipated states such as Ohio. Ohio was the one state all of the abolitionists believed would lead in the progress. After all during the heights of the slave days that state was reported to have more than two hundred stations of the underground railway. That shadowy secret abolitionist network created to ferry runaway slaves over Lake Erie into the protection of Canada. But everywhere there was still the system of caste. Will Hearndon was heard to say when he learned of his old law partner's death, "It'll change someday...It just might take longer than we thought. If it takes a hundred years...it'll change."

In the passing years, the accomplishments of Hearndon would fade into obscurity. It may have been because of his excessive use of alcohol or maybe just the relentless passing of time. When asked in his later years to help with preparing one of Lincolns biographies he proved very little help. His memory had begun to fail miserably. History would tell us precious little of the life and times of the great American that was William

Hearndon. Be that as it may to that select group of Washington denizens who are really "in the know" he will always be remembered as the driving force that convinced Abraham Lincoln to strive for the seat.

Abraham Primble

In another and much less important part of the world Abraham. Not Lincoln but Primble was becoming one of the great enigmas of his time in the west. For a black man to have reached his level of success in an area so steeped in prejudiced traditions was no less than astounding. Adding to the feat's complexity and noteworthiness was the fact that he had a white wife and neither of them had yet been hanged, shot or burned out. A remarkable victory in 1888 in the Kansas territory

This unlikely cohabitation was occurring at a time and place when and where racial prejudice was rampant. It always seemed to Abraham the lower the class of white men he met the more strongly they opposed mixed relations. Married or otherwise.

Abe was a tall and light-skinned man who exuded physical power as he moved about. His arms were heavily laced with sinewy muscle, and his chest was broad and thick. His wide face was open with pure honesty and a ready smile, and most people whom he met readily liked this good natured big man. But he was, after all, a Negro. White folks, even those of the lowest reputations, could only like him so much and still cling to their respectability.

Abe's success, though, fell on the fact that he had concocted a splendid, highly desirable product. If his product had not brought about complete forgiveness from area bigoted whites, it was certainly good enough to allow him and his bride to survive in a sort of armed truce arrangement. He had diligently, artfully combined the finest of local ingredients. He had so faithfully practiced his art that his results were approaching perfection. So salable was his produce and so respected for its quality that it had set him apart from other men of color in his community. This fine commodity had brought him a sort of reserved respect from even the most bigoted of the nearby citizenry..

As respected, that is, as a black man could hope to be. Most everybody liked Abraham Primble. Black or not. Even though there were some whites in his community who strongly resented his success, they never the less consumed his commodity with great relish. Primble was just another in a long line of men throughout history who had found their personal success in the distillation of fermented spirits. Abraham Primble had one thing in his favor that was uncalcuable...The protection of the Broken Spur.

It hadn't started that way. Abraham was simply fed up to the gills with treatment of blacks in those post Civil War days of 1866 and 1867. He had never been a slave to begin with. He had been born a grandson to slaves who were, strangely enough, manumitted by one of the south's greatest slavers, The family of the Tennessee statesman Henry Clay.

Curiously, although he was pro slavery Clay was one of the men Lincoln had so respected. When Lincoln had come forth with the emancipation proclamation Clay had begrudgingly freed his holdings from his shear respect for Lincoln and the Union. Even as he relented Clay thought slavery was good for the nation and also good for the slave. He believed the freed slave simply could not survive on his own. Lincoln had confided in only a few close friends that he often wondered if Clay could have been correct in his assessment.

It was a forgone conclusion to men and women of colour that there was more safety and refuge in the far north. However, a substantial number of blacks chose to look to the west for their future. True, there was at one time slavery in parts of the west but there was an also unfathomable expanse of space. The great vastness of open, unattended territory seemed to many to be the perfect place to lose one's self forever. The emancipation proclamation had done more towards increasing the population of black cowboys than any other single element. It was one of those great movements that often occur as man tries to civilize himself.

To add to the unrest more than a few white men of the north and south alike went about the practice of racial prejudice so freely it was as if there had been no war fought at all. And after all, who was to say the Supreme Court might not one day set aside all the previous efforts. It had been Abraham Primble's father, driven by fear and weariness of the day by day oppression who had said,

"Go to the west. Men are needed there to herd cattle. A black man workin' on a horse is a better thing than a white man loafin' on a stoop."

"But, Daddy," Abe had complained. "Texas is southern. Lot's o' Texans think strongly on ownin' slaves. Even with the war bein' over and all... Some of them don' really believe the north won at all."

"But Texas is different son... I don't know why but Texas is just always different... Ain't never been a place where men prize freedom so much as in Texas. I hear there's colored cowboys workin' those herds right now. Right along side of them whites. I'm too old now, Abraham, but you needs to go to Texas. True 'nuff you'se named after old Abe Lincoln but in Texas you gotta say you'se called after Abraham in the bible. Them Texans might hate a abolistionist but they truly loves they bible."

Abraham would always remember his father, a man who would have been tall if not so stoop- shouldered. Thin and angular, he was a man who had missed his own opportunities. Abraham had seen this reflected in his father's haunted eyes and docile demeanor.

It seemed Texas was an impossible destination. But maybe he didn't really have to go all the way. Kansas might do. The Union Pacific had promised travel in return for manual work on the section gangs. Blacks rode in separate cars it was true; but, at least, they rode. A few days of the back-breaking work of packing rail to the gandy dancers who spiked them in place, and Abraham had earned a ticket. He was given a round wooden token as large as a man's palm.

"Niggers tend to lose the little paper tickets." he was told by the florid, pink-faced, fat little man who was the ticket agent. The printing on the wooden disc told him that it would permit him to ride as far as Dodge City, Kansas. Someone said to him, "There's cows in Kansas... Cowboys too." It was all the recommendation needed. Abraham Primble was off to Kansas to punch cows.

If one had followed the course of old Caney Creek from Dodge City southwest, he would've found the original stream a bountiful one. Caney Creek was as pleasant to follow as any mid-western river in America. Its quiet flow moved lazily over a bed of sand and gravel. It meandered mile after mile, and its waters were as clear and fresh as any in the land.

Sometimes the Caney ran deep. In these locations, a man crossing it would have to swim his horse. For the most part, though, it was about chest-deep on a man and chin-high on a woman. It was about as far from shore to shore as a good man can throw a silver dollar.

Abe Primble had passed this spot on the creek three times in as many years now. He had found work as a cowboy without much trouble. A cowboy named Possum Victor had filled him in expertly on ranch hand job hunting. Possum was a successful cowboy in his own right and one who knew the ropes. Abe had spotted him right away in the Dodge Stock Yards where he had gone to seek work.

Possum was indeed easily spotted. A dashing figure of a man, he wore a bright crimson shirt and batwing chaps. Tall and straight, he was, indeed an exciting figure. He was neatly tucked under a large, white hat with broad, four-inch brim and embellished with a bright blue band. Abe saw him first at the edge of the cattle holding yards, sitting on a fence, holding the reins attached to a fine Pinto pony.

He made the definitive picture of the perfect cowboy. The colorful appearance was an accurate one. Possum Victor was a real cowboy. He was, further, a top hand and a good man with ropes, cows and horses. More importantly, he was black. Abraham walked boldly over to him, something he would never have done had Possum been white, introduced himself and immediately began to ply him with questions about the cowboy life.

"Ride with the Broken Spur bunch." He had been told by Possum. "The Scotsman is fair with his pay and the Mex is the bravest you'll ever ride with."

In asking more about this cattle empire known as Broken Spur, he at first thought he wanted no part of it at all. He was told that Juan Garcia would often ride a horse at full run through the darkest night. While some called this brave, Abe called it foolhardy. The stories of the hangings, though, distressed him the most.

"On three different drives the rustlers tried to get the Scotty's cattle," he was told by Possum. "Three times they tried his mettle. Old Garcia catched 'em he did. Catched 'em and hanged 'em right on the spot. Five men he's gone and hanged. Five men in three years. After that, them cattle rustlers steered clear o' Broke' Spur herds."

Abe wasn't sure he wanted to ride with some outfit that would hang so readily. That might not be the spot for a black man. Innocent black men had, more than once, taken the rope when a guilty white was not available. But when he went to the stockyards to look for work it quickly became apparent the Broken Spur was the top outfit around.

Further he learned right away that at least three other black men trailed beef for the Spur. Abe cornered one of these colored cowboys and asked about the Scotsman, Robert Trav and his top hand Juan Garcia.

"Won't abide no thief or a liar. Hangs them that steal from him he do. Garcia hangs 'em or rgw Scotty shoots 'em with a big old rifle he packs about. But he don' abide no slavers neither. Lot's o' black folk on the Spur. Come there as runaways, they did. Slave catchers say we comin' get them boys." Ol' Robert, he say, "Come on ahead... But maybe you' slaves don' be goin' back with you.... Maybe, Mister Slaver, you don' go back neither. Somebody... Anybody come messin' round with Spur hands they got to fight the whole bunch... Roundup time, that's a hundred men. Old Garcia can fight like ten. Ridin' the Spur is good for a workin' man... Black or white."

On his third drive for the Spur Abraham could resist the little spot on Caney Creek any longer. He found the owner, a thin, consumptive man who dreamed of returning to central Kentucky before he died. The land owner, it proved, was an impoverished horse trader called George Booter.

Abraham bought the little forty-acre plot for seventy-five dollars. Seventy-five precious dollars that would allow Booter to see the Green River and Mammoth Cave country again in his last years. Of course, Abe didn't have seventy-five dollars and so he asked Juan Garcia for a loan.

As in every matter that had to do with money, Garcia referred him to Robert. Old Robert, before committing to a loan, carefully looked over the forty-acre plat.

"It's a right pretty place, Abe." Old Robert said. "But how can you make a living on forty acres? That's hardly enough room for ten cows or so."

"Not raisin' cows, Mister Trav. Corn. Raisin' forty acres of corn."

"Well, Abe, the last time I checked corn was about thirty cents for a bushel weight. How would you ever live and still pay back the seventy-five dollars?"

"Don't sell no corn by the bushel. Runs it through a still, I will, Mister Trav. Make that good Kentucky whiskey that quality gen'emen drinks. This old prairie piss they sellin' cross the bar in Dodge ain't nothin'. Ain't even fit for drinkin' when you puts it next to the whiskey made from old Henry Clays 'receep'. Clay, he long dead. Folks still swears by his whiskey though Clays' old lead man, Pompeii, showed my daddy how to mix up the mash. Daddy learned me how to agitate it. How to let it set till it sours up and starts workin' real good and a-bubblin' and all. Then you fires it. Turns the mash into steam. Then you leaks the steam through a copper coolin' worm runnin' through acold water kettle. That steam cools into drippins of sweet 'brosia, Mister Trav. That's sippin' whiskey that does its maker right proud."

"Can you really make good whiskey?" Old Robert wanted to know. All Scots were interested in good whiskey. It was in Scotland, after all, that whiskey had first been invented. For hundreds of years Scots had sought the perfection that always, through peat smoke, grain or malt, seemed to baffle and elude.

"I makes it smoother'n honey and sweeter'n 'lasses. I c'n make it light and whispy or fiery as the hinges of Hell. I gon' raise corn here and buy more when I needs it. I gets Mister Henry Brooker up in Murphy Flat to gits me some sugar. I'll haul it down here by mule team.

"I'll make the finest whiskey ever Mister Trav. And just look at all this sweet water. This here Caney Creek water'll make a straight bourbon that jest shines. Once I gits 'er set, I believe I can run me fifty, maybe sixty bottles a week. 'Bout two hogheads a month I thinks." Old Robert thought over this proposition briefly.

"Tell Brooker I said to give you whatever you need and put it on the Spur's account books. We can settle it later. Abe I think you'll do well." Without another word, without the condemning loan terms, without the overbearing advice Abe had expected to be obligated to hear from a white man making a loan to a black; Old Robert reined his mount and trotted back to his herd.

With corn, sugar and credit, it came to pass that for more than twenty years Abraham Primble distilled the finest whiskey west of the state of Kentucky. For the first few years he lived alone with a couple of local white boys to help him. There are a lot of steps to take in the manufacture of fine whiskey. None so burdensome and back-breaking as the chopping of firewood

It's the chore that never sees an end. Abe cut wood right alongside his hired help. He treated them more than fairly and always remembered he was black and they were not. When he had to give instructions he was as careful in the wording as a politician is with promises.

He may have been the owner, but success was more important to him than ego. He managed to make others feel good about themselves while he concentrated on the manufacture and sale of more and more whiskey. His business grew and flourished; even in the face of his race. White saloon owners weren't always pleased to be dealing with a black, but they were interested in his superior product. It was called simply Caney Creek Sour Mash. All who tasted the amber ambrosia agreed that it was truly among the finest of spirits.

Abraham was an affable man. That gentle quality was certainly a help along the road to success. The Civil War was over, it was true. Still, if a black got too demanding or failed to realize his proper place, things could go badly for him in a hurry. Especially in Kansas or Texas territory.

Abraham was a big man who stood nearly six feet tall. His neck was thick and powerful and his arms were roped with heavy muscle. His broad brown face was a handsome one. His teeth were even and so white they gleamed when he smiled, which was often. He looked exactly like what he truly, was: A free man who made good whiskey, paid his debts and cared for his friends. He loved God and loved life and he was good at it.

From time to time, a saloon keeper might try to take advantage of Abraham by not paying him. Abe never made a scene, he just didn't sell that saloon any more Caney Creek. After a while it seemed good business just to buy Abe's whiskey and pay the bill. None of the tavern keepers, though, would ever have thought of permitting Abe to drink that whiskey within their establishments.

It didn't bother Abe. He kept salting away his money and improving his capacity for whiskey making. He paid Old Robert Trav back the seventy-five dollars from the first few batches he ran off. He tried to pay him extra, but Robert refused. He took a five percent profit on the loan and called it square.

For years to come, every Broken Spur drive that passed the Caney Creek Distillery received ample supplies of fine whiskey to carry back to the ranch. All in all, it was a simple and rewarding endeavor. Abe made the whiskey as fine in quality as he was able to. He made as much of it as day light hours and firewood would permit.

He also bottled the beverage, packed it in the wagon and peddled it himself. He sold to all the saloons within a day or two trip of the farm. He knew if he tried to travel farther, being the only colored in the area, he would surely fall prey to every bandit in the district. He was now making enough product that he needed more outlets for distribution.

Whiskey drummers were the obvious answer. These super salesmen of the frontier would pick up the amber liquid at Abes' farm in hard-topped peddlers' wagons. Sometimes these wagons were so large they needed a big four-horse team to draw them along. This was no place for light plains horses or even good saddle stock. These wagons were mammoth; large enough to require the service of the big draft animals. From Germany came the Belgian. England sent America the Clydesdale. The dappled grey Percheron was the French contribution, and immigrant Spaniards brought the war-horse called the Punch.

Never husbanded to pull wagon or plow, these gentle behemoths were the fighting horses of the long-gone days of knighthood. They were bred gentle and non-excitable so as to be under total control in the midst of a wild fighting melee. Their size and strength and attitude were vitally needed to accommodate a full-grown man in a heavy suit of steel armor, fully equipped with ponderous weaponry.

Once these gallant animals had settled disputes across the face of Europe. Now they were settling the land of the Americas. They were the most important animal citizens of the west. They could go where a train could not. They could plow the deep and virgin furrows required on the endless plains. They could deliver colossal loads of freight nearly anywhere a man could walk. They made fine, even royal, transporters of Abraham's good whiskey.

The cargo capacity of these peddlers' wagons that were in truth homes on wheels, was enormous. Loaded mightily with fine Caney Creek, they would carry it the two hundred miles to Kansas City. The drummers lived in their wagons and sold their wares all along the whiskey-starved trail. Some of Abe's spirits were, eventually, put aboard trains and found their way all the way to Saint Louis.

One single incident had given Abe a decided advantage over other black business men of the time. It further was the event that would change his life in a most unlikely way. Most blacks– whites too for that matter– who tried just as hard as he to engage in some form of business or another failed miserably.

White success was rare for all, black victory was ten times more isolated. Racial prejudices of the time were simply too severe to tolerate very much success on the part of a "Nigra". The thing that had given Abraham the most protection, freedom to trade as an entrepreneur, was the incident called, "The Hitching Post Raid."

Eighty miles south west of Dodge and forty miles west of Abe's farm there existed, on the bank of Caney Creek's outer reaches, a settlement called Rogers, Texas. Actually, no one seemed quite sure if Rogers was really in Texas or in Kansas or in the Nation. The local citizenry preferred to call themselves Texans.

The parochial saloon in Rogers was a low den of vile characters called the Hitching Post Tavern. The proprietor with the help of a few of his customers had taken whiskey from Abe and then refused to pay for it. Further, they had thrown him into the street after roughing him up considerably. They had broken his nose and cracked several ribs with their brutal kicks. When they left him laying in the dusty street of Rogers their spirits soared and they shared a great deal of laughter at their success of handling a "smart assed nigger". Battered and bloody Abraham had taken nearly three days to make his way back to his home.

The story spread far and wide that the boys at the Hitching Post knew how to handle "uppity Niggers." It was the fact that the local law did not one thing about the situation that gave Abe grave doubts as to the future of his business. If he could expect no more protection from the law than this, it was almost certain others would take advantage of him too.

Abe was deeply troubled and worried. It was one of the few times in his life that Abraham Primble found it difficult to smile. Bravely, he tried to forge ahead with a business-as-usual attitude. His mistreatment at the hands of the Hitching Post regulars haunted him and settled over his generally sunny demeanor like a great, oppressive shadow.

The incident at the Hitching Post had taken place in May. In the month of June, the Broken Spur herd passed within three miles of the town called Rogers. The herd that year was a large one. The drovers from the Spur were moving nearly four thousand head of cattle in this early summer move.

The cattle were broken into three groups and spread out on the plains for a stretch of more than twenty miles. Juan Garcia had understood the need for extra hands for such an enormous endeavor. The drovers that year numbered about sixty. Many were regular Spur hands, but a few saddle tramps and gun toughs had been recruited by Garcia to round out the company.

A few others though were not even that credible. Garcia had, out of desperation, hired a tough assortment this summer. There were gamblers on the move. Gunmen from the border towns trying to get out of Texas. A few were bona fide bandits on the run. All these were needed to handle this unusually gigantic herd.

Garcia had proven time and again that he could handle dangerous men. Yet it was not those wild and curly woods colts but the regulars who instigated the, "Hitching Post Raid." When these compadres heard of the abuse and mistreatment of their old saddle pal, Abraham, they paid a memorable visit to the Hitching Post.

They had told the night hawk in charge that they were riding in for a few drinks and a little fun. When they left Rogers in their dust, two men were dead and most of the town was in flames. Neither of the dead were riders of the Spur. The raid had been led by Juan Garcia himself. It would be a bloody night that all would long remember.

It had been the drifter that had actually caused the shooting. The drifter had instigated the conflict by merely being the bearer of the news. If the drifter had not brought the news, the raid might never have happened. He was nothing more than a down and out, bedraggled grub line rider.

He and his kind rode up and down the cattle trails doing minor chores or running messages for the men handling the big herds. A few would take steady work when it was offered. But most seemed to drift aimlessly, up and down, first one trail and then another. A few days work and a few dollars, and they were more than likely to drift away as quietly as they had appeared. The Indians who had domesticated enough to work as trail hands called them Shadow riders. It was a good name.

This Shadow Rider was called Emmett. He gave no last name, nor was he asked for one. Dusty from days on the trail, he was a short, powerfully built man of about thirty. He was as raggedly dressed as his kind generally were and his round face bristled with a frosted red beard.

He rode into the spur camp one evening just at sunset. Arrival time for these drifters was always at sunset. That was the way he could get a meal and know it would soon be too dark for him to have to work for it. At least that day. If the meal was not a good one, if he determined the cooking to be better further up the trail, morning would surely find him as long gone as last night's biscuits.

"Lots o' news up the way," Emmett had said to the Spur riders who were seated on the ground eating their evening meal. He whistled loudly when he pronounced the letter 's'. Garcia determined the speech defect was due to the front tooth that was so obviously missing.

The pot of Texas chili beans filled the air with a delicious spicy perfume. That familiar aroma was well punctuated by the more wonderful smell of brewing Arbuckle's. Emmett could see with a well practiced glance this was a well to do chuck wagon. He certified this observation, positively, when he was able to detect a sprinkling of rare cinnamon dusting the surface of the bubbling pot of stewing apples.

"Fellow name of Will Jenney just built hisself a skyscraper," the grub line rider said. He was launching himself heartily into a plate of the spicy beans and beef. He was readying himself for a really good meal. He was pretty sure from past experience that he more he talked the faster the food would be in coming.

"What is this thing... this skyscraper?" Garcia wanted to know.

"Why, it's a building, friend. A big old building made out o' bricks and stones. Goes right up to the sky, it does. This here building is up there in Chicago town. You know ever since that town burned down they been set on buildin' it up a sight bigger than ever it was afore. This here buildin' this Jenney feller has gone and put up is ten stories high." Before Will Jenny no such structure had existed in America.

"Ten stories?" The disbelief was obvious in Harlan Winsted's voice. "I ain't never heard tell of no buildin' that was ten stories high." Winstead pushed his dusty black hat to the back of his head and observed the stranger with honest doubt and amazement.

"Well, this one is. They tell me they's a fixin' to add two more stories to it, too. That's twelve stories. President Arthur himself is goin' out to Chicago to see it."

"Well ...," Winstead drawled, "...I guess if the President sees that twelve stories and comes back and says so... I 'spect I might believe it then. Tell you the truth though, I don't believe most of that bullshit I hear from Chicago. Matter of fact, I thinks most of the liars east of the Mississippi lives in Chicago."

"Well, I grant you they's a bunch o' windy boys livin' there." Emmett allowed. "Anyhow, they's excitin' things happenin' everywhere, friend. Not just only in Chicago."

"What else is happenin' then that I ought to be knowin' 'bout?" This came from the tough wiry little Bobby Baxter. At seventeen, youngest of the Spur riders, Garcia often thought the boldest. Through mouthfuls of the fine beans, flashing the tooth gap in the firelight, drifter Emmett told of the marvelous things encountered in his recent travels.

"Earp's left Dodge," he said. "Politicians put him right out. I hear he's goin' out to Arizona territory. That's a dangerous thing to do you know. What with Geronimo and them Mescaleros runnin' loose out there. And in New Mexico too. Guess old Wyatt can keep up though. He's a hard man." The Spur hands gathered in closer. Emmett was a walking newspaper, and whether he was all that truthful or not, he was a diversion.

"Garrett killed the Kid out there somewhere in Lincoln County, New Mex. I hear tell. I's just gettin' to like readin' 'bout the Kid, and now Pat Garrett done up and did him in."

A murmur of surprise and concern wafted through the gathering of Spur riders. The Kid had been dead for more than four years, but a personage such as Billy Bonny was still worthwhile talking about. Besides, perhaps some detail, omitted in the past, would now and then be brought to light.

"He was a tough one I suppose," Garcia said. Senor Billy... The senoritas called him El Chabito. It was their way of calling him a better name than just 'Kid.'" The drifter was into the cinnamon apples now. He smacked his lips noisily with appreciation of the phenomenal spiced flavor.

"They's tough ones 'bout everywhere I go, "Emmett continued. "I saw a nigger get a beatin' a few weeks back not five miles from here that was one of the worstest things ever I seed."

"Niggers get whupped all the time," Winstead said.

"Yeah. That's right. But this here's a pretty good nigger. I hated to see him get so beat up. Whiskey makin' nigger name of Primble."

Emmett didn't see the visual reaction that circled the campfire. Every Spur rider busied himself with his beans and listened intently. Each trying to look uninterested and yet hanging on every word. Even the newest employees had heard the name 'Primble'. Garcia leaned forward and cocked his head to one side.

"You say this good man of color was injured? Who would hurt a man who only makes whiskey? Was his whiskey not good?"

"Oh no. Not at all. Why he makes that Caney Creek panther piss. It's right good stuff alright. I've had me some of it when I had some money once. Them fellers at the Hitchin' Post tavern just ain't up to givin' a nigger his proper money. 'Makes 'em uppity,' they says. I cain't rightly agree though. Seems to me niggers ought to get paid rightly for what they do. Even if they is niggers.

Them old boys beat him up pretty bad, though. Matter o' fact, they kicked the livin' shit right out of him. I ain't drinkin' in there no more. If they ain't got Caney Creek you might get poisoned. Them saloons as serves trade whiskey could jest kill a feller right out, don' ya' know? 'Er... Mister Garcia sir... Do you think I might have another apple or two? They's right fine flavored."

A half an hour later Garcia was saddling his horse. Looking up he saw Winstead coming his way, his saddle slung over his shoulder. Behind him carrying saddles too was a contingent of grim-faced and determined men.

"Where you goin', Mister Winstead? Mister Baxter?" Garcia asked.

"Over to Rogers to have a drink or two," was the answer.

"These other hombres, too? They drinkin', too?"

"Yeah. They all mighty thirsty."

"You have guns?"

"One or two I reckon." Bobby Baxter said. A strange light came into the eyes of Juan Garcia. He made an issue of buckling on the famous Spanish rapier. The new riders had heard of this sword, but now their eyes widened. They were actually seeing this legendary and formidable blade for the first time.

"The Spur rides tonight." Garcia said through a grin, somehow evil and knowing. "Tell the nighthawk we'll be back soon. Saddle up compadres, pronto, pronto. We ride."

Garcia had left the herd camp that night at the head of seven other Spur riders. They had galloped over the plain as avenging angels swooping down on the little settlement of Rogers. Every man in this wild bunch felt exactly the same. Abraham was their friend. He was a Spur rider. Those who affronted a Spur cowboy did so at great peril.

No man could insult one of these or call him out without risking the wrath of these dusty fellows. Garcia, already dressed in black, had now pulled an ebony scarf across nose and mouth. He did this to avert the dust the stampeding horses were putting up. The result was a chilling one. In the moonlight, Juan Garcia created a terrifying sight as his ghostly grey mount swept his lean masked rider across the flatness of the plain.

This night he looked and felt the same as he had so many years ago. He was again the vaquero who had been another man. He was again the fearless raider of the Rio Grande. Tonight he was ablaze, fervent with the old familiar feeling. The posse behind him set their spurs hard to the flanks of their mounts and thundered into the narrow dusty streets of Rogers.

As a unit, they wheeled their mounts to rearing halts in the front of the Hitching Post. The horses, having been so abruptly stopped, snorted and blew noisily. The night was cool, and the Broken Spur mustangs felt good, full of life and exhilarated by the run. The horses had enjoyed the competitive wild flight over the flats immensely. Each animal was prepared to continue the run at breakneck speed. Now they blew through flared nostrils and stamped their hooves. Fighting their bits, they milled about in dancing circles. Their riders patted their necks, speaking in low, affectionate voices to them, trying to calm them with the intimate sounds that only master horsemen or lovers know how to make.

The animals' forequarters had begun to perspire heavily. The horsemen knew this to be a good sign. These mounts were only warmed up. Each had plenty of fire and vigor left in him. A horse sweating from the front, his neck and brisket, the powerful shoulder withers, is an animal cocked and ready for any challenge. Hindquarter sweat though is often the sign of a spent horse.

The pungent odor of the frothy horse lather enriched the night air. Garcia looked singularly to each of his men as they dismounted and tied up. Each had a hard set to his features. Narrow-eyed, with jaws set tight, almost as a single man they adjusted and saw to their weapons.

One or two wore open-topped holsters. Juan Garcia had a Colt .44 tucked into the sash waist band he always wore. On his left hip hung the fine Spanish rapier. Clyde Tudor carried a double-barreled Greener shotgun. Cyrus Hollis packed a short-barreled Merwin Hulbert revolver in each of his two front pockets.

The pistols' amber grips protruded obscenely from the pockets of Hollis's riding pants. Garcia thought they were the most intimidating guns he had ever seen. The rest of the riders were armed just as fearsomely. Pistols and bowie knives fairly bristled from their clothing. The Winchester rifles were carried at waist level, ready for the kind of heavy duty action only they were able to handle.

Parting the slatted batwing doors, the Spur cowhands stepped into the Hitching Post Tavern. The place was dim with a low roof. The oil lamps that lit the room were smoky and yellow. The air was heavy with the smell of stale beer, kerosene and tobacco smoke. The riders blinked to adjust their vision.

A tall heavy man in a dirty apron stood behind the bar. Arms folded across his large belly, he chewed the stump of a black cigar. He mopped his balding head with a damp bar towel. and eyed the riders suspiciously as they entered.

Two other cowboys stood, drinking beer from pewter mugs, at the bar. Garcia recognized them as point riders for a Red River ranch called the Turkey Track. They, in turn, recognized the Spur bunch just as quickly. The pair of drovers looked up in puzzlement as the Spur cowboys entered.

It was easy for the pair of T.T. men to see the Spur boys were lit with the hot fires of anger. Their display of weaponry left little doubt of forthcoming events. The two Double T riders looked at each other for a long, questioning moment. Then the tallest one spoke.

"Evenin' Mister Garcia."

"Evenin', Turkey Track," Garcia answered. Without another word the two from the Red River country pushed some coins out onto the bar. Hitching their belts into position, without a further pause, they left by the front door. These Double T boys had ridden enough trails to know a fight was spoiling here. You didn't get to be a point rider by being stupid. From the open display of weapons, this fight looked to be a serious one. Since it was not their fight, the Turkey Track men mounted up by the tie up outside and rode off swiftly into the darkness. Their horses' retreating hooves were the only sound now. The fat man clamped his teeth hard on the cigar.

Now the Spur men spread themselves out against the front wall of the Hitchin' Post. They stood, shoulder to shoulder, in defiant readiness on either side of the bat wing doors. Two tables of small stakes poker games were in front of them.

Each table held four men. At the farthest table a thin, red-haired woman was laughing and dealing the cards. Her laughter tinkled like a bell and was the only sound to break the ominous silence. The card games had stopped now, the players eyeing the list of armed men who seemed to be invaders.

The laughter from the woman faded and then halted completely as she assessed what she was seeing. At once the silence in the room became so heavy one could slice it with a knife. She gripped the wrist of the poker player on her left.

"Caldwell …," she said, as if alerting him to the men he had already seen. The gambler shook off her hand and ignored the intrusion.

"I think I c'n afford to raise on this hand a bit," he spoke loudly, trying to call the players' attention back to the table. "I don' think you boys got no cards near as fair as these. What do you say, Dan? You still in here with me?" His fellow players ignored him and kept a steady visage on the gunmen.

The red-haired woman looked up and down the rank. Finally her gaze fell upon the stern face of Juan Garcia. His eyes were narrow slits, and his hand rested on the hilt of what appeared to her to be a sword. She could never remember seeing anyone actually carrying a sword before. In picture books maybe, but this was a real sword.

Was he a Mexican soldier? A General maybe? She wondered nearly aloud.

Smelling danger, with the keen senses such women must develop in order to survive, she could hear her own heart pounding rapidly within her breast. Now she looked to the ashen faces of the men she'd been entertaining. They were frozen in fear and anticipation. The greasy lamp smoke hung against the low plank roof as a yellowed dirty fog.

Three of the gamblers quietly folded their hands. Neither wanted to appear cowardly. But they were acutely aware that serious trouble was in the air. The trio quietly made their excuses, pushed themselves back from the table and all, save one, eased themselves through the swinging doors between the flanking Spur drovers. Sharing furtive glances and nods of recognition of the trouble that was brewing about them the players at the second table continued their game but lowered their voices to mere whispers.

The red-haired woman and the dealer she called Caldwell stayed in their places and watched the exodus. Caldwell seemed greatly agitated at the interruption. It seemed his game had obviously ended for the night. The heavy bartender stood quietly at the far end of the bar, his slitted eyes fixed on Juan Garcia. The scene was an intimidating one, but the bartender stood his ground. He had seen bad men and bad situations before. No man could operate a tavern in this land if he was scared off each time a cowboy with a gun came to town.

"Puddin' Winslow," The woman said. "Are you goin' to serve these men so's we can get a new game started or not?"

"Naw, I don't believe I am, Annie. You and Jack'll have to wait till I throw them out of here. We'll have a game then I'd expect," the bartender said.

"Are you very good at beating men and throwing them out?" Garcia asked.

"I am... "I damned sure am. 'Specially, greaser Mexicans. I don't serve whiskey to no greasers."

"What about men of color?" Garcia was grinning now; but his smile, somehow, seemed mirthless to the red-haired woman.

"You mean niggers? No... I don't have no custom with niggers.... Indians neither if it's any of your greaser business." The bartender began to polish up the bar with his towel. He turned sideways to Garcia and the riders as if to ignore further interruptions. He kept up his polishing as he spoke.

"I guess I'm supposed to be a-scared of that big knife you're packin'. I really ain't much afraid of nothin' you greaser Mexicans can come up with. That is... 'cept that syphilis all your women carry. That scares me a little. I hear they get it from goats. How about you, Greaser? Your Momma got syphilis too? Your Momma keep a goat herd? You plannin' on stickin' somebody with that knife, Greaser?"

The words of Puddin' Winslow were, of course, meant to inflame the temper of Juan Garcia. Angry men often make mistakes. Mistakes that alter the course of advantage can prove fatal. The amateurish ploy didn't work this time of course. The raider of the Rio Grande had seen far too many battles to allow him to become entrapped by stupid, unguarded emotions.

Garcia looked first to the men on his right. He examined those standing at his left. All were alert; in a state of readiness. He withdrew the Toledo rapier and with a flourish that made the blade whistle in the air, laid it on the mahogany bar. Its gleaming blade pointed down the length of the bar. The thin vaquero stood near its leather and silver wire grip. He flashed the bartender a toothy grin.

"You can see, Senor Bartender... She is a beautiful blade. She is really more for looking upon than for fighting." The bartender kept up the polishing task. "I am interested in the way you treat men of color, though." Garcia went on. "If you don't let them drink... Do you buy their whiskey?" Now a sudden look of understanding came to the fleshy face of Puddin' Winslow.

"You must mean the whiskey Nigger. Are you talkin' 'bout the whiskey Nigger? What's his name...

A-bram somethin' or other?"

"Si, Senor. That's the man I inquire of you about. Abraham Primble. How have you dealt with him?" Bobby Baxter thought for some reason Garcia's Mexican accent seemed a great deal stronger than usual. It was as though he was deliberately using it to antagonize the Mexican hating barman.

"I told you. I ain't got no business with no Niggers 'cept for him. He's about a uppity sumbitch. 'Course he ain't as lowdown as a Mex, but he's still a Nigger. Whupped his ass I did. Just 'bout like I'm fixin to do with you."

The bartender struck both his beefy fists flat on the bar with a resounding thud. His left hand was nearest Garcia. His right hand began to slide slowly from the bar. Garcia suspected a shotgun was close at hand. A sawed-off Greener behind the bar would be nothing unusual.

Without a word, without waiting to be certain of the shotgun theory in a sudden flash Garcia batted the pommel of the rapier hard with his left hand, sweeping it powerfully. The sword flew down the bar point first. It sailed along the bar's polished surface, sliding with amazing velocity and accuracy. The sword had become a javelin, propelled at bullet speed over mahogany ice. Its needle point impaled the bartender through the center of the knuckles of the right fist. The double-edged blade was a razor in sharpness.

It pierced the clenched hand as if it were butter. The steel slipped deeply through the fleshy hand and wrist. The double edged rapier blade exited Puddin' Winslow's fore arm a full eight inches from its entry point. Its bloody tip protruded grotesquely through the savaged arm before its flying force was lost.

In pain and surprise the bartender cried out. He wildly slung his hand. Using his entire arm, he arced it about with all his might. He swung his limb back and forth, shaking his hand to rid it of the stinging blade. As he slung his arm about the pain increased mightily due to the twin edges slashing back and forth. It's heavy hilt added greatly to the leverage of the cutting edge. Panicked as the pain intensified, he shook his hand all the harder.

The move was a bad one. The razor-sharp blade, aided by the leverage of the slinging arm and the increased weight of the pommel, sliced its way effortlessly. With hardly a hesitation, the edge cut through the palm and exited though the edge of the hand, cleaving bones to make its exit.

The bartender roared in pain and seized the ruined right hand with his left.. At the card table, the man named Caldwell leapt to his feet. With his right hand, he clawed clumsily at a shoulder holster. The leather was buried too deeply within his coat.

From the riders against the front wall, the fusillade of shots came as a single devastating blast. The gambler was lifted off his feet by the surging lead. Smoke from the black powder rolled over him, completely obscuring him from view of the shooters. He dropped to the floor a full five feet from his seat. The red-haired woman screamed and threw herself across his bloody and fallen body.

At once her dress front was stained bright red from breast to thigh. Somewhat recovered now, the bartender made a grab at the shotgun beneath the bar with his good hand. Injured as he was from the sword's slash, he proved far too slow and clumsy. The drawn cocked and smoking arms of the Broken Spur were far too formidable.

Bullets tore through Puddin' Winslow as a leaden hailstorm. The gunfire drove him backwards and into his own back bar. As he collapsed, his falling body toppled the back bar. Over it turned. He was wetly buried under a dozen bottles of his own whiskey. Flowing blood pooled with the loose liquor under his fallen body.

The Spur men stood now, eyeing the small crowd before them. They were spring steel, coiled to strike again. Knees slightly bent and gun hammers thumbed back, they stood with their backs against the front wall. They were more than ready to continue, should one of the remaining patrons care to take up the fight.

Each man stood shoulder to shoulder. They were hard-eyed men who were fanned to flame by the blood letting. Earlier today they had been simple cowhands. That demeanor had fled them now amid the roar of the guns firing and the acrid fumes of black powder.

Now they stood together, united in the brotherhood of blood. They had avenged the disgraceful treatment of one of their own. It was obvious that they were willing, even anxious, to continue. Those before them were aware that a single sudden move would bring about instant death. The light grey gun smoke hung in the flickering firelight. Its sulphur smell was bitter, and the charcoal smoke stung the eyes.

"Vamoose," cried Juan Garcia. He had intended this call to leave for benefit of his own men. It was the remaining bar customers, though, that hit the front door in a cluster at a dead run. Now the Spur men walked out into the street and stood by their horses.

They watched and smiled to one another as the bar patrons fled down the dusty street and into the night. To a casual observer they would have seemed almost calm. The appearance was a remarkably false one. These riders were as tense and ready as a coiled rattler.

Garcia crossed the floor to the end of the bar and retrieved his fine rapier. Sheathing it, he strode to the fallen body of the gambler, Caldwell. The woman was still covering his body with hers. Her body jerked involuntarily. She was sobbing uncontrollably.

Garcia bent and lifted her gently to her feet. She fought him to stay by the fallen man, but he was insistent. He drew her near him and very nearly carried her out of the tavern and into the street..

"He should never have reached for his gun, Senora. It was not his fight." He intended to let her stand now, but her legs gave way under her. She fell into a disheveled heap at his feet.

"Torch it," Garcia called. Three of the Spur cowboys entered the tavern. With their pistols, they shot the remaining oil lamps, exploding them one by one. The flames leaped hotly and the Hitching Post was a den of fire in less than a moment.

"We ride," Garcia announced loudly. The riders of the Broken Spur swung into their saddles and in an instant were racing down the narrow dusty street of Rogers. Garcia turned his head and looked at the flames behind him. Nearly panicked by the shooting and the soaring flames, his horse raced wildly into the black of the night.

The final thing Garcia saw, as the posse cornered the last of Roger's shabby little hovels, was the red- haired woman. She made a strange and fearful sight backlit by the fire of the tavern as she was. Surrounded by the leaping inferno, she was trying to force her way back into the bar amid the seething holocaust. The fire though proved simply too much for her. She collapsed sobbing into the dust of the street.

They had burned the Hitching Post to the ground. They had shot Puddin' Winslow, proprietor and a three-card monte player named Jack Caldwell, to death. Amid the spreading flames and odorous gun smoke they rode out as swiftly as they had ridden in. It became apparent that night that to take advantage of Abraham Primble was to challenge the wrath of the Broken Spur. After that night, Abe's burgeoning business improved even more. Having the protection of the Broken Spur riders was a coveted boon.

The Hitching Post Raid though would have another effect on certain involved lives. It has been said that from death, life often springs fresh and anew. From the blood and fire that engulfed the low building at the end of the solitary dusty street in the town of Rogers, just such an occurrence would be spawned.

It was the death of Caldwell that brought about Abe's involvement with Annie Stinson. Annie had traveled all about the frontier with Jack Caldwell. There was very little to do with saloon life in the mining camps and cattle towns that Annie didn't have some experience in. When she was a younger and prettier Annie, she had worked in places like the Dodge City Birdcage and other rather classy bordellos. Age and the hard life soon robbed Annie of her fresh good looks though. Overnight it seemed she took on a hardened appearance.

Actually, she was more intimidating than seductive. Most men hesitated to hire a whore they were afraid of. Annie's customers were becoming fewer and her life was becoming harder. A Kansas City druggist had sold her some hair coloring. With a mighty effort she had changed her soft brown hair to a rather wire-like, blazing orange. Add to this her over applications of crimson rouge, and Annie's prospects were narrow indeed. She had taken up travel with the slight and skinny little tinhorn gambler, Jack Caldwell. Sometimes Caldwell acted as her pimp, letting her out for a few dollars when he found someone drunk enough to show an interest. But mostly Annie just looked after Jack.

Jack Caldwell needed a lot of looking after. In addition to the fact that he was a rather poor card player and therefore limited to games with rather small stakes Caldwell was an exceedingly heavy drinker. It was Annie's responsibility to see him home to bed at night. She kept him near his chamber pot and fed him coffee in the mornings to get him up and around again. Annie had known that Caldwell's money was running low before the shooting.

She was deeply troubled that he might not win enough to keep their hotel room. That meant more nights in alleys and livery stables. Annie hated that thought. Days without food were far easier to bear for Annie than a night without shelter. She was always afraid when they camped on the trail or hid out in some lonely and deserted barn. Annie had been a lot of places and seen a lot of things. Some of which were terrible. But she never trusted the dark. Annie had known all her life that if there was anything bad it was surely to be found in the dark....

The riders from the Broken Spur brought her worst fears to bear a lot sooner than she had expected. When Jack Caldwell fell, she saw her last chance slipping away. It wasn't much of a chance; but as slim as it was, it was all gone now.

Annie made a heart wrenching picture fighting her way through the flames and greasy smoke. She wanted so desperately to pull Caldwell's body from the fire into the street. Annie frantically wanted him away from the flames. It was futile. The heat of the inferno drove her back into the street. Puddin' Winslow, the corpulent owner of the tavern had been left inside to burn. She could swear she heard his fat frying in the fire. The sizzling, crackling sound made her cry for Caldwell that much harder. It was not so much love for Caldwell as it was knowing she was now alone.

The fight had been so sudden Annie could never be sure which of the Spur riders actually did the shooting. Puddin' had said something about Mexicans. She thought she heard him tell the riders he would treat all Niggers just the way he had treated the one who makes the whiskey.

Then the fight just went wild. Puddin' stood there, hollering in pain, she remembered. He had that big knife, that sword, clear through his hand. Jack had grabbed at his gun. Then some hot unaccountable wind had just swept him away. One minute he was standing by her, and the next he was lurching drunkenly through the air.

The Mexican, she thought. *I knew he was looking for a fight soon as he came in. All that grinnin'... and that big knife... He's a devil, that one.*

Guns had blazed. The flames of the firing black powder had leaped out three feet or more from the pistol barrels. Tables covered with whiskey glasses, cards and money were overturned. Lighted coal oil lamps were shot apart. They sprayed their oily fuel against paper dry walls and exploded in fiery shards. Jack had fallen before that she thought. Her mind was whirling now.

Annie's thoughts were filled with fire and smoke and the explosions of gunshots. The Mexican had dragged her into the street. She remembered that. He was thin. But strong. He had been very strong and the muscles in his arms had been hard.

When she had turned to look back, the whole place was a blazing inferno. Caldwell was still in there. What if he was alive? She had to get him out. It was hot. She remembered the skin on her face felt as though it were cracking open from the heat.

"Oh, God!" she cried out. "It's so hot. Oh, Jack, where in the hell are you?" She stumbled across the wooden porch and tried to reach for the swinging doors of the saloon., It was far to hot to allow her entry. One of the badly burned doors fell from its hinges in a shower of sparks and embers allowing her a final glance into the blazing barroom. Through the flame and smoke she spied the lifeless form sprawled on the floor that was Jack Caldwell. His sleeve was aflame and she saw that one of his trouser legs was burning hotly. She saw that the hair on his head had singed now. It had turned the color of ash and was a strange kinky curly wire.

She could see that he was dead. He made no move to protect himself from the fire that was torturing him. Destroying him. Annie resigned herself with a sigh. She watched as long as she could as the flames of the Hitching Post tavern became Jack Caldwell's crematorium. When at last the heat drove her away she fled to the street. She knew Caldwell was dead for sure now.

And so, thought Annie, *So am I.*

Annie

She sat in the powder dust of the street in the darkness and watched the Hitching Post level itself. The raiders had mounted and rode out by now. With no reaction to her whatever, they had galloped off into the darkness. They had paid less attention to her than they would've a town dog.

It was an attitude that Annie Stinson had encountered very often in her pitifully lacking life. She had a good many times before been completely ignored. Especially by men. At least most women hated her because she had been a prostitute. The men just didn't care that much one way or the other.

Sometimes the ignoring was so painfully total that Annie had to ask her self if she did, indeed, exist at all. It was as though she mattered no more than the dust in the street; that she was no more important than a tumble weed. When she suffered this treatment, it always made her feel lonely and desolate. There hadn't been much hope anyway with the likes of Jack Caldwell. There was nothing left now but the street. A small crowd of citizens had gathered now to watch the last of the fire. She saw quickly that there was not one trace of help for her among them. There was not even a single thought about Annie Stinson.

Abraham Primble found her along the road two days after the already famous "Hitching Post Raid." He believed at first she may have been drunk. She seemed dazed and was wandering about rather aimlessly, he thought. The front of her dress was a ruin of dried blood. He stopped his wagon alongside her. He climbed from the wagon seat and stood by her in the road.

He took off his hat and lowered his eyes as coloreds know to do when speaking to a white woman. As politely as he could, he asked if she would care for a ride to somewhere. After all she was a woman on a lonely road. She was at least seven or eight miles from even the nearest house.

"Don't take no help from no God damned Niggers," Annie snarled. Without a word Abe reclaimed his seat, clucked to his team and the slick, fat mules moved him down the lane. Later that night though Abe could stand it no longer.

What if a wolf got her? he thought. He admitted that he had never actually heard of a wolf getting anyone, but it was a scary thought. He re-hitched Bluegrass and Jumper and took his wagon back down the road to find her. She was sitting in the road center when he finally came up on her.

"Why's you in the road, Miss?" he asked politely.

"Lots 'o weeds along the road sides." Annie declared. "Probably there's snakes." Her defiant mood was softened now. Gone with the sunset.

Not so easy to be brave after dark when you alone, Abe thought. But he said, "I give you a ride if'n y'all just climb up here. Takes you where you wants to go."

She didn't speak but climbed aboard. Annie Stinson had lost all her fight.

"There is no where to go." She said in a low voice. "I'm throwed out of Rogers by the Constable... I ain't never been like this before... But there ain't no where to go."

He took her to the little cabin he had built on Caney Creek. She was tired and hungry and desperate. She made no resistance.

In the cabin, he assured her he had no intention of touching her In "that way," as he put it. Actually, he thought to himself that she was simply too ugly and bedraggled to have any appeal for him. Besides, white women could get you hanged. He believed that she was just a starving dog. That he would feed her and send her on her way. He brought to the rickety little table that sat in the center of the room that served as kitchen a pitcher of cool home brewed beer, a pan of corn bread with bacon pieces mixed right into the batter and a bowl of stewed collards with bits of salty hickory smoked ham and onion laced throughout. Annie, near to faint from hunger had never before eaten any food so delicious. Annie ate, she slept... and she stayed.

Annie was amazed at Abe's lack of possessions. The cabin was spotless clean, and the plain food was well seasoned. But he owned practically nothing. He had a home-made table, one chair and small narrow bed made of crossed strands of rope and a mattress of goose down and ticking. At one end of the cabin was a large open fire place with a black wrought iron kettle and a Dutch oven with a cracked lid.

"Makin' whiskey," he explained. No time for the makin' o' furniture. I gets to it sometime."

He treated her gently and made no demands upon her at all. At first she was aloof and referred to him as "Nigger" or "Coon" when she felt a need to hurt him. But then she gave that up and realized there was no worthy reason to hurt this good man at all. He treated her far better than any of the saloon or brothel men she had dallied with.

The most important thing was that he asked her questions. No one had ever done that before. Her life had been a series of 'do this', don't 'do that', 'bring more whiskey', 'take off your clothes'. Now he was asking her things. Truly important things.

Did she think the garden would get more sun if he planted it north of the oak trees? Would the bacon sides be tastier if he mixed some apple wood with the hickory? Did she think they ought to buy a cow? It was the asking if "they" ought to have a cow that let her know she was a partner around the Primble place. If she wanted to be.

He was impressed with the changes in Annie too. When first he had brought her here it was only out of pity that he tolerated her sullen insults. All of his life he had believed that people of his race were at the lowest rung of the ladder of human condition. Yet Annie Stinson had been far lower than any black person he had known in his life. It was true he had known colored prostitutes. That was often the only way of life available to prairie women, black or white. But Abe had never known anyone as beaten and as defeated as Annie Stinson.

She had come the full circle to his way of thinking. She was now at the bottom of the circle and could sink no lower. He sensed that she knew that, too. Her resignation to her defeat saddened him greatly, though he couldn't have explained why. She hardly ever said "Nigger:" any more, and the decent food had done something to erase most of the hard look she'd had. Her orange hair was gone now. It had grown out to a rich dark brown somewhat streaked with grey. Abe liked the way her wavy brown hair framed her face.

Little by little Abraham began to find time to manufacture a few more articles of furniture. Crude but very serviceable first was another cot that was Annie's. Then another chair and later a bench that sat by the fireplace to aid the cooking procedures. Annie thought how nice it would be if someday they might purchase some chintz for curtains. One day Abraham showed her a short three-legged stool he had made.

"It's for milkin' Annie. You know...For when we gets us a cow."

Without the rouge, the face began to soften and soon lost much of its former hardness. Abe began to notice that Annie seemed so very feminine now. Only once, in their time together, did the subject of the Hitching Post Raid come up. Abe dreaded discussing the subject but knew it had to surface sometime or another.

It hung between them as sharp and as intimidating as the sword of Juan Garcia. Abe wanted to put it to rest. If he could. He hoped it wouldn't turn her against him. The day she finally brought the subject up Abe's hands were unexplainably shaking.

"Them's your friends that burned the saloon, weren't they?"

"I wasn't there, Annie. I think I know who they was and why they done it. I wasn't there, though. I didn't never call for it. I didn't know it was gonna happen."

"Somehow, I knew that Abe. You just don't ask nobody to handle your problems. I never knowed anybody like you before. You ain't never asked for no help, but you always there a-givin' it." Abe thought for a moment.

"It ain't true that I never had no help Annie. Old Robert Trav, he borrowed me the money to get this here place. I owe him a lot. Niggers cain't gets money hardly at all."

"Don't call yourself Nigger, Abraham. I don't like to hear you say that."

"You says it sometimes."

"Yes. And I ought not to. I just forget sometimes. It happens when I'm just bein' slovenly. I swear, Abe,... I can be downright slovenly at times."

"You mad at me about the shootin' at the Hitchin' Post? Did you love that man what was killed down there, Annie?"

"Oh... I don't know. He was a man I guess. He had white skin, but he weren't really much of a man. I'm right sorry he's dead. I'm glad I ain't with him no more, but I never wished him dead. Tell you the truth, Abe ... I'd rather be here. Things with Jack Caldwell were scary sometimes. I ain't never scared here with you." She paused here for a moment. A bit dreamily she gazed out the widow that overlooked the garden plantings of squash and beans. After a moment she spoke resolutely, "I do think we gonna need that cow."

It was the last time they ever spoke of the Hitching Post incident. From time to time Annie still said, "Nigger." She always apologized when she slipped on that word. Abraham just didn't say it at all any more. It never angered him when Annie said it. He knew she didn't mean it. She was just being slovenly.

The air of tension that prevails between men and women was no stranger to the lives of Annie and Abraham. From time to time she noticed him looking at her, long soft looks. Looks of yearning. Looks from dark eyes filled with a sort of questioning, a wonderment. Nearly as often, it was Abraham who suddenly found himself aware that Annie was studying him just as intently.

As the days and weeks passed they felt themselves drawing nearer to each other. It was a confusing and fearful feeling. Each secretly avowed to leave the other. To go away before something dreadful could happen. But they stayed. Unexplainably and in the face of all tradition, they just stayed. Annie was beginning to fix meals, fix her hair and care for the little cabin in ways she thought might please Abe. When she first became aware that she was doing these things, her sensibilities were shocked. That she would exert such an effort in order to please a colored man puzzled her no end. It upset her and made her unsure of herself.

It was the day the Gitau family drove by in their clatter trap of a wagon that Annie became aware of what her relationship with Abraham really meant.

She heard the rickety wagon creaking and rattling its way up the dusty and rutted road a long time before it came into view of the cabin. Mostly, she heard the raucous laughter of the unruly Gitau children. Abner and Mamie Gitau were locally famous for their enormous brood of children. They had nine. They came in all ages, sexes and sizes. Most of the Caney Creek inhabitants considered the Gitaus' little more than white trash.

They attempted to farm a pitiful little dusty quarter-section. For the most part though, they worked out on other area farms and ranches. As soon as one of the children became old enough to find his way home from a neighbor's place, he would be assigned some effort that he, or she, was sturdy enough to handle. A few of the younger ones milked family cows or searched for hens' nests and gathered the eggs for neighbors.

Old hens, tired of having their eggs filched in a regular manner, soon grew wise enough to take to the brush. They would secret their nests among the Osage orange and Hawthorne. The Gitau children would forage through the wild brush, avoiding scorpions, rattlers and stinging nettle, in search of these treasure caches. They conducted their inspections with noisy laughter and the inherent "finding things skill" that come naturally to very poor children from very large families.

Older children helped to put up hay or round up livestock. When they had reached the ripe old age of fourteen or so, they were hired out onto cattle drives. Some left and were never seen again. Some occasionally drifted back home again. All in all, they reminded observers of a covey of skinny underfed quail. There was no order nor even attentiveness to the commands of their parents. There was simply a mad scramble of uncountable arms and legs clutching, grasping, struggling for survival.

All of this activity was commingled and punctuated by a nerve-shattering din of gleeful laughter and pitiful wailing. The sounds were loud but, for the most part, meaningless. The oldest girl, a raven-haired beauty named Claudette, had simply disappeared. The sloe-eyed and shapely sixteen-year old had just vanished. Right from the dusty yard in front of the Gitaus' tumbledown house during broad daylight. One moment she had been hanging some wash on a clothes line, and the next minute she was gone. The basket of clothing sat alone and unattended. Only a freshly washed calico dress was missing from the wicker hamper.

Abner and Mamie never knew what happened to the teen-aged "Cludy" as they called her. A big Texas herd had passed nearby that day. Abner knew of that passing by the dust out on the horizon... The immense cloud had risen from the earth to a height of forty or fifty feet. It had stretched in dusty waves across the prairie for a length of five or more miles.

"Maybe Cludy jined up with some trail hand," Mamie offered one night over an all to often groundhog stew.

"Mebe so." Abner answered, and the matter was put to rest. They were a helter-skelter bunch. They lived as wild as the game animals they ate for nearly every meal. They were often accused of stealing hogs or the occasional calf. A daughter gone, more or less, was no disturbance to the Gitaus.

Most of the victims of their thievery let the matter drop. After all, the Gitau children were near to starving. At times the neighbors secretly hoped someone from the clan would steal some food so the children would be better fed. And besides, the return of a skinny old range hog is certainly not worth having a barn burnt in the middle of the night. Most people simply shunned the Gitaus and that was that. When Annie had first learned of the family from Abraham she determined herself to do precisely that. Ignore them. Now on this scorching hot day she heard their approach while they were still more than a quarter mile away. She relented on her promise to ignore them based on two important factors.

I'll bet those children could use some cool water in this heat, she told herself. More importantly though was the fact she had not seen another living soul except for Abe for more weeks than she could accurately remember.

It'd be nice to pass a few minutes with Missus Gitau, Annie thought, trashy or not. 'Sides that I'll bet she's not so bad. Anybody might cuss a little, or even steal a little food, if she has such a brood to care for. Annie justified her thoughts with a final one. I'll bet she's not a bad person .. Just a good mother. With all them young'uns, she just has to do a lot of things folks don't understand.

Her mind made up, Annie fetched her largest milking pail and hurried to the tank. The water tank was in an inlet from Caney Creek that Abraham had dug with a spade and lined its squared dirt walls with logs. The tank had been strategically located at the source of a large rushing spring that fed into the Caney.

The water that bubbled from the ground was so cold it made Annie's' teeth ache when she drank it too fast. When it mixed in the tank with the creek's water flow, it was sweet and cool and delightful. The logs kept the mud down and made an easy place to gather up pails and even hogs heads of water for whiskey making. In short order Annie had a pail full of crystal clear creek water. Seizing a gourd dipper from the porch post, she hurried to the front of the cabin and stood herself by the gate; only a few feet from the dusty trail. She thought to offer them all water when they drew near.. Annie checked the cleanliness of her apron and tried, with her fingers, to replace a few strands of her hair that seemed determined to fall over her face. She was looking forward to company and wanted to make as good an impression as she was able. In only a minute or two the wagon was drawing near enough that she knew the man and woman on the high seat could see her.

Annie fixed a determined grin of friendliness on her face and waited for the woman or man to speak. They did not. Instead, their eyes stayed fixed on the road ahead and never strayed her way for an instant. The man spoke sharply to the children and their noisy glee stopped as abruptly as though he had turned a switch. They turned their soiled pale little faces to Annie and searched her very soul with large inquisitive eyes.

The wagon kept right on rolling. The mismatched and half-starved team of two old mules missing not a step. Annie widened her smile. She was not understanding what was happening. The thought raced through her mind that maybe the Gitaus felt inferior and unwelcome. She was sure after all that other neighbors had never made them feel appreciated. The wagon was almost past her now, and Annie felt she must not let this chance for friendship escape.

"Missus Gitau," she called through the smile, "...would you folks care for some fresh water?" She held up the dipper and spilled its crystal contents back into the bucket. The heavy woman on the wagon seat made a stern face at Annie and gave no answer. She tucked errant strands of wispy grey hair under the soiled bandanna she wore as a head scarf.

"Missus Gitau," Annie repeated. "I have some water for you here. This heat is terr..." Annie would never finish her remark; nor would she ever speak again to any Gitau as long as she was to live. The Gitau woman spoke to Annie through a mouth filled with rotted and blackened snags that had been teeth. Her words were as venomous as Annie had ever heard, even in her lowest barroom days.

"My 'chirren' ain't a-takin' no water from no Nigger's whore. Get yersef away from bein' so close to the road where 'spectable folks can see you. Whores' ought to know to keep out o' sight." Then she hissed, "Hurry up this team Abner... Let's git oursefs shed o' Nigger's whores." The hard-faced Abner, eyes dead ahead fixed on the mules' scrawny rumps, called to his team. As broken down and thin as they were, the two loyal animals tried to pick up the pace as well as they were able.

Tears burned in Annie's eyes. When she had traveled around the saloons she had often been called whore, harlot and worse. Somehow, that had never mattered all that much. She had in those days simply gone on about her business, and she never remembered paying much attention to those kinds of remarks. Now, as she watched the backs of the skinny Abner and his hefty wife retreat from her, she felt desolate.

The burning eyes of the children still bored holes through her heart as they stared from the rear of the wagon. Annie Stinson had spent a lifetime being injured by others. Mostly she would admit she had been insulted or humiliated only because she had let herself sink low enough to merit such treatment. This was

different. These words from a woman at least as low down as a bar room strumpet had stung her to the quick.

Blindly she dropped the bucket, splashing water over the lower part of her dress. She, staggered more than walked back into the cabin. Annie slumped at the single table where she and Abe took their meals.

She felt dazed and alone. For a long time she looked out of the cabin's front window. She could still see across the flat plain the Gitaus' wagon moving off onto the horizon.

At last she laid her head on her arms and cried. Her tears came freely. It was a cry that should have come a long time ago. Now it burst forth in pitiful and uncontrollable sobs. She was deeply wounded by the remarks of the Gitau woman, but for the life of her she couldn't imagine why. It was nothing she hadn't heard before. Why was it hurting her like this? Then it struck her. In those bar room days people called her a whore because she was one.

She wasn't now. She had done nothing here at Caney Creek to earn that salute. Neither had Abe. Now she began to realize she was madder and more injured for Abraham's sake than she was her own. He was a good man. He was caring and generous; a hard-working man who asked nothing from the world. He only wanted to be left in peace and to make fine whiskey.

How dare that heifer call Abe a nigger, she thought. *That old slut ain't fit to tie his shoes.*

The warm tears of sorrow were rapidly being replaced by hot ones of anger. The self pity she had felt now gave way to blinding fury. The rest of the day she flew about the cabin in a rage, doing the only things she knew to do in order to gain some control of herself. She cleaned the entire cabin until it fairly shone. Looking at the mantle clock, she realized it would be three hours before Abraham returned from his peddler's route. Unable to calm herself, she cleaned every square inch of the cabin over again. She had just put her cleaning rags into the lye soap pot to soak when Abe walked in.

"Don't you never sell the God damn Gitaus no whiskey, Abraham Primble." Annie fairly shouted. "They ain't fit to drink the fine shine you makes up. Pig slops is more their fare, I thinks."

Abraham was physically taken aback by her outburst. It had been a long time since he had heard her curse. And she had never addressed him by his complete name.

"Why, Annie, I didn't sell them no whiskey." Abe lowered his eyes as if he were apologizing for some transgression. "They ain't got no money for buying spirits. When I heard that little Thaddeus Gitau was all sick and croupy, I gave his Daddy a jug. I thought the little boy could use the medicatin'. Was I wrong to give them folks some shine, Annie? Did I hurt somethin'?"

Annie stopped her tirade and looked at the plain and common man before her. In all her years, and for all her travels, she had not met a man as good as this. The Gitau woman had called him nigger without hesitation. Yet, he was the one who thought about the wellness of her smallest child. Abe had given, not sold, them the only thing he had to give: whiskey.

As she looked upon Abraham's questioning face, she felt her heart melt inside her. She walked directly to him now. She stood before him for a long moment. The two looked at each other with confusion glazing both their eyes. At last, Annie took his face between her hands.

Startled, he attempted to withdraw from her, but she tightened her clasp. Now for a moment she looked into his dark eyes. She saw that he was, at once excited. She felt an unexplainable movement low in her abdomen. She understood his fear, for she was feeling it too. It was all mixed up with other feelings she couldn't seem to put a name to. Annie had thought; been taught, all her life that kissing a black man was certain to be a dreadful experience. But now as she pressed her lips against his, she found it was not so offensive at all. In fact, his kisses were warm and comforting. His powerful arms made her feel safe and somehow, feminine. Annie could never have explained it if you would have asked her to, but she somehow instinctively knew his kiss was filled with love for her. Annie had met bad men all over the land west of the Mississippi. At last, she knew she had met one good one.

"Are you scared, Annie?" Abe asked. His lower lip trembled slightly. This was dangerous business. A colored man kissing a white woman. It was a role he had never prepared himself for.

"Of course I am, Abe. Not of you but of the Gitaus. Of them and their kind."

"I guess if I gets hung on a tree for lovin' you, Annie, I cain't complain none. I guess you all I ever really wanted. If I knowed you cared for me, I guess I could die alright."

"No dyin', Abe. Don't be talkin' 'bout dyin'. We ain't done no livin' yet. Besides, we got too much whiskey to make." She stopped here and then spoke reflectively. "I think I can get along just fine without the approval of the Gitaus. A smile spread across Abe's broad brown face. His white teeth glistened, and his eyes crinkled with an inward humor. Annie liked the way he looked just now.

"It's our business, Abe. Mine and yours. It's always gonna be just that way." Annie kissed him again. There were still some fears and apprehensions. Each was afraid they would cause the other grief in some form or another. It was safe here in the cabin, but outside its walls was a world of uncertainty. They knew, even now, they would face that together when the time came. It was still frightening; Terrifying, But it couldn't be helped. Not now. Things had gone too far and they were not about to stop. Abe and Annie sensed that from this moment on they would always be together. Only death could part them now.

That was the night they had become lovers. They had pushed their homemade single beds together and silently climbed into them. They lay quiet for a long time, naked in the darkness, just holding hands. only their ankles touching. As their bodies touched, at last, there was no further thought of color. The harsh words of Mamie Gitau were forgotten, as though they had never been spoken. There was no whore here, nor Nigger. Only a man and a woman. A woman with no past and a man who was no particular color, were here, alone and together in the night.

Frogs, on the banks of Caney Creek, sang all night long that night. Abraham listened to them right up until dawn. From time to time he put his head against Annie's breast. He could hear her steady heartbeat. The bobwhite quail kept their covey together out in the honeysuckle., signaling each other by their pretty little two-toned whistle. Cicada harmonized in the live oaks. The air was as still as death and heavy with the summer's oppressive heat. From time to time the distant flashes of heat lightning faintly illuminated the room.

In the brief flicker, Annie's form was a slash of silver against the darkness. Abraham's brown body was a dark phantom lingering within a deep shadow. In the distance Abe could hear the low growling roll of the thunder. "A storm out on the prarie." He thought. From time to time a whippoorwill called to the night. Abraham believed the night bird to be pleading for the rain the distant rumbling promised. There would be no rain that night. It was a night of dark and the fleeting glow of the heat lightning. It was a night of miraculous sounds.

During the next weeks, Abraham was as happy as he had ever been in his life. He wasn't so foolish as to let his guard down. Abe knew there was more to be done. There were plans to make. Things to figure out. Abraham knew this new relationship could be dangerous. They both conceivably could even be lynched. The idea of a lynching was pretty far fetched, but stranger things had happened. Lynching aside, he just didn't want Annie hurt any more. Physically or mentally. Annie had been hurt enough in her lifetime, he determined. He vowed he would do for the rest of his life all he could to keep her from further hurt and pain.

There was the thought in Abe's mind too that they ought to be married. It was what good people did. Regardless of color. Good men and women who lived together needed to be married. A preacher that would marry these two though might not be so easily found. For the next weeks Abe searched for such a clergy.

No less than three times had Abraham been refused. Indeed, he'd been sharply rebuked by the white ministers when he had asked if they would sanction the union of himself and white Annie Stinson. A colored preacher's ceremony he knew could be held groundless. To be legally valid, this wedding needed to be officiated by a white man. Finally, after much pleading and a bribe of twelve full jugs of Caney Creek's finest, a most unlikely Justice of the Peace from Rogers, Texas, had agreed to perform the ceremony.

Clement Harkens was an unusual Justice to say the least. Old and fat and foolish, he claimed to have journeyed from Tennessee to Texas "to at least eradicate a portion of the excessive sin," as he had put it. Harkens fully believed it was his destiny to save the western lands. He had acted as minister, doctor, veterinarian and blacksmith in the little settlement at various times.

Now though he was the Justice of Peace and a Deputy Sheriff as well. He often wore a judge's robe for evenings of drinking at local taverns. On Sundays he frequently delivered stirring, impromptu sermons within the same saloons. Very often he wore his judicial robes at the same time. Somehow the black raiment's lent an air of authority to the unlikely scene. It was said he could preach the fire and brimstone as well as any man could be expected to with a whiskey glass in hand. Strangely for all his time spent in barrooms no one ever remembered seeing Harkens drunk. But then as one citizen so astutely opinioned:

"Maybe he's drunk all the time.... Ain't nobody ever seen him sober, either." The Justice had at first wanted Abe and Annie to come into the town of Rogers for the wedding. Neither Abe nor Annie ever wanted to be in Rogers again after the Hitching Post incident. Then too, the idea of taking a bi-racial wedding to the site of that infamous raid seemed like a very bad idea. A wedding trip to Rogers was ruled out.

The Justice had been about to cancel the wedding altogether until he was reminded by the county Sheriff that Abraham was a protected friend of the Broken Spur. A repeat of the Hitching Post incident would not be a welcome event. The Justice had at last relented and rode out to Caney Creek in the Methodist Preacher's borrowed buckboard to conduct the ritual.

Abe and Annie had needlessly feared this jeopardy from the bigoted and prejudiced. No danger was forthcoming. Instead their neighbors seemed placated that the two were 'off the streets' so to speak. The women rested easier knowing that the orange-haired whore– well, it had been orange for a time– was reduced to living with a Nigger and that must surely be God's punishment visited upon her. The men were quietly relieved that the handsome and successful "Nigger Primble" was not running around free where he might tempt a wife or daughter. All concerned just sort of settled back into life and the lazy patterns it will provide when given an opportunity. Additionally, all were aware of Abrahams relationship to the riders of the Broken Spur. All agreed it was better to have no problem with the Primbles than to court a set to with the Robert Trav congress

Then came the girls. Not many things that had happened in Annie Stinson / Primble's life had been a total surprise. When one had lived as Annie had, there were certain expectations that went along with the life style in general. She knew she would be left by one lover after another each time the wind blew in a different direction. She knew that run-ins with sheriffs and other constables were just to be expected. She knew that prostitutes often came up with horrible infections and that sometimes they even became pregnant.

Certainly, Annie had had her share of being deserted and left destitute. She also unfortunately knew most of the lawmen in a four-hundred-mile circle to the Primble cabin. But somehow, she had avoided the infections...and the babies.

The realization of what was happening to her came over her ever so slowly. At first she just could not imagine why her stomach was so upset every morning. Sometimes the nausea was just overpowering. She thought it must surely be some sort of ague or something similar. Then one day, out of a clear blue Texas / Kansas sky, it hit her: She was with child!

She thought of all the times this could have happened but didn't. She was scared at first. Could there be something wrong with a child of hers, giving the way she'd lived? Was God handing her a punishment...or was it a joke? She slumped down in one of the chairs in the cabin kitchen and just began to think it out...Then it came to her. It was Abraham...It was because he was a good man and God wanted to bless him with a child. Of course that was it. She hugged herself, and Annie Stinson / Primble was happier than she had ever remembered being in her entire life.

She was going to have a baby, she was going to have Abe's baby. She and Abe were going to have a child. Annie Stinson / Primble was a whole woman...She was going to be a mother. Who could've imagined? She ran out of the cabin and ran up the dusty road as fast her bare feet would carry her. She had to find Abe. She had to tell Abe!

First born was Rachel. A lively girl filled with fun and forever laughing. She had the good-natured humor of her father but had Annie's blue eyes. Rachel was a mischievous child who neighbors called "bright as a penny." The precocious child loved music and, even as a very little girl, sang loudly in Sunday services. Of course, she sat in the rear pew of the little clapboard church with her family. The rear pew was considered to be the Primbles' seats. This fact was unspoken but it was a fact.

Abe and Annie were the chief financial supporters of the little church, and without their contributions any church at all would've been impossible. For as unlikely as it seemed, the black man Abraham Primble was financially the most successful member of the congregation. Certainly a pew in the rear was not all that outrageous. There was after all a double space left between the Primble pew and the next one forward. This quite noticeable gap was important. It was enough of a separation that the rest of the congregation didn't feel they were really going to church with Negroes. All of this political maneuvering, however, was lost completely on the Primble child with the lovely voice.

Lovely little Rachel with her copper-colored hair, ivory skin and blue eyes liked the services well enough. But, mostly she loved the singing. She could lift her childlike soprano above all the other voices and it would soar like a halo over the little congregation. A few of the truly bigoted members were, at first, offended by this child who was becoming a minor celebrity by way of her voice. But then, they too became victims of Rachel Primble's whimsical charms. How could anyone not like such a beautiful and gifted child, they would ask themselves. As she grew older Rachel was often called upon to sing solo at services. This duty she performed in such a sweet and demurring way that Abraham would sit in the rear pew and just beam with delight.

"That's my little girl," he would whisper smugly to himself. "Mine and Annie's'."

He longed to take Annie's' hand in his own during these special minutes. He dared not. The affections between a black man and a white woman were still not something to flaunt. His acceptance had progressed. but not enough for all to accept unconditionally. He sat beside his wife in church but he never touched her in any way in public.

It was the second daughter, Laurel that had proved to be the student. She read everything she could get her hands on. At the little school house at the crossroads she was called 'the student' by Olive Brandly the teacher. Laurel was especially astute at reading bible passages. The "Thee's and Thou's" she encountered seemed not to deter her in the least. Olive Brandly thought that Laurel also enjoyed a feel for phrasing in her 'aloud' readings. It was as though the child could instinctively punch or emphasize the most meaningful words in a verse. Laurel was only a little above average at mathematical problems, but in the field of literature, precious little escaped her steel-trap mind.

Both girls were lovely to look at. Their skin was light coffee and old ivory. They both had their mother's soft brown hair, though theirs was richly embellished with unusual and attractive copper highlights. They enjoyed Annie's' delicate facial features. Rachel's blue eyes were bright and probing. Laurels' eyes though, were the deep brown, livid pools that were her father's.

Annie and Abe alike had feared the girls would be mistreated at school simply for the fact they were mulatto. It hadn't worked that way at all. It was true, Tal Winslow, the nephew of the infamous and now deceased Puddin' Winslow, had tried to ridicule the girls' heritage on at least one occasion. Other students had come swiftly to the girls' defense. Their protectiveness reminded Winslow that it was he who was little more than white trash. When Winslow failed to find the support bullies and bigots need to thrive he was crestfallen. Once it became apparent he was alone in the proposed mistreatment of the Primble girls, the threat of trouble had simply ended.

From time to time Annie and Abe wondered together what they would do when the girls were old enough to marry.

"Maybe we send them to Boston," Abe had said. "We got mo' money'n we need, and they needs to be away from the south. Mo' tolerance in Boston I thinks."

These were the very thoughts Abraham was pondering as he turned the mule drawn wagon down the little lane that led to the cabin. He'd worked hard that day and was looking forward to spending the evening with his" three girls" as he had come to refer to his family. He expected Annie would have supper ready, and Rachel would be funning about some thing or another. No doubt, Laurel would have learned a new word to baffle him with. She played this game with her Daddy nearly every day. It was when he came to the fence corner that he saw old Ned.

Raiders

The redbone hound that he used sometimes for hunting raccoon but mostly as a pet, lay dead in the center of the lane. He stopped his mules and fairly leaped to the ground from his seat. In the failing sunlight, he knew right away the dog had been shot. A hole in the front of the dog's chest had long since stopped leaking and the pool of blood under the hound was a great one. Taking the dog's still paw in his hand, Abe moved the animal to the side of the lane. He noticed the leg was stiff, and he knew the dog had died hours ago. Bottle flies, too, had come to taste the blood in the road. Like lightning the realization struck him. If someone had killed his watch dog, it may have been in order to get to his family.

Abraham Primble deserted his team and wagon in a flash. Afoot now, he ran as swiftly as he was able down the lane to his cabin. He was praying as he ran that he would find everything to be all right, that supper would be ready and that the girls would be waiting for him on the little porch. He was running so hard now that his lungs were about to burst. He was at his top speed when he ran directly into the .44-caliber rifle bullet.

His instant death was a blessing he would not ever realize. His legs went to water under him and his ears were filled with a strange unrecognizable ringing. A searing burn invaded his chest. It made him think for a moment of the times he had accidentally swallowed scalding coffee. Only this was worse, and it just kept hurting without relief. Something was the matter with his eyes, too. The focus seemed all wrong. The colors were not what they should be.

When the bullet struck, he had been running full speed forward. Now he found himself, unexplainably, driven backwards. He was ripped from his feet by the violence of this rearward propulsion. The force of the slug drove him down and back into the dust of the road. For a moment he felt confused and greatly disoriented. Purple and silver lights flashed within his brain right behind his eyes.

Now he was skidding; sliding on his back. He felt the gravelly surface of the road grinding the shoulders of his shirt. The dust of the road was gritty mud in his mouth. There was no pain, only lack of understanding.

What the force could be shoving him against his will he couldn't imagine. Baffled, he felt his body was completely out of control. He had been stepping forward, but now he found himself hurtling backwards as though his body were responding to some mind, some will other than his own. His head swam with a mysterious lightness, and he tasted the salty iron flavor of blood mixed with the grit in his mouth.

At last his skid halted, and he tried to compose himself. He looked up into the glassy blue sky above him. The heat waves shimmered over him more thickly than he had ever seen before. He tried to open his mouth to speak, to reassure himself he had only fallen somehow. When his mouth opened, the blood gushed forward.

My God, he thought. *I must be shot! I walked into an ambush and now I'm shot! Oh, Annie... What in the world?... What's happening?* He looked up at the sky again. searching wildly for the answer. Somehow the sky was dimming, fading away. He struggled mightily to clear his vision and to understand what was happening. He blinked his eyes rapidly trying to bring them into better focus, but the sky and clouds kept fading.

At last a warm and wonderful darkness fell over him. It was somehow comforting, and he gave into it. He allowed his eyes to close and knew this feeling, whatever it was, would vanish in an instant. *When this passes*, he thought, *I've got to get to my girls. This spell's gon' be over in a minute. It's goin' t' pass.*

His body felt wet and sticky, but it didn't seem to bother him. Quite to the contrary, the wetness was warm and soothing. The blackness rolled in over him like a warm, prairie wind. The concerns and thoughts of Abraham Primble were washed away in a dark and gentle zephyr of balmy and wonderful, cloudy ink. Abe would never know how fortunate he was to die in the road this way. His death at ambush would save him the pain and suffering of seeing the death and destruction that had befallen Annie and his beloved girls.

Beaver Parker levered a fresh shell into the chamber of his rifle. He called aloud to his comrade:

"Hey, Weasel. You see how I kilt that big Nigger? I tol' you all we's in for some fun here, din't I?"

The thin-faced man with the eyes of a mink grinned and nodded. He held a skinning knife high as in a victorious salute. Beaver could see his shirtfront and trousers were crimson with fresh blood.

"We got another girl to do, Beaver. When we gonna do her?"

The two men were shirtless as they stood on the porch of the Primble cabin. Their white, fish-belly skin was somehow obscene in the full sunlight. Their laughter was different than had been heard in recent years on this porch.

In the rear bedroom the lovely child lay bound hand and foot to the oaken bed her father had made for her with his own two hands. She heard the laughter and knew the men would come for her soon. She had seen everything they had done to her mother and sister but now, unexplainably, she was no longer afraid. Her blue eyes were glazed over and her mouth was slack. Her terror had driven her so deeply into shock that she was only barely aware of her surroundings.

Then, almost in state of coma, she felt her voice welling up inside her. Words kept invading the dimness of her mind. They were words of songs. Songs that she knew, had sung before. The rawhide bonds at her wrists and ankles cut deeply into her flesh, but she didn't feel it anymore. She, lost in a twilight, heard the men coming through the little cabin toward her. They were coming for her now. The way they had for her mother. And then her sister. Now... for no reason she could think of she began to sing. "Je-sus loves me—This I know—For the Bi-ble tells me so—"

Chapter Twelve

Danger on the Trail

Pamela and Colin sat side by side on the high seat of the Conestoga on this beautiful September morning. It had been several days now since the encounter in the pecan grove. Nothing even slightly romantic had happened since. Both Colin and Pamela seemed determined to treat each other with enough coolness that the other travelers might not suspect their true feelings. Yet, obvious to all, the bond of closeness between the two was growing daily.

Each member of the convoy had become alert to the fact that something special was happening between Colin and Pamela. There were sly little glances between the two and the occasional touching of hands. It was easy to detect that the two kept their eyes on each other as the day's travel unfolded. It was true, they were not physically very demonstrative, but their glances spoke volumes. To even the most casual observer their feelings for each other were becoming more apparent.

This included Justin. The boy seemed filled with joy that Colin and Pamela were seemingly growing closer. He hadn't completely given up on Colin as step-father just yet. He rode alongside them with a knowing smile affixed on his sunny face. He still missed his own father desperately, but Justin liked the way his mother looked and acted when she was near the cowboy.

Chinagirl had a better idea of what had happened in the pecan grove than anyone. The pale glow of that dawn had lighted the area around the grove just enough that she could recognize the figure of a woman deftly slipping back to the Conestoga. She now greeted Pamela with good natured knowing smiles and titters of indiscreet laughter. It never failed to make Pamela's face blush a hot crimson.

Justin rode his pony at the head of the oxen. The plodding, stolid draft animals moved along slow and steady. Shaking their great horns and switching their tails endlessly against flies, their pace was steady and uneventful. One of the great burdens that tormented the western settler who traveled by oxen had been the unrelenting monotony and boredom.

Rather than boring, however, Pamela described the oxen as dependable. So dependable in fact that Pamela and Colin were able to talk endlessly without having to pay much attention to their wagon responsibilities. The weather had cooled a bit. While midday was still hot enough to send heat waves shimmering over the dirt trail, the mornings and evenings were a delight. The boy kept the oxen headed southwest, and Pamela talked with Colin of every subject imaginable as they shared the wagon seat.

"Tell me what the Broken Spur is like." Pamela asked.

"Well it's beautiful I can say for sure. It's big, too, by the standards of other ranches I know of. About six- or eight-hundred thousand acres I think. Half a million anyway." Colin was rolling a tight morning smoke. "Old Robert has held onto all the land he ever crossed. His foreman, Juan Garcia, has helped him hold it against some pretty rough characters over the years."

"Oh, Colin, tell me about old Robert. You keep referring to him. Is he really that old? What's he like anyway?"

Colin was thoughtful for a long time. "I don't know if I can really describe him or not Pam. I've never tried. He's pretty old, but he gets around real good. He doesn't leave the Spur very often, but that's just because he doesn't want to. He once walked about a thousand miles... all the way from north Colorado to Texas. He did that leading a horse or two because he'd rather walk than ride."

"That's funny." Pamela said.

"I guess the best thing about him is he thinks most everybody is worth somethin'. After the slave trouble in the south, lots of coloreds came around lookin' for work. Old Robert would always help them in someway. He never talked rough to them or made them feel he was a Master or anything like that. I used to watch him deal with those folks, and I knew I was lookin' at someone good. I guess you could say he's got a good heart."

"Alex had a good heart, too," she said bitterly. "It got him killed."

"Well, Pamela, you got to understand that while Robert is a good man, he takes no nonsense from anyone. He won't abide a mean or cruel person. He says there's some folks too mean to live. Several people don't live anymore because of that feeling."

"You mean he's killed?" Pamela sounded aghast.

"He never killed nobody that didn't need killin'. But yes, Pam, answerin' your question, he's killed before. Some folks wouldn't be alive today if he hadn't. I'm one of 'em"

"You're his only son?"

"Step-son. I was a prisoner of a Comanchero when I was a button. "

"A what?"

"Comanchero... Slave trader. Mostly they're half breeds. Maybe not...Just ne'er-do-wells. Drunks and bandits...Go around the country stealin' children– women or horses too sometimes– then they sell 'em off as slaves to Kiowa or Comanches or maybe in Mexico. They butcher up wagon trains or little settlements. They're a bad lot, Pamela, more dangerous than the regular tribal Indians by a long shot."

"And you were one of those captives? Oh my, Colin, that's a terrible thing!" Pamela was at once interested and horrified. "How'd the Comanchero get you? Where are your real parents?"

"Don't rightly know. Can't remember. I know there was me and my sister or at least a girl was there. I'm not so sure she was my sister. She couldn't be saved. Guess I'd've died too if not for Old Robert. I can't remember anything much before him and Garcia. Garcia says that happens a lot. Things just happen to some folks they don't want to remember. So they just don't."

"Then, Colin... You don't really know who you are, do you?"

"Sure as hell do." Colin grinned. "I' m Colin Trav, step-son to Old Robert Trav and adopted nephew of the Rio Grande bandit, Juan Garcia. I'm also the trail boss of the best danged ranch in Texas, The Broken Spur. Oh, and I'm the man who loves the lady horse trader from Illinois." It hit him quickly that for all his years, he had never before told a woman that he loved her. It frightened him just a bit. He changed the subject quickly.

"We'll be at the Primble farm late today. You're gonna like Annie and Abe Primble and their girls. I think I ought to tell you before we get there that Abe is... well... colored."

"Why ever in the world would I need to be told that in advance, Colin?"

"Well... Annie ain't colored... Annie's white."

"That's not so unusual, Colin. It happens pretty often in Illinois. Don't worry, Colin. I won't act shocked."

"I know that, Pamela. I don't know why I felt I had to tell you that. You're just a good person, Pamela. I... I've got to learn to have more confidence in you. I don't know why I felt like I had to tell you."

"Because," Pamela said. "You're in love with the lady horse reader from Illinois... And she loves you back."

From the head of the lead oxen, Justin Carstin turned in the saddle to see what was bringing about all the laughter from the wagon seat behind him.

It was about midday when the heat shimmers reappeared that Colin saw the far-off flicker. Just a little wink of light far out on the plain. He called Chester Crawford to his side.

"There in the due west. Can you see that glint? Just happens from time to time. There... See it?"

"I do see it, Mister Trav... What is it?"

"Well, thirty years ago it may have been a Comanche signal. I don't know what it is now, but I think it's not somethin' good. It's been with us all morning. Now it's still here in the afternoon. If it was a friendly rider, why hasn't he ridden in to us? It could be he's afraid of us, but I doubt it. I think we're being followed, and it may be the horse thieves that shot Mister Carstin."

"What do you think we should do, Mister Trav?"

"Well, I'm not really sure, but I think I want you to slip away. Whoever it is probably knows were heading for the Primble farm. By the time we get there I want you to be gone. If you rode out due east from here sort of on the other side of the wagon, that rider probably wouldn't see you. He's out there a far piece. We can't see him except for that glint. Ride east two miles or more... then turn southwest and try to cross a ways south of the Primble place."

"Where do I go then?" Chester asked.

"Get over on the Broken Spur cattle trail and stay right with it. Old Henry Brooker sent a wire to the Spur, so I think you'll come across some Spur riders down there somewhere..."

"Are we sure the Spur men will use that trail?"

"No. No, I'm not. But they probably will. It's the best travel and fastest even if it ain't exactly closest. Problem is we've come a far piece and still are a long way out. Dependin' on how fast the wire got there and how serious Garcia took it, the Spur bunch could be nearly on us or as far as seven or eight days back..."

"It don't matter Colin... Mister Trav..."

"Colin's all right. You can call me Colin, Chester. You ride till you find them and then start them back this way. I'll keep the women and Justin holed up at the Primble place until we find out who is out there. It'll be a sight easier to take care of things there than out here on this open prairie."

"I'll tell Chinagirl and then try to slip out." Chester said.

"Don't tell anyone. Just take one of the rifles as if you were goin' huntin'. No use to scare anyone and I don't want anyone gettin' upset. That might alert whoever's out there, and if they watch us any closer, you may not get away. You got a pistol too?"

"No, I ain't got no short gun... The rifle ought to be enough though..."

Colin opened his saddle bags and took out the Colt. "Here. If you have to make camp at night keep this close. Folks can get in mighty close in the dark. One of these can be a powerful source of comfort. Now start lookin' for a chance and get goin'. Take a little food along with you. Somethin' you can eat cold. No fires."

In ten minutes Chester was gone like a shadow. Colin looked at the others and realized no one had seen him go. He adjusted Henry Brooker's Smith-and-Wesson in his belt. He had to admit it felt very reassuring.

The rest of that day Colin stayed on the wagon seat close to Pamela and Justin. Whoever was out there on the prairie had him worried. If it was Amos Younger and his gang, it was surely a fact that Amos wasn't himself these days. It was hard to imagine an experienced outlaw like Younger getting involved in such a brutal killing over a horse-rustling scheme. Colin was keeping his senses sharpened now. He continued to talk with Pamela about many random things, and the Broken Spur in general. More than anything, he wanted the group to appear totally calm until they reached the Primble place. There would be enough cover there, he thought, to protect everyone.

"Is there a town near the Spur?" she wanted to know.

"Well... about eight or ten miles from the ranch house is what some might want to call a town. Old Robert gave a German fellow name of Huffenbarger a little plat near the south end of Spur and north of the river. Matter of fact, it's near the land claim you have mapped out for the horse farm. Anyway, Huffenbarger wanted to open a store, and Old Robert thought the area needed one.

Now this German fellow is really good at running' a store. He knows how to make good sausage and smoke hams. He can make beer and butcher hogs. He sells wire and dry goods... Even boots, hats and ladies' dresses. Pretty soon, we got us a store about as good as any town. A colored man named Oscar Flowers comes along next and he's a blacksmith. After that, we get our first tavern. Now Old Robert has a thought on taverns. He only lets the town folks build one tavern if they agree to build two.

He says when men drink, there's bound to be trouble if you only have one tavern. It seems that two bars gives the drinkers who cant stand each other a chance to drink with their own friends. That way enemies ain't in each others faces." Old Robert says you gotta have two saloons and three is probably better. Thing is though, by the time you get a second tavern, you've also got a church and maybe a school too. After that happens, the wives put a stop to the men havin' any more saloons."

"You have a school on the Spur?" Pamela asked.

"Well not exactly. Missus Huffenbarger turns out to be a right smart school ma'am. She opens a little two roomer up in the old slaughter house. Fixed it up real nice and pretty too. Then the Post Office people come along and tell her she can get government books 'cause there's Indian children goin' to school there, too. Then they tell her she cain't have the books unless the store, school and taverns are a town. She say's, "All right it's a town. Let's call it Trav, Texas." Well strangers can't seem to get onto that Scottish name. About the first letter we ever got in that Post Office was made out to "Travis', Texas.""

"And so the town is Travis?" Pamela asked.

"Yep... Travis, it is. Same name as the Alamo hero. Anyway, Old Robert don't mind that at all... Juan Garcia teases him about it though." He paused in his story telling long enough to call out for Justin to head the lead oxen a bit more westerly.

"Are you rich, Colin Trav?" Pamela was being brazen and knew it.

"No... I don't think so. We don't talk much about that at the Spur. I guess Old Robert's rich... Maybe Garcia too. I don't think I'm rich, though. I guess there's some money, Garcia tells me, that Robert has in my account at our little bank. I just never thought about finding out how much I guess."

"You own a bank?" Pamela asked incredulously.

"Well it's not much Mostly it's a cattleman's bank. It's there 'cause Robert thought we might make mortgages on land and cattle. I guess we do that a lot. But it ain't nothin' big. Just a little bank you know. What about you Pam? Are you rich?" Colin turned the tables now.

"Collie, I'm sure my Daddy thought he was rich... I've got a feeling that my Daddy's not rich at all... Not compared to Robert Trav."

He saw the glint again. Just a second of a pin point of light far out in the sage. Then it was gone. It was true; Colin hadn't seen as many killings or ridden into as much danger as Henry Brooker. Nor had he lived by his wits as long as Old Robert. But his many years of trail bossing and the few he'd spent as a Ranger had made him an expert in the prediction of trouble. He smelled it now.

There was something wrong here. He wondered if Chester Crawford had eluded whoever was out there in the high sage. It may have been a mistake to send a fighting man like Crawford off on an errand. Colin couldn't help but think that Chester's gun might soon be needed. He touched the Brooker pistol at his waist for comfort.

"Do you think Juan Garcia will like me, Collie?" Pamela interrupted his thoughts. She had begun to use the nickname and Colin liked hearing it from her. It made things seem closer somehow.

"Juan Garcia has never met a woman he didn't like. More than that, there's never been a woman who ever met Garcia who didn't like him. He's got lady friends and senoritas stashed all over the territory and treats everyone of them like a queen. He still gets slicked up now and then and will ride two or three days to attend a Fiesta or a barn dance. When he gets home sometimes, you can see he's been fightin'. Ask him why and he says "It's a matter of honor and men don't discuss such things". Old Robert says he's been chasin' again and caught one with claws."

"He sounds like a swashbuckler. Has he never married?"

"No. Him nor Robert nor me. Old Robert's the oldest but were all gettin' along on the calendar. There's lots of women on the Spur, though. Ranch hands been bringin' 'em around for nearly forty years, now. Marrying them and havin' their kids right on the place. I guess, all told, there might be more'n a hundred people livin' and workin' on the place. We three just never got around to gettin' wives. I think Garcia had too many women to ever think about just havin' one. Old Robert had himself a woman once, they tell me. Things went so badly he just never tried again. Nobody knows about her. Well... Garcia knows but he doesn't talk about it."

"She must have been quite a woman. From the things I hear I've concluded that Robert Trav is quite a plainsman."

"I think sometimes he is the plains." Pamela looked questioningly at this.

"I think he's all of Texas, somehow... He's the plains and the wild horses... He's the wind...I can't explain myself very well when I think about it... He's the wind that cleans up the prairie... I guess if he ain't all of Texas, then he's the best part."

"You love him very much, don't you, Colin Trav?" Embarrassed that he had spoken so emotionally, and without an answer, Colin stared straight ahead.

Far out on the flat, three riders merged in a deep gully. Silently they looked one to the other and checked the loading of their rifles. Charley Stone rubbed his sore back and longed for the ride to end. Willy Parker licked his lips. His eyes were wide with excitement. This raid on the Primble place has been the most stirring thing Willy had ever done. He was glad Beaver was the new leader. This new direction of attacking deserted farm houses was a lot safer that stopping a stage coach or entering a bank with gun in hand. There had been only one man about.

"Just an unarmed Nigger," he said aloud to himself. "A stupid Nigger what walks right into ambush we baited with a dead dog." That was an easy shootin'. Willy had to admit, too, that he liked the things they had done to the women. Beaver was a far better leader, he thought, than Amos Younger had ever dared to be.

Beaver Parker was actually sweating with anticipation. He had been totally committed to the proposition of killing the men in this group of travelers and having the light-haired woman for himself. He would kill Charley and Willy too if they dared to interfere. Now there was the bonus of the Chinese girl. Thinking of her, he felt his palms go damp and sticky.

From various vantage points while spying on the group, he had seen Chinagirl rather closely a time or two. The thought of her lithe, small body caused him to shudder with delight. He thought of her ebony braids framing that strangely colored beautiful face. He wanted her almost as badly as the blonde woman.

He wanted the group to get to the Primble farm. Along with Charley and Willy, he'd be waiting there for them. With only two other guns, an assault out in the open was too much of a risk. That would be nothing more than an open gunfight. Beaver was interested in killing, not fighting. At least, not fighting out in the open in the broad daylight. That was foolishness. There was a better way. Beaver's men could keep them pinned down in the farm house. They could lay a siege that would last as long as it had too.

The food and water had been taken from the house, and the surrounding terrain was all quite high. Perfect for rifle men. Once inside the house there was no way out except over the hidden guns of ambush. Beaver also wanted the travelers to find what he and his associates had left in the farm house. He wished he could see the faces of the two women when they found the bodies. The thought brought a shudder low in his abdomen and thrilled him delightfully. Also, he knew that once they entered the house he would have them trapped if he handled it well.

"What if they don't go in? What if they stay outside?" Charley Stone wanted to know.

"They'll go inside alright... There's somethin' 'bout a house draws folks inside... 'Sides they'll want to see what's happened to the Niggers and all. They'll go inside... You'll see. All we'll have to do is just wait."

If Beaver Parker was slow, even retarded, in most matters, he was displaying remarkable generalship now. He was carefully covering every detail in the strategy and planning of this rape and murder raid. He might not always have been in full control of his own mind, but for the task that lay ahead he seemed amazingly alert and vital. He thought of the dark girl called Rachel he had destroyed with his hunting knife and again felt the thrilling tremor. Now, he thought of the exciting contrast of the two women who would soon be in his trap. One so very fair, long light hair, so vulnerable. The other dark and exciting, exotic looking, yet childlike in her raven braids…

"All that hair." Beaver breathed aloud. "What am I gonna do with all that hair?"

Unaware of the presence of any danger, Pamela continued to question Colin about their destination.

"What are the stories I hear about the big house? If Robert has no wife, why does he live in such a mansion?" Pamela sensed that Colin was somehow uncomfortable about this change in the direction of their conversation.

"He don't live in it. He built it, and it's big all right. But no one lives there. He keeps it empty. Who told you about the mansion, anyway, Pamela?"

"Well, Henry Brooker told me first." Pamela was open and matter of fact. "He just casually mentioned it as I remember. He didn't let on that there was some secret or a mystery about it. I think the Sheriff might have said it was a fine house, too. I'm not sure. But why would Robert Trav keep it empty? Why would he do that?"

"Whoever told you about the big house should have told you that no one knows why he built it or what he intends to do with it. It's the Travis, Texas mystery." Colin smiled. "It's called the Red River Riddle, even if it is on the Canadian." Colin gave some thought to the subject. After a short pause he went on.

"Personally, I've always thought that maybe he built it in case… In case the woman he loved so much ever came back into his life. He'd give the house to her I thought. I asked, though, one time; and he said the woman he had known wouldn't have an interest in the house at all., or any house. I don't know what to make of it Pamela. But it's a dandy. Most beautiful house I've ever seen."

"Colin," Pamela was being kittenish. "Tonight, try to sleep aways from everyone else. I think it's time for another late-night visit. I've been thinking about it for some time now."

"I've thought of nothing else." Colin replied. "Have you really thought this out, Pam? What with our age difference and all?"

"Colin Trav, if you mention age one more time to me, I'm going to take this team whip and cut your britches off. I need you, Colin. A man. Not some boy… you. Justin needs you, too. He carries that harmonica around as if it were gold. Damn it, Colin, can't you just shut up and let people love you when they want to?"

The thought of another night alone with Pamela was a thrilling one indeed. But even savoring this projected pleasure, Colin was having trouble keeping his mind on Pamela and the small talk. His survival senses kept over-riding his anticipations, sending him signals of impending danger.

When the oxen turned into the lane he heard Justin's call. "Look, Colin. Look here in the road. It's a dead dog."

Chapter Thirteen

Massacre

Colin dismounted his little group and called them together. Justin tethered the horses and oxen, and Chinagirl tied up the team and the Studebaker.

"I don't like finding that dog in the road. Flies everywhere. That dogs' been dead a spell. I know Abe Primble would never stand for somethin' to be unburied on or near his place. He'd bury it. If he was able…"

China girl's eyes were wild and darting. Furtively her eyes flicked first in one direction then the other, probing, searching, her face a mask of anxiety. Like Colin, her instincts were telling her there was something to dread here. Pamela held Justin near her and clutched at Colins' arm.

"What should we do, Colin? What's next for us?" she asked.

"We'll go the rest of the way on foot," Colin said. "It's just around this bend in the cottonwood and then up the road. Not more than fifty or sixty yards. We won't move slow, but we won't run either. Leave it all here." He said gesturing toward the wagon buckboard and horses.

"Leave it all here except for the guns and ammunition. We'll carry that with us. All of it…. And the water bag. Justin, you bring the water." The boy fairly leapt to accommodate. "If we don't need it, we can dump it and freshen up the bag at Abe's well tank."

Colin went on issuing orders. His eyes narrow and intense, he was trying to cover all the bases. He was a bit surprised that he found himself remembering his Ranger days. He thought of Henry Brooker and wondered if he were handling the situation the way that proven fighter would.

"Now… Stay close behind each other in a single file. We'll stay close to the edge of the lane. If you hear or see anything, dive right into the brush and hug the ground. There's probably nothin' wrong at all, but it never hurts to take care… We'll worry about how foolish we look later."

At a moderate pace the file of four moved up the trail towards the Primble homestead. All concentrated on looking straight ahead trying to show no signs of suspicion. Chinagirl though stole anxious glances up and down the road, as alert, Colin thought, as a bobcat.

We must look so obvious, Pamela thought, *...leaving our stock and wagons this way and carrying all these guns. We must appear like we're ready to raid this place.* She looked now at the small corral that lay midway between the house and barn.

A few horses lazily milled about; their tails busily switching at the bothersome flies. Even from a distance she could see they were excellent horses. The kind of stock Alex would've appreciated. Then the terrible realization of what she was truly seeing crept over her. Suddenly, she froze in her very tracks.

"My God, Colin," she said. "Look at those horses. Those are my horses, Colin! Those are Alex's mares." She chastised herself severely for not instantly recognizing her own string of breeders. Colin took her roughly by the arm.

"No time right now. Move to the house." His voice was low and urgent. The fact that the horses were here at the Primble farm confirmed his suspicions of impending trouble. Glancing swiftly towards the corral, he quickly determined that Pamela was correct. Even at this great distance it was easy to recognize the tall Kentucky horses. It would've been obvious to the most untrained eye that these were blooded mares. Unlike any plains' mustangs, these were brood mares intended to couple with the best wild mustang stallions that could be found. Hopefully a foal would occur that would be the best of both.

A colt that would be rocket fast and flint hard tough. This was the reason the Carstin family had brought thoroughbreds to Murphy Flats ion the first place. These were among the first and finest Kentucky horses to find their way to Kansas and the west. Their presence here, at the Primble farm, was mystifying to Colin... But he knew they meant trouble.

Why were they here?

He couldn't give himself a suitable answer. His own rational mind could, in no way, have grasped the madness of Beaver Parker's intentions toward Pamela. Even had he known who Parker was or about him, this murderous insanity would've been beyond his comprehension. Colin was simply not capable of thinking the way Beaver Parker did. Had he known of Parker's motives, he would've been incapable of understanding them or even believing them. What he did understand though, was there was trouble somewhere nearby. He was sure of that. The appearance of the horses had intensified his caution.

He now carried the Brooker gun in has right hand. The hammer was thumbed back and the big .44 was in a state of readiness. He hurried his group along a little faster now. The pressing urgency of getting to cover was a far more important consideration than stealth for the moment. Shaken, as she was, Pamela staggered along as directed. She moved as in a bewildered daze, trying to comprehend the full meaning of the presence of her horses. She wanted to run to the mares, to inspect them and ascertain their conditions. But Colin would have none of it. He gripped her arm, almost too tightly, and shepherded her, none too gently, on to the house.

Now Colin spotted Abe's wagon and team of mules standing at the end of the lane by a wooden trough filled with water. The animals turned their great ears forward chewed at their bits and starred balefully back at Colin. They were obviously on their own and wandering around still in harness but unthethered. They seemed to be searching for direction. Then Colin saw the arm. It was, unquestionably, the arm of a man. Clothed in a faded blue work shirt, the arm, visible from about elbow to wrist, stuck awkwardly skyward from the bed of the wagon. Colin knew what it was.

The arm and hand of a man, extending up above the sideboards of the wagon… It's unnatural, lopsided angle told Colin instantly that the man on the other end of the arm was dead. He could see the hand and exposed wrist were deep brown in color. Colin reasoned the hand was that of Abraham Primble. He wanted to go to the wagon, to see if he could help his old friend. But that would mean moving out in the open. Besides, he was sure he could be of no help to Abe now. He moved his charges more directly now to the cabin.

Upon entering the house it was instantly apparent there was something seriously wrong here. Furniture lay in disarray, and the central table was overturned, its contents spread before the upset top on the floor. The smell of something recently on fire permeated the living room of the small low-roofed structure. Colin moved through the front room and adjoining hall with a caution born of the plainsman. His eyes narrowed against the dimness of the room, he kept the Smith and Wesson ready in his hand. The ivory grip was warm to the touch. Like something alive.

The weight of the revolver was reassuring. He knew at such close range the only weapon equal to, or superior to, the .44-40 and its heavy leaden slugs would have to be a shotgun loaded with buckshot. He felt well armed. The short-barreled revolver was quick and deadly.

The scream of discovery came first from Chinagirl. More of a gasp than scream, it was as though the voice of Chinagirl had locked itself in her throat and could only escape a bit at a time. Her cry startled Colin, and he wheeled in her direction, gun ready. Pamela uttered a cry of surprise. She was not terrified as she thought she might be. Nonetheless, the choked cry from Chinagirl startled her and made her skin crawl on her back like live vermin. She felt hollow in her lower stomach. Still, she thumbed back the hammer on the Winchester. She heard it click twice very audibly and knew she was past the safety notch on the hammer and in firing position. She peered into the small front bedroom immediately off the living room and saw the vision that had stunned Chinagirl. Sprawled on the floor, obscene in its nudity was the wasted and bloody body of little Laurel Primble.

It was only a split second later that Pamela glimpsed the tortured remains of a mature woman she knew must be Colin's friend, Annie. She half sat, half lay there. Legs and arms akimbo, she was pitifully exposed and lewd. Her body was covered with knife slashes and fiery, water-filled blisters. Across her stomach, in a cruel arc, the flesh had been so badly burned that the skin had simply sloughed away. Rolls and patches of the loose flesh clung to her like formless, crumpled paper. It hung there in sickening flaps still partially attached. There were bruises too, the color of ripe eggplant. The battered areas were grossly accentuated by the stark white of the naked woman's skin.

She was slumped against the wall, not quite sitting yet not quite laying. Her bare legs and feet jutted out across the hallway, her jaw hung slack and her glassy eyes stared sightlessly at those who had found her. Revolted, beyond belief, Colin saw that the soles of her feet and the tips of her breasts had been tortured by fire. Colin ripped a quilt from one of the beds and threw it over his friend. It was an effort to help her preserve, at least, some of her remaining dignity. He brushed tears from his eyes with the heel of his hand, and a cold hatred welled up deep inside him. His mouth went dry and tasted like old iron.

He found another coverlet and spread it over Laurel's thin, pale form. They lay like broken dolls with arms akimbo and no longer able to protect their modesty. Pamela stifled the scream welling up inside her. She vowed she would not cry out. She bit her knuckle forcefully to choke back the sounds her heart told her to make. She knew instinctively this day would be with her always. It was a terrible thought....

How can I live with this? she thought, almost aloud.

It struck her then that she might not live at all. That the fate of this woman and this thin girl might also be hers. She knew, though, if she did survive, she would never forget those dead and vacant eyes; the slack and silent mouths that could not protest this onslaught to their dignities. It was at this point Pamela saw the boy, Justin, had moved alone down the hall. She saw him now as he stood motionless peering into the back bedroom. It was the room that held the remains of Rachel Primble, still tied to the bed her Daddy had made for her. Pamela had never seen her son so white; it was as if all the color had completely drained from his face. Startled by his waxen appearance Pamela called to him.

"Justin," she said.

"Oh, Momma." His answer was not a reply but a low moan of horror and pity. Pamela rushed to her son's side. She looked into the room and saw the carnage that had left her son so desolate. Bile rose in her throat, and she pushed the boy's face into her body, shielding his eyes. She spun her own face from the scene of horror at the same instant. She felt her nerve slipping now. She had encountered more than she was prepared to bear.

"Colin," she croaked searching for her own voice. "They've all been murdered." She pulled her son closer to her and continued to shield his face against her body. It horrified her to know that he had seen such charnel. With the near panic caused by the discovery of Rachel, Colin decided to move outside. He felt that being inside this house of horrors was too much for his group of charges. He determined to find cover for them away from these grisly scenes.

Near the barn or by the corral, he reasoned. Got to get them out of here before all control is gone.

He herded them together and moved them back to the door they had entered. Just as he stepped into the doorway, the wooden frame exploded with smashing rifle bullets. Eight or ten shots hit the door casing seemingly all at once. The air was filled with flying splinters and chunks of wood. The fire was relentless and withering. The hail of lead drove the quartet back into the cover of the living room of the small house. Now Colin quickly dispatched the two women and Justin to different defensible areas.

"Justin," he called, ...bring your rifle and set with your back to this wall." He indicated the front wall of the house. "Don't move and don't show yourself. Keep low but keep your rifle ready." More shots spattered the house. The surrounding cover of brush and trees was thick, visually impenetrable. Colin was having trouble determining the bullets' places of origin.

"Chinagirl...Take your rifle to the rear of the house," he called. "Try not to look at the bodies. We'll cover them as soon as we can. If you see anyone moving out there, shoot them. No waiting...just shoot as quick as you can."

"But Mister Trav... Chester is not here yet," she protested. "Don't shoot Chester."

"Don't fret," he told her. "Chester's gone for help. Just shoot anyone that moves back there. It won't be Chester. Pamela, take the side window in the front bedroom. Keep your head as low as you can. All of you try to tell me where the shots are coming from."

He levered a big rim fire shell into the chamber of his old Henry rifle. Now the shooting slowed, and for the next hour it was sporadic. A shot, now and again, splatted against the door or shattered the glass of a window. Suddenly Colin became aware that Chinagirl was somewhat exposed at her place of appointment near the rear door, and yet no shots were coming her way.

Now he looked to Pamela's' place of defense and realized that she too was not being fired on. The shooting was nearly all being directed at him. He had pondered this turn of events for only a moment when a memory came flooding back too him from his Rangering days. He remembered now, with clarity, Charley Goodnight, leader of the Duro Palo Canyon riders. Goodnight had given a little impromptu speech one morning while on the trail of marauding Kiowa. Colin vividly remembered the telling.

"When Kiowa and Comanche are on a raid and don't shoot at the women, it's 'cause they want those women alive and unharmed. When you see this happenin', you got to fight that much harder... We can't be lettin' Kiowa bucks take women alive. Better we kill the women ourselves first. Better for the women by far..."

Colin knew now, for the first time, that these raiders were after Pamela and Chinagirl, not just horses as he had originally thought. These riders were not horse thieves. They were rapists and murderers. He checked the shells in Henry Brooker's Smith and Wesson. Colin knew that there were two things that could happen in his favor. Either he could get lucky and spot the ambushers and be able to return disabling fire; or Chester Crawford could appear with the Spur riders. This latter perchance seemed the safest for the women. Once Colin himself were killed, as he might be if he made a red-hot fire fight out of the situation, Chinagirl and Pamela would have little chance of survival all. He thought of Rachel Primble, and a cold hand touched his heart. The boy might be of some help but he was very young...

These thoughts all served to bring Colin to the conclusion that standing off the raiders and just surviving was the most important thing. He wondered whether or not Chester Crawford had gotten through the waiting bandits...if he were able to locate the Spur bunch. He wondered if Henry Brooker's wire had ever reached the Spur to begin with. All of these were remarkably slim chances. They were however the only chances he had. He couldn't trust his life to an open gun fight. Not with the women and the boy to think of.

For his own part, Colin would've preferred to locate the shooters and charge right into them. Juan Garcia had said to him many times that an attack was nearly always more effective than mere defense. For the safety of those in his care, however, an armed charge seemed the poorest of options. For now he would need to bide his time. Stay awake, stay alert and protect those who needed him. He correctly assessed that this was a siege. He reasoned that whatever food and water that may have been in the house now lay out in the thick cover with the attackers.

He was glad they had brought the water bag. It wasn't much but better than no water at all. He hoped this situation would end before that problem had to be dealt with. Looking about he saw Pamela was watching her window position intently. Chinagirl, too, was diligent in protecting her post. The boy Justin was checking his rifle. He seemed brave enough, and he was holding up well. Colin worried about all of them if the shooting really got hot. Or if there was a sudden rush...

During a long lull in the gunfight, Colin gathered up more of the bed clothing and covered the bodies of Annie and her daughters. The sight of their mutilated forms made him furious. He could never remember wanting a fight so desperately. He had loved these people for years and cared about them. Old Robert and Juan Garcia had cared about them. He had played with these girls when they were mere babies. He had known the Primble girls all his life. As for Abraham and Annie Primble, he had never had better friends. His years of trail bossing had brought him in contact with them at least once yearly. Frequently more often than that. They were visits each had come to expect and look forward to. Colin recalled Abe's wonderful musical ability and how he could make bright lively music on the fiddle.

He could just as easily create lonely and mournful sounds on the harmonica. Abe called it the French Harp. He could make it sound like the freight trains as they sped through the lonely prairie nights. When he played the Red River Valley, it was hard not to cry a bit. The sounds created by Abraham were so reflective. The notes told the story of every cowboy who had ever found himself totally alone in a land so large it baffled the senses.. And indeed, every cowboy had at one time or another. Colin's very spirit cried for revenge. With every fiber he longed to punish those to death who had assaulted his friends.

Yet he knew full well if he were killed or wounded, the boy and Pamela and Chinagirl would be, for the most part, defenseless. If he failed in his assault on the killers, it would be those who needed him most that would pay the dearest price. He could face death so easily for himself. Certainly, he had before. But he couldn't have this for Pamela. Not for the boy. He had come to love these two so dearly by now that it wrenched his heart to think they might fall to a fate similar to that of the Primble's. He thought of Chinagirl too. He couldn't allow any of these to fall into foul hands. Whatever the price he must pay it. This woman, this boy, they were his. They had to be protected by him and he vowed they would be.

He knew they were brave enough and would no doubt fight with their rifles till the very finish. But, he thought, in the conclusion they would wind up as Annie, Rachel and Laurel Primble had. They would end up dead. He had to resist the urge to fight it out. Rather than try to end the fight, he had to keep the killers at bay. He had to hope for some new development, some break-through in the standoff. Mostly, he wished for Chester Crawford and the riders of the Broken Spur. He realized that was not likely to happen, but there was the chance of some passerby discovering them and sending help.

Another bullet slapped into the open door casing, sending a shower of splinters into the room. This time Colin thought he saw a puff of smoke from the base of a hedge apple tree some ninety or a hundred yards out. He decided to wait for the next shot to confirm the shooter's location before returning fire. For now he sunk lower against the door frame and resigned himself for the long inevitable wait.

Could this be the Amos Younger gang? he wondered. When had Amos become interested in rape and the murder of families? He was deeply troubled by this. He felt his enemies were wholly dedicated to the taking of Pamela and Chinagirl. He couldn't help but wonder if this siege might not be a long one.

He had been taught warfare and survival tactics by two of the very best in those fields. First there was Juan Garcia. If the local legends of this vaquero were to be believed, he had once been among the boldest of bandits along the Rio Grande. And then there was Old Robert. Colin was amazed at how little he really knew of the old Scott that was his stepfather. It was for certain that Robert Trav had been a man of the plains. He knew the wiles of Indians and Comancheros. He was, for the most part, a quiet man; but Colin had never doubted that he would fight.

He had fought off bandits and land grabbers, Indians, renegades and rustlers. With his old Hawken rifle he had filled a number of graves in the little cemetery that served the Broken Spur. Garcia had said the truly bad ones had been dragged off into the sage to feed buzzards and wolves. Colin could not help but wonder how Old Robert would handle the situation he now found confronting him. He knew, for sure, that if Robert Trav were here it would not be enough to merely escape. Like Charley Goodnight, the old Scot would've wanted these attackers' dead. Colin closed his eyes for a just second. In his memory he could plainly hear the old man's voice saying the words he had uttered so often.

"There's some men that just aren't fit to live."

Looking at the death and destruction around him now, seeing how villainy and brutal meanness had taken the entire Primble family, Colin was sure that Old Robert had been right.

Part two: Old Robert

Chapter Fourteen

The Walk to the Sea
Scotland to Texas 1836/1888

He stood on the bare earth on the high wash above the river. No grass grew in this heavily eroded spot where, for eons, the rushing waters of the Canadian river had cut the land back and formed this high bluff. Old Robert had always thought it was the loveliest place on the Spur. He hated the thought of ever leaving the Spur again. Now Garcia had come with a wire that said Colin might be in trouble. What was a wire anyway? How did they send words along a wire? he had often wondered. No matter. If Colin needed him he would, of course, go to him at once. He would go anywhere to help Collie. There weren't many other reasons that would tempt him to leave the Spur.

How could this place have stayed so beautiful? the old man wondered. How could it have kept this look of peace and beauty when he and Garcia had shed blood upon it so often?

He brushed some unruly grey hair from his face. The evening breezes caused it to wisp a bit. His face was weathered and lined with age. Rather thin and hawk-like in appearance it may have been, but the light blue eyes were clear, cold and piercing. His senses were as alert and keen as they had ever been. When he stood here on this high place, looking north over the Canadian, he always felt his heart swell a bit with his love for this land.

If there is a place worth killing for, he thought, *this is surely it.... It may be even worth dying for.*

It was high here indeed. From where he stood he could see the junction of the Canadian river and the big tributary that flowed far to the south to join with the Red except in the dry season. Once it mingled the runoff waters of north Texas with the waters of the Red River, they meandered a thousand miles through hundreds of smaller streams and brooks before ending, eventually, in the Gulf of Mexico.

It was late summer now and the wash was a dry, wandering arroyo. The main channel of the Canadian flowed deep and peaceful to the southeast and it's destination with the Arkansas River. From the heights where Robert sat, he could see the river divide the land as a silver slash against the sage. One couldn't see all the Spur from here. Not even a tenth of it really. But what was visible clearly revealed the nature and character of the spread. Vast and untamed. The few human hands that had touched the land hadn't changed it much in the last ten thousand years.

From here you can see the feeling, Robert often said to himself.

Old Robert liked it wild and primitive. However, he had, for private and secret reasons, built a lavish "big house". Rumor told that it was furnished and appointed beautifully with lavish style and even fashions imported from Europe. But no one knew for sure. Probably Garcia knew. Maybe Colin knew. That would be all.

The big house was kept closed and shuttered. Strictly forbidden to all ranch hands, the occasional visitor to the Spur could only stand in the trim little yard that surrounded it and marvel at its mysteries of wealth and silence. Even Robert himself would only enter the massive structure and prowl about its empty hallways for a few hours once or twice a year. Though the ranching and cattle dealings of the Spur were honest and open books for all to see, the house remained a ghostly puzzlement.

Its ominous facade lay forbidden behind gaudy, Corinthian columns. Its presence betrayed the expected appearance of the landscape as its three vertical stories stood alone without so much as single tree or even a bush about. The jutting upright structure seemed foreign and somehow alien as it sprang suddenly skyward from the open prairie. An eruption, disturbing the flatness that was the surrounding endless stretch of grassland. When strangers looked upon the gaudy mansion, the remark most often whispered was,

"It's so out of place."

The other ranch structures, the old house, the bunkhouse, horse sheds and hay barns were of the simplest and lowest forms of architecture. They ranged from lean-to sheds to flat-roofed pueblos. Robert hated pretension; and he had to admit too, that he despised progress. It was progress, he thought, that had always taken away the things he loved most. Other than the "big house," austere would've been the word that best described not only the Spur but Old Robert, too. No one knew just how wealthy The Broken Spur had made its owner, least of all Robert himself.

He didn't bother much about money and other than the big house he had spent precious little during his lifetime of accumulating so much. More than the assets, he loved standing on the rich earth of the Broken Spur in his old, familiar moccasins. He had never given up the old ways of the Rockies, and there would be no high-heeled riding boots for him.

Not ever, he thought. He had come to this country in the clothes and trappings of the Long Hunter. The free trapper of the Hudson's Bay Fur Company. He loved the vaqueros and the cowboys, but their ways were not his. They would never be his. The owner of the greatest ranch in Texas was a mountain man at heart.

In his seventies now, Robert was still an imposing figure. The sharpened features of his weathered face made his steel-colored eyes somehow more deeply intent and remarkably perceptible. He carried his angular body ramrod straight. His steps were steady and sure. The arthritis stiffened him now though, and when he rose from sitting, he was often visibly pained for a moment. He called it "shakin' the kinks out." Thin as he was, there was still a masculine strength that refused to be trifled with.

"Like a longhorn range bull ," his friend Juan Garcia had said assessing his long time compadre. He referred to the bone-thin, tough-as-wire, range cattle. The Longhorn, whose very wildness and will to survive and multiply had been the most important singular driving force that had brought about the enormous financial entity that was the Broken Spur.

"Everything on the Spur is tough," Garcia had often said. "...its cattle...Its horses...Its men. All tough and hard. The gold of the Spur is from the seed that lies in the belly of the bulls. They are the toughest of all.... except for Senor Trav."

It was near sundown now, and the breezes of the evening rippled the surface of the shallow water. Robert watched as a man entranced. This had always been his part of the day. Beyond the river lay more land than a man on a good horse could cross in three days. The old Scotsman knew it was his. All his, if at a terrible price sometimes. How long had it been since he walked down from the mountains?

Driven by anguish and all alone he had walked steadily south on the vast prairie until he had at last come to the water's north edge. A strange sight he had been, indeed. This buckskin-clad young man with hair down his back and below his shoulders. Dusty and trail worn, he carried the heavy Hawken rifle and led his string of four ponies. Exhausted as he was, an observer would've noticed the determination in his step, the steady alertness of his gaze.

Robert had ridden his horses only when exhaustion dictated it. He had yet to come to grips with riding the horses so vital to western life. Indeed, Robert would never completely trust, nor ever be at ease with a horse. It felt to him now that those happenings were ages ago.... And yet each detail was etched so deeply in his mind that the events of years past were as vivid as yesterday. The one woman of his life had been left behind so many years ago. Still the loneliness was as intense as ever. True enough, he had learned to live with the loneliness, but the memories had not faded. The longings still lingered. He could still close his eyes and see her face at any time he wished. Just as clearly in fact as he had been able to do those countless years before when he had actually held her lovely face between his hands.

How startled she had looked the first time he had pressed his lips against hers. The Crow people had known nothing of kissing until Robert Trav had come among them. When he thought of her and of the Rockies he felt as though there was a hollow spot in his very heart. He had tried to fill it with the Spur. For the most part he had succeeded. Except for a few vivid memories of the woman.

He sat now on a fallen log thinking old thoughts. It was an activity he had come to indulge in more and more as he had aged. Mostly he thought of Colin. But every time he came here the thoughts of his past became overwhelming. It was a familiar and favorite resting place. Down the river bank a short way, his hawk- like vision caught a flicker of movement.

Just slight...Not much...But even this very slight movement here on his own ground triggered, instinctively, those survival sensors he had lived with for so very long. His hand, gnarled but sure and steady, moved slowly a scant inch nearer the rifle. The rifle, like the buckskin clothing, was a reflection of the man. It was not the new Winchester repeater that was so in fashion, nor even the old Spencer carbine the left over militia favored. Rather, his rifle was the old cap lock, full stocked Hawken that the mountain men and fur traders had treasured more than four decades ago.

In truth, it had once been fired by the primitive striking of a flint stone to a steel frizzen. The rifle had been originally conceived and constructed as a flint lock. But by now the arm had been converted to the more modern and reliable percussion cap ignition. The little caps were a bit more reliable he supposed, but Robert Trav still trusted good flint with a great deal more faith. The standard half-stocked Hawken rifle was seldom seen in these times. The rifle's hey day had been half a century before, and the gun was now considered rare.

Old Robert's beloved full-stocked version, the one with wood all the way to a browned steel-nose cap right under the muzzle was even more scarce. He would never give up this fine old fifty-caliber muzzle loader. Jim Bridger had owned one. Kit Carson had one... And by God, Robert Trav had one and that was that. Now he saw the disturbance in the river brush a bit more clearly and as suddenly as he had tensed, he now let down his guard.

A coyote, he thought nearly aloud. *An old coyote with a frog supper on his mind.* He went back to dreaming...

How young had he been when he left his native Scotland ? He couldn't remember for sure but he might have been fourteen or so. Now he was more than seventy, but he couldn't remember how much more exactly.

His father had been a game keeper to the squires and local gentry. He recalled that well enough. As he had followed this tall, angular and heavily bearded man about through the moors and thickets, Robert Trav, even as a boy, had become able in the trappers' trade.

"How different from all these cows," he heard himself say aloud...

Scotland—Inverness to Glasgow - 1836

"'Tis piss!" How well he remembered his father's heavy brogue. "'Tis piss that takes the fox. You'll catch him not with the dead fowl nor sheep brains. But give him a whiff of his brother's piss, and he'll throw himself amongst your worst trap."

Old Robert remembered, even as a boy, how he had thought it terrible that the urine of a fox would be used to trap its brother. Somehow, he remembered that more clearly than all the rest of the ghostly memories of his father. His mother he remembered scarcely at all, just a formless shape hoeing in the tiny garden or standing by the wood stove stirring who knew what? It was his father, though, who loomed the larger in his mind.

The mother he remembered was a silent form that moved about in the smoky light of the peat fires. She was a specter that carried a Bible and worked with her hands. Always there were busy hands: Hands that spun yarn, snapped beans and stitched seams in rough woolens and suedes. Far back in the recesses of his mind, somehow there was ever the smell of haggis.

He could still see it in his mind's eye: The chopping of the sheep's heart, liver and other vitals. The methodical mixing of the meats with the boiling barley and onion. The rich porridge was then stuffed into the stomach membrane of the sheep and baked somehow. He wondered often if the haggis was really as good as he remembered. Perhaps it was like all things past, the flavor, somehow, becoming sweeter and more delectable with the passing of time.

Time had made many of his pleasant thoughts richer, his hardest ones bearable. Time had changed him into an old man. It had been a friendly change. Filled with understanding, tolerance and warmth. The sun was gone now. The river and the prairie were only illuminated faintly by the receding twilight. He shifted his shaggy head so that he could peer over the lone ponderosa nearly directly in front of him. There it was. Just as it had always been. The north star....

It was the same star that had guided him from the north of Scotland to the Mohawk River Valley nearly a lifetime ago, then on to the River Niagara. Next to the deep hardwood forests the earliest settlers had called New York after the home they had left in York England more than an ocean behind. From there the star and the search for fur had borne him west to the shores of the sweet sea called Erie. He would never forget Erie. That great, mostly gentle lake could charm the most savage heart with her crystal loveliness. Then, in a furious and sudden swift reversal, could bring forth storms of such ferocity that she could break the very hearts of those who loved her best.

He had been mesmerized by his first impression of the pure and peaceful Lake Erie. Its waters teemed with the finest of fish. The heavily wooded shores held unlimited numbers of game and fur bearing animals. Then her dark and fickle ways had crushed his hopes forever. Like men who had come a thousand years before him, it took only one heavy storm for him to feel the sting of the grand lake's betrayal. The wind assaulted him as meanly as a warrior. Here he learned the bitter lessons taught by the fury of Erie's famed "Nor' Easter squalls."

Erie's shallowness would ever be her greatest fault. Because of her shallow waters, ferocious storms could come about with no warning at all. The gale would be upon one far more quickly than would be whipped up in the deeper, more reliable waters of Michigan or Ontario. Her great black storms could destroy whole trap lines in the twinkling of an eye. Shorelines could be swept away and even entire islands swallowed whole by the relentless tempest.

Her enormous and adamant breaker waves could smash the strongest boat into pieces, and her rushing waters were unrelenting. It was the north wind that propelled the storm and had driven him from Erie's shores so very long ago. Yet storms as he had seen there were not so easily forgotten. He clearly recalled that when the blows had taken his all, he had given himself over to the star. The star carried him onward, away from the place the Ottawa and Shawnee called Sandusky, the land beside the shining water.

As usual his reminiscing was, for the most part, thoughts of fair and pleasant times. From the darker side of his life, though, were memories of blood and fire. He thought of Kahn-ee-wa, the wild goose, and his strong sister nearly always. Then there were the memories of Fletcher Harris. It was Harris who would become the first enemy that Robert could remember.

It was Harris who had made him a fugitive when he was but a boy. Yet how could he hate Harris after all these years? It was after all his flight from Niagara to escape the abusive and dangerous Harris that, years later, would bring him to this land. The land that now held his very heart. Fleeing Harris and his threat of life-long slavery, he had driven himself to the south. He strove mightily to put as much distance between them as he could. Yet, he longed to stop somewhere. Flight promised him safety from his enemies, but at the same time he knew he couldn't run forever. He felt he needed to start building a life of some sort.

It must be my Scotch showing, he had thought. He believed, since trapping was his only skill, that the answer for him lay in furs. The Long Hunters had said in the trading post and at their campfires that the land of the Mingo and Shawnee still held vast stores of skins. He had heard all the stories, many times, of the great fur caches of the south. They were to be found south of Spay-Lay-Wi-Thee-Pee, that twisting, winding river that split the eastern quarter of the continent and was called "Ohio" by the whites. The days of Tecumseh were long gone now, and Daniel Boone, Simon Kenton and Ebeneezer Zane no longer ruled the vast wilderness called Kentucky.

Robert vowed to see her fur, yet when he arrived he was dismayed to discover her wilderness had already begun to vanish. To be sure the rivers and streams still held fur, but it was scant compared to the stories he had heard and to his anticipated expectations. It seemed to Robert that even the deep forests were filled, or were filling, with people. People were there and building things. Churches, schools and even towns. It was no longer the land of the Long Hunter. These were citizens.

The buffalo crashes still could be seen in abundance along the river. Those huge, barren gaps where the brutes had shoved through the brush to drink. But the buffalo themselves were long gone. The last of their kind had been shot off the river bank back in the 1740's. The sound of the land now was the ring of the hammer on the nail, the yawn of the saw and the jingle of the trace chains as mighty horses snaked logs through the woods. These powerful dray animals brought the timbers to a place where a buzz saw would sing its song night and day for a hundred and fifty years. Buildings would spring up and the forest would retreat.

Searching for the peace and solitude that all trappers must love in order to become trappers, yearning for the mother lode of pelts, he had traded some poor, early fall skins to an old Negro for a canoe. A spindly and leaky affair made of skins, bark and cedar ribs. The boat trade came about on the north bank of the river. It was near the Ohio's great and dramatic junction with the Mother of North American rivers called Mississippi that Robert encountered a place that was to bring about an enormous change in his life. Robert would learn more of men, women and life in the brawling, muddy river port called Evansville. River traders called it "Evil-ville"

Even the very origins of this wild and sin-filled river town were questionable. Reportedly, Evansville, of the Indiana territory, had been founded by Hugh Mc Gary who named the are after Robert Evans a hero from the war of 1812. Mc Gary himself though was reported to be an Ohio frontiersman of such low morals he had been previously ordered out of the Ohio region by the famous, buck-skinner, Simon Kenton. This banishment of Mc Gary came repotably after he had shamelessly tomahawked an old and handcuffed Shawnee chieftain to death. The vicious attack came even after the aged warrior's surrender. Kenton, striving for peace with the Shawnee had sent him straight away.

Since the mid-seventeen hundreds, trade had taken place on this muddy bend of the Ohio. The Shawnee camps gave way to an unnamed trading post. That bartering camp would evolve to an anonymous village. And so, on it grew. By eighteen-nineteen the settlement was being called Evansville, named after an obscure militia colonel.

No matter who her founders were, by 1839 Evansville had become the talk of the river. What Louisville, Cincinnati and Saint Louis offered in service and culture with their great keelboats industries, progressive banks and land speculation and even something of a frontier elegance, river front Evansville had naught.

It was true enough that a mile or so north of the river a rather genteel Evansville did truly exist. The front on the Ohio though was a different story completely.

Here she offered boisterous auctions of cotton brought up the Mississippi river. Other goods and services found their way to Evansville, too. She became the Ohio River's Mother of Trade. It was at Evansville that the rivers Wabash, Green and Ohio converged within a thirty mile area and emptied into the Mississippi. Of the settled part of America, all water travel and trade converged at Evansville. Her greatest asset though would come about some years later; the mouth of the Wabash and Erie Canal, Gateway to New York, the Atlantic Ocean and the world's greatest markets.

Here now were stockyards, filled to overflowing with southern cattle, squalling hogs and the worn out dairy herd culls of the surrounding German farmers. Furniture factories had begun to bristle with activity along the river bank. This trade brought the town more than her share of woods -tough lumbermen. The factories were a natural progression to the discovery of another major resource of the area: Black sunshine... coal.,

the fossil fuel that has eternally been the creator of industry, was generous here. In most areas the thick ebony veins were close enough to the earth's surface to mine quite handily. Some of these courses were, literally, miles wide. One had only to stab a shovel blade into any hillside and would likely turn a spade filled with this black blood of industry and travel. To be sure, the good and sturdy German stock that were the principle settlers here tried dutifully to keep about them a clean and law-abiding community. They built their churches and followed the creed of their great hero of church reform, Martin Luther.

Their farms of course were their second love, and these gleamed spotless in the southern Indiana sun. They built their schools and kept their sons and daughters off the streets after sundown. In short, they were the salt of the earth. They were strong and good people. But they were few. Evansville at this time in her childhood was as two completely separate landscapes.

In the saloons and brothels of the river front lived another type of citizen. They were bold enough in the broad daylight but totally shameless when the sun went down. These were the River Rats. To them belonged the span of waterfront to the south, west of the auction rings. That, and for more than two miles due south of the stockyards. When the sun began to set, out would come the fiddles and banjos, the mouth harps and the street dancers. Their merry sounds and scenic diversions were to cover the activities of the cut purse, the strong-arm boys, the grifters and the harlots.

Each doorway for a seven-block stretch offered gambling, the soft arms of the wanton and the very fuel that made that corrupt machine operate so slickly, whiskey. Good, Kentucky whiskey made foul by those who watered it to reap a more plentiful profit. Whiskey was for sale here by the drink, bottle or barrel. It was the drinking man's choice. For those who drank too freely and lost their way or their common sense or their caution, there was often the promise of a quick and violent death in the muddy streets of the West End.

Mornings often found the lifeless body of a drunken gambler who had taken his losses poorly. As often it would be the savaged body of a street whore too young to know how to survive in her chosen profession or too old to matter much any more to the fancy man who was her pimp.

It was just under a mile across the river at the big bend. To the south lay the neighboring settlement that would become Henderson, Kentucky. There was little law on the north side of the river and even less on the south. Lawmen who tried to rid the settlements of the undesirable found only bewilderment. It was a simple matter for the panderers and grifters to move back and forth across the river at the slightest imposed pressure.

The Kentucky town hadn't the industry that was to be found on the north bank, yet it fairly bristled in bartering trade. Coal was to be found on the south side too, but no one mined it. At least, not yet. Kentuckians were more interested in that territory's three greatest commodities: Horses, whiskey and tobacco.

The tall horses of Kentucky could, and did out run, out jump and out distance any horses in the world. Because of his tall and lanky appearance, the Kentucky thoroughbred may have been misjudged in looks by the uninformed horse breeders of the world. But they were never underrated. Their performance was legend. These were the fastest horses in the world. They caused the horsemen of Europe to die of envy.

The sour mash bourbon whiskey first distilled by the settlers Daniel Boone had brought into Kain-tah-key was a staple. Like bread and meat, bourbon was at all the tables and side boards of the Ohio and Mississippi Valleys, elegant and common alike. Here gents and ladies, too, would often take "a sip of the amber."

The first settlers made their spirits in the Hudson River Valley. It was here they copied the Scottish style of whiskey made from barley malt and cured with peat. It was close enough to the smoky Scotch they had left behind. After they crossed the Appalachians, however, corn was far more plentiful than barley. Corn whiskey aged in a charred, white-oak barrel was given the French name, Bourbon. Like the great horses, Kentucky whiskey was a grand American original. Those who coveted the smooth liquid fire of Kentucky and neighboring Tennessee found it abundantly on the Ohio's south bank.

As to the tobacco, Kentucky was fast becoming a rival to Virginia as the leading producer of the world's highest quality and tastiest leaf. Packed in hogshead barrels, the river demand for this staple created a lively trade and generated thousands in gold. The green plant and the yellow gold brought the abundance of colorful traders. It was the same gold, though, that brought the gamblers, the thieves, the killers and harlots. Both sides of the river offered the traveler the riches of trade or the pleasures of sin. The latter was most often selected as a more tempting option.

It was into this raucous life, on the north shore, that Robert Trav eased his battered canoe in the spring of 1839. He was less than twenty years old and was already a fugitive. He was, indeed, a stranger in a strange land. He was a lean and impoverished youth with a keen and lively interest in this rough and tumble river port. Spring upon him and no trapping for many months to com, for fur is only fine in the cold.

Robert determined to look about for work in this bustling anchorage. A long way from the Niagara now, he was still living as a fugitive. He was still fearful of capture by his pursuers. The profusion of people here, he felt, offered some anonymity. He would hide in this crowd if he could strike work. He looked first to the boats. He saw men working with tar and oakum making keelboats as watertight as they could. Here and there ship-rights laid out the keels and hulls that would soon become keelboats, river ferries or the like.

Suddenly he realized he was being borne down upon by a group of ten or so wild looking cattle with great white eyes and long, dangerous horns. The cattle were being forced squarely upon him by three men on horseback. Terrified, he leaped from their path. He saw then that these horsemen were easily the most colorful men he'd ever seen.

"How dashing!" he thought. He'd never seen cattle driven any way except on foot. Scottish cattle were so valuable they were treated as gently as household pets. Only the richest of Lairds had cows. These men in their leather breeches and big slouch hats moved the cattle along with the cracks of whips and a good deal of yelling and shouting. Their shrill whistling pierced the air and offended the peace of the day. The whole scene looked so intriguing that he thought for a moment he might seek work of this type. But then he began to look closer at the horses. Big they were and powerful. He noticed, too, that when the drovers and horses took to the street they were given total right-of-way.

"Tis maybe a fine job of work," he thought. "But maybe there'll be a more proper time to see to the learnin' of horses." He returned to his thoughts of working on the boats.

Robert knew scant of boats. One had, of course, brought him to America. He had hated that voyage. On board, he had languished with the length of the voyage, the roughness of the Atlantic and the infernal sea sickness. There would be no such sailing here among these sweet rivers.

he realized. He despised the travail that was ocean journey. He had to admit, however, the ship herself had been interesting. In fact, it had unreasonably fascinated him. He had found her as graceful as a bird in the hands of her good and able seamen. After all, it was boats that had, in a round about way, brought him here and that might even be an omen If one believed in such.

As a boy, Robert knew that Scotland had her great cities like Glasgow and Edinburgh, but he knew of no one who'd actually been there. And then, just as suddenly, he was going to Glasgow himself. The trip, thrust upon him, at once thrilled and terrified him. A favorite old uncle had brought it about.

"Colin," he had said to Robert's father, "I'm too old to poke about the countryside alone. If I'm to see to the familiy's needs by this journey, I'll need a good hand. It's Robert here that I want, for the fetchin' of my tea and layin' out my ground bed at night. For these many days I'll need a hand, and the lad here is likely."

At the word "likely," Robert had tried to puff his thin chest. He brushed the straw-colored hair away from his open honest face with the back of his hand. He recalled his mother saying that clearing his face made him seem so much more alert. If there had been anything Robert had longed for in his short span of years, it was a journey such as this one to the outside world. He felt his heart rush at the very name, Glasgow. And so it was that Robert, now at the end of his fourteenth summer was handed over to the old uncle, Clyde Alexander Trav.

The foot journey from north of Inverness to Glasgow is a long and wearing one. if for no other reasons than the damp and cold. Robert lost count of the days but recalled they might have been near ten. At last they crested a hilltop that seemed as though it might well be the roof of the world. Robert felt a wave of exhilaration rush his thin stomach as he looked down now, for the fist time, on the city Glasgow.

"There she is." The old uncle spoke as a merchant unveiling his fine wares, as though the city were his alone. Robert strained to see the great city all at once, but the fog and mists were so heavy that at first he saw very little. Gradually his eyes began to focus against the mist, and the true majesty of the view spread itself slowly before him. The first penetration of the fog was a slim silver stripe so far below.

"'Tis the river Clyde," the old man said. "'Tis the fair river that gave me her name." Robert had never realized, until this very minute, that his uncle even had a name and that it was Clyde Trav. It was the name of the great Scottish river that split in twain the majestic city of Glasgow. Now Robert's vision was clearing rapidly. As they descended the hill, the mist began to thin. From what he saw, amazement and awe overtook him. Here were houses and shops and public buildings by the score. And here were people, People maybe by the hundreds. Ceartinly a dozen score or more.

The streets were alive with the bustle of the throng of these. They swept their way through the crowded narrow alleys yelling, calling and signaling each other. The air was alive with waves and whistles as the dealers went about their transactions and affairs of trade. And then, grandest of all, Robert saw his first Cathedral. His father had shown him a drawing or two of the great churches, but they had not come close to expressing this sort of grandeur. Typical of the popular Gothic styles of the day, the church was a miracle of points and spires soaring to the skies. The doors and windows, with their pointed arches, seemed centuries strong to Robert. Through the designer's guile, the whole work seemed somehow rooted in the supernatural. Robert imagined it was the kind of structure God Himself would build. Or at least, approve of.

He looked skyward to the steeple and it's crowning Holy Cross finial. He pondered the copper Cross seeming to disappear into the heavens. He thought he could somehow hear his father's voice commenting on Angels and Archangels. He felt like a grain of sand in this mighty presence. His head was spinning as he and the old man maneuvered their way through the living throng. Robert, suddenly, caught a most unlikely and unfamiliar odor. No, it was a taste he was experiencing.

"What?" he whispered. "What uncle, is that smell?"

It was much stronger now and as the breezes freshened each zephyr brought the odor anew and more potent. Robert found it intoxicating. He felt in it a great mystery.

"The sea, Lad...You're smellin' the sea. You were to follow the river less than a day to the west and she's there... The great ocean sea. When the wind is strong from the west you can smell her from here. You'll hear its songs soon enough now." He rubbed his whiskered chin and smiled a toothless yet radiant beacon.

"'Tis the sea, Robert... The splendid, maddenin', ever-callin' sea."

It seemed to Robert that every man in Glasgow had a boat. The city was about equally split north from the south by the river. The Clyde made a vigorous short run through the city and then gave way to the forevers of the north Atlantic. Men and women sold vegetables from boats, shoes from boats, fish from boats. Robert could scarcely fathom the enormous variety of goods and services marketed, all by boat. Here were the crafts of peddlers and merchants of all types and sizes. They ranged from the meanest prams to the great tall ships making ready to unfurl their canvas wings. These world travelers stood at the mouth of one of the busiest harbors in all the world. He was baffled and mystified by the huge black piles he saw everywhere. He knew, of course, they were coal, but never had he dreamed there was so much coal. It lay in great rows of mountains so shiny black. It gleamed now and glistened in the mid morning sun. The sun that had finally burned away all the morning mists.

Robert was overwhelmed by this abundance. But at least he knew what it was. What could this white ever be. White mountains were here too. Rows and forever more rows of snowy bales partially wrapped in the meanest of burlap. As he drew near it revealed itself to him and brought about further astonishment.

"Me Lord!" he thought. ""Tis cotton…'Tis great bundles of cotton!" His jaw gaped as he stared now at cotton bales measured by the mile instead of the rod. As with the coal, he could not fathom the world could hold so much cotton.

"Where Uncle?" he sputtered. "Where can so much of these wares come from...what do they here...Why?"

"Hold, Laddie." Old uncles' eyes were strangely aglow now. On his face there dwelt a distant dreamlike quality Robert had never seen before.

"It comes from 'round the world, Laddie. 'Tis truly the white cliffs o' Scotland. They brings it here from everywhere, Robert– Egypt among the pyramids, And Affry too where lions live about. Mostly though, son, it's here from America. From the great plantations, once our colonies, when we was English anyways. They grows it by miles and we brings it here. Black mens grows it."

"But why, Uncle? And why so much?"

"Look, Robert lad. Raise your head and look above the city." Robert saw then what he had missed before. He had been so intently interested in the water and the boats, he had not looked up at all. But now he saw a great forest of soaring black smokestacks. They surrounded the city and stretched off into the horizon like a gigantic leafless, prehistoric jungle. It was early morning now but already they were painting the sky with their black and greasy soot.

"It's a good thing, Robert, the winning wind here blows from the south and out to sea. Otherwise, you'd fair choke by now. These then, are the Glasgow mills, lad. It's this city alone that mills the world's cotton. All the men you see here, e'en those that sell fish, live because of cotton. The mill gathers up the fibers here and spins the white gold into fabrics worn about the world by kings and beggar men. No drop of blood flows here at the River Clyde without it flows for cotton. This is where your father and I came from, Robert. We toiled here as wee lads. Would've died here too if the Laird had not taken us to learn the gamekeeper trades. Your father and I were the lucky ones. Mostly, those who work the mills die soon enough of the bloody cough..."

"Then you were lucky, Uncle...to have been picked by the Laird I mean."

"Talk no bloody foolishness about me, Rob!." Robert had never heard his uncle speak so harshly. His voice was truly venomous.

"It's not luck what got us picked...It took every cent your grandfather had...And he threw a sweet daughter and my sister into the pot too, lad. 'Twasn't luck that let us live son. 'Twas greed and evil– evil of an unspeakable kind. Your grandfather saved us, he did, but he gave his meager wealth and a special piece of his soul to do it.

He gave an evil man his only daughter for who-knows-what corrupt plans. Did it so his sons could live, he did. Girls don't 'mount to much they says. Not so much as sons. But I think of her, Robert. I think of her often, I does. The old man did too I'd 'spect... Well, he's dead now these long years. We think died of guilt and sadness, maybe shame... 'Tis good that the old Laird is dead now, too. Maybe they'll meet in Hell".

Stunned, Robert felt the same quiver in his knees as he felt when he was afraid. He had never known this terrible secret. He knew it made no sense, but somehow he felt a pang of shame as though he too had gained from the gift of the money and of the girl, his unknown aunt, to the lecher Lord. It was the first time ever, that he had realized that the character of men in high places could be suspect. Even abominable. It was also the first time he realized that people could be bartered or given away if they had been born in one of the unfortunate categories. It made him ashamed to think of the uses the Laird had found for the girl, his aunt. He vowed later that night, just before sleep, to remember it always.

The next days, old uncle Alexander Clyde Trav went about seeing lawyers, solicitors and the like. It was taking care of the family business that had brought him here, and it's what he would do. Robert, during these times, explored the harbor carefully. He was thrilled by it all. He especially loved the great sailing ships and how could anyone, he wondered, stare at them for very long without feeling a sense of wonderment. He pondered now over the strange and marvelous places these ships had been and whence they were bound on the morrow. He loved the clippers and even the slow freight sail vessels.

Thrilled by the sight of his first Man O' War, he was even more dazzled by the great Chinamen, the oriental aristocrats of maritime trade. He knew from his lessons, these sailing mercantiles plied the seven seas in search of spice and silk. They sailed on, endlessly, searching for the black rose. He knew that was the name these adventurers had given to the clove, most important spice of all in trade.

Fur: the Ancient Gold of Kings

It was on a clipper though that a friendly sailor on watch had let him steal aboard that he would see the amazing thing that would completely spellbind him and shape his destiny for years to come. The sailor was an American, but the ship was Russian. Neither was as captivating as was the cargo. The American allowed the Scottish boy to peer into the open hold. When his eyes became acclimated to the darkness, he realized he was looking at an entire ship's hold, filled to the running over brim, with fur! Here was the fur of the Americas: Bale upon bale of otter, lynx and fox. He saw the bulk of the cargo was beaver.

The sailor allowed Robert to lower himself into the hold, and he browsed among the priceless cargo, touching here, feeling there. Running his hands about its luxury and finally caressing his own cheek with a fine beaver. It was wondrous soft beyond description. He breathed in it's slightly musky smell. Nothing had ever so moved him. At last the sailor, bored with waiting, called him from the hold.

"Where could it all have come from?" asked Robert. "'Tis the most wonderful things I've seen ever!".

"America," answered the sailor. "The colonies England lost. Richest land in the world, I'll tell you. Not just in furs, but there's tobacco there. Too. Lad; and corn and whiskey and lots o' prime stuffs. America, boy, that's where we all needs to be."

It seemed to Robert that all sailors talked about America. He had to admit it all sounded wonderful, though he wasn't sure about his interest in tobacco and whiskey. But furs?

Ah, there, he thought, "Is a sharply different matter." He queried further.

"My father," he began, "My father trapped the Laird's varmints all his life. Yet in three lives or even more, maybe a dozen such lives, could never put aside such a store of fur as this. Who takes this much fur? Who could own this cargo? Is it near all the world's wealth?"

The fur and its ancient mystery had his heart in it's grip . He was caught as surely as any man who'd come to worship fur since the dawn of time. And many had, indeed. It was the coinage of the rich; its mystery and lure was far older than even that of gold. Ancient Chieftains had killed for fur eons before silver and gold had merit.

"Why, it's the Long Hunters lad. The Long Hunters and free trappers. They live in the wild and do as they will. A year or so and they sell their cache to the old Hudson Bay Fur Traders company. It's the biggest in the world ye know. 'At's why they calls it a company I 'spects. It's all mixed up in English money and 'merican fur somehow that's far beyond the likes o' me; but it's them Long Hunters as takes their fill o fur. They gets rich you know? Just a year or two and they gets richer'n Captains."

"Long Hunters?" Robert asked softly, already captivated by the sound of the words and what he suspected must be their profound meaning.

"Aye, lad. Calls 'em Long Hunters, they do, cause they hunts a year or two at a time. Lives in the wild, they do, and fights bears and wild Indians. And...and... most days they kill or be kilt they own selfs. Long Hunters they calls 'em...That and free trappers." The sailor was being carried away now by his expertise in the matter and the romance of the subject.

"How...?" Robert fought for the words. "How would someone get to America and see...see...or be one of these Long men?

"Hunters, son. It's Long Hunters... And ye says it just that-a-way cause they ain't jes' men. They's wild men, I tells ya. Wild and special, too. They's many a way to get there I'd reckon, lad. Most are just plain old slavery. Slaver, bondage 'n such...Too hard I'd reckon for the likes of you. To be a trapper, though...I guess you'd need to talk with Harris about that."

"Harris?"

"Fletcher Harris it is. He's the man, leastwise, tells me what to do with the furs. His, he calls 'em. He's a hard-old bat, but I 'spect he's somethin' pretty high with Hudson Bay. Aye, lad, he's the man you'll want to ask about trappin'. Be mos' careful now, boy...He just might take you to where the wild Indians'll trim your hair fer ye." His weathered face split with an sly grin.

"My hair?" Robert was baffled.

"Talk to Fletcher Harris. He'll tell you about scalps and scalpin' 'n such. Heathens, lad. They's heathens about near everywhere. I reckon they kills Long Hunters most o' the time. Cooks 'em too..."

Robert gasped. "Cooks 'em!"

"'At's right boy. Scalps 'em 'n cooks 'em 'n eats 'em, too. I heard 'bout it many times. Have yourself that talk with Fletch. He'll give 'er to ya straight...I reckon if they don't eat ya' up, you just get lost anyways. Wild it is, boy...!" His face was contorted now as he was lost within the rapture of his storytelling. "…wild, and it goes on forever. Rivers deeper'n oceans and forests a thousand leagues across. Mountains, too, lad. Some as called Rockies, they say, cain't be crossed 'cept by eagles 'n such. Talk to Fletcher, lad. He'll tell you tales 'at'll scare your pecker off. If it don't, and you go to the woods? Indians probably get that, too." He guffawed and Robert's face flushed red at the sailor's ribald joke.

That night Robert rolled in his blankets tight against the old uncle for warmth. A fog had rolled in and sleeping on the ground was a cold and damp proposition. That was the eve he dreamed all through the night. For the most part fitfully. So much so, in fact, the uncle scolded him twice for his writhing. The hard dreams were of Father and home and the smell of haggis. Troubling was the sense, somewhere deep inside him, that he may never see that home again. The sweeter side of his dreams were of rivers deeper than oceans… of forests ten leagues across…of mountains with eagles in attendance. And, mostly, of fur.

Rivers, oceans. mountains of fur filled his dreaming. And he, Robert, saw himself controlling this vast fortune. He dreamed of other men who would call him Long Hunter and look at him admiringly. They would be envious of this frontiersman. This pathfinder.

It was very near full dark now on the Canadian River, and Old Robert stirred himself from his river bank seat. He shook himself against the evening chill and to dispel those memories of so long ago in Glasgow. It seemed as though he fell into these trances more often now that he used to. He shook his head to clear his thoughts, and he was back now, back in Texas, back on the Canadian. Tomorrow would find him and Garcia heading out. They would be traveling up a trail he had helped to blaze so many years before. All he really wanted now was to find his son, Colin, unharmed.

The coyote saw his movement and like a shadow slipped easily back into the greasewood. Old Robert rubbed the stiffness from the small of his back and his buttocks. It hurt him now to sit so long. His arthritis may have been slow coming, but he sensed it was making up for lost time A horse snorted and nickered in the corral, and he thought it must be the little roan mare. He'd never really learned to love horses very much, but he had to admit this three-year old filly was about as sweet as a horse could be.

The evening damp began to set in, and he headed back toward the little adobe house. The adobe stood some distance away from the main house, but he liked it better and considered it his real home. After all, it was here years before the pile of plans called "The Big House" was ever built. No one had ever lived in the big house. No one could even fathom why Robert had caused it to be built. The little flat -roofed adobe was home to him and had always been so. He and Juan Garcia had stood off raids of Comanches, Apaches and border raiders from the stout little adobe casa with the sod roof.

Others had fought there too. Good friends they had been who had helped him build the Broken Spur. Friends who stood by his side when it had to be defended and protected. Fierce battles had happened here and old and trusted comrades had died in this place as well as enemies.

As he walked up the slight incline to the adobe, he looked over to his right as he always did. He gave a little salute to the small cemetery. There were eleven graves, barely visible now in the failing light. The final repose for the special ranch hands and vaqueros, all friends who had helped him, in one way or another, to build the Broken Spur. Of course, not all were killed fighting. The creation of a ranch from the wilderness has other ways of taking men. The Broken Spur, Old Robert realized, was purchased with the lives and blood of brave men.

Estes Cotton had died in the big flood. Little Jim Parker fell, horse and all, into a forty-foot gully while night-hawking. Some, like Wade Wills, took sick with fever, pox and the like. No question about it, Isaac Turner, the black runaway slave from the Louisiana cane fields, just got too old to breathe anymore. But there were others there, too. Others who had died by the rifle, the tomahawk and the knife. Old Robert remembered them all, loved them all, and saluted them all when he passed their last little bit of Broken Spur: the grassy knoll that would always be theirs...It seemed when one came to work at the Spur they just never left. Even in death their bones were interred within the borders of the Spur for eternity.

Robert entered the door of the cozy adobe. Juan Garcia had a small but warm fire of greasewood softly flickering. By Robert's chair was the pitcher of toddy. Juan Garcia knew, by now, just how hot to make the water, how much sugar to use to cut the fiery clear corn liquor. Garcia didn't like for Robert to drink as much as he had been lately. But on the other hand, he was the Patron. He was the Broken Spur. And he was old. And the joints and back and legs ached and yearned for rest. The whiskey gave him that rest.

And he was the best friend Juan Garcia had ever had and the best man Garcia had ever known. Tomorrow Garcia would place him in a horse-drawn buggy and start out to who knew where. He hoped his old friend would bear up well on the journey.

Old Robert sipped at the toddy, and Garcia covered his shoulders with the elk skin the old man loved. He was a bit tired now. The fire and the whiskey soothed him. He thought now about Colin as he sank deeper into his chair. He wished the boy were home. He chuckled then, at his own foolishness.

"Boy, indeed!" he snorted. Colin was more than fifty years old. Maybe nearer to sixty. To Old Robert though, he would always be the son he and Juan Garcia had raised. It seemed now Colin was gone a lot. Well, that was his job. He was the trail boss of the Broken Spur. Colin loved the trail more than anything else in the world. And, by all standards, he was so good at it. He had a natural way about him when it came to the handling of cattle, horses and men.

"That's what trail herdin's all about." Robert spoke to no one. "Trail herdin's about cattle, horses, 'n men." He missed Colin though. He wished he were home. Robert sank deeper into the robe now. Soon, sleep would be upon the old long hunter cowboy. The blessed sleep of those who have tried it all and have never been afraid.

Chapter Fifteen

Fletcher Harris
1836 (From River Clyde to Niagara)

Fletcher Harris was the most terrifying thing young Robert had ever seen. Terrifying yet exciting. Colorful and dangerous looking. He wore the buckskin clothing of the American frontier. Great sheets of fringe cascaded from his arms and legs. A ponderous mane of shaggy grey hair hung about his shoulders and blended so perfectly with his beard it gave the impression that this wild-eyed bundle of energy had no neck. He moved like a cat, smooth with a stalking motion.

His limbs were powerful. Even covered as they were by the buckskin, his calves and biceps were clearly visible. Somehow, despite his look of power. he still appeared lean and hungry. He for all the world gave Robert the impression of a ravenous lion. He roared orders to the hands that brought the furs from the hold of the clipper.

"Damage one beaver," he bellowed, "...only one, and I'll have your arse on a plate for my dinner and I'll make you eat with me. Look to it lads... Not a one of you has a pelt worth the lowest skin I own. Treat me badly once," he cried, "and the Hudson company'll have your eyes!"

The men Harris bellowed at seemed huge and brawny to Robert. They worked bare chested and Robert admired their powerful glistening arms and barrel chests. They were a dangerous looking group of five. Two wore rings in their ears. Great curving knives were thrust in their waist sashes, ready for action in a blink. Yet, these men fairly leaped when Harris spoke. The boy could see they were under his control completely. Harris moved about through the men as they worked. He paid them no more mind than if they were chickens in a barn lot. He stopped only now and then to cuff one of the men or to swear a vile curse at another.

Robert had thought fitfully between snatches of sleep the night before of taking the sailor's advice. He wanted nothing more than to ask Fletcher Harris to tell him of the Long Hunters. Now, here he was. Suddenly it came to him that he wasn't sure at all that this was really a good idea. This Harris man was quite a sight.

Harris's shoulders were so wide Robert could hardly believe it. Then his body tapered downward into a sharp v where it was gathered into corded muscle at his waist. That waist was girdled with a belt that appeared to be made of some sort of colored beads. Tucked tightly into the belt was a large bore pistol and a wicked looking, gleaming knife. A hatchet was there too, but it had a strange shape. It was like no hatchet Robert had ever seen. Most frightening of all, though, was the man's hat.

It looked to be the head of a wolf! Its yellow eyes, fixed forever, in the cold stare of the predator. Its mouth was open and revealed gleaming razor teeth, the lips pulled back in a relentless and constant snarl. Robert had never seen such a headpiece. He decided it was surely the mark of a Long Hunter.

Then, as Robert tried to summon up the courage for an approach, Fletcher Harris gave his head a mighty shake and the great shag of grey hair flew about his head as a dog's might when shaking water. As the hair fell away from the right side of his face Robert saw a small pucker of pink flesh where an ear had once flourished. The boy recoiled in horror at this sight. He felt his jaw drop open. At the same time, he tasted the sour vomit in his mouth. He fought it hard and at last came composure. He watched the loading of the ship a long time. He was, at last, losing some of his apprehension. He sat quietly on a cotton bale and watched intently as Fletcher Harris went about his deeds.

Nothing in Harris's life ever went unnoticed for very long. He was a bundle of alertness and observance. With his woodsman senses, he picked up the slightest motion… the faintest sound. The attention of this young and watchful boy was no exception. Just for a moment Robert let his eyes wander.

For an instant he glanced away from Fletcher Harris and looked down the weathered planking towards the end of the dock. Out to the sea. When he turned his face back his heart leaped in his chest. Harris had moved directly to his side and was not two feet away. Robert recoiled instinctively.

"Here boy…What're you about?" the trapper demanded. The wolf's head appraised Robert with a hungry stare.

"No harm, good sir! No harm!" Robert blurted. He jumped clearly three feet away from the fierce face that was thrust at him. "No harm meant here, good sir. It's just watchin', I am… Watchin'…wishin'…That is, wishin' to talk a bit. Are you Master Harris? Master Fletcher Harris?"

Chapter Sixteen

Bloody Evansville
1840

Robert lay on the deck of the keel boat in the warmth of the spring's noonday sun. Hungry flies had disturbed his dreamless rest. They buzzed about relentlessly, hoping to make a meal of the glossy, dried blood that matted his hair to his scalp like plumber's putty. He heard the strained grunts of the pole men as they forced the keel boat to their will. For the longest time he couldn't imagine where he might be or how he got there. He touched a spot above his ear gingerly, and pain fairly bolted through his head. Now he took notice; it was a pain reflected throughout his whole body.

What in the world is the matter here? His thought was random and disorganized. He began to try and clear his head and take some kind of an inventory. He groaned aloud. The multitude of hurts and aches was burdensome.

"Look here, boys, our sleepin' beauty is about wakin'." The voice was not unfamiliar to Robert, yet not so common to him that he could quite place it. He tried to raise his body up on his elbows but a new pain stabbed him now. It sharply gouged him somewhere low in his belly. He at last brought himself to rest on an unsteady elbow and craned his neck for a look.

The front of his buckskin breeches was dark and caked with dried blood. Great multi -colored bottle flies were busily searching for any blood that still might be liquid enough for their grisly diet. Their blue and gold metallic bodies glistened in the sun light.

My God, thought Robert, *It's me manhood. My God, I've lost me powers!* Pain or no, he sat bolt upright now.

"Be easy, boy. Ease into it. You don't need to recover yer'self all at once."

It was the voice again. And there was the sound of laughter too, men laughing... big hearty voices filled with mirth. Roberts' thoughts were too blurred to understand. His head was swimming. As he tried to find the source of the laughter he suddenly realized he wasn't seeing very well either. He tried to rub his eyes with his fists but when he touched himself he recoiled in agony. His whole face was swollen, even torn in places, and sore beyond understanding. Then he realized his eyes were nearly pasted shut. Glued shut as they were with dried, caked blood....

He was becoming desperate now for some understanding, some bit of orientation. He groaned aloud, and his plea was answered by a full pail of cold river water thrown directly and none too gently into his face. Some of the Ohio River found its way up his nostrils and down his throat right in the middle of a substantial groan. It was one of the shocks Robert would always remember. Through the coughing and gagging, though, he finally came around a bit. He felt himself being lifted into a sitting position now by a strong and steady arm. A gentle but deep, powerful voice seemed to be trying to comfort him. In the background, though, behind the voice, he could still hear the laughter. The water's dissolving powers began to work now, and he found he could open his eyes to the full. Then he saw the face. The face...He knew that face...It was the Evansville face, the trapper. Was it Barker? Parker?... No.. It was...Baker.... That's it. It's Hubert Baker.

Piece by piece it started coming back now: It was the west end of Evansville. There was a place...a dark place that smelled of whiskey. A colored man with a banjo. He had never heard of a banjo. It made a merry tune he recalled. The thoughts flooded in faster now, but he was still totally baffled as to where he was or how he came to be here.

He remembered meeting Hubert Baker though. What was the name of that place? Coongetters? Was it Coonget...No...? Coonhunters Tavern. That was it. That's where he had met Baker. Coonhunters Tavern in the west end of Evansville. It was at the mouth of the creek, where Pigeon Creek fed into the Ohio.

The meeting had indeed been an eventful one. Here was Robert, totally dissatisfied with the furs of the Ohio valley, and who should he meet but a real Long Hunter. Hubert Baker was home from the Rockies to recruit a band to trap the high Crow country. The land where the Rockies crossed the border of American territory and swept up into Canada.

Robert and Baker had casually met at the bar of the Coonhunter. Over smooth Kentucky whiskey, they had talked and talked. Robert had been invited to join the band of six that now tried merrily to drink up all the whiskey on the river. Now that they knew who he was, and from where he had come, he was exactly the experienced trapper the Baker band was looking for. Robert recalled now, he had drunk more than he'd ever allowed himself before. But it was the company, not just the whiskey. These men were not fat bellied, Dutch farmers with a few traps in the local ponds. These were Indian fighters and explorers. These were, By God, Mountain Men. The very men Robert had crossed the Atlantic to find.

Now the trappers, in their drunkenness. began to dance with one another to the thin twang of the banjo. They whooped and leapt about, filling the cavernous tavern with their laughter. Suddenly the one they called Axel was standing on the bar crowing like a rooster. He held a gleaming ten inch knife in one hand, with the other he held his brass-trimmed flintlock rifle aloft. In his fringed buckskins and a hat made from a wildcat, he was the most colorful and wonderful thing Robert had ever seen. At least, since the talks with Fletcher Harris back in Glasgow. That was long ago. So very long ago. Now Axel began to crow again.

"I'm half horse." He bellowed. "Half horse on my Momma's side and my Daddy was a full growed, Seminole gator. I got the fastest horse, the purtiest wife, the ugliest dog and the surest rifle in the By God Rockie Mountains. I eats bears and injuns for my brekfas and I can whup up on any man what cain't out run me. When I walks, I sounds like the thunder. When I drinks whiskey there's lightnin' about ..."

It was coming back to Robert now in vivid detail although his head hurt like the hinges of hell. There was a girl too, a girl called Anna. And more whiskey and more dancing. And a big fellow, too. He was a.... gambler. He was the gambler from the tables. Robert had grabbed at Anna. She was kissing...and touching... and laughing....and she was a swirl of hair...and eyes. She whirled in a dance, and her skirt billowed. He recalled bare legs and more laughing.... now her arms were at his neck, her lips brushing his, and she was touching him...touching him here then there... that private place. He felt her tight against him, soft, molding herself to him.... Then something slammed his head.. And there was a knife. Was there a knife? Yes, a knife. A big knife. And a gun. That's it. There was a gun, It fired. Smoke and flame in the dark tavern and a stabbing searing pain deep inside. And blood...And blackness. Blackness...black...His thoughts were interrupted.

"River rats cleaned you out I guess, Rob." The voice was strong and steady.

"Leastwise, they got to yer' canoe and took whate'er you had in her."

Feeling an instant wave of panic, Robert's hand went swiftly to his waist. It was still there. Thank God it was still there. He felt the reassuring weight of the buckskin money belt.

"Your money's still all together, boy. If it is money in that belt. Me and these here boys don't go round stealin' or peekin' into things ain't our'n." Roberts' hands trembled with relief.

"Me'n the boys just kinda' fetched you along. Figured if we left ya' there, that big card playin' man would-a sure kilt your skinny ass. Course had we left you with that purty li'l tavern gal, she'd-a prob'ly drained you down to just a shadow. She'd-a prob'ly kilt ya' too had she known about that there belt. We just dragged you here to save you from all that sinnin' and them men with big knives and guns and such." Robert heard the laughter behind the strong voice. "We can let ya' out anywhere along the river here you say. We been draggin' your canoe along a'hind us... We can sit you out anywhere's you say. But you have been shot. You might want to lay about a day or two. That's alright, too, Rob. It's up to you."

"Am I...?" Robert was afraid to ask.

"You're in one piece alright, boy, though I sure'n hell don't know why. He tried his level best to shoot you in the balls, but I reckon his aim was just a bit high. Pistol ball jus' sorta' bounced off your hip bone I'd guess. I'd say he had a few buckshot mixed in his load considern' 'tother wounds too. I'm pretty sure you're in fair health though. Hell, he shot you three days ago. Yo aint dead yet!"

Me and the boys plugged up the holes. Tamped 'em with some rags and poured on a little kerosene an' some whiskey. Must a burned like hell. You did some fair, pissin' and moanin'. Even bein' out near cold like you was. But after three days? I'd bet on you. Damn if whiskey don't make you 'bout as feisty as they come. You right sure you ain't a Irishman 'stead o' Scot?" The frontiersman flashed a wicked grin.

"Lawd sakes, child. You just get a little whiskey and right away you start wantin' to feel up them little bar gals. I tells' you, Rob boy, that makes for a passel o' trouble. 'Course you can handle it.. Your old head bone dulled that feller's knife up to a fair-thee-well."

"What about my head?" Robert gingerly touched his scalp. It stung like fire.

"Head's fine, too. Them damn knife slashes about the head near always bleeds just somethin' fierce. We sewed you up some, where we could get a sail needle through. Me'n the boys talked about it. Your old head hide is tougher'n a gator's back. You'll live, Robert. Just toughen up a bit. How's for a big drink o' genuine, river water and some Kentucky race-horse piss whiskey?" Robert nearly gagged. The word "whiskey" made his stomach lurch.

"Well, I'm interested in livin' right enough, Hubert, but as for bein' tough, I 'spect right now I'm a little too delicate for more whiskey." It was the one called Axel who spoke up now.

"Count yersef lucky you didn't get out there west o' Pigeon Creek. One o' them big stout German farm gals was to wrap her legs about yer scrawny ass and you'd be done to where we couldn't save you with no sail needle." The trappers broke out in hearty laughter at this bawdy remark. Though it pained and embarrassed him some, Robert eventually joined their noisy guffaws.

Hubert Baker and the Trapper Band

The next days were long and lazy as the keel boat drifted along with the Ohio's current. Robert lay on the little deck crowded by supplies, wicker baskets of steel traps and the shuffling feet of the pole men. It had been a long time since Robert had been this inactive; and, even though he needed this rest for healing, he began to be a bit listless.

He watched Hubert Baker every day and came to a new understanding of this burly frontiersman. When he had met Baker first, at the Evansville tavern, he had assumed him to be a brawler and a hard drinker. Now, he began to see him in a different light. Hubert Baker, Robert was finding out, was a hard working and intently industrious man.

Much larger than the wiry frame that was Robert; the muscular Baker seemed tireless, almost relentless in his labors. He was in total command of his men, too, but Robert noticed he never abused anyone. The commands he gave commanded respect and yet somehow were respectful. He found time to look after Robert, too. Fetching him food or water and helping him to the rail when needed.

Some days in the warmth of the afternoon Baker would shed his weighty buckskin shirt. Robert saw then just how powerfully built was Baker. His arms were roped with corded sinew, and his wide shoulders and deep chest gathered at the waist in hard muscular knots. His straight black hair was worn shoulder length or sometimes gathered into a tail at the back of his head. On these days, he wore a leather band about his brow to hold back the unruly mop. It seemed to Robert that Baker's eyes were the darkest he'd ever seen. In further contrast to Robert, whose pale body was nearly hairless, Baker's swarthy chest was a virtual blanket of thick and black curly hair.

"Is they beavers back there in that Niagara River you talks about?" Baker asked.

Robert sensed it was a test question. Baker was trying to find out if Robert was truly an experienced trapper or only dreamed of being one.

"Naw," Robert replied. "Big river. Fastest river, too. Big and deep. Too much water in the main river for beaver. Creek's though. Feeder streams and such hold beaver in fair amounts. You know how beaver are I'd 'spect. They look for waters they can block up and make they pools. Sure not the Niagara. Big water 'n fast as anything. Get back on the creeks, though, with a little castor 'n you can do right well sometimes".

It was the right answer.

"You know about castor?" Baker's face was entirely a great grin. His strong white teeth contrasted, gleaming against his coaly beard. Good trappers knew there were many baits that might attract a beaver but only one that would work every time: Castoreum.

It was from the scent gland contents found at either side of the root of the beaver's tail. The strong smelling, amber fluid found there was the beavers' mating call. When the beaver lay down castor by spraying it about as a skunk leaves scent, it would attract breeding beaver for incredibly long distances. As a trapping lure, it was close to fool proof. When Robert recalled how castor scent drove beaver beyond reason and into the waiting deadly steel he, for some unknown reason, thought of the saloon girl named Anna. He remembered how she had felt, pressing her body, against him. Somehow this recollection made him, further recall his father's advice of years ago. The talk they had concerning the use of fox urine to bait his traps for foxes.

" It's the things we know best.," Robert thought. "The things we know, and sometimes the things we love, that are our undoing." He made a secret vow to always do his best to keep his head and heart separated. The festered and slow healing bullet wound in his lower belly seemed an adequate reminder.

In truth, Robert did know a lot about beaver. He knew, for instance, the real name of the secreted liquid was Castoreum. Castor was the gland's name that manufactured the magic scent. He knew that both male and female produced these tantalizing scents and were interchangeable as trapping lures. Robert thought beaver to be one of God's most fascinating creatures. Unlike most wild animals that give birth to their young in spring, beaver utilized the coldest of months for whelping, January and February. Beaver matured for breeding at two to three years. After that, a female in good health could have an annual whelp of two to eight pups every year. She could maintain this proclivity for about sixteen amazing years.

"It's eatin' 'em I likes." It was Patch speaking now and intruding on Roberts' thoughts of Beaver. Patch was the Long Hunter from Kentucky.

Nearly everyone listened to Patch when he spoke. After all, it had been his granddaddy that followed Daniel Boone over the Allegheny and through Moccasin Gap. He and Boone had been among the very first white men into the sacred territory of the Mingo and Shawnee. They had named the land, Kain-tah-kee, the Shawnee words for "dark and bloody place." From Kain-tah-kee came the word, Kentucky. Patch still carried the respect his ancestor had earned for all his descendants.

"I eats them beaver's tails when I can," he allowed. "You jes' lays that ole tail on a flat rock by a good fire. Purty soon the outer skin starts to blisterin' away. The meat inside is all white and flaky like. Jes' sweeten' pie...specially if you got some salt. 'Bout ever' body I know loves them tails. All them Catholic farmers back in Ohio got the priest to say beaver tail was fish. He said that alright cause with the skin still on it is kinda' scaly. That made it fine for them to eat tails when they wants too. You know, Fridays and such. We get some beaver soon an' old Patch'll show you how to cook it up right enough."

Robert was coming to like this group of self-reliant men more each day. He liked the way they stuck together and looked one to the other. Though they were close as comrades could be, yet each seemed to respect the others' space. Robert had come to feel that part of this mutual respect was built on the fact that each of his new-found companions was just a little bit dangerous. That and the fact that each one knew that fact about the others.

"Look up the high bank there, Scotty boy." Hubert Baker called out. "That there is Cave in Rock. That's where, they say old Sam Mason and the Harpe brothers killed mor'en forty folks. This here is called Shawneetown area by some. I'd reckon some of them Ohio Shawnees have been here alright...Mingo too probably. Them there pirates though...they was all white men. You know. Je'ss lowdown murderin' scum. Jim Ford too. He was another bad one. Worst of all maybe. I went up that high bank to see that cave for myself once two or three years back. That old hole goes back 'bout a hundred feet or so. Mason, he sets himself up a tavern in that rock. He offers the river travelers whisky, cards and women. What they got though was their heads bashed in and a long sleep at the bottom of the Ohio. Spaylaywethepee the Shawnee's calls her. Seneca's say Ohiyo...Means beautiful. And she is a fine river ain't she?"

The pirates of Cave-In-Rock had terrorized river traffic from the time of the American revolution right up to the eighteen thirties. Preying mostly on unwary settlers moving west along the "Ohio Corridor" on their keelboats. Many of these river travelers just disappeared, never to be heard from again. From time to time, some of their identifiable belongings would show up at various river trading posts. The bearer of these suspicious items always had the same story:

"Got it from the Indians in a trade." It was heard so often it would've been laughable had it not been for the tragic fact that innocent people were being murdered, their livestock driven off, personal property stolen, and their keelboats burned to the water line. Sometimes, it was rumored, the women and girls were kept alive for long periods of time, serving their captors in various forms of slavery that usually had more to do with the captive's personal beauty and youth than any other factor. Robert shuddered even when he thought of it. "What happened to them?" Robert wanted to know. "The pirates?"

"They just got too greedy. See that south bank over yonder?" He motioned with a sweeping arm. "That there is Henderson County Kentucky. One of the first places on the river to have any law that really amounted to much. They got themselves a sheriff and he did the one thing that just about always wipes the noses of the really bad men. He posted a bounty of a thousand dollars on Sam Mason. One thousand cool American dollars dead or alive. Doesn't take long afore the Harpe brothers started countin' that money. Knifed old Sam in the back. They took his head to Henderson in a basket figuring to collect that reward. Only that sheriff? Why he recognized the boys right off. Big double hangin' they had that day in Henderson. That cleaned up the river."

"What about that Jim Ford fellow?" Robert asked."

"Oh, they got him too." Baker went on. He was havin' some supper with a woman he favored in a little shack when a Kentucky posse tracked him down. Come out of there they holler. Go to hell he hollers back. That posse just opens up with them Long Tom Kentucky rifles on that little shack. I heard tell old Jim was shot about twenty or more times. Anyways, what was left weren't fit for hangin. Dangdest thing though and best part of the story, I heard was when they was buryin' him the day was a rainy muddy one and the coffin slipped from their hands and fell endwise, head down right into that open grave. Seems with the mud and all it was just too hard to right that casket so them sextons just covered it up like it was. They told everyone that Jim Ford went to hell head first." Robert sniggered at the macabre tale and at once was ashamed of himself to laugh at a man's death no matter how humorous.

Baker went on, "Oh there was a few bad ones still tried to feed of the settlers movin' west on the river but after about eighteen thirty things were pretty safe along here. You still have to watch out though. This is wild country. Best not to forget that."

That night Robert's sleep was a restless one as he dreamt of piracy, treachery and the double hanging in Henderson County. Most disturbing thought was the vision of the head in the basket.

Wings of the Carousel

The Old Uncle moved slowly and alone back up the trail from Glasgow to Inverness. He wondered how his brother, Adam, would receive the news that Robert was gone. The trapper, Fletcher Harris, it turned out, was looking for a new apprentice at precisely the time he'd met young Robert on the docks at Glasgow. Robert had never been a lad to deceive anyone, and so the first thing he had done was to bring Harris to their campsite along the road to meet the Old Uncle.

"He'll do fine, Master Trav." Fletcher Harris was a gifted and persuasive speaker. "I'll care for him as my own. He'll work by my side along the fair streams o' America. All days he'll be in the fair sun and learnin' the ways to have wealth of his own. The work is fair, the pay is high and, if sir you'll permit a small boast, he'll be a learnin' from one o' the very best. It's the way I started, sir, and today, be assured, I owns a penny's worth and more o' my company's stocks and credits."

The Old Uncle could see that Robert was certainly ready to go. The thrill of fur and its riches had firmly gripped his heart. If those stories the sailor had spun of wild Indians had been intended to frighten Robert, they had failed. In truth, they had only served to sweeten the pot and whet his appetite for this adventure more sharply.

"But his father," Clyde Trav had tried to explain, "...the lad's father has trusted me with the boy and his return. Can't it wait until the next voyage? Can't I bring the lad back here then for another trip?"

But he concluded he was pleading a losing cause. In truth, Clyde and Adam Trav had previously discussed the boy's future. Eventually they knew he'd need to be on his own. It was just that neither of them was prepared for this turn of events right now. It just came about too soon.

"Good fortune ne'er waits, as you know, Master Trav. Nay, I fear it'll be this voyage for Robert nor none. But fear not, Master Trav. 'Tis a year we speak of not eternity. A year it is, two at the very most. Five year is what the company insists on, but I'm willin' to make an exception to young Robert here. And, bye the bye, Master Trav, families' general pays me an apprentice fee for turnin' their lads into men. On this one special occasion, however, I'll agree, if somewhat reluctant, to take the lad aboard at my own expense. It's that I've taken to him, ye' know. It's that, and his obvious love for furs."

"Please, Uncle." Robert pleaded. "Just tell Father I'm off to become as good a man as he himself is. Tell him and Momma I love them, Uncle. I love them and that's why I go now to the Americas."

"The Hudson Bay Company, you say? He'll be workin' for the Hudson Bay Company? Apprenticin' that is to say?"

"You're right as rain, Master Trav. Its real name is Hudson's Bay, you know. With an "S" at the end. Nobody ever says it that way though. Everybody jus' says Hudson Bay or even just H.B.C. And a fine old company it is, too. I'm hopin' soon to be a Factor."

"A Factor?" The old uncle asked.

"It's what we calls our leaders. Our bosses, if you don't mind. I'm already a Minor Factor in the Niagara trade. And I hope to be a regular company Factor any season now. That's why they send me so many places. I know most of the company's business, I do. That's why they sends me everywhere. Why, I been to Nova Scotia and clear west to Winnipeg. Seen me the Rocky Mountains, too, I have. Been to San 'Frisco. Lots o' places sir. I seen lots o' places."

"But I thought the Hudson Bay, 'er that is to say, Hudson's Bay Company, was just only up in Canada. Maybe even by the north pole." Clyde Trav was more than curious now.

Fletcher Harris carefully considered his answers now. He knew that a prudent Scott was liable to check up his story. He was determined to tell the exact truth as temptingly as he could.

"You're right again. From Lake Superior, Lake Huron too… north is where the bulk o' the company lies. But I'll tell you, Master Trav, we's everywhere. We got traders and trappers in America, too. That 'Merican, John Jacob Astor, thinks he can do as well with the 'Merican Company." as he call's it. There's a North West Company too, I guess. I ain't heard just who's at the helm there. Their piddlin' small you know? Wont 'mount to much I 'spects. Astor, too. They's jes' small besides the H.B.C. We got us a fine, big place at Albany. 'Course, I runs the hide yard at old fort Niagara. "Course we pays duty on the catch we take in 'Merica, but we trade everywhere there's pelts.

"Ain't just pelts we're about neither. We do trades in sugar and tea. Got us a whiskey and rum business goes clear to Cape Horn in South America. That's the end o' the world you know? There's big warehouses in Virginia with Hudson's Bay tobacco fillin' 'em to the seams. King George smokes Hudson's Bay tobacco and old Frenchy Napoleon, too, I hears. We holds big land grants from the King himself all over Canada and way north to the pole herself. Why I tell you, Master Trav, The Hudson's Bay outfit ain't truly a company at all but it's more of a kingdom. Mints our own money, we does. And trades big in salted salmon and arctic whale bone and ivories from Russian Alaska." Fletcher Harris was moved now by his own rhetoric. As he spoke, he became more colorful and dramatic by the moment. His audience, of two, were spellbound.

"Why, there on the 'Merican sea coast they's a town called New Bedford where our whalin' men sails out and kills big whales. Like swimmin' barns, they are. Biggest things in the whole world. Not just in the Atlantic, mind you, but in the world. These men sails clean around the horn and kills whales off Mexico and California. Russia, too. They cooks them whales into oil right on the ships. We owns much of that oil, Master Trav. It's us what sponsors them ships. We owns some, too, I'd reckon. We fills up lamps around the world, we do.

"But they's nothin' we covet as we do the beaver. I'll tell you true sirs, it's that little flat-tail river rat that puts the big ships to sea, and brings men to the froze up north and makes 'em rich. Was a time we had to take the beaver through the ice with harpoons and the like. Men froze to death, drownded too, but they never quit huntin' the fur. Catch was mighty poor that way you know.

"Things are a might different now though. Just about ten year ago or so....1823 I thinks, maybe, a fellow from around Onieda, New York, In amongst them finger lakes goes and invents the steel trap. His name was Newhouse I remembers... Yes, it was. Sewell Newhouse. Anyways, since then, the beaver catch gets good enough to build a grander and richer company on. It's the steel what takes 'em by the thousands. Nobody drowns no more while tryin' to harpoon beavers. Now they's real money afoot for them as can catch beaver. That's what it is about them compeeters. Before the steel trap, the Hudson's Company was the only outfit with men enough to man the harpoon. Now, with the comin' of the trap, we starts to hear of Astor and his likes. They weren't there when the hunt was a rougher game." Harris could see his knowledge was captivating to the listening pair.

"Fine gentry wears them beaver hats, and make no mistake about it, I'm the one what ketch's 'em. Its beaver we'll hunt, Master Trav. It's gold That's a-walkin' on four paws."

"How many beavers are there? Can the world use so many hats?" Old Uncle asked.

"Beavers spread south from the North Pole way the hell down to the Rio Grande River; which I hears is off in Godforsaken Texas. I ain't sure where Texas be, but they say beavers live in half the world. Last year, just in London, the Kings Auction was of more'n five hundred thousand skins and that there's a half a million!" Both the Uncle and Robert gasped at such a figure.

"I tell you, Master Trav, your boy'll do just fine with us. They's none alive can say what we can, good sir. Here it is barely 1824, and the Hudson's Bay Company's nearin' a hundred and fifty years old. Who else can claim as much? Got us a passel of Scots a-workin' with us too. Them Frenchies, you know, thinks they own all the fur. But for me, I'll hail the bonnie Scot. They all's make the best trappers don't you know." Harris knew that he had spun a mighty yarn...A lot of it true. He also new he was near to acquiring a new apprentice.

Finally Clyde Trav could hear no more. He had to admit Fletcher Harris knew more about the beaver trade than he ever dreamed there was to know. He knew that men had been made rich by fur, but Harris had overwhelmed him with the adventurous potential. He made success sound more of likelihood than a gamble.

"Leave us, Master Harris. Leave us to family talk. If this thing is to be, I'll have the boy at your ship at first light. But there's family matters here that men must be alone for."

"Understands completely, I does. Lad, I'll say good night to your uncle and you and leave your good fire. It'll be with a glad heart if I spies you on the morrow's early light. It'll be you 'n me boy. We'll catch the beaver together. We'll see the great forests and trade with the red man. Join me if you can, and wear a wolf head of yer own."

As silent as a shadow, Fletcher Harris withdrew into the darkness. That night Robert and his uncle lay on Scottish soil under Scottish skies and talked until dawn.

How can an uncle tell a boy all the things his father should tell him and do so in the span of an eve?' Old Uncle worried.

When they were at last talked out, Clyde Trav gave his nephew a leather sack. It was not very large, but Robert knew it contained gold.

"Rob," he said, "I know you feel you know this Harris man and its maybe that you do. But hear me well now, son, for these are the very words your father would speak were he here: Wait till you know him a lot longer before you trust him, boy. Keep your eye on him and see how he treats others. Mos' 'specally look to how he treats them below him in station or those weaker than himself. Watch him too about the traps lad. Trappin's rough enough as it is, but there's men who hurt caught animals more than what's vital.

Cruel men, son have no place in this world. Cruel men and liars are the Devil's own children, Robert. Your father and I want you always protected from such. 'Tis gold in the bag, boy, and a fair amount of it, too.

There's more than enough to bring you home to Scotland if need be. I tell you now, nephew, no matter how you come to care for this Fletcher Harris, ne'er tell him of your gold. You'll see it soon enough, boy. But mark: It's whiskey, women and gold that makes tall men stoop low."

When Adam Trav received the news of Robert's departure for America, with the trapper Fletcher Harris, he said nothing. Clyde Trav had really expected to be chastised sharply or at least upbraided somewhat for returning home without his brother's son. This silence was the last reaction he would've expected. Adam heard it all without interrupting or even speaking once. Then, without a word, just walked out of his small house and sat on a stone bench at the side of the garden. He seemed just to be staring off into space. Clyde Trav felt confused and disoriented. The silence of acceptance was mixing him up, and he felt like crying or laughing at once. His heart was a stone in his breast. He felt the urge to flee. The silence of his brother had become an unbearable weight

.Then he heard a slight sob. Looking into the shadows by the fireplace he saw the soft cry had come from Robert's mother. He had scarcely noticed her before. The delicate crying broke the spell though and brought back some reality. It relieved the pressure just because it made sense. It was right to cry for an absent son. Old Uncle was grateful. He felt better now.

It was now late at night, and the moon was high over Scotland. Adam Trav sat alone on the stone bench at the precise moment that his son, Robert, stood on the gently rolling deck of the clipper Carousel. Her sails were spread against the night winds. She was a dancing, graceful bird on the crests of the foam. Neither Robert nor his father could possibly know that they were both contemplating the same moon at the same time.

Alike, they had been told Fletcher Harris's story of "Only a year...two at the very most." Neither believed the tale. Somehow, deep down inside, they both innately sensed they would never see each other again. The night was colder now. Adam Trav pulled his neck deeper into his high, coat collar.

Somewhere out on the Atlantic, a thin, young boy looked into the wake of his ship. He realized, somewhere, back there in the dark was Scotland. He was leaving everything behind he had ever known. He understood, full well, that he had to steel up his courage now. It was time to be a man.

"Damn," he said. "Damn and Hell." He never cursed but did so now in frustration. He could be a man tomorrow. Tonight, he allowed him self to shed one single tear. "t is a small tear, he thought. And the ocean sea is so much larger than ever I had thought.

Chapter Seventeen

Saint Lou, Big Muddy and the Hawken Rifle
1841

The Ohio River, for the most part, is a gentle flowing ribbon of water. Nearly a mile wide, it runs clear and cold in the northeast mouth. Her founder is the expulsion from the fork of the Allegheny and the Monongahela near old Fort Pitt and Pittsburgh settlement. From this point, called Three Rivers, the Ohio meanders to the south and west more than a hundred and fifty leagues. The water's browning some as she flows, and at last she becomes a wide, deep and sweet sister to the Mississippi. It pours its sweet, green- brown waters into this vast muddy waterway just north of Memphis, Tennessee, and south of Saint Louis, Missouri.

For most of its thousand-mile odyssey, she drifts along in an aimless gallivant to the southwest. Her lazy currents are bordered by the wooded and often wild territories of Pennsylvania, West Virginia, Ohio, Kentucky, Indiana, and Illinois. It's only the stretch of water that spans from the port of Louisville to the little burg of Yellow Banks that the river was known for her rough currents and dangerous eddies. Many thousands of years ago a deep waterfall had existed here. The millennia of flowing currents had eaten most of the falls sheer drop away, leaving a swift running and treacherous spillway.

"Falls Rough," the river men called her at this point. Louisville became known as Falls City, and it's here in this stretch that many settlers bound for the west would lose their keelboats or flat-bottom skiffs or perhaps their lives. Finally she slows again and runs, headlong, into the continent's largest waterway. She finds and joins the Mississippi at the Missouri border.

Spay-lay-we-thee-pee, the Shawnee would call her, the water with no end forever. To the white settlers she has been called the link between the eastern shores and the Louisiana Purchase land, the mid-western third of America. A sweet waterway, her only curses were the treachery of the Falls City flume and the periodic ambushes of the Shawnee and the Mingo. These were small prices to pay when river travel is compared to the burdensome overland expeditions through the thickest hardwood forests yet seen in America.

For a time, all who would journey west must first ride upon the wild wake of the Ohio. For ten miles or so the river was fearsome and frothy here. Other than this short span and the constant watchfulness for hostile Indians or river pirates, it was an easy and pleasurable keelboat ride down the Ohio. Since the ride from Evansville was already a hundred miles south of Falls City, Robert found these days of easy travel truly a pleasure, even restful, if somewhat lackluster. He was about mended now from the Evansville fight, and there was little to do except keep the boat to the channels, avoid floating debris and wave to the occasional passing steamboat.

"Will we ride currents clear to the Rockies?" he asked Hubert Baker.

"You'll wish that before we're done," Baker answered. "When we hit the Mississip' we turn north agin the current for a spell. Lots o' hard pullin' there. Real back breakin', it is. After we get to Saint Lou we'll look into storin' this here keeler. We'll lay 'er up somewheres. That or maybe sell her to some river man.

"Once we get this here boat business settled up, we'll take passage up the Big Muddy on a steamboat. That current's too mighty for a boat like this one. And don't be forgettin' that ole river's more'n two thousand miles long. We'll be travlin' most near all of it.

"I've done it before in canoes and the like," Baker continued, "...but we're a big party. Too many hands to spread out in canoes. That Missouri river pours all the way from the Yellowstone up in Montana. It'll be runnin' agin' us all the way. We'd be all wore out afore ever we saw a Rocky mountain. I guess I ain't got no interest in ever canoein' it again. Tell you the truth, Rob, we'll start to droppin' our men off when we hit the Platte over in Nebraska country." Baker had Robert's full interest now.

A river of two-thousand-mile length seemed incredible. That was nearly the distance he had traveled across the Atlantic.

Baker went on with the authority of one who had executed his plan before. "We'll drop 'em off one at a time and sort of feel our way to the Colorado territory. I figure me 'n you'll go to the end of the line if it's right with you."

Robert agreed wholeheartedly with this part of Baker's plan. He longed to see all the river and its wild lands.

"We'll be better off travelin' with the steamboat too on account o' the Indians. They're just camped 'bout everywhere along big Muddy. They ain't much danger to a big party, but when you're down on the river in canoes, and if you get all strung out... Well, you just never know."

"What kinds of Indians will we be seeing?" Robert wanted to know. He had lived four years among some of the eastern woodland tribes when he worked along the Niagara with Fletcher Harris. Or, rather, had slaved for him, which was a sight more correct. He knew the Delaware, the Chop Tank and even the Iroquois pretty well, he thought. These western redmen were a different matter. He was anxious about them and what to expect.

"You'll see a passel of 'em 'fore we're through, Scotty. Buffalo hunters of the big plains mostly. Cheyenne, Arapaho, Mandan. Some Blackfoot. And of course, the Crow. You'll catch on soon enough, Rob, but I'll tell you right now, them Crow are a pain. They're just everywhere and into everything. Mos' unreliable folk they are too, Rob. They's all sweet 'n friendly one minute, and the next day they're paintin' their faces, poundin' hell out of a bunch of drums, and they're just meanern' hornets. The young women all want to bed with you, the young men all want your scalp; and the old folks all want to cook you over a slow fire.

Hear me good, Rob, Arapaho 'n Flatheads; that's where to spend your time. They don't do no warrin' lest you really put 'em out. They's good to trade with, too. Believe me, Rob, was I never to see a Crow again it wouldn't pain me all that much."

It took sixteen days in Saint Louis for the party of Long Hunters to complete their arrangements for the trip up the Missouri. Hubert Baker was experienced in this endeavor. He seemed to take a genuine delight in showing the sights of this exciting, western outpost to the wide-eyed Robert Trav.

Robert, for the first time since he left Scotland, allowed himself to spend some of the gold Old Uncle had pressed upon him the night before the trip on the Carousel. He dared not spend too much. He knew not when he'd likely see money again. There were many German and Dutch in Saint Louis residence now, and the two travelers ate their fill of the finest sausages Robert had ever tasted. Scrapple, too. That rich, Dutch mixture of cornmeal, spices and pork reminded Robert of haggis, but he had to admit it was more flavorful. Robert believed there was no flavor, however, to compare with Saint Louis beer. He drank it readily. But he never forgot the Evansville beating. At the very first sign of intoxication he would shut off the beer drinking instantly. He, at the urging of Baker, Patch and Axle, visited a brothel for his first time, too.

"It's the thing to do before a trip as the one we face," Patch had told him. "Long Hunters allus' does this, an' I'd be hard pressed to trust a man who didn't."

Robert selected a rather plump German farm girl who seemed a bit better scrubbed than the five or six other offerings. He well remembered Axle' descriptions of the German girls west of Pigeon Creek and wondered if this comely and pleasant lass could, indeed, be so dangerous.

When he left her, he was one of his precious coins short. But there was more to it than just the coin. He wondered, nearly aloud, so great was his confusion. This was it? This was the thing that all men seek so relentlessly? Was it this coupling of bodies that had driven Fletcher Harris mad and nearly caused his own death in the Evansville river saloon? It was true the whole affair had been a pleasurable one. But he failed to see what the fuss was all about.

The girl was lively and jolly and did all the things she knew to bring him pleasure. The act of intercourse itself had been without fault or flaw. It had gone about as he had anticipated that it would. Why then did he feel so vacant? Was it for this simple, physical gratification he had nearly lost his life in the Evansville fight? Indeed, was this experience something to die for? Or to kill for? From what he had experienced thus far, he knew many men would answer this question with a resounding "Yes!"

He felt there might be something wrong with him. He had found the occurrence sweet and memorable: But worth risking life for? Or taking a life for? Somehow it seemed so much less important to him that. The act seemed so much less vital than he had imagined that it would be when it finally took place. The feeling bothered him greatly. It even caused him to question his own manhood. It was the next day he bothered Patch with this dilemma.

"Nothin' wrong with the way you feels, son. It has to do with the difference in men. Why there's men what can lay about with any female they can find. They's the ones who love the huntin' of women to bed with. Not the actual beddin' itself. But that ain't you, I'm thinkin'. You're apt to be one of those men who might like that sort of dalliance somewhat. But I'm thinkin' to really feel it, the way you think you ought to, you wants to be really lovin' some old girl, sure 'nuff carin' 'bout her and all." It seemed ludicrous to hear this crusty old trapper speak of sentimental subjects like love and caring. Robert had to stifle an embarrassed snicker. He felt his face flush, and he knew his ears would soon redden.

"Laugh as you will. I'm tellin' you Old Patch knows a right smart about love, I does. 'Course, I ain't never been in no love but I got me a pretty female cousin what's a school ma'am. She knows all 'bout love and stuff like that. Tol' me mos' all I knows, she did."

Robert came closer now. If a school ma'am had said these things to Patch they must be so.

"There's men about who feels different about women than my gang. The band I hangs with are called whoremongers, Alicia says. That's my female cousin's name, Alicia. But you're not one of these." Patch continued. He was speaking slowly now, instructing the youth in a serious matter.

"There's nothin' wrong with them, and there's nothin' wrong with you. You'll just have to come to terms with the fact you're different than me. That fact alone ought to pleasure you a great deal." He grinned a wide beam, displaying numerous gaps caused by missing teeth. Both men laughed aloud.

Walking away, Robert gave great weight to the advice of such an experienced sage. There may indeed be something in what he said. The German girl was pretty and pleasing, but Robert didn't even know her name. Or, if he did know, it he had already forgotten it.

Perhaps it was as Patch had said. Some men do better with one woman than with many. He was pretty sure his one woman, if he ever found her at all, would not be last night's sweet and stout strumpet. He might have to look a long time to find the one that suited him. He vowed he would do just that.

But then, what if he didn't suit her? His mind was reeling now with too much thought. It would be a good idea not to think any more on the subject for now. Perhaps he should go and have a mug of cooled Saint Louis beer. That, he thought, might clear his head considerably.

He had to admit, though, that if he hadn't taken last night's occurrences quite so seriously, if he hadn't tried to analyze the situation, if he had simply enjoyed himself like Patch, he would've certainly relished the occurrence a good deal more. Taken honestly, without all the needless questions, he had to admit the ordeal would have qualified as a rollicking good time. It was his own soul searching that was diminishing the experience.

Suddenly, and for no reason he could explain, he had flogged himself for taking on the burden of so much perplexing thought. He had nearly forgotten the indefinable pleasure of that all-too-brief and devastating final moment. Those unbridled short seconds when he had lost all command and reason. Those incredible feelings were very difficult to explain, or to even understand. It was just too much to think about. He had spent a coin last night and now he proposed to shed another. This time on a venture not so thought-provoking.

He set his cap for beer and more German sausage. He'd ponder on love and such, he vowed, another time. He bought only one fine thing in the city of Saint Louis. Robert Trav, who had never before had any fine thing of his own, spent three more of his precious coins. He bought a rifle. It was the rifle of legends.

The rifle shop of Samuel Hawken was near the river, and it was, in truth, one of the busiest shops in Saint Louis. Hawken rifles were the most prized of all on the western frontier and up and down the Big Muddy. To be sure the Kentucky and long rifles of Pennsylvania were more decorative and likely to be more beautiful, but the Hawken was made short, powerful and famous. The Long Hunter of the west was faced with different challenges than those of the eastern woodlands. The rifles of Hawken were shortened so they could better be used by a man on horseback. The long distances faced by the western trekker made walking all but impossible.

Further, these guns were made thicker and more durable to accommodate extreme roughness in their usage, such as being dropped from a horse or bouncing about in the floor of a wagon with iron rimmed wheels. And then there were the calibers. Big and powerful, they were suited to the larger, stronger animals that made up plains and mountain game. Elk, buffalo and the dangerous grizzly bear were far different in temperament and tenacity than the eastern whitetail deer. Woodland deer were often killed at twenty or thirty yards. A prairie rifle needed effective ranges of two- and even three-hundred yards.

The typical eastern rifleman may have been served well enough by the .36 or .44 caliber. These Hawken rifles were of .50 calibers and up. The .50caliber bullet was a full one-half inch in diameter. It weighed nearly half an ounce. When powered by a charge of eighty or ninety or a hundred grains of black powder, the Hawken could stand up to the most formidable challenge.

The only rifle Robert had heretofore was the ancient trade musket that Fletcher Harris had allowed him to use. It was the same gun he had stolen when he fled Harris's tyranny. He supposed it was now in the hand of the Evansville river rats. It had been among the belongings he had thoughtlessly left in the long since burglarized canoe.

As Robert looked over the rifle racks in the most famous gun shop in the world, he knew he'd have to have one of these fine weapons as his own. He selected a .50 caliber., full stocked, with the wood running the entire length of the barrel and capped in iron at the muzzle. To assure expert accuracy the rifle sported double set triggers. Once these were set it took only the slightest touch to fire the piece. He had heard them called "hair triggers". He had the rifle fitted with an oversized frizzen. When struck soundly, by the powerful lock, with an amber flint the spoon shaped frizzen sent forth an amazing shower of spark. Robert had never seen a rifle so resolute and imagined misfires would be nearly non-existent. The gun was plain and finished in brown iron. It carried no ornamentation at all except for an oval-shaped patch box inlet into the stock's right side.. Two extra flints and a few greasy patches reposed here. Now, with a horn filled with powder and a soft leather bag of round, lead bullets swinging from his belt, Robert took his place at the rail of the wilderness-bound paddle wheeler. With the Hawken cradled in the crook of his arm he felt, for the first time ever, that he was truly a Long Hunter.

The trip up the Big Muddy was a long and lazy one. Baker had told Robert to get all the rest he could now because these peaceful times were to be short lived. The steam-powered paddle wheeler labored against the currents which varied from no current at all to swift and dangerous torrents of rushing, white water. Robert was impressed with the power of the steamboat. The steam engine was relentless in its efforts. It was just as demanding in its hunger for firewood. Countless stops were made to take on firewood. It amazed Robert that the captain knew exactly where the next stack of fuel would be waiting.

"Trappers and hunters," he was told by Baker. "Some settlers too. They make extra money by cuttin' this wood and stackin' in spots along the river. The captain leaves 'em some money hidden someplace or else gets it to their tradin' post and puts it in their account."

The engine, when filled with a hot fire, was a marvel of power and efficiency. The white wood smoke billowed from the ship's twin stacks and streaked along the wind. When the fire was truly a hot one, Robert could see a foot or more of fire leaping skyward from the pipes. That was when the vessel really moved, he discovered. It pushed a wall of water in front of its bow that truly dazed the young Scot. Sometimes it looked to be a full six-feet high. Its surge into the headwaters was remarkable, and Robert wondered how Baker had ever had the strength to handle this river by canoe and paddle.

The days were spent in caring for traps and gear, cleaning rifles and talking about the brothels of Saint Louis. There was also time now to assess the other passengers. There was a missionary bringing God's word to the Blackfoot and the Crow. There were two families of settlers, a blacksmith, a whiskey drummer and a gambler. The latter was accompanied by two of the flashiest and most interesting women Robert had ever seen.

"These women," he thought, "Could not have an interest in fur. Nor these others about me." He could only wonder what his fellow travelers hoped to find at trail's end.

It's so very strange, he thought. Each going up the same, watery path to the same destination. Yet, each looking for something so different from the other.... Robert wondered how all these desires, so varied and different, could possibly exist at the end of the same river. All of the river travelers evoked curiosity from Robert, but the gambler and his two girls were absolutely fascinating. The man was large and fleshy. He wore his coat open and the buttons on his grey waistcoat were strained to popping.

Even considering his imposing, size, Robert felt his belly was two or three sizes too large for the rest of him. His face and hands were the color of white library paste. This paleness was greatly accentuated by the contrasting black suit he wore. If it had not been for the myriad of purple and red and blue veins crisscrossing about his large nose, the man would have had no color whatever.

The black suit was badly worn. Threadbare at the elbows and knees, the card man, nevertheless, brushed it daily and made himself appear as well as he was able. Robert's attention was drawn to the celluloid shirt cuffs that gleamed so whitely, protruding two or more inches from his coat sleeves. The cuffs were apt to stand quite stiffly in a circle not touching the wrists themselves. When they did this, Robert could see a soiled expanse of the man's wrist and a bit of forearm. The grey and dingy wrists gave mute testimony to the lack of bathing facilities, both aboard the stream boat and where ever this player had dwelt before.

The man told Robert that he was Alphonso Crane from Chicago. He said that, while it was true he was a man who lived by the taking of risk, he was also a showman of national renown. He professed to knowing magic tricks of alarming stature. He said that he could eat fire and catch bullets in his teeth. Robert never saw any of these feats performed. He did, however, hear the gambler strum the banjo. Robert had heard better banjo players along the Ohio, but Crane was good enough to provide a pleasant diversion. The two women, though, were far more interesting than Mister Crane.

One was a rather, thin woman with flaming, red hair. She wore the same dress every day, a pinkish affair, trimmed out with blue ribbon bows. Robert noticed that the hem of the dress was rather well worn from dragging about the ground and the bows were somewhat faded. Her face seemed to have been coated with a colored oil that made her facial color quite different from that of her hands. Robert was nearly sure that her eyebrows were colored on by grease pencil; So black were they. The mouth was a painted slash of vermilion, colorful, yet somehow ghastly. Robert was certain the mouth didn't quite create the effect the woman had intended.

She didn't smile or laugh very often, but she did sing a bit. When Mister Crane would take out the banjo, she would sing strange and wonderful songs that riveted Robert's attention to her. Some were sad and mournful. They were songs of lost loves and suicide and graveyards. On the other hand, she knew some songs about race horses and dancing girls and barroom fights. They were the jolliest sounds Robert had ever heard.

Once Robert had asked her if she knew any Scottish tunes. She nodded to Mister Crane. He strummed some chords on the banjo for her and, finding her key, she launched herself into a soul-tearing tragedy called "The Wild Colonial Boy." Robert recognized it right away as a famous Irish ballad, not Scottish at all. But she sang it so well. She put so much of her soul into it. Tears streaked her painted cheeks as she sang of the Irish misfortune. Robert thought it so well done, he decided not to correct her for singing a lyric of the wrong country. When she finished the sorrowful hymn of the young freedom fighter that lost his life in the eternal Irish struggle, Robert applauded vigorously. His own eyes heavily misted, the taste of salty tears at the corner of his mouth.

The second woman was large. Indeed, she was a sight larger than her male companion. She had, at least, two dresses which she rotated each day. One was a shiny green ankle length dress trimmed out in delicate ivory-colored lace. Both the dress and the lace were showing signs of heavy wear.

Robert liked the yellow dress she wore on alternate days. The neck of that frock was square cut across her high, ample bosom. The white flesh of her breasts spilled generously over the top in a most delightful display. Robert especially liked it when she jig danced to the banjo a bit, for this caused the white flesh to jiggle and quiver in a most spellbinding manner. Most impressive though, was the big woman's smile. Robert loved it when she smiled, which was often. Indeed, she smiled and laughed uproariously. She slapped her knees and let out with resounding guffaws. She was noisy, good natured and vulgar.

Robert felt himself blush hotly when she would lewdly wink at him. It was a smile such as Robert had never encountered. Right in the middle of her mouth was a tooth that appeared to be of solid gold. When she threw back her head in resolute laughter, there would be that startling tooth. A gleaming, beckoning flare that Robert found mesmerizing.

Robert liked the tooth more than the banjo or the ballads or anything. He believed he would miss this colorful trio more than any of the sights he had seen thus far. Often, at night, he lay in his blankets and wondered where the three were going, how they had come to be together. Like himself, what would be their fate? As always, his questions were lost in sleep.

At length, the steam boat reached the Platte. Now they began dropping off trappers at strategic places along the river. Each man would leave the vessel as it came close to shore, leaping into the water and wading up the muddy bank. They were heavily loaded with trap baskets and possible bags, rifles and the like. They waved and goodbyed vigorously with shouts of, "See ya in the spring!" or "Bet I'll take furs more'n you!" They were laughing, shouting children off to Sunday school and the picnic of the wilderness.

As the paddle wheel turned, the number of travelers aboard noticeably dwindled. The blacksmith departed first. The gambler and his ladies left ship near a muddy, mosquito-ridden flat graced by a few run-down shacks. It was a mean little settlement named for the Indians who had, many years ago, deserted the hostile place called Omaha. The trappers gathered at the rail to watch the two pretty ladies gather their skirts up around their waists to help clear the mud. The preacher left soon after, and then there were two.

"Way I figure it, Rob, is that we'll leave the boat somewhere about the Colorado territory. Buy us some horses. Then just head west the rest of the way to the Crow country," Baker declared.

"Horses?" Robert asked suspiciously. "You never said anything about any horses."

"Damnation!" Baker exclaimed. "Don't tell me you're afraid of horses. Great Heavens, Rob, you're the man that fights guntotin' gamblers with your bare hands. And now you're tellin' me you're a-scared of a horse?"

"I ain't rightly scared o' no horse, Baker...It's more like I'm scared o' bein' on top of one of 'em. Them's big scary bastards, and I ain't sure men are s'posed to be ridin' somethin like that."

"Well, I'm tellin' you now, Rob boy, this ain't no little walk down through Ohio. And it ain't no social dance in Saint Louis with your fat little kraut cutter. This here's the genuine Rocky Mountains. And you cain't no ways make it without some horses.

"Horses?" He emphasized the plural. "My God, you mean I got to put up with more'n one?"

"I think maybe four oughts to serve us pretty well. Money's already earmarked by the sponsors for horses, Rob. So don't go clutchin' at that precious money belt o' yours. You hear me now, Scotty, and hear me good: It's horses, Rob. Horses and me and you and the by-God, Rocky Mountains."

They left the steam paddler the next day at noon. After some spirited dickering, they bought four horses at a river landing named Wolf Head Creek. The name reminded Robert of Fletcher Harris and the wolf's head hat. The horses were of course, the wild mustang variety of Indian pony. Every horse trader in the west relied on these wild ponies. They had, in fact, become an acceptable form of ready currency. They roamed the west in great loose herds. Indian traders captured them in blind canyons or rode them down to the lariat. These were the great grandchildren of the horses of the Spanish Conquistadors.

The Spanish Knights had left them here, not by choice, more than three hundred years ago. These bold adventurers, their passions and greed inflamed by Christianity and riches for Isabella and Ferdinand, marched north from the Yucatan rain forests. Fierce and ruthless fighters, they pushed their way to, what is now, the northern border of Colorado. The Iberian treasure hunters faltered and died along the way. As they had killed the red man, so they too were killed. They fell to arrows, starvation and sickness. As an eternal reminder of their presence, their horses were left behind. These did not die as their masters, but multiplied into the greatest wild horse herd the world had ever known.

The cayuse. The mustang. The only legacy remaining from the incredible search for El Dorado, the lost city of gold. Of course, when the Spanish brought about their mounts to the new "Empire of the Americas," given them by Christopher Columbus, they were the finest horses in the known world. These were the ancestors of the fine Andalusian, and later, the Arabian.

After the Conquistadores were nearly all dead and, at last, admitted defeat in the search for the city of gold, they deserted their horses. The few explorers that remained alive sailed back to Spain in disgrace at having failed. They gave no thought to the horses or the cattle they had brought and now abandoned. The animals they had transported by sail all the way to the new world, as work stock and for food, were forsaken and left to fend for themselves. Only a few of the Spanish Knights survived. The animals did better, and they did it so well. They thrived far better than their masters had.

The Spanish adventurers would eventually find the gold and silver they had pledged to Isabella and Ferdinand and, later to Phillip and the kings of Bourbon. All those years they had gone the wrong way. El Dorado was not to the north as they had thought but, rather, the true riches lay in the Inca treasuries of Peru. By now though the American horse-and-cattle saga was fifty years underway.

The food supply and natural terrain was perfect for the building of vast herds of cattle and horses alike. The deer, elk and other grazers and browsers proved no competition for the existing food. With the possible exception of the buffalo, these aggressive horse and cattle herds had the grass and water of the Great Plains to themselves. They reproduced until they were abundant. The immense distances across the plains proved to be their greatest ally. Their numbers might grow incredibly in herd size; but try as they might; they simply could in no way over graze. With no herdsmen in attendance, of course, the animals inbred one generation after the other. The normal black-colored, medium-horn length cattle of Spain became the calico and roan longhorn., the wild cattle that free grazed from Colorado south to Old Mexico.

It just may have been that the cattle with the most horn and a bit of color were, in some ways the best equipped to survive. Whatever the case, they were never native to America. Now, three hundred years later they dominated the plains, flourished in the thickets by the thousands.

The horse took on some changes in appearance as the cattle had. After generations of inbreeding the clean, intelligent look of the Andalusian gave way to a short-coupled, mean little brute. He was prone to having rounded facial features. That quality gave him the name "hammer head". His lower lip was almost always extended. This gave him a look that acutely belied his true intelligence. More importantly, though, his most striking feature was that of wildness. A horseman could ride one of these horses all day, every day, but every morning the animal had to broken to the saddle all over again. It was said they never calmed down. The sight of anything strange or unusual, such as a rattle snake or a prairie dog, could send these animals into headlong flights of terror during which the rider on the topside usually found himself on the bottom.

Robert noted after a few days that it didn't have to be anything as dramatic as a snake to upset a mustang. A blowing leaf, a crack of thunder or even a dust devil was more than enough to assure an unsuspecting rider that he was in for the thrill of a lifetime, a few panicky seconds aboard the hurricane deck of a wild bronco.

For the first three days Robert didn't ride. He walked along leading his two mounts and letting Hubert Baker get far ahead of him. At the end of the third day, his traveling companion was so far ahead that Robert had to guide himself to Baker's camp long after dark by the light of Baker's campfire which, though small, showed itself for miles across the open plain. It became obvious that a man just couldn't walk as far or as fast as a horse. On the fourth day, at Baker's urging, he gave riding a try. He had to admit it was so much easier on his moccasined feet. But now other parts of his anatomy began to pay a dear price. It was after a spring rain shower he rode several hours in a wet saddle. He learned that very day about saddle sores.

He was starting to wonder if this horse riding would ever be really worth it all. About the time he was ready to give it up for good, though, it just suddenly fell into place. Not that he was truly comfortable around horses— he doubted that would ever happen. But at last his body toughened to the saddle. He and his two mounts came to a sort of uneasy truce. It wasn't a perfect relationship, but it would have to do for now.

As on the river, they, from time to time, passed bands of roving Indians. Several times they rode in clear view of small Indian campsites. Robert saw that some of these Indians were indeed the noble savage of the plains he had heard of, just as regal as he had come to expect. It was true some of these men and women they passed on the trail were handsome, well fed and dramatically garbed in the colorful beaded buckskin-style of the plains warrior. But, far too often, Robert thought they had the appearance of beggars. He had seen the same look of resigned subjugation on the faces of the Delaware when they had been forced to accept unfair dealings at the hands of Fletcher Harris. He was surprised and disappointed to find it here, too.

"Hubert," he said when he could be quiet about it no longer. "Look at these people, Baker. They're poor to starving. More'n that, they looks about like they've given up all hope."

"What you say is the truth, Scotty. There's somethin' amiss in the way we're dealin' with these folks. O' course now, Rob, when we hits the mountains, things are a world different. These here are trail niggers. They done give up the old ways o' the huntin' warrior. 'Stead o' that, they hang 'round where they can trade for somethin' cause it's easier livin'. Course, if they cain't trade for somethin' they wants, they's likely to beg for it. That don't work, they try to steal it. It wasn't like this when I came here some ten year ago. This is "trail tendin'" as I calls it."

Baker went on with his explanation. "They just hang around trails and roads, lookin' for a traveler to feed 'em a handout. They didn't use to act like this. This just seemed to happen overnight. You'll see a different Indian soon, Rob, just you wait a few days. Once we clear these trail tenders you gonna see some, By God Rocky Mountain red men."

Even though Robert knew Baker was probably right, the whole scene of ragged people and hungry children left an uneasy feeling in his breast. It was Fletcher Harris all over again. A shudder ran through him again when he thought of that name.

Chapter Eighteen

The Niagara, Erie and Ohio Flight
1838/1840

The Carousel had hardly cleared the Dumbarton port when Robert began to feel he'd made a serious mistake. The error lay in his assessment of Fletcher Harris' character. Harris, it turned out, was a bully when he was sober and a cruel and wretched taskmaster when he drank spirits. Robert was to learn that he drank a lot and he drank often.

The voyage was hard on Robert. He was ill prepared for the sea sickness. It came swiftly to the uninitiated on a clipper ship rolling about on the high seas. The Carousel was one of the better clippers and her hold was filled to the brim with fabric from the cotton mills. The cargo weight and steadiness– for cloth doesn't shift about in the holds as some cargos do– helped to make the ship ride the sea a good deal easier than others. Still, the relentless roll was more than enough for a greenhorn sailor like Robert. On top of this discomfort, there was Harris and his constant demands. The friendliness had vanished now, and Robert began to see his predicament as a hard one.

At voyage end Robert would learn soon enough life on shore was no better. Harris had whisked him off to a trapper's camp on the Niagara and his days were filled with the meanest labor. If anything added to his broken spirit, it was his initial sighting of the Harris home base camp.

It was a ramshackle assortment of tiny cabins and lopsided shacks in various stages of disrepair. There was a pen filled with noisy hunting hounds that became frantic when anyone approached their lair. Robert understood immediately they were hoping for food. The hounds were so thin as to appear starved. In the rear of the tumbled down barn stood a small hog pen. Here a mud-covered sow stood up to her belly in mire and stared balefully at the men working in the hide yard. Robert saw about five men there. Shirts off, they were toiling at mixing tan and lacing hides tightly into the skin stretchers. His first observation was that they, too, were a sorry lot.

In days to come he feared he would soon be one of them. He stretched and scraped skins and boiled steel traps in acorns and skunk scent. In the winter he broke ice on the streams for the beaver sets. In summer he labored with the axe. Robert felled the trees for cabin building and shed enlargement. He was not paid, and was underfed and overworked seven days a week by Harris. Robert had now come to consider his overseer an unquestionable tyrant. He was beaten, too. Not often, but when Harris had a certain amount of whiskey, the boxing of Robert's ears was a very likely occurrence.

When his year of servitude was nearly up, he had queried Harris about his promised return to Scotland. At first, his questions were met with stalling, then laughter, and at last with temper tantrums, threats of beatings and indignant outrage.

"How dare you speak of leaving?" Harris had roared. "You owe me more than a thousand dollars towards payment of your apprenticeship sir! You'll not be leaven' here, Lad. Not for two more years. And maybe not at all. Boy trappers sometimes disappear in the great woods, ya' know...Could happen to you, too, boy. So I'd just be quiet about this leaving."

One day a rider came on a grey mule. He was a fat man with a pink face. He wore a black frock coat and wheezed when he spoke.

"I'm Constable Alton Woods," he declared. "I'm here to see this Robert Trav." Robert gave up the steel trap he was scouring for rust and approached the mule and rider. The man removed his hat to mop sweat from his brow. He revealed a bald head as pink as his face and rimmed with wispy, white hair.

"You this Trav boy?" He wheezed.

"I am Robert Trav."

"This here Mister Harris been your friend and your mentor too, I understands. He tells me you think you might run away or somethin' bout that silly." Robert blanched at realizing someone could know his thoughts so well.

"Apprentices round here don't fare too well with runnin'. We always catches them we do. After we gets 'em..." The fat man leaned forward in the saddle to make his point. He stared into Robert's face with watery blue eyes and the suggestion of a sneer on his lips. "...we whips 'em real good with a rawhide strap. Whips 'em every day for five days. That's when we puts 'em in debtor's prison to work out the learnin' fees. I'd think real long and careful 'bout any runnin' boy. You'd best be a man and keep the bargain you made with Mister Harris."

Harris had come from the darkness of the shack now and stood beside Robert. He had arrived in time to overhear the end of the fat rider's remarks. His face split in a triumphant grin. He was bareheaded now, and without the wolf-face hat, the missing ear made a lewd display. He'd tried to comb some of his hair down that side of his face as cover. That effort had failed; and the puffy, proud flesh of the missing ear was as pink as the constable's face. Fletcher Harris helped the fat Alton Woods from his mount and escorted him into the darkness of the shack.

Now he was loudly commanding Robert to water and care for the mule. Later Robert heard the sounds of tin cups, clinking jugs and raucous laughter coming from the cabin's gloom. His life had not been a long one at this point. Robert understood that he had a long way to go in living and gathering experiences. But, for the moment, he never remembered feeling so completely defeated.

Robert temporarily gave in. At least he surrendered outwardly. Deep inside though, he swore to escape; and if he were able, he would reap a terrible vengeance on this man who had befriended him, betrayed him, and had now become his nemesis. Robert had told most of this tale to the trapper Hubert Baker.

"I tell you true, Hubert. It got harder for me each day. He treated the Indian families we dealt with so badly, too. They had no control whatsoever. They were totally dependent on him. As far as trapping' went, he was in control of the river. If they didn': do just everything he said, he'd just pull in more white trappers and starve 'em out. He tricked em' too. Sold them whiskey and cheap rum. Most always he'd cut it with kerosene and water. Gave 'em junk trinkets and untempered knives. Iron axes with no steel at all in 'em. Traded 'em those gee-gaws for prime fur. Sold 'em gunpowder cut with sand. Tear up a rifle barrel in just a few shots. Then he could sell 'em a new barrel you see. He made their women share his bed, too. Hubert, I could feel God was offended in my very soul when he would do that.

"I'd see him trade some trinket or a pig or a cured ham to a good man for his daughter; sometimes even his wife. He never cared for these women no how. He'd sleep with 'em for sure. Mostly he'd just beat 'em around. Cuss 'em and kick 'em and such. 'Bout three or four days with one and he'd throw her out. Send her home in shame and disgrace; go pick out another one. I know now the Hudson Bay people had nothing to do with this. Fletcher was acting on his own and if the Factors had found him out he might even have been jailed. I'm sure he'd like me dead or anyone else that knew about his doing's."

There were things about his servitude to Harris that Robert never told anyone, not even his friend Hubert Baker. These were the stories he considered too dismal. He was also ashamed. Ashamed of the fact that Fletcher Harris had so terrified him he couldn't find the strength or courage to resist, to fight back. Now much later, and with the Harris years behind him, he understood full well that death was the better alternative to fear and cowardice. Under Harris' watchful eye, he had simply cowered and hoped for a better day. He had never been as terrified as he was the night Harris got unusually drunk and grabbed him by the arm as he tended the fireplace.

"Sit here!" Harris had commanded, and he had fairly thrown Robert to the floor on a pile of skins.

"I seen you." Harris's voice was a furious snarl. "I seen you readin' them labels on the supply boxes. Thinks you're pretty fancy 'eh... readin' and all. I hates them that can read. They always thinkin' they so much better'n me". He took a razor-sharp skinning knife from his belt and used it as a pointer as he spoke. Robert felt the running droplets of sweat trailing between his shoulder blades.

"I can read too, you know. Not fancy readin' like I 'spects you do. I can read cargo bills and fur credits. I can count sponsor money. I can read whiskey labels to a fair-thee-well," he guffawed at this big joke. "I got me a way of takin' care o' them that gets too uppity around me, boy. Just ask the other boys round here 'bout the Algonquin. They'll tell you how old Fletch deals with them as crosses him." Robert already knew the story. The other hands who worked in the hide yard had made sure to terrify him with the ghastly tale soon after he'd arrived.

She was far more beautiful than the other Indian girls about. She was small and they said she belonged to an Algonquin. an Indian man who traded furs with Harris on occasion. The Algonquin trader was a tall man who would stand shirtless in the small yard of the shack in his breech clout and leggings as he traded with Harris for tobacco, cloth or a knife blade. She would stand dutifully beside him in a stony silence looking only at the ground as the business was transacted. Fletcher Harris could not take his eyes off her. He was mesmerized by her lovely face, her petite but well rounded body. She gave him a feeling he could neither control nor understand. The Mohawk called it the 'feeling of fire.'

Fletcher thought of her often. Day after day, her memory assaulted his very sanity. The Algonquin had made a small dry camp less than half mile from the Harris cabin. Early one morning the Indian trader had called on Harris to buy a few bullets for the rusty old trade musket he carried. Harris could tell instantly, by the way he was packed, this Indian was off on a hunt.

"Back this many days," he had said, holding out four fingers.

It was late that evening when Fletcher Harris lost control. He had been drinking all day. Drinking and thinking of the girl in a hunters camp just a short distance away. Around midnight he could take it no longer. He charged through the dark woods as wild as a bull.

Branches whipped and stung his face as he pitched headlong through the darkness. Briars tore at his shirt and cut little rivulets in his flesh. These pains only served to inflame him all the more. He grabbed the girl from her sleeping robes, and holding her by the wrist he ripped her out of her small clothes.

Panic stricken, she began to fight back. She screamed, too. For an instant the sound jolted Harris. He paused for a moment, and her nails raked his cheek in bloody, ragged lines. With a thunderous blow of his fist he broke her nose. The second blow, harder than even the first, rendered her unconscious. He threw her back onto her sleeping robes and fell on top of her comatose body.

"Crazy Goddamned Indian!" Fletcher was wild now in his drunkenness and rage. He was waving the knife around about as he told the story to Robert. The knife flashed in the light of the fireplace as though he intended to behead Robert. The boy withdrew further. He sunk back on the floor until; at last, he was wedged into a corner. He kept his eyes fixed rigidly on the plank floor. Nearly trembling he could not bring him self to look up at his tormenter. Now Fletchers occasioned feet came into his view. Too terrified to raise his eyes he studied the moccasins. A tear was evident into the buckskinned heel and Robert fixed his gaze on that small rip as he tried to compose himself.

"Just cause I had me a little fun with that there woman he carried about, that crazy Indian comes up here and calls me out, he does. Believe that? Comes right in my camp and starts wavin' his damned old rifle roun'. Hell, I just thought he wanted some money for me a-usin' his squaw. I tries to be a good feller. I been tryin' to be good to you too, Scotty. Anyhows, I offers him two jugs o' whiskey...And a powder horn too, I thinks. Well he ain't wantin' no powder horn. 'Fore I could compose myself he grabs out a tommyhawk and hits it at my head. I can feel this blood on the side o my face, and I looks on the ground... and there's my Goddamned ear! I din't know at first what I was I was seein'. It's my ear...My Goddamned ear! Well, I tell you now, Mister Robert Trav, when I seen what that "Gonk" did to my ear, I pulled my skinner. I hauled out my Sheffield and jest went right to work. That woman o' his, she's there a-watchin' and a-yellin'. I kilt that" Gonk" in short order I did. Cut his liver out, too, and throwed it in the dog pen."

Robert was horrified at the grisly tale. His stomach moved as though it were alive.

"Them hounds, they go right for that liver too. And this little "Gonk," wolf bitch, she's decidin' now she's goin' to get even. Got 'er own knife, she does. She jerks out this knife and comes onto me. Smacks the shit right out of her, I did. Took her own knife away from her and marked her good. Marked her so she won't be forgettin'. Dragged her back hear too I did. Thought she might had 'nother ally near the camp. No help for her here though, No help. That's been five years or more but I bet she ain't forgettin' who it was cut her ears off...Yeah and her nose too. Just cut' 'em off I did, with her own knife, too. Then I kicked her ass out of here."

Harris pointed at a dark stain on the pine flooring of the lodge. "See her damned old blood there? I let them hounds come in and lick it up. Hell, they eat Gonk blood same as if it was people leakin's. When this she- wolf bitch goes back 'round her people lookin' like that, no nose and no ears neither, you can bet old Fletch don't have no more trouble. No more trouble at all."

The brutality of the story had taken all the starch out of Robert. If he'd had any will to fight at all, it was gone now. It took some time for Robert to screw up his courage again. But eventually, it started to come back. But he vowed to remain cautious. There was no reason to be stupid. But he also determined himself to be unafraid.

The day finally arrived when Robert had tolerated his situation as long as he could. After nearly three years of brutal treatment and cruelty he had, at last, just walked away. It was a strange way to initiate his flight. He had lain awake nights dreaming of elaborate plans to affect his escape. When the time came though, he forgot all the detailed scenario he had imagined and just walked away. The only part of any plan he salvaged was the waiting. Waiting until Harris was drunk. He knew Harris would be upon him quickly if he faltered. He further knew Harris to be the best tracker along the Niagara.

Robert had patiently waited for one of Harris's big drunks. He knew one of these binges would come sooner or later. And, at last, it did. He'd even helped by fetching Harris additional liquor; even after he was more than a little drunk. He'd seen Harris take two or even three days to recover from a drinking bout of this magnitude. Once Harris had fallen across his bunk in a drunken stupor, Robert had moved swiftly. He had taken the trade musket and the pitiful little collection of possibles he could rightfully call his own. With a few flints and a steel, some fish hooks and a knife he just slipped into the night.

He traveled by night for a few days to be sure he was out of Harris's territory. He knew where many of the trapper camps were located by the maps that Harris had kept in their shack. He had studied those maps intimately. He walked from camp to camp, getting a little food here and a blanket there. He never rested and wasted no time that might cause him to be caught. Robert knew, full well, that if Fletcher Harris were to tell a court he owed for an apprenticeship he would be taken back to the hide yard instantly, or worse, thrown into prison. For no one would be likely to take the word of a Scottish immigrant youth over that of a man as important to the economy of the area as Fletcher Harris.

He committed himself to a westerly flight. Following the Niagara upstream the better part of nine days, he came, at last, to the rocky eastern shore of Lake Erie. He was glad his point of origin had been to the south of the Niagara Falls.

It would be a bonnie wonder to see those great falls, Robert thought. The risk of travel in that district, however, was an immense one. The Niagara Falls region was infamous as a veritable tangle of swirling eddies and creeks. It was a perplexing maze of tangled waterways that went everywhere and nowhere. The area was a jumble of hundreds of tiny islands that could befuddle the most experienced traveler. Stories and tales of those lost in the misty web of the Falls territory were legion. Avoiding the Fall area was a prerequisite for a clean escape.

It was nine days Robert would never forget. It was the first time he had been really alone in his life. He was so unsure of himself at first that he wondered if he could really survive this wilderness. Almost at once, though, he learned that his time with Fletcher Harris had made him a skilled woodsman if nothing else.

He began to gain in confidence immediately. He learned, soon enough, that he was in possession of all the skills necessary to live off the land. Actually food, water and firewood were plentiful. The weather was fair and, had it not been for the apprehension of Harris' pursuit, the sojourn might even have been a pleasant one. It was during this nine-day period that Robert would reflect, in later years, he had become his own man.

Utilizing the Long Hunter skills he had learned from his recent associations, he stayed away from well-used trails. He traveled, still mostly, by night and used the north star as his only compass. The river was a better and more reliable guide. He feared straying too far from the shoreline, afraid he might not be able to find the river again. And so he traveled through heavy brush that grew right on the bank. This was, from time to time, exhausting. As hostile as the thickets were, he bulled his way through them.

It was his way of knowing his travel would keep him within sight or earshot of the flowing waters. The brush tore his clothing and flesh alike, but never once did he feel he was straying too far from the guiding currents. He tried hard to avoid Indians. They were supposed to be friendly enough in this area, but if a lone white were to encounter a hunting or gathering party of three or four in this desolate country, who could really say for sure? Robert vowed he would not be the daring one to discover the answer. He determined that he might, from time to time, approach a white should he encounter any along the way. But only after long observation from hiding to assure their presence was not of Fletcher Harris' doings. He would approach no Indians whatsoever. That risk would've been outlandish.

A journey like this was unheard of back in Scotland. There a walk such as he and his uncle had made, from Inverness to Glasgow was considered a most unusual feat, generally undertaken by madmen. He observed pretty quickly that in America, though, these Long Hunters and others as well, would set out across country on foot for what seemed a ridiculous distance with hardly so much as a thought about it.

Even women, with child in arms, would join their men with hardly any provisions at all and at anytime of year. Summer or winter they would embark on a foot trek of a hundred leagues or more. This with no more concern than if they were embarking on a Sunday stroll. When someone had asked Daniel Boone if he thought he might have walked as much as a thousand miles, he answered by asking,

"Which year?"

Robert soon learned that he could travel far and fast when he felt he was being pursued. On the shores of Erie he decided to rest a bit, fish, and run a small trap line for a day or two. By now he needed both rest and food supplies.

He built a small smoker of driftwood and covered its sides loosely with bark and grasses. The small but delicious yellow perch were easy enough to catch from his little raft. Like all frontier travelers of the time, he carried a few fish hooks wrapped in buckskin in his pockets at all times. He felt for a day or so he was on a holiday. Then he learned firsthand of Erie's storms.

Vicious and violent, the wind bore down from the northeast. In what seemed like seconds, the peaceful calm of the great lake was whipped into a frothing maelstrom. The waves crashing the shore were higher than

Robert's head, and his little smoke house was quickly swept away, along with his three-day catch of fish.

The furious nor'easter storm rapidly robbed him of the little raft he had crafted so carefully to help him trap and fish. It washed out the few snares and deadfalls he had placed so mindfully among the pockets and indentations along the shoreline. He had diligently searched for these select locations of spring or creek inlets or of marshy quiet flats, places he knew would likely yield the foolish and easily caught muskrat, a useful animal of wonderful fur and delicious flesh. Wire snares were the simplest method to take a few of these, and he had set the three snares he had squirreled away from Harris. Pursued as he was, he knew he had no time for more elaborate trapping schemes. These three precious wires, too, were lost in the violence of the storm. For two days the storm raged on. At last, his every possession gone or totally drenched, a bedraggled Robert turned away from the once inviting shore.

It appeared to Robert these driving winds would never relent. It was this storm that drove Robert on his trek to the east and then to the south. Robert was not the first man to quit the Erie region because of its legendary and mighty nor'easters He would, in no way, be the last.

He had been traveling much longer than a week, he determined, though he had lost track of actual days and nights. Now he sensed he was being followed. Several times he doubled back onto his own trail. He knew that deer, fox and even rabbits would do this when they were pursued to throw off the hunter. He felt that the few days spent at the Erie shore might have been a drastic mistake. He might have lingered long enough to lose his head start advantage. His pursuer, after all, was a skilful and accomplished woodsman and tracker, perhaps the best among his peers. Each time Robert had backtracked he found the foot prints of Fletcher Harris nearly within his own tracks.

He would recognize that moccasin spoor anywhere. Plain as day there was the mark of that revealing tear in the heel. He would not forget that he had stared so intently at it while being upbraided so horribly by Harris. He had to somehow survive long enough to get to a stream or a river. He believed water travel would hide his spoor. Was it possible that Harris had pursued him this far? He determined, indeed, it was possible. The tracks of his feet were there and were not to be denied. Fletcher Harris had as much resolve as any man Robert had ever encountered. He was determined and would never relent until he caught his quarry or had driven Robert completely from this country.

If he got out of the woods and into water, he reasoned, he just might outdistance this relentless pursuer. He knew enough about local geography to understand that if he walked due south, sooner or later, he'd cut a river. Walk southeast though, and he'd probably hit it sooner. He chose the southeast, bearing very hard to the east.

Finally he came to the river he sought though he didn't know its name. He walked the shore of the unnamed river for the better part of a day encountering no one. The river was as lonely as the forest around it. Robert was surprised to be so isolated on this swiftly moving stream. It was obviously navigable given its width and depth. He had considered wading in the water to alleviate his tracks. The bank was a steep one though and in places the currents undercut the shore deeply. Considering the currents, the water simply appeared too treacherous for wading. The absence of river travelers also was troubling.

On the Niagara, travelers by boat were a common occurrence. He began to realize that he was now in country far less traveled. It was a more desolate place and probably more dangerous as well. At last he found an old colored man fishing near the shore from a battered canoe. Robert hadn't seen many coloreds in his life and he proceeded with caution.

"Halloo," he called to the fisherman. "What river is this?"

"Mongaheeler," came the answer.

Robert had heard the Long Hunters talk of geography and waterways often enough that he knew the man was saying Monongahela in his own backwoods jargon. Robert was astounded. He knew he'd been traveling in the direction of that river, but it never occurred to him that he had covered that great a distance.

He had gone a lot farther than he'd thought. A lot farther. Now for the first time he began to relax a bit from the anticipation of Fletcher Harris' pursuit. He knew to remain cautious, but now his complete escape seemed a distinct possibility for the very first time. What he needed now was a boat...

"Come ashore and talk some trade with me," Robert called. "I have a good knife, a powder horn and a coin of gold."

At the mention of gold the old Negro took up his paddle and stroked silently. Three or four powerful strokes brought him to the shore. After some lively trading, Robert owned the canoe. He also still had his knife and his powder. The Negro though had a glistening, gold Scottish sovereign. The old man tested the authenticity of the lustrous coin with his teeth. When the soft gold yielded to his bite, his face split with a wide and toothy grin. This piece of gold was worth far more than a hand-made dugout canoe. a crudely made one at that. The Negro knew when he had the better end of a trade. He was also wise enough not to gloat too much. A colored besting a white in a trade, here in this lonely place, could have some danger as well as reward. It was better to appear a bit unhappy. He protested he should have the horn as well. Robert refused, and the Negro made no further complaint.

Robert took up the canoe and sent it to the river's middle. On his knees now, as Fletcher Harris had shown him, he dug the paddle in deep. His aim was distance now. Distance and speed. The little boat responded true under his mastery. When he looked back the old man was gone. He had taken his golden future and slipped away into the forest before the foolish white boy could change his mind.

He had the canoe now, and life became considerably easier. Travel with the water was pleasure, and the avoidance of river bank thickets was a great enjoyment. Had the old Negro only known it he could've held out for more than one of Robert's precious coins. Robert had never considered parting with even one of them since his uncle had presented them to him that night so long ago. But the canoe wasn't just a whim; it was vital to escape, *to life*. Now he was on the river. He couldn't quite believe it, but it appeared that he had outrun the Long Hunter, Fletcher Harris. The river was filled with bends and turns.

What, he wondered, *waits for me down this swift and crooked stream?*

Chapter Nineteen

The Goose and the Crow
1841/184 –

The two buckskin-clad adventurers guided their horses to the west. The journey was a pleasant one. They shot game along the way for their food. One early morning, the air filled with mists and morning fog as they approached the top of a ridge, Hubert Baker urgently shushed Robert. Once quieting him, he motioned for him to dismount and follow him higher up the ridge. Near the top Robert became acutely aware of strange noises. There were grunts and snuffles. He could hear the rumblings of a hundred great stomachs. He was working hard in his mind to identify the sounds of a multitude of enormous animals, many breaking wind and blowing their nostrils clear. His heart quickened, and he gripped the big rifle tighter. When they topped the ridge, Robert peered through the quiet morning mists, his eyes slowly adjusting to the magnificent sight that spread before him.

Buffalo! A gigantic herd he believed; but, as he raised his head and looked deeper into the mists, he saw it was a hundred times larger than his first impression! They stretched for miles across the open plain. His breath caught in his chest as he realized there were thousands of these great shaggy black/brown beasts in this herd. Such a sight made his heart beat faster in his chest. Robert could only think," How wonderful!".

Huge, they were. Like buildings. Covered in brown to black curly hair. They seemed like a part of a dream for they slowly milled about, unconcerned and at peace with the world. Robert tried to drink it all in at once. There were cows with calves by their sides. Old bulls slowly circling the perimeter of their private stock of cows. Stout groups of young bulls bawled softly and stared after these harems enviously.

Some of the calves looked as dainty as the pronghorn antelope that also were a shadowy presence scattered throughout the herd. Many of the big bulls though, Robert knew, would exceed a ton in weight. Several looked as though a ton-and-a-half would've been more accurate. Now Baker was nudging Robert, bringing him from the spell cast by so many buffalo. He was gesturing towards the Hawken. Then barely moving his head, he nodded to an animal that had singled herself out of the herd. Robert saw she was a young dry cow, and she was close. Very close. He understood now: Baker meant for him to shoot this animal.

He vigorously shook his head "No." Baker eased his own rifle into position. He aimed a long time Robert thought. Just when he believed Baker wasn't going to shoot after all, he was startled suddenly by the 'skitch-BOOM! that was the sound of a firing flintlock. The cow fell as though she'd been struck by cannon fire.

The rest of the herd moved away only few feet. They observed the fallen cow and her few feeble kicks. When she was silent they went back to their browse. Only when Robert and Baker showed themselves in order to approach the dead cow did the heard show any thing like alarm, though that didn't last long either. The nearest animals just trotted off a few yards, some as much as fifty perhaps, and they quickly settled back into their pattern of walking, grazing and walking some more.

"Why in the world would you kill an animal as large as this?" Robert wanted to know. He was nearly angry.

"Fresh meat, Rob. Just wait till you try some o' this tongue. You'll eat no finer fare, e'en in Scotland."

"Don't doubt its fineness, Baker; but, Lord, look how much meat is here. We'll never eat so much. It'll waste."

"Haw!" Baker snorted loudly. "Don't you be a-worryin' none about waste. Come help me take the tongue and hump, and you'll soon see."

Robert detected quickly that Baker wanted to take the select cuts of meat, mount up and be away from there with all haste. When the butchering chore was finished and the two had ridden something like a half of a mile, Robert looked back towards the fallen carcass. He was stunned to see four Indian braves hard at work with knives and axes. They were taking the rest of the meat and the precious hide.

Robert asked, "Where did they come from? I had not the slightest idea that any Indians were near."

"They's always about, Scotty. This here herd's their farm. It's their bank. This herd's everything those people own. They tend to it just the way you told me your Ma looked to her garden. This here herd is their garden. Without it there ain't no winter food, nor warm robes, or tipi covers. Without this herd, there ain't even no tomorrow. There ain't nothin'."

"They use the buff for all that?" Robert asked.

"That and a whole lot more. They burn his droppings as fire fuel. His sinews are thread for sewing. Cure the buffalo hide right, and it makes a shield so strong it'll turn an enemy arrow. It's all there is to these people, Rob. You know when I hear tell of some settler being killed by Indians or some mass-a-cree takin' place; I usually know 'thout askin' that somebody got into the herd, or maybe just stayed around the herd a little too long.

You'll do well Rob, and you'll keep your hair a sight longer if you learn to avoid buffalo herds. 'Specially big herd like this one. There just ain't one chance in Hell o' findin' a herd like this one 'thout a few Crow or Arapaho or both findin' you."

"I'll remember that, Baker. It sounds like real fine advice."

""Nother thing, Rob. Even if those braves didn't clean up that cow like I knowed they would, I reckon it wouldn't hurt none to shoot one o' these critters now and again. Just look out there, Rob...Did you ever see so many of anything in your life? They're breedin' faster'n the Indians can eat 'em. I guess you could shoot buffalo for a hundred years, and they'd still be plenty. I wouldn't worry 'bout it very much, Scotty. One thing we got forever's buffalo."

Robert look out over the herd that stretched as far as he could see.

That Hubert Baker's a smart man, Robert thought. "Guess he's right again."

The trip was well into the fourteenth day on horseback when the terrain finally told Robert they were entering the Rockies. He had been astonished at how long it had taken. They began to see the mountains on the horizon more than six days ago. They looked so close. Robert had thought a half-day ride would bring them to the mountain range. Now, as they drew nearer, he was overwhelmed by the mountains' size. He understood, at last, they only looked so close because they were so large. They loomed high above the riders' heads. As they drew nearer it seemed as if the mountain tops would block out the sky.

Their colors were breathtaking. The dark green of the heavy forest grudgingly gave way to the light, yellow green of high grasslands. Higher yet, above the growth line, there was the profusion of mottled colors supplied by the rock itself. Looking even higher, Robert was amazed to see snow, pure and white and touching the late summer sky.

Now they sought passes and gullies that would let them travel deeper into the wilderness. They sought to penetrate the very heart of this wild place. Robert had come to see the benefit of the nimble footed little mustang horses. Tough and sure, they could survive where grass was nearly nonexistent, and they could walk just about anyplace a deer or elk could find a path.

Mostly the riders traveled in stream beds, always moving uphill. It took determined men and special horses to negotiate the steep slope day after exhausting day. Robert remembered now, that Baker had warned him of these hardships and had cautioned him to rest when he had been able. The gullies and washes were immense, some impassable. Robert found the high rock faces thrilling and awesome. For sheer beauty though he thought the fairest sight of all were the high meadows. It seemed they would travel for hours through thick timber or heavy brush, over rocky faces and stone laden trails. Then, as from nowhere, there would suddenly appear one of these lovely little oasis of light green. Some though were quite large and contained a hundred acres or more. These places of lush grass and sunshine almost always held deer and elk. Wild flowers abounded and monarch butterflies added their gaudy orange-and-black to the swirling collage. Sometimes even a small buffalo herd would be found quietly grazing here. For the most part though, it was too high for these lumbering giants. At last, they found a meadow that was perfect for their purposes. It was high but had a few large level spots; places where a lean to or cabin could be built.

Rushing streams nearby gave the promise of a good water supply, for it was now late summer. Any stream still running was unlikely to dry up. A big cliff offered its south face as a building site. Its loft would protect them from the north wind, and its southern stony countenance held a promise of sunshine, even in winter. They went to work now, felling logs and gathering foundation stone from the stream banks. The mustangs proved their worth again. In hastily made rope and rawhide harness now the tough little horses easily tugged log and stone that would cause the strongest man to falter. The work was exhausting, but both men reveled in it. And then came the Crow.

Hubert Baker and Robert Trav were both on their knees worrying a tenoned log into another log's prepared mortise. Quietly, the sudden sense of another's presence came over them simultaneously. Easing themselves to their feet they looked into each other's eyes and both knew they were being watched.

They turned slowly and there, not fifty feet from them, were the four Crow warriors. Robert's first thought was that they were striking and handsome. Not the 'trail niggers' he had seen previously. Not by a long sight.

They stood motionless. Not a hint of expression on their faces to betray their thoughts.

Robert thought they were as stone. They wore the colorful buckskin garb of the high plains warrior. Each had his hair fully roached out, decorated with brass wire, colored horse hair and hawk feathers. From head to toe they were covered in beads, fur and buckskin. Two of the warriors wore bright red blankets about their shoulders. Robert knew these were the most important of the Hudson's Bay trade goods. These red blankets were to be found anywhere the Hudson's trappers had ventured. Robert could not help but wonder if Fletcher Harris had somehow been connected to the blankets.

As Baker knew the Crow, he wasn't so interested in feathers. He did take intent notice however of the fact each wore a different painted design on his face. Baker knew the paint of battle when he saw it. He was keenly interested in their weaponry, too. His own rifle was right at hand. He eyed it warily. A quick glance and he saw Robert's Hawken, too, was in easy reach. Without looking, he knew his own skinning knife was in his belt, and he held a short broad axe in his hand.

He saw that the two Indians at the ends of their line carried long buffalo lances. They were brilliant spears, long and lithe. Wrapped in crimson flannel and decked out with braids of horse hair, snake rattles and plumed feathers. The largest brave was in the center. He was the one armed with a bow and a quiver stuffed with white, fletched arrows. Baker noticed the bow and quiver, though, were slung across the warrior's back and posed no instant threat. The smallest warrior of the center two, though, was a different story....

Baker's eyes fixed on his belt. Held there, in an otter-hide sash, were two fine Kentucky pistols. They were matched flintlocks; the type cased together and sold to wealthy gentry as duelers. Baker was quick to ascertain that both pistols were fully cocked and could be in deadly play in an instant. Only a man who expected danger would resort to the dangerous practice of carrying a cocked pistol in his waist band. Now he surveyed the same Indian's third weapon, a fine Pennsylvania long rifle. It was beautifully German silver mounted and stocked in elegant hand-carved and checkered curly maple. Its hickory ramrod was burned with a candy stripe pattern.

From the corner of his eye Baker saw that Robert had spotted the weapons also. Without knowing what the other was thinking, each was curious as to the fate of the gentleman who had given up these splendid guns. Neither Baker nor Robert had very much hope for his present condition.

The Indians stood a long time. After several minutes Baker realized he knew the tall Brave with the bow and quiver. He didn't know him well. He'd never spoken to him, but he'd seen him and somehow he remembered his name. He forced a smile and spoke. His voice, breaking the silence of the interlude, made Robert startle and jump. He fought for composure.

"I know you," Baker said. "You're the big brave called Bloody Shirt."

"It is a name white men have called me by."

"I am told you are big boss over all the buffalo." Baker was overjoyed with himself. This breakthrough made him feel as if he were the most important of Indian traders. He felt his recognition of the Crow had placed him in somewhat of a position of authority and leadership. Puffing his chest a bit he went on:

"They say, low on the mountain, that your voice is the thunder, that your arrows are the lightning of the sky. They tell how you kill all the enemies of the Crow with the touch of your mighty finger." Sensing the Indian was succumbing to his flattery, Baker swelled with pride. He was somewhat overcome by his own oratory. Further, he thought this flattery was bound to endear him to the Crow.

The four warriors looked one to the other in silence. They looked back at Baker and at each other again. Wordlessly, they turned their backs and, shaking their heads, walked back toward the forest. As they moved away, Robert heard one say something in a low mutter. He knew just enough Crow talk to know they were saying something about talking with fools. How these two whites were not smarter than turtles.

Now Robert and Baker saw the ponies the warriors had tied a short way back into the trees. The Crow mounted and, without so much as a backward glance at the two who were no smarter than turtles, vanishing into the trees as quietly as they had come. Robert turned to look at Baker who had turned to look at him.

They stared at each other nervously. Each was visibly shaken by the encounter with the painted Crow. Now the tension broke. Relief stirred in Baker's lower stomach; and at last Robert dared to breathe fully. Finally, the stress washing away, as if by signal, each fell into a nervous and uncontrollable fit of laughter.

The next weeks were busy ones indeed, for now it was late summer. Winter comes early to the high country, and Robert and Baker knew they had to be ready for it. Survival of winter in the Rockies only came to those who skillfully readied themselves. Further, they knew the pelts would prime up in the cold weather. The Rockie mountain beaver is the finest in the world when winter thickens his luxurious coat to an almost unbelievable fullness. There would be no time for working on lean to's or laying in supplies when the snow began to fly. They would be out in the elements every day that a man could stand the weather.

That required heavy robes of buffalo and elk. High moccasins too, water proofed with bear grease, were a must for outdoor work in the heavy snows. Meat and firewood had to be laid aside in vast quantities.

While one man worked on the shelter, the other shouldered his rifle and went for a hunt. Wild currants and fox grape were sun-dried into raisins. Long, thin strips of salted venison were dried and smoked into jerky. When this dried meat was combined with the raisins and pounded together with a stone hammer it became the life-sustaining pemmican.

The Crow came every day now and watched the two white men at their labors. Sometimes they laughed a bit at their goings-on, but mostly they just stood or sat and watched. Robert soon got used to their presence and he, good naturedly, smiled and waved at them. They hardly waved back but would react to his friendly "Halloo's" by looking sourly, one to the other.

Robert may have been a bit lax in their company, but not Baker. When the Crow were near, he was a coiled spring. He stayed close to his weapons and kept his eyes on them at all times. He pretended to ignore them, but they were in his peripheral vision every moment.

At last Bloody Shirt, who this day had shed his shirt and leggings and stood before the trappers nearly nude began to speak to Robert. He made a point of haughtily ignoring Baker who was not smarter than a turtle.

"My name is Sawn a watoe," he said to Robert one day. The remark was completely unexpected and Robert was startled by his voice.

"You're not Bloody Shirt then?" Robert asked.

"I have been Bloody Shirt to some whites. As I have been Red Tailed Hawk to the Arapaho...Sawn a watoe is the name my mother and father have given me as my own. When I speak to a fool or an enemy, I am the Shirt or the Hawk. If I only talk with a man...If I talk with men I wish to hunt with, I am Sawn a watoe."

It took Robert back a bit when he realized he'd never once thought of this half-naked warrior of having a mother or father. It started to dawn on him, for the first time now, that there were bona fide similarities between himself and this high plain savage.

"You speak good American," Robert said. "You know many words to say. I will call you by the name your mother and father gave you. I will hunt with you when you want. I am called Robert."

"Robert. Sounds good. What is Robert?"

Robert was confused.

"Robert is..." He groped for something to say. "Robert is my noise," he said finally. "It has no meaning but is the sound men I hunt with make when they want me to come."

"Do you come when they call?" the Crow wanted to know.

"I come," Robert said. "I come if they call in need or friendship. I come when they have shown me the open hand." Robert eyed the brave closely now. He saw that the Crow was as handsome as any man might be. His hair roach gave him an unusual look, but his features were finely chiseled. His face and body were nearly hairless and caused Robert to think of his own body and sparse blonde beard. Mostly, Robert observed that the Crow carried about him an air of quiet nobility. It was as though he knew precisely who he was and was at comfort with that knowledge. He was just what he was...No more...Certainly no less.

"It is good that you come to hunter friends with open hands. But Robert should be more. Not just a sound. I will give a true to Robert. We will say Robert when we..." his voice trailed off.

The Crow glanced now at Baker hard at work on firewood with a bucksaw.

"A good man with a big heart who rides with a turtle, that is a Robert." Robert was glad Baker was out of earshot.

"It is a good true, and I like it a lot," Robert said. "When next I hear the word Robert, I will think of this true. I will think of the Crow who knows many American words. I wonder two things big in my head, though: Where the Crow found so many American words...That and the true for Sawn a watoe. What is it I say when the sound I make is Sawn a watoe?

"It is a part of a goose," the Crow said. "It is the part that lives in the heart of the goose, that makes him watch his flock and go with them to the far places and to bring them back again. It is more brave and a better honor to be a goose heart than bear's claw or the teeth of a cougar. The clans of bear and lion makes the war and kills the enemy of the Crow. The spirit of the goose leads them back and forth, always together." The warrior paused here to be sure he was being understood. Satisfied at Robert's attention, he said,

"For a thousand seasons the goose flies with his band to the south place before the snows. But he leads them back every new grass. He is a strong leader. He has kept his band while the bands of men have come and then gone away and are seen no more. The goose is good and strong and is forever. If in the spring some time the goose does not come back, the Crow will know he is dead; and the Crow will die too. "Bloody Shirt" is a poor name. It is a name for death and war. Sawn a watoe is a name that lives on the wind. In the sky. It is a name of far places and forever."

Robert somehow felt touched by the words of this man who was so different and yet, so much like himself. They were poles apart in lifestyle and philosophy, yet somehow Robert understood everything the Crow had said. More importantly, what he had meant.

That night Robert told the story of Sawn a watoe to Baker as they sat by their evening fire. He was careful to leave out the part about the turtle.

"And when I asked him how come he could talk so good, he said the words come from Hudson fur men. I'm sure he meant the Hudson Bay Fur Company. I guess they got free trappers and Long Hunters 'bout ever'where. You know Baker, I had a belly full 'o them already. I sure wants to avoid seein' anymore of them."

" We'll have to sell to 'em, Scotty, but don't worry about it none. They ain't goin' to know you from Adam. Not likely they can tell that Fletcher Harris where you are now. But they got buyers in here all the time buyin' pelts as well as trappin' on their own. I ain't worried none about them holdin' you to an apprenticeship or even knowin' who you are. 'Sides that, if it'll make you feel better, I'll do the dealin' with 'em and you can run off and hide with the goose if you want." Baker's face was an open grin.

"Seriously though, Robert, I ain't near as concerned with Hudson Bay as I am you gettin' all friendly with a Crow. I'm tellin' you, Scotty, they just different in ever way than you and me. There ain't one single thought you have that a Crow can understand. They think and feel different ' bout all kinds of stuff."

"You really hate them don't you?"

"Hate? Hell no, I don't hate them. Could I hate a rattler for eatin' a squirrel? Rattlers eat squirrels all the time. It don't mean he's a bad critter...It means he's a good rattler. You can't hate rattlers for bein' rattlers. But you don't go pettin' 'em neither. If you tried to take a buffler calf, the cows and bulls would stomp you into solid rock. Don't mean the cow's a bad cow; it means she's a good Momma. Foxes got to be foxes, Rob. They cain't be nothin' else." Baker halted his talk now and drew nearer to Robert.

"I don't hate the Crow, Scotty, but I knows 'em pretty well. I know they don't feel the same about things as white folks do. That don't make 'em bad, but it sure makes 'em different. Scotty, you got to get onto this. You're buddyin' up to that Crow, thinkin' your makin' a friend. I don't know what he's thinkin'. But I can damn sure tell you it ain't what you're thinkin'." He paused again now, and placed his hand on the Scot's shoulder.

"I'm warnin' you Rob. Let's be alert. Let's be careful and save our hair 'till were 'bout ninety.... Me 'n you, Rob. Let's just stay in our own places. Let's catch some o' these high-country beavers and let the Crow go to hell."

That night Robert thought a long time before sleep. He pondered over Baker's remarks. He certainly respected Baker for his wisdom and experience, but maybe this time he was wrong.

After all, he told himself, Men are men. Maybe Baker's not so right just this one time. Could be the Crow're just lookin' to be friendly. A night of restless sleep came after long hours of hard thinking.

Baker and Robert came out of their bedrolls just at sunrise. Looking to the edge of the forest Robert saw that the Crow warrior, Sawn a watoe, had already taken up his daily vigil. But this time he had brought the woman.

Chapter Twenty

Juan Garcia, Bandito!
1836/1888

Garcia laid another thick, stick of greasewood to the small fire. He removed the empty toddy cup from the hand of his sleeping friend, went to the window and stared out into the gathering darkness. Stars were now appearing in the night sky. He always marveled at their brightness.

He was hopeful that Long John and the other ranch hands were making ready for the long trip that would face them tomorrow as he had directed. Hopefully it would be nothing. Maybe Colin was in no danger at all. Henry Brooker, though, was not a man given to foolishness. If he thought Colin might need help, then the prudent thing to do was to see about offering it.

The stars, he thought, *...cover all the land that is the Spur at the same time.* He wondered for a moment if Colin might, at this moment, be looking at the stars too. Garcia wasn't too sure about how land was measured, but he had heard talk that the Spur was about one-half million acres. He knew enough to know that was big. He knew the big spread was bordered on all sides by free range. Or at least it had been. After the big drought of 1868 things had never again been quite the same. The land had survived that most terrible Texas drought ever recorded.

But the drought brought on the deaths of a few million head of the wild long horn. The crossbreds died by entire herds at once. The lack of rain had paralyzed dozens of smaller ranch operations. Along with their once proud herds, these ranches vanished into the Texas dust. When Garcia thought of the type of cattle called "breeds," he always smiled to himself. The cross between a wild Texas longhorn and the sweet-natured English shorthorn made almost the perfect animal for this wild country. They had the survival instincts of the longhorn and his amazing foraging ability, but the wildness was contained. No longer were these animals as difficult to herd as deer or buffalo. Additionally, the great horn span was considerably shortened. Besides being a more civil animal, they produced the first real quality beef America had known.

But they are weaker, Garcia recalled with a sigh. The droughts, the heavy winters, the herd bosses who attempted to push them too hard had brought the breeding traditions to their knees. In recent years bigger, hardier stock was being introduced. Most prevalent was the Hereford.

A big white-faced, heavy-boned animal that did well if feed and water were available. They were docile and easy to handle, but in fly season they suffered terribly from eye infections. They didn't trail all that well either and the overzealous trail hand who hurried their cattle had to be toned down or fired. The Hereford made excellent beef though when the living was easy. They were still not tough enough, was Garcia's assessment.

Then came the introduction to the Brahma. The big fierce cattle from the continent of India. With them came fly resistance. No one could explain this phenomenon. The relentless flies of Texas would worry men, horses and most cattle to death in the fly season. No one could explain it, but these voracious pests would simply not land on a Brahma. The cross breeds carried this same fly resistance and therefore were stronger, healthier and had a much better weight-gaining metabolism. Good foraging ability was another plus.

Unfortunately, the Brahma brought along a return to wildness. The Brahma was bigger, meaner and wilder than the longhorn but simply lacked the longhorn's stamina. Like the shorthorn and the Hereford, an unrealistic trail boss could push them to their death. At last, after three decades of trial and error in animal husbandry, a three- or four- or even five-way cross of breeding provided the cattle Texas needed. Long drives and herd survival were the only way to the eastern markets. These lay vast distances from the Texas plains. That meant that if whatever breed crossing carried the survival traits of the old longhorn, they could prevail.

Men had to change too. The longhorn drives of the 1860's were nothing more than headlong stampedes. They were uncontrolled marches of cattle, horses and men all totally committed to the wild. The cattle though, were only being marketed at this time as a source of hides and tallow. It was after the great Civil war that Americans east of the Mississippi river developed a yearning for Texas beef.

These specially bred cattle that provide all the desirable traits had to be handled by men who were special too. The Spanish called them Vaquero. In Texas they were the cowboys. It meant the same thing: Men who could think like cows. Men who could live on the ground or the back of a horse. Cowmen who could push two thousand cattle at a time up fifteen hundred miles of trail to the Kansas rail heads. The trip took three to five months of bone-jarring, back-breaking work. It meant breaking horses to ride every day on the trail, while living on bacon, biscuits and stewed apples. These coupled with beans and the strong Arbuckle's coffee were the daily fare unless someone shot a deer or killed a crippled cow.

Night hawking, to prevent straying, meant the job was twenty-four hours a day. These great herds lumbered at a snail's pace, barely making ten to twelve miles on good days; a lot less in weather.

To see themselves through the day, a biscuit or two would be squirreled away in a saddle bag or pommel sack. Supper was a sundown affair of beans with salt-cured ham or beans with salt-cured side pork or beans with fresh beef. The beef usually had been taken that very day from a cow or steer that had lost the look of survival.

Cornbread cooked in a Dutch oven and spread with blackstrap molasses rounded out the meal. Always, there was Arbuckle's. The coal black, evil brew that was a mixture of strong Brazilian coffee and Louisiana chicory. Mostly it was chicory with a bit of coffee for flavoring. The cowboys laughed as they made their morning toilets that they had drank so much Chicory they were passing tree bark. It was beans, bacon and Arbuckle's that was the fuel that moved the great herds. The cowboys were the machines. It was, for the most part, a proposition of man against nature.

Juan Garcia had observed to himself, more than once, that the driving of cattle in a herd for a long distance, is as unnatural as a fish with feathers. It was Texas that had given the men the horses and cattle that would constitute the grand herds. Yet, it was Texas herself that threw up their greatest opposition. Without doubt, the long distances that faced the trail herds was far and away the single most discouraging factor. Simply to look upon a herd of two thousand fierce, wild and dangerous cattle and to realize they would have to be moved more than a thousand miles overland through the most hostile country America had to offer was disparaging to the gamest heart.

But distance was only one of the obstacles. There were rivers too. Sometimes they were so dry that even the diamondback couldn't find a swallow of life-sustaining water. That same river would, when it desired, swell into an angry torrent that could, and would, in an instant, drag man and horse together to a watery death.

Weather always played a major role in the success or agonies of trail life. Texas weather was totally unpredictable. As one trail hand observed to Juan Garcia, "It just ain't reasonable." He was reflecting on the May storm of 1874 that simply appeared from nowhere and froze to death their entire remuda of seventy-eight horses. Drover, Tom Arnette had been found on the prairie in June of 1875, beaten unconscious and near death, by hailstones as large as pigeon eggs. His face and head were shredded to the bone by unrelenting hail. The incident had prompted old Robert to warn his herdsmen, in the face of hail, to dismount and cover their heads with their saddles.

Blizzards so intense as to be unbelievable came all the way from Canada. Alberta clippers, they were named. The really bitter ones became the famous blue Texas norther. Borne on the breast of the North wind, these squalls killed horses and cattle in astonishing numbers. Then they vanished into nowhere as suddenly as they had come. Along with their heavy winds, they brought temperatures so cold that the air indeed took on a blue cast. Even their name was terrible.

Heat killed horses and cattle alike when the broiling Texas sun brought about temperatures exceeding one hundred ten degrees or, often as not, even higher. The summers of Texas are long ones. They linger about with no relief, the very hottest days coming as late as September and October. When many other places in the world are exhilarating in the friendly temperatures of fall Texas offered no such relief. It was this time of the year that drove Robert out of his favored buckskin clothing. In this intense heat he donned the cooler, more practical light cotton garb of the Mexican farmer. Even the beloved moccasins gave way to the cooler hurachas, the Spanish sandal of Mexican peasants. He thought often of donning again the breech clout of the Crow but in the end he did all he could to put those days behind him.

Charley Goodnight, leader of the Duro Palo Canyon Rangers, had opened the old Goodnight trail from the Pecos River to El Paso. He had marked the trail north all the way to Cheyenne, Wyoming. It was Goodnight who had described the Texas heat as, "Greasy....So greasy you can hear it poppin' in the skillet." Men suffered and cattle fell before this "greasy" sunshine.

The problems that had to be worked out in herding cattle were legion. Of these none was more critical than some form of marching order.

"Soldiers can march a straight line'" men like Charley Goodnight allowed. "Even those stupid cavalry, horse turd soldiers can follow one behind the other. But tryin' to drive cattle's more like tryin' to drive a covey of quail. Like herdin' cats,"

And it was true. For a mounted group of men to fall in behind a herd of a thousand or more was, at best, comical. At the worst, tragic. The cattle would stray and wander; a cow running here to a calve, a steer leaving the herd to investigate a likely looking clump of green grass. It appeared, at first, no cattle would ever be driven more than a few yards from their starting place. The first attempts at herd-driving were disastrous. When Robert saw this futility, he called his cowboys together. They sat on their haunches around the cook and medicine wagon, and Robert observed his casually assembled band of misfits.

They were a bit ragged, he had to agree. But there were men here. Men like Juan Garcia who showed a natural ability for leadership. Juan never seemed to boss his men about. Rather, he helped them decide what he wanted them to do. Robert had caught the fact he got the required work done and more. More importantly, men liked Juan Garcia.

Garcia was, without question, a cut above the others. He dressed as the traditional Mexican Vaquero: Chaps, boots and Spanish spurs. He had a sombrero, too, but rarely wore it. The big hat truly provided an amazing amount of protection from the weather. Even in summer, its high crown was a cooling insulator. Garcia just thought its incredible size looked absurd. Instead Garcia elected to wear the flat crowned, straight brimmed hat of the vaquero. He felt it offered enough protection from sun and rain to suit him and was not so ridiculous in appearance as the sombrero. So this was this hat he chose. Generally, in black. Often as not though, the hat was not worn on his head. Rather, it hung carelessly down his back from the chin cords. Held fast, in the sash at his waist, was a heavy caplock pistol. Plain and strong it looked, as though it may have come from the Hawken store of Saint Louis.

Sometimes Garcia did not wear the sword. Generally though, it swung gracefully at his left side. He was a lean and hard man. Dark eyed, his even, white teeth gleamed against skin burned olive-brown by the sun. Garcia found the sideburns and moustache that many Mexicans adored to be hot and uncomfortable. Once, when he was very young, he had seen a poster picture of a famed Spanish Matador. The young man's handsome face was drawn on a Seville bullfight poster that someone had shown him as a curiosity. Looking at the face of the young and handsome Torero, Garcia felt he was gazing in a mirror. The drawing of the bullfighter's face so reminded him of his own appearance. There was no indication of facial hair on the drawing. Garcia took this sign to support the way he personally felt about facial hair.

Spanish Toreros were considered by most Mexicans to be heroes. Certainly, one who had his face on a poster must be so. An example to follow. Someone to emulate. Garcia elected to go about clean shaven when he could. Of course, it was not always possible, given his duties in this wild country. He wore his hair though at shoulder length. He cut it straight across with a knife when the length annoyed him. His long hair and dark skin always reminded old Robert of the Crow people.

Garcia despised the "bowl haircuts" that displayed the gleaming white skin at the back of the neck and above the ears. With his hat thrown back so often, he usually wore a blue or red bandanna as a head band. Sometimes, he used a leather strap to hold the glossy thick crop in place. He sat his horse straight and tall. His walk was sure and steady. Powerful.

Robert thought of the cougar when he saw Garcia striding about the corrals and feed lots of the Spur. Juan Garcia was not a vain man but he might have been called fastidious. He daily brushed the trail dust from his clothing. He shined his riding boots with lamp black and oil, and he bathed when he found it possible. These acts alone set him somewhat apart from the typical cowboy. Robert decided that day that his old Scottish uncle had the precise words to describe the appearance of Juan Garcia. He would've called him "a dashin' one," to say the least.

Garcia had been with Robert the longest by far of any of the hands. Robert often thought of the day he had found Garcia so badly wounded on the plain north of the river. It was a day neither would ever forget and, in truth, a day that changed the lives of these two forever. As badly wounded as Garcia was, Robert had wondered for all these years whether this bold brigand was shot while running from men...Or maybe a woman...Or maybe the man of some woman. One thing was sure: someone had tried to kill Garcia. And nearly succeeded. With Robert's help though, he had beaten the odds. He had survived his grievous hurts.

When Garcia had recovered from his wounds enough to ride about or walk along the river with Robert, the Scot noticed a queer thing. He saw that this obviously fine horseman and particular dresser rode with only one spur. With the attention Juan Garcia seemed to pay to the detailing of his gear this seemed, to Robert, a strange thing.

"Mister Garcia," Robert had asked. "Where is your other spur?"

"In my pommel bag, Senor. The spur is a good one, but I broke it on a stone." The Vaquero rested easy in his saddle. "I hope soon to have some dinero...Money. I will fix the spur when I can pay. I will fix many things with money when I get it." Robert wondered if this last remark had anything to do with unfinished business Garcia may have left behind in Mexico.

Robert looked out over the vast spread of wild Texas land, its only shelter at this time, a rude tipi in the Crow fashion.

"Mister Garcia," he said, "I think this here ranch is pretty much like your spur...It needs fixin'. It needs a heap o' fixin'. I reckon you and me ever get the money, we'll fix it up real nice. That is, if we live long enough."

"I understand, Senor Robert," the slim Mexican grinned. "This ranchero. She needs some fixin' pretty good. She is like a broken spur."

"Broken Spur…" Robert repeated to himself. It sounded right somehow. In some mysterious way it reflected on Robert's very life to this point. Like the land– like the spur– his life could stand some mending.

This land, he thought, …could be the bonding material my mending needs". And on that day they christened their home "The Broken Spur."

The others who came weren't so attractive or trustworthy as Garcia. Nor were they nearly so astute. Here was an assortment of runaway slaves, Mexican banditos, genuine Texas outlaws and a few starving sod busters. Ragged, hungry and dirty, they sought food and refuge for many reasons.

Little Joe Coulter, who was all of fourteen, had simply been told by his father that the family could no longer feed him and still survive. The family had agreed that, since he was oldest, Joseph had better find another place to light. His mother had stood in the doorway of the rude sod shanty and waved goodbye as his father turned the frightened boy with the pleading eyes away. A pitiful sight, with his little poke of corn dodgers and a few apples, the boy had nearly starved out on the plains. Twice he was nearly detected by the Comanches, or maybe they were Kiowa, he wasn't sure. Joseph Coulter had been terrified, cold and hungry when he finally made it to the Canadian River and Robert Trav's Broken Spur.

The others weren't that much different. They may have been older; more experienced perhaps; but they shared the common bond of desperation with Little Joe. Like him, they had come from everywhere when they heard of the Rockie Mountain fur trader who was paying real gold to men who would help him bunch cattle.

Here are the orphans of Texas, Robert thought. Their very lives have been broken into by storms and drought and Comanches. It was a gathering of men with nowhere to go. Hope had been replaced by raw courage; faith with the desire to survive. As he watched them, though, Robert found no sadness nor dejection here. They may have, by their clothing and worn trappings, appeared humbled; but these men walked tall. They were bright, not with intellect but filled with energy and a knowledge of the out of doors. A lot of this exuberance for life was given over to good-natured horse play and constant joking.

Robert often thought, tough times may have been their lot, but you'd not know it by these laughin' faces. Bruised they may well be, but these are not men near to beaten. If the men had any problem at all with Robert, it was trying to understand his sanity…. or the lack thereof.

"Why in the world," they questioned, "…would a man pay out real money to men for helping him gather up these pitiful Texas longhorns?"

They were, after all, worthless old hunks of hide and bone. Nobody owned them and nobody cared. The riders had to question the soundness of Robert Trav's mind.

Scottish cattle are worth their weight in silver, he reasoned when he came first upon this land. These are poor by the standard of the Scot, but, my Lord, they're cattle. There's such a great many 'o 'em,. I'll gather up these wee beasts and see how we fares....

"Senor Robert'" Garcia reported to him one morning. "We have three arroyos filled with the cows and the box canyon too. The men, Senor Robert...They want to know where they go now."

"North," Robert had said. "I heard that Charley Goodnight and that Oliver feller...You know. Oliver Loving from down by the Red. They was a-sayin' back in 1849 the Union Pacific crossed the whole country north of here somewhere. I figure we just head these cows north, and sooner or later we'll strike that track. When we do, there'll be folks there a-wantin' cattle. Maybe for oxen and hides and tallow and such. That's the way, Garcia," he pointed. "We headin' north."

"Sooner or later?" Garcia queried.

"That's the way of it, Mr. Garcia. North to the tracks. All we got to do is live long enough."

"Boys," Robert began explaining to his new trail hands. "Back in the Rockies there, I met up with a Crow chief who was a big boss because he was a true. That's what the Crow call men big with honor or wisdom. It's like when we say a feller is straight, or walks tall, or the like." The men listened intently.

"This here Crow chief tells me that bears and catamounts and such ain't so near powerful as leaders as is the goose." Garcia would never forget the quizzical, almost amused looks on the faces of the men. These were hard-bitten men. Foolishness wasn't their chosen fare.

"Seems this goose leader picks out strong ones in the flock to help him lead his band. Then he strings 'em out in the sky in a long line or in a big V. Then these leader geese try to hold that together. That way, they can see each other...They each know what the other ones are doin'...They...sort of...depend on each other. What I'm thinkin' is we stretch ourselves out in a big V. Like the geese. Only we fill in the middle space with cattle; so it's more like an arrow head. I made me a drawin'."

He passed around a crudely drawn diagram made with the stub of a pencil and a piece of paper torn from an Arbuckle's sack.

"You can see the point of the arrow is long and thin. We don't get into the big bunch of cattle till pretty far back. That's so we can swing the point when we make a turn. We can turn that thin line and only have to worry about half as many cows till we get 'em goin' in the right direction again.

"I'm thinkin' that cattle, and geese alike, need a strong leader right up front. So I'm puttin' Juan Garcia up there in the lead. He's gonna have the medicine wagon right up there with him. The wagon might get a chance to break far up in front. Get ahead o' the herd two, three miles maybe. That'll give the cookers a chance to get ahead on buildin' fires and such, gettin' the food ready. But Garcia will stay up there where the cattle and the other men can see him. We'll look to him for our directions.

We'll call Juan and the wagon our point. About a quarter of the way back we'll put a rider on the east. Then, one on the west of the herd to make the point stronger. I didn't know what to call them riders. Then Tom Arnette spoke up. Robert gestured toward a thin, dark man in a buckskin shirt, Arnette said.

"Maybe they should be called the 'swing riders. 'cause, when we got to make a turn they'll have the whole weight of the herd to hold. It'd be easy for the cattle to break out during a turn between the swing and the point. We got to make them turns big and slow. Sort of... swing. the cattle around instead o' turnin' 'em." Robert nodded his head in ready agreement.

"That's good Tom. Swing riders it is. Back another quarter mile or there'bouts we'll put out another team of riders, both east and west and I thought we ought to call them our flank riders. Right in the very tail of the bunch we'll bring the rest of the riders together to help push, look after the remuda of horses and fill in when we get a hole in the line. These will be our drovers. "

"When we start a turn or when any cow breaks out of the arrowhead ,one o' these drovers will get out in front of her and head 'er in. We'll need good riders for our drovers. Mostly the point-and-swing will be ridin' along at a walk. These drovers will have to push their mounts fast to catch some of these old wild cows. Some o' them are faster'n deers. Ridin' and pushin' from the back, we ought to be able to watch each side o' the line pretty good. That's gonna be tough place to be boys, mostly on account of the dust. "

"Specially that drag rider on the down east tail. What with the wind prevailin' from the west as it does, that rider is gonna eat all the dust every day. We got to spell that man. We'll all take a turn at ridin' the downhill drag. Better cover your faces with bandannas and such 'cause that'll be the roughest place on the drive. Now, boys, I know this plan ain't perfect....

"It would be if the damned cattle would listen to it!" The men roared.

"I'm gonna act as trail boss...They tell me that's what Charley Goodnight call hisself. Trail boss. Reckon I'll be four or five miles up ahead of you and Garcia. You got my word, boys, I'll try to pick you a soft path." The men looked one to the other. They nodded to each other and in a stoic; silent way affirmed the commitment to follow Robert Trav. Garcia sensed these men would ride into hell for this young Scot. He knew he would. Here was a man who made it a point to treat half breed, Mexican and Negro all as his friends. More importantly, as his equal. In this part of the world he was a rare man indeed.

With only slight variations on the Trav plan, all the herds that would come out of Texas for the next thirty years would depend on the marching order laid out by Robert Trav. Oh, Charley Goodnight would call his medicine wagon the "chuck wagon."

Oliver Loving and John Chisholm would hire "outriders" to protect the herds with their guns as they moved north. But for the most part, the method of trailing beef stayed pretty much the same. You could see it on the Pecos Trail, the Chisholm, the Red River or the Goodnight. Wherever one looked, he would encounter cattle moving in the order prescribed by Robert Trav that day, so long ago, on the Broken Spur. Mostly the workers were very young. Cowboys often ended their trail careers early and moved on to better lives.

A few, like Colin and Juan Garcia, stayed in the saddle well past their prime. Garcia, now in front of the fire in the little adobe, thought of Colin who was on the open trail this very night. He looked over at old Robert who was dozing quite soundly by now. He would in a minute help his oldest friend to his bedstead in the corner of the adobe. For now though he was enjoying his thoughts and memories. The night was full, black now and each star was a point of brilliance against the dark sky...

Colin was a man who truly loved and understood cattle and horses, Garcia knew. Old Robert, too, was revered for miles around as a true cattle man. Though Garcia knew Old Robert had not yet come to terms with horses. Garcia, on the other hand, loved the horse almost as much as life itself. The times he had spent in the company of horses, he felt, had been the best of all his life.

"Old Robert," he mused, "...he is true Vaquero. Colin too. Colin is cowboy."

Without it ever having been said, Garcia knew that part of the Spur was his. His life had become so intertwined with that of Robert Trav there was no way they could ever have lived one without the other. If Old Robert Trav was the father of Colin, then so was Juan Garcia. Both of these men had pasts they would try in vain to forget. Yet both of them knew it was the past that made them what they were this day.

Then he remembered, I too...I'm one of these. I could never be better than Vaquero...There is no better thing to be than Vaquero.

He had these thoughts often. But he could never shake off the memories that nagged at him deep down in spirit. Now he was a totally respected rancher. A leading member of a community even it was spread out over so many miles. But it was not always so. He hadn't always been a cowboy. There was a time when Juan Garcia had lived an entirely different life. He had not been called "cowboy" then. He was Bandito.

Chapter Twenty-one

The Ride from Alamo
1836/1846

Although it was March, it still was unseasonably warm that morning in 1836. The boy felt uncomfortable and overly warm in his ill-fitting uniform. The heavy brogan shoes, worn over stockingless feet, were hard and unsparing. The acrid smoke from hundreds of pounds of burnt gun powder hung in the air as grey and poisonous vapor. The boy was only thirteen. He had not really seen anything like this before. His father had consigned him, for a few pesos, to the infantry of Antonio Lopez Santa Anna more than a year ago. He had carried ammunition, water and even dispatch through several skirmishes but they had been mere hostile forays. This was absolute carnage.

The north wall of the old mission had been completely breached by thirteen days of unrelenting cannon fire. Now the mission's ramparts were a crumbling disarray of rubble. The boy was part of an army made up of more than five thousand battle-hardened Mexican Infantry troops.

It was said that, within the remains of the fort like walls, were the one hundred and eighty dead rebel dissidents... the Texicans who had dared defy so great a personage as Generalissimo Santa Anna. The boy, as ordered, entered the split and broken gate. He carried a large bundle of bandages to serve the wounded.

He nearly dropped his burden when he first he saw that there were far more than one hundred and eighty dead. Inside the remains of the walls, the slaughter was terrible to behold. The hundred and eighty had fought like tigers. It would appear each Texan had killed four or five of his attackers. These once holy walls now steeped in blood-spattered stone, unholiness and defilement, encircled the remains of more than a thousand valiant men, of two separate persuasions, who had fallen that sixth day of March, 1836. It was the day Texans would never forget.

"Bring me Crockett! Bring to me the soldier Crockett!" The boy heard the barked command over and over. "I want the head of the Green

Mountain leader...Bring me the head of Crockett...Bring me his long rifle to spike his head on..."

It was the voice of Captain Ricardo Herrera. It was Herrera who had sworn vengeance on the former American Congressman. It was Davey Crockett, Herrera believed, that had held the rebels together. He knew for sure it had been the long range of the Kentucky rifles used by Crockett's' sharpshooters. That sniping had been the most harassing single feature of the thirteen-day siege at Alamo. The search was made for the body of the Tennessean, but the utter devastation of all the bodies of the dead offered Crockett sanctuary against final indignities. His identification was lost among the carnage.

The boy watched the grisly work of war with spellbound eyes. He was unable to look and yet could not turn away. He wondered what it must have been like here, among all these dead, in the final minutes. There had been the ceaseless roar of the cannon, then the breech of the north wall. This, followed by dozens of scaling ladders against the walls of the enclosure. Then there was the pouring of troops over the wall and into the courtyards. How fearsome that must have been. Musket fire and long rifles gave way to hand guns. Then to the Toledo steel bayonets.

Now it was a battle of blades. Old Spanish rapiers, sabers and bayonets challenged by the Bowie Knives and Arkansas Toothpicks of the Texicans. Wide eyed now, like an animal confused by the smell of blood and death, the boy could only wonder if he would've been afraid. His Captain had instructed him never to fear.

Obeying his Capitain, he knew, was the right thing to do. It was the thing he wanted more than all others. To be brave. To be a man. An hombre. Now, amid this butchery, he wondered if any man could have been a part to this melee without feeling the rank sweat of fear. Of knowing the bitter metal, the coppery taste, of fear. It was that day Juan Garcia learned how to win a battle. He saw the results with his own eyes that come from using all the force you have as fiercely as you can. No mercy, would heretofore be his policy. For a dead enemy was little threat. He vowed to grant quarter to no man who offended him.

It would be these legacies he would use so many times later in his life. He would call this battle wisdom to mind whenever it was needed. The thoughts came as a conditioned reflex when interlopers and invaders made it necessary for Juan Garcia to defend the Broken Spur.

Once the Alamo had completely fallen; once the bodies were burned–for Santa Anna had proclaimed that no Texan was allowed to be buried. He would permit no graves to exist that might someday be places of reverence for the worship of these fallen heroes. The cremation pyres darkened the skies over San Antonio with a black greasy smoke and the smell of burning hair and flesh for days upon days.

Word circulated throughout the bivouac that soon Santa Anna would meet Austin and Houston on the field of battle. At last the dissidents would be crushed forever. Perhaps, the war would culminate in another battle at Goliad where in 1835 a poorly equipped and out manned Texan company had claimed its first victory over a Mexican force. Now However, Santa Anna had vowed to wait at San Jacinto. Here he felt he would end the revolt finally and forever. The Alamo victory had whetted his blood lust and he felt spelled doom to all in his path. Of his army most felt it would hardly be a skirmish worthy of being called an actual battle. After all, even the Indians who loved Houston called him "Big Drunk." Surely pit him against the hero of Alamo would be a disaster for Texas. Yet even at such a tender age Garcia had a nagging feeling of guilt. A sense that said these Texicans had done nothing to him. And why should he fight with them? And could Santa Anna really succeed against these dedicated fighters a second time? What if the next battle were more evenly matched?

He was committed now to killing his enemies, but he wasn't sure these fierce fighters of Texas were, in truth, his enemies. He was positive he never wanted to see human life so ruined again as he had at Alamo. He was sickened by the Captain he had always admired and respected; now searching so churlishly for the head of Crockett.

Juan Garcia, after much deliberation, came to the first important decision he had ever made in his life. The night of the twenty-sixth of March he stole a horse and a small bag of assorted possibles. He took his Spanish musket along with a fine Toledo steel rapier, also stolen. Under the cover of a starless night, he deserted the Army of the Mexican Republic. He made good his escape with no elaborate planning or skilled and devious execution. He got away cleanly by just riding off into the darkness. Now, for the first time, he was on his own. He was alone.

It is not easy for such a young boy to be alone. Not when he is in the endless tract of wild land that makes up the Rio Grande Valley. It took all of Juan Garcia's instincts just to survive. Those, and the fact that many of the Mexican families he approached for help gave it to him.

It seemed to Garcia that any of the Mexicans he approached were more than willing to assist him. They were, indeed, his salvation. From those few who refused him help, he simply stole whatever he asked them for. Most, though, were willing to assist him, even knowing him to be a deserter and a fugitive.

The tyrant, Santa Anna was not in high regard with the middle and lower classes of the Mexican people. After all, what was wrong with Americans? Wasn't it the Americans who had brought the only prosperity to the Rio Grande Valley that these citizens of Mexico had ever known? By defeating the Americans, the Generalissimo was depriving his own people of sorely needed trade and employment opportunities. The Mexico of 1836 was made up of the haves and have-nots. There was nothing in between. The have-nots were finding more opportunity among the immigrant Texicans, by far, than they were from their own ruling aristocracy.

With the vast amount of natural resources held in the Texas lands, the Mexican needed no charity. What they needed was a chance to exercise trade and commerce. This had never come from governing Spain, but these Americans, with their perpetual thirst for development, seemed to offer some genuine economic advancement. Many Mexicans, in dealing with the "Gringo," had achieved some financial success through trade. It was for the first time in three hundred years. Spain offered commerce only to her aristocracy. Santa Anna and his royal associates were fast losing support among those who saw themselves starving in the midst of plenty.

Further aggravating the situation was the battle at the Alamo. What Santa Anna's troops saw as a great victory was beheld by Americans as a massacre. The very name, Alamo, so inflamed the hearts of Americans that those who had cared not a pittance yesterday now readily volunteered in the great "Texas Assist."

They rallied from all over Texas and surrounding territories to assist Sam Houston, each pledging his fortune and his life in support of Houston's attempted retaliation against the cruel Spaniard Viceroy. The great Generalissimo was about to fall victim to his own conquest.

As a deserter from the army of Santa Anna, Juan Garcia had little trouble finding the support of friends. Living as he was, mostly hiding out and avoiding people when he could, it would be months before Garcia would hear of Santa Anna's crushing and humiliating defeat at San Jacinto by Sam Houston. Young as he might be, he sensed the revolution was over. The Texans had won. He never regretted having missed it.

Chapter Tweny-two

The Crow and Robert Trav

Two years came and quietly passed now in the lives of Hubert Baker and Robert Trav. They were the same close friends they had been from that first meeting in the Coonhunter Tavern except for the fact Robert had moved into the crow camp some four miles higher up the mountain.

The day Bloody Shirt had brought the woman to the trappers' camp, things had begun to change.

"She is sister to the wind," Bloody Shirt had said. "She is my sister too. She has another name that no one may say. It is because her man has fallen before the enemy in battle. She is alone now, Robert Trav... And you are alone... Her man is dead and she is alive... And you are alive... I have brought her to you, Robert Trav. That is my true."

She stood apart from the men as they talked. It was apparent her brother, Bloody Shirt, was handing her over to Robert. He was giving her away as he would've a gift pot or fox pelt. Robert noticed that her stare was fixed on the ground. She seemed totally without emotion. He had been around enough Indians by now to understand she was forbidden to look into the eyes of men while business was at hand. Yet her silence was deeper than that of respect or custom. She was feeling something. Something deep and dark that Robert couldn't understand. He stood, confused and mesmerized by the whole proposition.

He looked at her. Even with her bowed head she was tall like her brother. She wore a light grey dress of smoked elk skin. The supple pelt had been worked until it was as soft as any fabric. Robert felt his face flush hot as his eyes drank in the generous curves beneath the clinging elk. Even hidden as they were by the folds of her garment, he found her compelling.

Her hair was so glossy black that Robert could detect little glints of reflected sunlight. She raised her head only slightly, and from the corner of her eye she caught his stare. She showed him the suggestion of a smile, and he fixed on the sight of even white teeth and flashing dark eyes. It was her first indication of acceptance of him. Embarrassed now for this moment of boldness, she quickly recovered her composure and assumed her proper downcast stare. Robert felt something move in his stomach that reminded him, somehow, of a hummingbird. He stood silent, rooted to the spot, and he felt his mouth go dry.

"Take her back! Take her back to the camp of Crow. We have no room for slaves here!" It was Hubert Baker who spoke first, his voice revealing just how much he distrusted the Crow.

Now Bloody Shirt coldly regarded Baker but spoke directly to Robert.

"When I speak with you, Robert Trav, why am I answered by the turtle? My sister is no man's slave. She is a warrior's wife. She is of great honor. Her man was of the Mandan, come to live among the Crow for a great true in his heart. A great love for "sister of the wind." They marry in Crow council and he is big honor to the Crow. He steals many ponies from the Arapaho. He kills deers and elks and once a great bear. At our council fires he makes big magic songs. His voice is thunder. Then he falls to the arrows of the Arapaho. It needs be six arrows..." He held up the appropriate number of fingers. "...to make quiet the voice that is thunder." Bloody Shirt lowered his head as he recounted the sadness of his story. "Now his wife and my sister comes before the fires and makes a mighty oath ..."

Baker moved forward and started to interrupt, but a steely glance told him Robert would hear this tale.

"She tells the council that she will avenge the Mandan stealer of Arapaho horses. Before the sun crosses the sky eleven times she comes and brings me this." Reaching into his belt pouch he produced the long black hair with the dried skin attached that all men in this wild country recognized.

"She carried great wounds of battle and was near death when she returned. She cried aloud. Not as a woman. She sang the death song as a big warrior. She too strong... Never die... Never cry. She stands before the council fire and shows this big true... this Arapaho hair. She is her dead man's big magic. She carries the spirit of the Mandan horse stealer. We vow to speak her real name no more. She is Iron Woman!

The turtle calls her slave. Hah!" he spat. "He calls her slave and she take big knife to his man parts. He is turtle. Iron Woman is a big true... She is no slave to you either, Robert Trav... Friend... She big friend for you. Winter soon, Robert Trav. Winters here long and cold with no woman. Long and cold and dark. Her arms will warm your lodge, Robert Trav. Her eyes will light your cold, dark mornings. Bloody Shirt brings this fine thing to you. This big true."

"I want her out of here!" Baker was angering now. Robert ignored him and let his gaze drink her in. It started at the small, moccasin clad feet and strayed upward to the fullness covered in the smoky elk leather. At last, his gaze fell to rest on her face. It was a face which he found lovely. Her high cheeks and dark eyes held a promise of mystery. In his stomach, Robert felt the bird again.

"She stays." Robert spoke with such firmness that it jolted Baker. He had never spoken this way to Baker or to anyone. His candor made it obvious. This arbitration had ended before it stated. Baker was stunned. He had never known his friend to be so firm with him or, for that matter, so brutally blunt.

That night, Iron Woman and Robert Trav stayed together in the lean-to. Hubert Baker, filled with his mistrust of the Crow, sat a hundred yards above the little shelter on the side of the slope. He held a loaded rifle. It was like the Crow in his judgment to use the woman to orchestrate treachery. The rifle felt comforting to him.

That long cold night, as Baker looked down from his vigil on the rude hut, he could not help but think of his friend inside with the Crow woman. He pictured them warm under the buffalo robes together. He felt a cold stab of jealousy. More than jealous, though, Hubert Baker had to admit he had never felt more alone. He reflected that he had never known a night to be so cold this time of year. Along with the thoughts that he feared and mistrusted the Crow, he was afraid he'd lost his finest friend. Lost him to the Crow. He felt hollow. Hollow, cold and alone.

The seasons came and went peacefully. The change, though, in the relationship between Baker and Robert, was a severe one. The two were of course, still the best of friends, but now they lived apart. Baker had taken up the camp site and the lean to. Robert had gone up the slope four miles or a bit more into the Crow camp. He had moved into the tipi of Iron Woman. The same one she had prepared and then shared with the Mandan horse thief. On the day they had moved from the trappers camp the woman had led the way up the grade. Carrying a small burden of possibles Robert had followed her to her lodgings. As he came into the sight of the Crow camp for the first time he felt some apprehension of danger of course for these were the fierce warriors of the hills. More than that though he was prisoner to an overcoming of curiosity. It would be the first time he had genuinely seen how these people of the forest and mountains really lived.

Men and women walked about in the clearing. They were tending fires, stirring cooking pots of hot food and generally going about the day to day business of living. They barely looked up or in anyway acknowledged the arrival of this strange pair. A few dogs barked at the approaching couple and one or two even bared teeth as they issued low growls. For the most part though the entrance of Iron Woman and her white man lover attracted very little fan-fare. Robert could only assume the gossip had started long ago and by now he was old and even somewhat stale news.

The encampment was not a large one but Robert had counted more than twenty visible tipis. He knew more might well be secluded back deeper into the forest. Robert had come into her lodge filled with misgivings and doubt. Perhaps even a bit of fear. Now, try as he might, he could never remember a time he had been happier or more content.

Robert and Baker ran a fine trap line. They covered twenty miles of wilderness that had never before seen a steel trap. They took fine big catches of beaver as well as mink, otter and even a few choice pelts of fisher, bobcat and ermine. The furs were so pristine and richly filled out that they always brought premium prices when delivered at the Landing.

The Landing as it was called was the fur market trading post. Located on a wild branch of the river the currents here were swift and barely navigable by cargo canoe. Baker and Robert shared such a river craft of more than fiveteen feet long. They had traded ten knife blades and two steel axe heads for the birchbark and deer-hide affair to a group of meandering Flathead Indians. Baker simply would have none of trading with the Crow people.

The eager water raced headlong through a narrow gorge. Its excited currents sprayed forth in a frothing boil of white water the traders and Indians called "Horse Tail Flume." Baker and Robert did not visit the Landing often. It was more than twenty-five miles away from their camps over torturous trails. It was usually Baker who went to Horse Tail Flume to do the trading every month or so. He kept his visits timed by the fullness of the moon. Each half moon meant it was time to sell hides or buy supplies. Then Hubert Baker would set out in the big canoe for the dangerous exodus. Often he would portage the boat on his strong shoulders a mile or so around impassable waters. It was hard and dangerous, but Baker was as hard. He was used to the frontier ways and the trip was something he just did… without much thought.

Robert, unquestioningly, turned over his half of the pelts to Baker, helped him load the pack horses and sent him on his way without any thought of mistrust. Robert knew full well that his part of the fur cache or the money that it brought, always in pieces of gold, could be in some jeopardy at the landing. There was whiskey available. And gambling. Sometimes, an enterprising trapper or gambler would find a woman brave enough or desperate enough to come this far upstream.

He would bring her to the landing. There, for a week or so, he would put her out as an entertainment to the visiting trappers and traders. The whole proposition reminded Robert of the Evansville experience. He found it easy to relegate that part of their business to Baker and keep himself away. Other than Baker, Robert neither had nor wanted relationship with any whites. Day by day, he was living more and more as a Crow. He hardly ever wore his own clothing now. Instead he went about day by day wearing only the breech clout and moccasins like the other men of the village. Baker was highly distressed by this. It reinforced the feeling that his true friend had vanished among the primitive Crow.

Robert knew that Baker must deduct a certain share of their money. This he would send back to Saint Louis to dividend their sponsors. Robert had never asked how much the investors were to receive. He simply never cared. He understood it was these men willing to gamble on beaver and men who could catch them who had brought him to this high place. He just was disinterested in the transaction made between the investors and Hubert Baker. Each time Baker returned from marketing their pelts he would hand Robert a small leathern sack of gold pieces and say, "Count it." Robert always gave the same answer. "I'm sure it's all there, Hubert." And never once did Robert look inside the little pokes.

Robert began to wonder what he needed the gold for at all. Iron woman had no interest in it. Neither did Bloody Shirt or any of his Crow friends. Robert had by now very nearly become Crow himself. There were things about this life he had come to love. Although he wasn't sure all the time that he knew, precisely, why his newly adopted people were doing the things they were.

He let that confusion slide and gave himself over fully to the things he most enjoyed. He assumed he would come to understand these little mysteries eventually. Still, it baffled him when he saw a warrior walking backwards for a whole day. He was puzzled when he observed a pregnant woman crawling about on all fours and mimicking the horse. There were a lot of things he admittedly, hadn't learned about yet. Iron Woman, though, had taught him a kind of love he had not known before. The most puzzling part of their relationship to him was her silence. She spoke so little. When she did speak though Robert was impressed that she knew so many English words. When he asked her about it she told a story quite different than that of Sawn a wato.

"Trapper come long ago. We watch and let him stay. Then he shoots buffalo...not eat just shoot...leave meat and shoot more...We take him and cut off his nose. We take his ears and see if he will die. He very strong...never dies. We keep him long time. See that he is wise and knows many things. We let him be free but he has no nose and can't go by his people so he stay here. He very wise. He is in the council many many years. He knows many things good for Crow. He make peace with Mandan...All Crow know American words from him.

"Where is he now ?" Robert wanted to know. "What is his name?"

"He die...die long time go. We call him shooter of buffalo." She nor Robert ever mentioned the captive trapper again although the tale and its brutality upset Robert not a little.

Sometimes Iron Woman sang. Often she laughed. But as far as declaring her feelings for him, it seems she preferred him to sense or feel them rather than to be told. He adapted well to her, though. Just seeing her each morning, watching her sleep at night. It was her presence that brought feelings to him he had never known before. This seemed to him to be the most important thing of all. He tucked the buckskin sacks of coins away among his possibles and forgot them.

He had been brought before the Crow council when he first arrived in camp. Here the leaders had told him, in sign language mostly but with some words in English what they expected from him and how he should govern himself in their presence. Now, two years later, he was a council member. He was a part of the decision making that took place around that fire. The things decided before that crackling blaze affected all walks of life in the camp. Perhaps it was because of Iron Woman and her mystical powers, but he was now helping to make those decisions.

He hunted and fished with the men. He wrestled and brawled with them. He joined in their stag functions where they made jokes so bawdy that the women were not allowed within earshot. More and more he was liviing in the way of the Crow. The camp's men and boys laughed uproariously when they first saw how pale his body was. The women lowered their eyes and blushed a hardy, deep red. In response he would slap his white belly with his hand and call out, Kahn-ee-wa. This name he had learned in this Crow camp meant "White Eagle". When he called himself this, the laughter was uncontrollable. Now after many months the sun had darkened the skin of his body considerably. He was still not dark enough to be confused with a Crow but he was no longer White Eagle either.

Most of all, he felt an uncontrollable passion for Iron Woman. The fascination he had experienced the day Bloody Shirt had brought her to him had not diminished. It had, in fact, given way to deeper, more profound feelings, feelings he had not the skills to express. His heart leapt when she spoke. He was entranced when she danced with the other women after the council fires. Waking in the mornings, he would pull her close too him under the robes of fur. There in the dark and warmth his life was complete. His love for her was an uncomplicated, uncluttered primitive ardor.

They could sit quietly for hours enjoying something as simple as watching a mother porcupine shepherd her brood. They could, just as easily, give themselves over to a form of passion that could range anywhere from tender to absolute savage. Robert always found those times to be intense, exhilarating and exhausting. Every time they were in each other's arms Robert felt new thrills and excitements. He had no problem with Iron Woman of any kind. Except for Hubert Baker.

Iron Woman hated Baker just as her brother did. She also called him the turtle. When Baker was around Robert she noticeably absented herself. When Robert would ask her why, she would only wrinkle her small nose as if to indicate a bad smell. Baker was more open in his assessment of her as well as all the Crow in general.

"I'm tellin' you, Scotty, she's a Crow. You think your lovin' her and she's lovin' you, but I'm tellin' you that ain't what's happenin'. These Crow folks just ain't like any other people in the world. Whatever you would expect a body to do ain't what a Crow thinks about doin' 'at all."

"You just don't trust 'em," Robert said.

"You're wrong, Scotty. I trusts 'em completely. The difference is, I trusts 'em to be Crow. You're thinkin' they's white, maybe even Scotch. You're actin' like she's a wife or somethin'."

"She is my wife!" Robert fairly exploded.

"Goddamn it, Robert, she's a war chief!" Baker exploded right back. "Do you think them Crow up there in that camp would let a woman into the council if she weren't big magic? Do you think other Indian women go around taken down Arapaho braves and scalpin' 'em? For God's sake, man, do you think they call her Iron Woman cause she's just a squaw? I'm tellin' you here and now she ain't no squaw. I don't know what she is, but she's a hell of a lot more than just your bed warmer! Medicine they calls it... That and Shaman... She's like a spirit or a ghost or somethin', Robert. Like a witch."

The words stung like fire. Robert spun on his heel and walked away. He stalked back up the mountain to the Crow camp. The friends didn't talk after that for nearly two weeks. Robert was still sullen when Baker came into the Crow camp. Robert sat on his haunches as Baker stood before the tipi of Iron Woman and broke the silence.

"I want you should go higher up the mountain, Robert."

"Why's that?" Robert queried. His anger at his old friend had long since vanished. He sensed a kind of urgency in Bakers' manner and speech. It was obvious this was not to be a continuation of their last conversation. Something new was afoot.

"Hudson Bay men, Robert. At least six of 'em. They down to the landing now. I was with 'em day 'fore yesterday. Nearly ran all the way back to tell you. They's Hudson Bay men here for fur buying. I counted six; might be more." Robert felt a pain knot his stomach.

"Any one of 'em wearin' a wolf head?" He wanted to know.

"Didn't see no wolf hats around, Scotty. I reckon that hat's a long time gone by now. But there's one down there in a black frock coat kind of thin like a hatchet. I was close to him as I am you right now. Matter of fact, I traded him two good rifle flints for a little poke 'o salt. I looked real good, Robert, and I can tell you for sure…. He ain't got no ear on his upside."

Somehow, Robert felt his life was about to change and he hated it.

"I tell you true, Robert. They's no good afoot. These men's tryin' to act like they would around tame Indians. They done been up in the Mandan country swappin' shit for fur. They's cheatin' them Indians, Rob… Givin' 'em whiskey, gettin' 'em drunk, and then just robbin' 'em blind. They sleepin' with their women, too…

"I heard 'em a braggin' on it. You know that ain't gonna work 'round here, Scotty. Hell, this ain't New York 'er even Saint Louis. These Indians round here gonna start sharpenin' knives and paintin' up. Anyway, Robert, you gotta clear out for a while. Too many for you and me to fight. That is. less'n you think your Crow friends here gonna help you."

"Sounds like Fletcher Harris sure enough," Robert allowed. "I wouldn't think he'd still be after me even if he knew I was here. But I can't let the Crow know. They would, I think, cause big trouble in order to look after me. Maybe you're right, Hubert. Maybe I better move up the mountain for a while. I guess I can't really even imagine that they're here. I know Hudsons' Bay men are everywhere; I just didn't never expect to see them 'round here."

"Reckon I can tell you right enough what brought 'em. It weren't you, Robert Trav. Hell, I reckon they ain't thought of you in a lot of years by now. It ain't you bringin' them kind out of the east out here to the Rocks. It's John Jacob Astor. He's what brung 'em here as I see it."

"Who in blazes is John Jacob Astor?" Robert wanted to know.

"Onliest man about that can challenge them English and Canadian sons of bitches. Been a lot of talk about it at the Landin'. I never paid it no mind. I only thought it was just back in the east they was talkin' 'bout. I tell you true, Rob. Beaver brings men everywhere. They's a-sayin' now that Astor's American Fur Company is gettin' bigger than old Hudsons.

They claim Astor's the man that controls fur all around the Great Lakes and all the fur on the Mississippi, from Minnysoter clean to the Gulf of Mexico.

I reckon the Hudson men are having trouble fillin' a trap. They a-sendin' men everywhere now I reckon. Even here to the Rocks. They got to try and hold on to all the fur territory they can for Hudsons Bay. Them men'll go anywhere to find a beaver. I hear they calls they'selves the Company of Adventurers. Hell, fur pirates is more apt." Baker fairly spat his words.

"You make it sound like a war with us in the middle of the two armies. I guess I never heard o' no John Astor. Where's he come from?"

"He's a German, Robert. Right there's most o' the problem. You know when them Germans get started fighting with the English, they just don't know when to stop. I swear they's the most all-out people I ever seen. Anyway he's from this big German clan and now they just about own New York City; and I 'spect they want the by-God Rocky Mountains 'fer a back yard."

Robert was devastated. He only cared about Iron Woman, Hubert Baker and Bloody Shirt. That was his whole world and really all of the world he wanted. Now, he found himself thrust back in time and once again running from Fletcher Harris.

In addition, he now had this John Jacob Astor to ponder on. His head spun with dizzying confusion. He cared nothing for this competition between two eastern factors. It seemed fairly likely though, that his world was about to be upset. And not by himself but rather in two warring factors searching for pelt.

"You'd better be a-goin' soon Rob. They right behind me a-headin' this way. Said they gonna get some skins, Beaver and Crow, too. Reckon you know what they're meanin'. They gonna try and bed down some Crow women. Mandans might put up with that a while but not these here Crow. There's gonna be some killin', Rob. Them Hudson men just ain't knowin' 'bout Crow. There's six of 'em, Scotty. Six, and they got a whore with 'em, too. She's just a little thing, a little red-headed tricker. They find you here there's sure gonna be fightin'. 'Course, I think they's headin' for trouble if you here or if you ain't. "

Robert knew he was no longer afraid of Fletcher Harris. He knew further that he was safe among the Crow. There would not be even a slim chance that Bloody Shirt and Iron Woman would give him over to six Hudsons men. But there was the thought that one of his Crow friends could be hurt or killed. Maybe even Iron Woman.

That very morning he gathered his few belongings together into his possible sack. He thought he might surely need the Hawken and a knife. For some reason he would never understand he added the leather bag of golden coins to his possibles. He told Iron Woman a lie about visiting a new stream farther up the slopes for a few days. He knew from her stoic expression that she did not believe him, but she said nothing. He pointed high and to the east as an indication as to where he was going. With no further explanation he moved, alone, up the mountain.

The Way of The Crow

After four days in hiding, Robert had had enough. High up the ridge and late at night, Robert could see the glow of the Crow camp fires. During his nights of exile, Robert had huddled in his bedroll. He lay alone in the darkness and longed to be back in the tipi with Iron Woman. In the cold blackness of night his body ached for her touch. For her warmth. He was impressed that the distant fires were as bright as they were. Against the darkness of the surrounding forest, the luminescent flicker was keenly visible. A time or two, when the wind was right, he thought he could hear the distant drumbeats and the plaintive shrill of the flute. Those sounds would have meant the Council was meeting. He dismissed it as imagination. The camp lay a very great distance below him.

Too far to hear the council drums, he thought. He had never considered the glow of the camp could be seen at this considerable distance. Robert recalled the fires that Hubert Baker had built to guide him into camp when they were at the foot of the Rockies, before he had decided to ride the horse. Those fires had been visible for miles too. They, however, were far out on the open plain. He had not believed that the gleam could be seen so far through this dense mountainside forest. He vowed to remember that enemies might easily detect the Crow camp location by these fire lights.

He would talk to Bloody Shirt about lighting decoy fires. Or using rock shields to cut down the distance the flickering glimmer could be detected. The fires seemed brilliant to him, and it appeared there were more fires

lighted than usual. Gazing down the slope at the bright pin points, he wondered if the fires might not be built up higher than normal.

Perhaps Iron Woman, he thought. Perhaps she's put out a beacon for me. Maybe she's buildin' up the fires, hopin' I can see 'em."

About midnight of the fourth day he left his little camp on the high slope and began to work his way down and around the mountain side through the darkness. He vowed caution in his approach, but his yearning for Iron Woman nonetheless drove him downward.

The slope was steep in places, rock-strewn and slippery with damp moss. Moving through the pre- dawn darkness would've posed quite a problem for most tourists. Robert had been with the Crow long enough, by now, that he navigated the mountain side with ease. He could feel each stone or twig through the soles of his elk-skin footwear. His steps were firm and steady. He glided down the incline with the sureness of a mule deer or wild turkey or the Crow dog soldier, those mysterious commandoes of the clan.

These were fearless warriors, driven into secret battles by the voices that came to them while they performed the ghost dance. Robert had learned many of their night navigational methods. He employed them now as he slipped through the gloom. The dark yet spangled sky was just cracking the first silver. Slashes of dawn were slicing across the sky's dark mantle when he arrived at the outskirts of the Crow camp. He could move so quietly by now that even the camp dogs were unaware of his presence. Those noisy and vicious, living canine alarms only stirred and grunted in their sleep when his odor settled about them. With no noise to punctuate the smell, no indication of movement, the half wild animals tucked their noses deeper into their own bodies and, whining a bit in their dreams, continued to enjoy their laziness. Robert slipped by them as if they were sleeping stones.

Prudently, Robert decided to watch the camp for a while to be sure the Hudson Bay traders were not here. He couldn't believe they would still be here. Not after four days. Still, he thought it better to be safer to watch a while than run the risk of a headlong confrontation with Fletcher Harris and his men.

He could see shapes and silhouettes that he couldn't recognize in the shadow of dawn. Not people. Just things. Things that looked out of place or foreign. Somehow the camp he had lived in for nearly two years was now strangely unfamiliar. The morning light was getting stronger now, and he could see the entrance to the tipi of Bloody Shirt. Strange... it appeared there were horses tied in front of the lodge. The horses were always kept a few hundred yards to east of this spot. He thought he could count the horses, even in this darkness. He believed there were four. He heard an unusual sound at this time too. It was almost indistinguishable, but it sounded as a low moan. He saw on the earth in front of the dying embers of a campfire a form flat on the ground. At first, he couldn't be sure he could identify the shape. Although he feared he already knew what it was.

Then it came too him that the fire was in the wrong place, too. Something prompted him to look up to the low limbs of a tree over hanging the fire. There was something there. Another shapeless mass he couldn't recognize at first. He strained his eyes against the darkness, and now it began to come to him. It was a man... It was a man. A man hanging upside down.

He felt the shock go through him like a bolt. He knew now what he was seeing. It was a dead man. Robert held his place of hiding. As the sun's rays slowly got stronger, the revealing light brought before him a scene of such horror that he felt the bile rise in his throat. The man was not alone. Two men hung there. Stripped of their clothing, their bodies hacked and ripped beyond recognition.

At that moment the entrance flap moved backwards from the tipi of Bloody Shirt, and a familiar form emerged. The form went to the fire and picked up a cherry red faggot. The figure held the glowing brand up and blew briskly on it to rekindle its dying flame. As the ember sprang to life, Robert saw the face that was so familiar to him. It was Iron Woman. Robert pressed himself closer to the ground, making himself invisible.

Iron Woman bent over the form on the ground. Robert could see now it was the form of a person staked to the earth before the fire. His fears were at last recognized. It was a small person, maybe a child. Now in the firelight he saw the glint of auburn hair. It was the woman he reasoned that Hubert had told him of. Fletcher Harris's woman Baker had seen at the landing. It was the red-headed whore.

Iron Woman leaned over the staked body, and Robert heard a groan. He knew that Iron Woman was burning the captive with the firebrand. He was horrified that the prisoner was still alive. Robert reasoned that she was moaning only because she was too near death to scream. Iron Woman entertained herself with this ghastly torture a few more times. Suddenly she cast the flaming branch away and strode back inside the tipi of Bloody Shirt. Robert waited in total revulsion. He was close to vomit, to tears. He could never have imagined the woman he loved so could be involved in this horrid torture.

Strangely though the strongest feeling that was creeping over him now was one of intense anger. He felt his very being starting to cry out for revenge. That he would avenge this woman on the ground against his chosen people, the Crow, seemed impossible to him. Yet these were precisely his emotions.

He lay secreted in his hiding place for what seemed an hour but really was only a fourth of that span. The sun was bolder now and Robert could see all too well. Without fear or concern for himself, he stood up from his place of seclusion. He could no longer bear this scene. His face flushed hot from his burning, rage.

He padded swiftly in his moccasins to the side of the pathetic woman by the fire. Her small ruined body was staked, spread eagled, to the ground. Her thin pale legs were bound to stout green hickory stakes with rawhide thongs. The stakes that pinioned her arms though had been driven completely through her narrow wrists. He saw that her eyelids had been cut away so that she could not hide from pain behind them. Her appearance was of a form in ruins. Her face, breasts and stomach had been slashed and burned beyond all hope. He felt her looking up at him with those empty, lidless eyes, vacant, hollow and ever so glazed in pain.

He knew the low, barely audible, moans were her only way of pleading for death. It was obvious that her tongue was gone. Robert didn't hesitate for a moment. He brought his rifle to his shoulder and, placing the bullet as carefully as he could, shot the devastated wretch before him squarely in the forehead. Her body lurched against her bonds in a final death throe. She lay there quivering for a moment, and then was still. Robert's eyes were wells of burning tears. His heart was as heavy as solid stone in his breast. The rifle report brought the Crow camp to life now and, instantly, the camp dogs began their senseless yapping.

Tent flaps were thrown back almost in unison. In a moment, a ring of Crow stood eyeing Robert Trav. Yesterday's brother was now an interloper. The White Eagle was not welcome here. Not among the secret doings of the Crow. He was asking for his own death by slaying their prisoner. Every warrior, Robert noticed, gripped an axe, knife or gun at the ready. The air was electric with tension. Each faction tensed and waited for the other's first move. The seconds moved by slowly. The wait was a long and anxious one. Robert looked now at the two bodies swinging gently from the limb. They were violated beyond recognition. As revolted as Robert was, he could not turn his face away from the carnage.

It was really no surprise, but Robert could not help but notice the body of the thinnest man hanging nearest him. The shape was a familiar one. He had seen this man many times before. Once, for a time, he had even believed him to be a friend. Without even looking, he knew the swinging corpse would be missing the right ear. He knew now that his long-anticipated confrontation with Fletcher Harris would never take place. Robert realized he was being confronted by a form of cruelty and inhumanity he could never accept. That he never even knew existed. Then he remembered Hubert Baker's words:

"Rattlers eat squirrels all the time. It don't mean he's a bad rattler, but he's only doing the things that are the way of rattlers. Rattlers are not evil... but they are rattlers." And then Robert said to himself, almost aloud, "Blame not the fox for being a fox."

He fully understood that what he was seeing was the way of the Crow. It wasn't evil to the Crow. They would have expected no different treatment for themselves had they fallen prisoner to a great enemy. It was simply the way of the Crow. A great true. Robert understood that, at last. Finally, he knew what Hubert Baker had tried to tell him.

He further knew that the true life of the Crow could never be his way. The same as it could not have been Baker's. Between his culture and that of the Bloody Shirt lay a great and forever impassible chasm. At that very moment he knew he must lose Iron Woman forever.

Now the Scot looked squarely into the face of Bloody Shirt. Then his gaze shifted and locked with the eyes of Iron Woman. They stared into each other's faces for a long time. Their mutual gaze was filled with anxiety. Each wanted to run to the other. To take the other in a deep embrace. To hold. To touch. To kiss. Yet, they stood there. Helpless to cross the line drawn by tens of thousands of years.

At last she broke the gaze and fixed her eyes on the earth. The same as she had the day he first saw her; more than two years ago. He felt empty and lost. He had loved this woman, and now... He had to break off his thoughts. He now noticed that the four horses in front of the tipi were his own and Hubert Baker's. He walked directly to the horses' heads, untied them and, stringing them together, he led them away.

During this operation he fully expected, at any moment, to be stopped or just killed outright. But the Crow warriors stood back, and he quietly walked the horses past them. Only once did he look back, and he saw Bloody Shirt half-heartedly raise his hand. It was not a wave. It may have been a dismissal.

Iron Woman stood over the small body of the girl with the red hair. She seemed angry that the girl's life was no more, irate that her amusement was dead. Robert tried to catch a deep breath to steady himself. It surprised him that it turned to a sob...

A mile down the mountain side Robert found the rest of the Hudson Bay trading party. They had been stripped of their clothing and then bound tightly to trees. There they had been shot full of arrows. Robert knew how that had taken place, too: One arrow at a time; with all the captives watching and waiting as they were dispatched singly and in turn.

He had expected he would find four bodies, but now he counted and became aware there were not four but five. Afraid, and fully knowing what he would find, he began his grisly investigation. Upon examination he saw the fifth naked body had its head turned away from him.

Robert did not need to see the face. He recognized the powerful and muscular frame. He saw the familiar and generous coat of black and curly chest hair. Robert knew instinctively who it was. Here was the frontiersman who had been his trusted companion of so many trails. Maybe the only true friend Robert had ever known now hung pitifully ruined before him. Here was Hubert Baker. Robert fell upon his knees and gave way to a wracking cry that lasted a long time. His lament echoed resoundingly through the surrounding hills. Many Crow heard his cry but it meant nothing to them. It was not the way they reasoned. It was not a sound they made. It was not a big true.

The rest of that morning he spent preparing a grave. He only made one. As he scooped out a shallow hole, he was aware of the Crow watching him from the surrounding forest. When the burying of Baker was finished, he sat and wept again. Silently this time. It was now as he sat in sadness and despair that he spied the bag of gold coin that was his friend's. It lay on the ground near the burned out lean to half buried in ashes. It

really had little importance to him in the face of all that had happened, but nevertheless he brushed away the ashes and added the hefty poke to his possibles bag.

He hadn't been so alone since he stood on the rolling deck of the clipper that cleared him of Scotland. He recalled again Hubert telling him how the Crow were different from himself and Robert. But that he could never hate them for being what they were. Robert wondered If Hubert Baker had kept those feelings as he faced his death. Somehow he was sure the brave trapper had....

Robert led his horses down the mountain now, for it was too steep and rough for riding. With his gaze focused on the broad flat plain below him he thought of three things mostly. First, he realized that he was quitting the mountains forever. He would never be back here again and he knew it. It pained him to leave this fair land behind. He knew too, that he would never trap another animal of any kind for only its fur. He had seen enough pain and suffering he felt for the whole world, and he would bring about no more of it than he must. He would not kill another beaver that an English dandy might sport a fine hat. Life was too precious to trade a beaver for a hat.

Lastly, he thought of Iron Woman. He resigned himself to the fact that he would be alone now. He knew that she would be forever in his heart and that he could never love another. His very being would always belong to the little Crow who was big magic. However, after what he had seen in the Crow camp that morning of horrors, he also had come to grips with the fact he could never stand to be in her presence again. He fully understood that these thoughts compounded themselves into a life sentence of loneliness.

There would never be another woman in the life of Robert Trav. There would never be another love. This thought overwhelmed him. It brought about such a great and profound sadness his knees felt about to buckle. He turned then and, for the first time, he gazed back up the trail he had just traveled. Perhaps he thought he might see a glimpse of Iron Woman again or maybe of Bloody Shirt. What he saw instead was a party of three Crow warriors just starting to unearth the body of Hubert Baker.

Robert knew there was nothing he could do about it, nothing at all. He turned his tear-streaked face away and proceeded down the steep slope. He understood for the first time now everything that Hubert Baker had tried to tell him. He and the Crow would never truly have a common ground. He also knew he must resign himself to being alone. It was not in Robert Trav to love more than once. Iron Woman was gone from his life and there would be no other.

This is, he thought, *what Bloody Shirt would call, a big true.*

Chapter Twenty-three

Garcia's Run
1846

Garcia's saddle was slippery with the gore that had leaked from the musket ball hole in his side. He had attempted to stem the flow by plugging wound with twisted cloth torn from his shirt. Thick dark blood would stop leaking from the hole in his side momentarily but it would start again the moment his horse took a jolting step. The Federales could not be far behind he reasoned. It puzzled him that they would still dog his trail this far north. He had been running now for days. As for how many, he had lost count. It was not the first time he had been shot. It was the first time, though, he thought he might die. His biggest problem for now was stopping the blood flow before he was empty.

Horses, too, were always a problem. A hard man on the run could use a good horse for a day or two; even less if he had to put up a hard run. This far north of the Rio Grande, Mexican villages were few and far between. When he was fortunate enough to encounter one of these widely-scattered havens, he could always count on the impoverished inhabitants for help. All of the villagers knew him or knew of him. They also knew he never come empty handed. He considered his territory a fifty-mile stretch of the Rio Grande valley. He had left coins and script in many places along this trail, and those who lived there were his confederates.

If they had horses, they would sell him one. If they had none they would, for a coin or two, help him steal one. For the most part, they were nearly always starving. He had learned early in his career as a bandit, that a few coins of gold could buy stolen horses or sanctuary in the blink of an eye. When he robbed, he spent freely. He very often gave much of his wealth away. But always he reserved his emergency fund should a purchased escape become a priority.

He knew better than to count on any help from the Gringo. The whites hated him more than the Federales, if that was possible. But the Mexican people of the valley looked forward to assisting this young outlaw. Rapier thin and armed with a flashing smile, his pleasing nature and generosity had assured him of friendship among these poor farmers and goat herders. He enjoyed stealing from the Gringo. After all, they had a lot to steal. Certainly, more than his own people. He could not bear to steal from them. Not anything. They had so very little.

From loss of blood now he swayed in his saddle. His head was swimming. He knew he had to recover enough strength to gain some distance from those behind him. He pushed on hard, sometimes bringing his mount to the brink of death. It was a big black horse with an enormous amount of heart and courage. He loved horses like this one and cursed himself for abusing the gelding so. He reasoned as he fled north, he might outdistance the Mexican troops that were now eating up his trail. Even if he could shake them, he would still have to deal with the Rangers perhaps. That possibility didn't frighten him unreasonably. It was early yet in the organizational period of the Texas Rangers.

For the most part, they were still just a bunch of disorganized farmers. He was pretty sure he could slip by them if the horse held out and he didn't bleed to death first. The only real problem with the Rangers was they were nothing more than an enthusiastic legalized lynch mob. It was too far between jails and too long between courts here in early Texas. The Rangers figured the best way to get rid of a problem was to hang it and worry about guilt or innocence later. After all, they reasoned, the men they caught were probably guilty of something anyway. Though Garcia had little respect for the Rangers' talent as lawmen, he knew that to be taken by them almost certainly meant hanging.

The Rangers were a rough and dangerous bunch, but in cleverness no match for Garcia. He had lived as Bandito a long time now. Those far smarter than Texas Rangers had sought his head. He knew he could avoid them all if he could just keep this horse under him.

If it had not been for the woman, he thought... If it had not been for the widow at Saint Theresa, this bitter cup would not be mine to taste. Like all Mexican Catholics, he sprinkled his speech liberally with biblical sounding phrases.

The lovely Carmelita Ansura, her husband dead, had welcomed the young bandit into her casa. She readily took the dinero he gave her. She fed him well, and often they were lovers. He would visit her only on nights with no moon. He would appear at her door late at night and always leave just before daylight for those many weeks. Then the Federales came to her and told her they knew.

They told her that if she didn't tell them when he came to her the next time, that they would execute one of her two children. She would be forced to make the choice of the one to die. It was an old form of Spanish- Mexican blackmail, as old as the Spanish Inquisition at least. They told her that if she refused to make such a choice, both the boy and the girl would die while she watched. She may have loved the bold bandit or maybe not. It could've been only that she depended on his gifts— his dinero and kindness to make her survival a bit easier— and his hard, lean body to comfort her... his open laughter to bring a little gladness into her dreary widowhood. And when he made her feel like a woman, it was as though a new life was being breathed into her very soul. It may have been love. Maybe it was something else. Even Carmelita Ansura herself could not be sure. Nonetheless, faced with the death of her children, she readily betrayed the outlaw without another thought.

"Juan Garcia," she told them, always came to her tiny casa during that part of the month the moon was dark. Sometimes he stayed for awhile, always leaving before the light of the sun. Armed with this information, it was decided that four of the Federales would keep vigil from the grove at the rear of the casa on each moonless night

How happy he was as he rode through the darkness on his way to see her. He had money for her, money that would make her glad. When he thought of her pretty face breaking into laughter, a warm feeling spread throughout his body. He knew she would be delighted to see only him, but in addition to himself he had something else, too: Dinero he had stolen from the fat and wealthy. Money, that she would use to feed her children. In his saddle bags he carried small gifts for the children, too— a good quality knife for the boy and lovely fan carved from bone for the little senorita.

The soldiers watched intently as the silhouette of a horse and rider came closer and closer to their waiting rifles. Juan Garcia was beginning to realize a family here. He loved the little boy and his sister as though they were his very own. The beauty of Carmelita took his breath away; He had begun to think, lately that he must surely love her, too. It was with these happy thoughts on his mind that he rode headlong into the ambush of withering gun fire. The muzzle flashes from the willow grove in the rear of Carmelita's little casa lit up the darkness like a hundred fireflies. In a flash Juan Garcia knew he had been betrayed.

Wounded badly in the very first fusillade of shots, Garcia wheeled his horse and raced off into the cover of darkness. It was the speed of a fine horse and the inky blanket of a moonless night that gave him his escape. Looking back over his shoulder as the horse sped through the blackness, he could see the muzzle flashes of the muskets that sought him in the gloom. His side was a stabbing flame as he headed north to quit the Rio

Grande. In less than a minute the big horse and the cover of darkness had taken him out of gun range. He spurred the big animal hard, and through the darkness he could hear the angry shouts from those of the ambush. He knew they would be mounted and on his trail in an instant. He knew now his only hope was for the cover of the night and the spirit of his steed. He said a little prayer to Saint Maria that the horse had not been hit by the wild gunfire.

Garcia was good at running, good at eluding pursuers. He had been doing it since he had deserted the Mexican militia soon after the fall of the Alamo. He had been a mere boy then, but he took readily to stealing and running in order to survive. It was when he stole his first horse that he truly learned about freedom. The mobility the horse gave him opened up a whole new world for him. He set himself to the task of learning everything he could about horses and horsemanship. In short order it was as if he and the mount were in the same skin. He became a bold and fearless rider who seemed able to coax the impossible from his mount.

He learned, too, that armed robbery was far more lucrative that burglary. Stealing at gun point brought about instant money. Foot padding only yielded goods. Goods that had to be sold somewhere. That was not only risky, it was low paying. He experienced another trait of armed thievery, too, one that he found quite amazing. Men feared his pistol. That was true enough. But never did they show the fear at gunpoint that they displayed when he held the rapier at their chests or throats.

The pistol scared his victims; the sword terrorized them. At the very first sign of the Toledo blade, his victims seemed almost anxious to hand over their valuables. Some were so paralyzed with fear he had to lift their purses from hands so trembling they could not seem to let go on their own. A few men even wet themselves. Garcia was amazed that any man could humiliate himself in this way. He concluded knives promised a far more terrifying death than bullets.

For his first few robberies he had covered his face with a bandana to protect his identity. It was soon enough though that he was recognized anyway. Not many men could set a horse the way he did. His horsemanship was so distinguished, his identity was soon common knowledge. He gave up the idea of the cumbersome mask and depended more on flight and hiding for his success and survival.

His daring and cunning soon became the talk of the tiny villages along the Rio Grande. In his own small way, he was becoming somewhat of a celebrity. Other road agents and shop robbers contacted him and tried to join up with the mounted swordsman. He was totally disinterested in this proposition. He rode alone. Juan Garcia had no interest in a band or gang. He robbed freely but harmed no one at first. It was when the Federales began to chase him, that he first understood the game he had selected had a dangerous and deadly side to it. It was not long after that he spilled his first blood. The incident, as he called it, happened right after Juan Garcia had held up a Mexican Army pay wagon.

He had left the robbed escort afoot by running off their horses. At least he had thought they were afoot. An outrider he hadn't spotted suddenly was riding after Garcia with a pistol blazing between the ears of his frantic mount. Instantly Garcia was in a breakneck horse race with a young Federale Capitain. After a mile or more of hard running, Garcia had snapped a pistol shot over his shoulder at the pursuer. He was astonished to hear him cry out. Looking back, Garcia saw the rider slip from his horse and fall headlong upon the ground. Garcia was dumbfounded. He couldn't believe that this carelessly fired shot had struck home.

He reined up his horse and sat watching the fallen soldier. The soldier lay very still. Garcia was just about to believe that he had indeed killed this lone pursuer. Then he saw the trooper struggle to his knees. His mount had returned to his side, and the wounded man used the stirrup to pull himself up. Garcia watched him now; standing slumped and disabled alongside his horse. It was obvious he was wounded. He was able to stand but that was all.

"Vaya." Garcia called loudly. "Vaya Con Dios, amigo."

"Vaya Con Dios," the wounded Federale called back. Garcia had wheeled his horse and raced off into the Rio Grande desert. Soon after that occurrence, in a running fight near Matamoras, he killed for the first time. He instinctively knew it had to happen sooner or later. He was too infamous. Too bold. He robbed so often a fight had to take place sooner or later. It was pre-ordained

Now the bold robber who had been so elusive and brave was fighting for his very life. The musket ball from a Mexican militia rifle is more than .50 caliber, and the wound it creates is a ghastly one. More, the bullet is lubricated with a coating of rank and dirty animal fat. The infection that accompanies it is as deadly as the bullet strike. Garcia was reeling in his saddle. His body was wracked in fever and fading from blood loss. One moment he was chilled to the very marrow; an instant later his body broiled with raging fevers.

Looking at the wound in one of his lucid moments he saw that the purple bullet hole was surrounded by an angry rainbow of red, yellow and blue streaks. The blood had stopped flowing now but the wound had begun to leak a yellow viscous fluid so foul that Garcia believed, now for sure, that he was to die. Help was scarce for the bandit as he made his way north, traveling through this lonely country mostly on courage, sometimes in a stupor.

From time to time he got a bit of aid from Mexican families when he could find them. This far north they were few and far between. Here and there he got a day or two of rest. Sometimes a bit of primitive medical treatment. On two occasions, a fresh horse. He looked for missions, small cathedrals and any place that Catholics might gather. There he reasoned he was most likely to find his own kind and perhaps willing help. Yet he was sharply aware there was danger in this reasoning too. A half century before many Texas men had married Spanish and Mexican women in order to obtain one of the generous land grants from the king of Spain. Not only were these Texicans required to marry Mexican women but further they were required to embrace the Catholic Church.

It was these very unions that had built the tiny missions scattered all over Texas. In the following fifty years and after the victories of Steve Austin and Sam Houston the king of Spain had no place in the lives of Texans what so ever. While it was true that many of the progeny of these original settlers kept to their Catholic faith a lot more had not. Garcia knew that though they had Mexican grandmothers and wives they were still Texans and could be dangerous. Especially those that still remembered Alamo he knew were likely to deal harshly with a Mexican bandit on the run.

The Federales gave up on him at about one hundred miles north of the Rio Grande Valley. The Rangers didn't even know he was in Texas. In later years his valiant escape would become famous. Those who knew the legend would call it "Garcia's run." In his terrible condition Garcia drove himself twenty miles north of the Red River and to safety. In the end his unbelievable run had carried him more than four hundred miles.

When Robert Trav found Juan Garcia he believed Garcia was already dead. He lay sprawled in the dust, his body clothed in bloody rags, far closer to death than life. He had been there a long time. His blood had caked in the sandy earth beneath his still form. Robert had earlier found his saddled horse wandering miles from where the circling vultures had told him to look for the rider. As Robert approached the fallen bandit, he caught the smell of the terrible wound and its corruption. To Robert it was the smell of death.

Vultures, too, smelled it. The huge birds flared their wings and hissed angrily when Robert approached. They stretched out their long necks displaying their angry red heads and croaked threateningly. They strutted about and raked the earth with carrion filled talons. They protected their prey with an unnatural boldness. Their coal colored eyes were fixed upon the dying Garcia. They became furious when they sensed this intruder might cheat them of their prize. From the fallen vaquero, Robert detected a slight groan. Then another.

He sensed this downed cowboy had a spark of life left in him somewhere. He covered Garcia with his bed roll blanket and bathed his gore-spattered face with water from his canteen. Robert drove off the vultures and built up a fire of greasewood. He made a wild sassafras tea for himself from his traveling stores and sat down beside Juan Garcia. He, additionally built up a rich tea of dried blackberry and some heavily smoked antelope jerky. From a small capped clay jar, he broke a large piece of honey comb and dropped it, dripping with amber sweetness, into the seething pot.

If the Mexican died, Robert allowed he would give him a decent burial. Away from the vultures. If he lived– which wasn't likely– he would offer the wounded man some comfort if he could. It was several hours later when Juan Garcia began to stir in his agonies. He revived just enough to sense someone was standing over him. Through hazy eyes he made out long light-colored hair and a white American face.

Not Comanche, was Garcia's first thought. He was fighting now to regain consciousness. He struggled to sit up but a shocking pain told him it was futile.

"Easy old fellow," he heard someone say. "Here, Compadre, sip a bit of this." He felt, more than tasted, a hot liquid in his mouth. The first few drops that slid down his throat were agonizing. His throat was sore beyond belief. Now he caught the flavor. The second swallow of blackberry tea actually soothed his throat. His recovery was a slow one, but Robert sensed he was coming around a little. It still looked doubtful that he would survive.

"Where am I?" he croaked in his poor English.

"I ain't rightly sure where we are," was Robert's answer. "I think we're on the south edge of the Canadian river. Unless that water out there is the Red. I just ain't too sure which river it is." He helped Garcia with another soothing sip. "You're in bad shape, laddie. I'm wondering what I can do to help you."

Garcia was stunned that this, or any Gringo, would have even the slightest interest in helping him.

"That's a mighty big hole in your flank, friend. It's got pretty messy, too. I'd say if you're to live, we need to clean that up a bit. I guess you know it'll take some hard doin' on your part?"

"Are we to burn it?"

"Reckon I would if I had somethin' to do it with. That hole is plumb through. I ain't got a rod of any kind that'll reach."

"My horse," Garcia said, none too clearly. "My horse, Manana, he is here?"

"I have your horse. He's hobbled right over there."

"On the saddle horn, Senor. The rod you need should still be there."

Robert hadn't seen anything like this since he'd left Scotland. He took the long razor-sharp rapier from its scabbard. He knew nothing of swords but easily recognized that this was a fine and deadly piece of work. Now he built up a fire and steeled himself for one of the hardest ordeals either man would ever face.

Robert first boiled his old, blue bandanna. After several minutes of hard boiling, he fished the bandanna from the boiling pot with a stick of greasewood. He pushed it, dripping with the steaming water, as far into the festering wound as he could. Garcia groaned and tried to roll his body away from the invading fire. Robert clutched his shoulder hard and held him tightly in his grasp.

"Hold on now. You can't pull away. Lean into it." As if by command, Garcia gritted his teeth firmly together and pushed his arching body against the scalding cloth. The rapier was hot now and Robert withdrew it from the coals of his fire. The Scot knew about good blades. He had brought the steel to a faint and dull red glow. Hot enough he thought to cauterize the wound but not the scarlet or bright straw-colored glow that would draw the fine temper from the precious blade. Now came the sizzling. The frying. Little clouds of rancid vapors. The smell of frying flesh.

Both men gnashed their teeth and equally cried aloud. Tears streamed their faces equally. Their white teeth gleaming, lips pulled back sharply in the shared grimace of pain. Light headed, they both fought for composure. Bile was sour and rank in the mouths of both men. It was as though the pain was a shared thing that ravished them together. Garcia was lying on his side so Robert could see the sword tip as it exited his back. The blade was so sharp he had to use care in his withdrawal so as to not cut another wound.

The ordeal probably took less than a minute, but the time passage seemed excruciatingly slow. At last it was done. Robert collapsed on the bare earth next to Garcia. It was in God's hands now. He held Garcia's hand and the two, resembling dirty and exhausted children, slept for a long time.

"How is it that you found this place, Senor?" Garcia would ask some days later. The healing was going well now, and Garcia was looking southwest off the grassy knoll above the Canadian. He was well enough to appreciate the splendor of what he saw.

"I came here after a long walk," Robert said. "I just thought it so fair I stopped here. I suppose I'll go no farther. Tis' home for me now. Such as it is. I was buildin' m'self a shelter when I found you. The tipi ain't hardly enough, but I guess I'll finish up a proper hut some time soon."

"Senor Robert, how is this land yours? How do others know it belongs to you?"

"I claimed it."

"Senor Robert, can you just 'claim' this land as you say? How do you mark it for others to know?"

"I claimed it. I went around the part I wanted and built up some stone piles. Some day there may be a better way, but for now there's stone piles every four or five miles apart."

"Four or five miles?" The number sounded huge to Garcia who was more accustomed to the Mexican farms of three or four acres' total. "How big is this piece of land you have claimed, Senor Robert?"

"Well, I ain't much on measurin', but I started at the fork where the Canadian run off heads towards the Red. I just claimed all the land in the wedge of that fork back upstream for 'bout forty miles".

Garcia gasped.

"It's three or four days across at the wide part of the wedge. It's about the same lengthwise, too. I met some settlers while I was comin' here, and they told me the names of the rivers and how to go about this claimin'. I met some Indian fellows here, too. Comanche, they were. Finest horsemen as you'll see anywhere." Anyway, we smoked some. Comanch' talk ain't that much different from Crow, and I know a little Crow.

They said not to kill no buffalo north of the Red and south of the Canadian. Only kill within the wedge. Course it ain't no true wedge. The rivers never come closer together than fifty or sixty miles. Least ways that's what I think. Then as you move east the separate for many more miles that that. Hundreds maybe. Anyway, they said just to kill what I need to eat. They said not to cross no rivers on a hunt. If I'se to do this, they reckoned they'd be satisfied. If I stays in the wedge for my huntin', we gets along pretty good."

"You talked with Comanche's and you're still alive?"

"Reckon so. Anyways, here I am. Indians ain't such bad folks you know, Garcia. They's just different. Had a friend once told me that.

"Different", he said. They don't think of the same things in the same way we do. Anyway, they's different that's all."

"These monuments of stone you built, Robert; how big are they?" Garcia wanted to know.

Robert scratched a whiskered chin.

"Well, I'd say about waist high if stones were about. Maybe knee high for some when rocks was scarce."

"They'll tear them down." Garcia said.

"Who? Who will tear them down?" Anger was already creeping into Robert's voice.

"Men," Garcia said. "I've seen it all my life in Mexico. When a man has some thing, some really fine thing, they will come to take it. Banditos, Indians or even men from your own Government. Someone will come and take down the stones. It is greed or hate or something I don't know; but they come. They always come."

"If they come here, I will be standing by the stones." Robert's voice was flat. "If they take down the stones, the price is a dear one."

A smile split the handsome face of Juan Garcia.

"I too, Senor Robert. I too, will stand by the stones with you. They will come I know, but when they come they will find us. We will stand by the stones together."

"My question for you vaquero is just how in the name of the Laird did ye manage to ride so far to the north shot up as ye were?" Garcia thought for a moment.

"I was to sick to know I was too sick to make it." He grinned widely showing those brilliant teeth.

Garcia put out his hand, and Robert took it. Some how these two men, each so very different from the other, recognized that they were embarking on the bond of what would become a great friendship. Their lives would forever more be entwined. It was the bond some men make that somehow is made up of blood and earth. A bond of the land.

They both felt something was happening but, as men always have been, the feelings weren't easy to express. Running through Garcia's mind was the word "Compadre". At that very moment Robert, thinking like a Crow, was contemplating a "big true."

The days stretched into weeks and then into months. The two friends worked side by side every day. It was one spring morning in 1851 that the pair first realized how long they had been cut apart from the civilized world. They were hoeing a little garden spot with the idea of planting a few potato eyes when Garcia suddenly asked, "How long has it been since I have seen a face other than yours, Senor Robert?"

"Well... I can't rightly say. Been a while though, I do know that." Robert leaned now on his wooden spade. "That war with Texas and Mexico, the Mexican war. Do you think it has ended?" Garcia wanted to know. Robert thought on this for a moment.

"I guess I don't know how long wars can go on. But it seems to me to be an awfully long time. I'd expect it's ended."

"Who do you expect won? Who is the Presidente of the United States anyway, Senor Robert?"

"I guess I don't know that either. Maybe it's Jim Polk still... Damn Garcia we're pretty poor ones, ain't we? Neither one of us even knows whether we're in Mexico, Spain or Texas."

"Or in the United States at all. Or who is Presidente." The two men, their questions unanswered, went back to their gardening. They were for sometime to remain unaware that Zack Taylor was the new President of an ever growing Union, and that Santa Anna's Mexico had been soundly vanquished. From where Robert and Garcia stood, it made precious little difference. The business of survival was just too important. The proposition of staying alive was too demanding. The two simply could not allow themselves to be bothered about the far less important political events. If it didn't happen on the Canadian, it would have to wait.

Garcia taught Robert how to mix the river mud into adobe. Together they built the little cabin that would be their house for so many years. Robert showed Juan how to hunt for food, both game and fine edible plants alike. Garcia was suspicious of the plants at first, but now he thought they were elegant. He thought nothing was so fine as polk greens and vowed someday he would try them with a little vinegar. Robert had said they were delectable served this way. Garcia hoped someday soon they would have some vinegar. Garcia's imagination told him it was probably true. Someday he would have some vinegar for flavoring. For now he was glad he had a bit of salt. Sometimes they discovered that a bit of wood ash could be used to flavor their bland table fare.

Garcia had said others would come, and they did. Some were just tramps looking for a handout as they followed the river course to some unknown appointment with their destiny. Others, more determined, were the settlers. From time to time Robert or Garcia would discover these prairie nomads setting up housekeeping, sometimes in clear sight of one of the stone pile monuments.

Many times, when the settlers were told the land here was spoken for, they moved on without a worry. Other times, though, they were more tenacious. Threats and even sometimes actions were needed to convince them. Robert was not good at threatening. Soft spoken as he was, his words carried little intimidation to the determined. Garcia though was excellent at this vocal chore. He could leave the air fairly blue with Spanish curses and biblical quotations. His promises of mayhem would generally encourage the startled squatters to move on quickly. More than once a wagoneer, encountering a fellow traveler, would warn him away from the land by the Canadian.

"They calls it Broken Spur," they were apt to say. "Crazy Mexican lives up there with a big knife. Got him a knife longer'n your arm. Just itchin' to stick somebody with it if you ask me. "'Nother 'un up there, too. All hair 'n whiskers he is. Got his'sef a old timey bear rifle and just stands around real silent like. My wife say's the hairy one's the ghost o' Dan'l Boone. He's a strange one a'right. Better stay clear o' the Spur. Real crazy ones up there." It was talk and rumors like this that helped Robert and Juan Garcia keep and protect the Spur.

It was growing day by day now. Both in land markings and captured cattle. Some came and just stayed. Robert still had his Scottish gold along with the tally of the trap lines he and Hubert Baker had tended. This he used now to buy the vitals needed by working ranch hands. However, it was a twenty-mile ride to the nearest Mercantile. That store was just as likely to be sold out of everything when one finally arrived at the end of the long dusty trip. Robert vowed that there would one day be a trading post or store located on the Canadian to serve the Spur. He would somehow find the right man for such a project; and whatever aid that man would need, Robert would see to.

Robert and Garcia supervised the men in the building of sheds, the gathering of cattle and horses along with hunting and gardening. The saddle men hated gardening even though, with the farm backgrounds most of them shared, they were excellent in this endeavor. Some of the men only stayed for a week or two and then drifted off to who knew where. Others though with nowhere to go at all, found a haven at the Spur. They were, for the most part, hard-working settler stock that somehow just lost themselves and their dreams in the big empty land that was Texas.

From time to time, others came who were far more dangerous and posed a more serious threat. Outlaws and saddle trash criss-crossed this back country that knew no law. Many were busily looking for what they could steal or kill for. By now the Spur had three full time riders collecting mustangs and wild cattle. Mostly they patrolled the monuments and gathered up horses as they came across them. All hands were riding the south edge of the river the day the first bandits came. Robert and Garcia were alone near the adobe. It was a fine June day, the sort of day that promised peace and tranquility.

The air was alive with butterflies. The peppery smell of blooming sage spiced the light breezes. Phoebes and waxwings filled the air with their noisy chatter. Robert had just lifted his head in order to comment on the day's beauty to Garcia when he saw the riders approaching the little yard of the adobe. He clucked his tongue to alert Garcia and the two men stood side by side as the riders approached. The three saddlers declared they sorely needed food and water; that they had been on the road two days with neither and hope for some relief was the reason for the visit. Garcia sized them up instantly.

The leader was a fat man on a dun horse. He had dirty yellow hair sprouting from under a slouch hat. When he smiled, his grin was full of holes. He wore a staind vest that would not fasten across the wide girth that was his belly. He had tied a string from button to hole to keep the ragged garment from flapping as he rode.

One was obviously a Mexican and the other seemed a mere boy. Dark faced, he could have been Mexican too or maybe Indian. Garcia saw the boy kept an old Spencer repeating rifle across his pommel and ready. Robert had given them the smoked ham of a deer and was gathering some greens in a sack when the three dismounted as one. Garcia tensed as they advanced. Robert's back had been turned, but now he felt someone's presence and he turned.

The fat man grinned, "We do thank you, sir, for this fine piece o' venison. But as me and these here boys' see's it, maybe we'll just take your guns and saddles along, too. I 'spect we needs 'em a heap more'n y'all." Without another word Garcia took two quick steps forward.

Robert would never forget the look of surprise on the face of the fat man as he looked down at his shirt front. He had seen Garcia step forward without realizing what was happening. Now, for the first time, he understood that Garcia had plunged the rapier cleanly through his chest and out his back.

There had been little pain from the razor-sharp instrument. It had slid neatly between his ribs and out the middle of his back, ruining the man's heart in the process. The fat man tried to speak, but no sound came forth. The attack had been so sudden that even Robert had been caught unaware. Seeing Garcia had committed to battle though, he recovered quickly.

Robert was ready to fight in an instant. The Hawken was never far away from Robert's hand. While the dying man's companions stood stunned and gaping at their fallen comrade, the big rifle exploded. The boy with the Spencer went backwards a few feet and fell; dead when he hit the ground. Now the Mexican gained composure enough to see what was happening. His two friends were dead in the blink of an eye. He wheeled to run, but Garcia was ready now with his pistol. The fleeing bandit was only able to make a few steps. He fell before the smoking pistol barrel with the back of his head destroyed.

The two friends stood poised, knees slightly bent and feet wide apart. Their senses were keen and alert amid the acrid smoke of the blackpowder. Robert now had his knife in hand, Garcia was again ready with the rapier. They waited for any sign of life from the three men on the ground before them. The boy groaned once, and then all was still. The three were dead. When Robert and Garcia had composed themselves they methodically took the scant belongings of the three dead. They turned the dead mens' horses into their corral and looked over the little assortment of three rifles, a cheap pistol, two pocket knives and a silver coin.

"These Banditos are poor ones," Garcia said. "When I rode the trail of the outlaw I carried mucho dinero. These three must only rob horses of their turds." He was grinning now that the tension was released. Then his eye caught something from among the possibles of the youngest of the three.

It was the boy Robert had killed with the Hawken, the one with the Spencer rifle. From the youngster's open vest pocket, Garcia had detected a glint of metal. Drawing it out, Garcia discovered a small, silver harmonica.

"Look, Senor Robert. This one was a player of music."

"I wonder if he knew any hymns," Robert said.

Later that morning Robert and Garcia rolled the three bodies into a roaring hot greasewood bon-fire. They had built up the big blaze about two miles from their adobe house. The fire was as hot as a smithy and, fueled with its new fodder, sent angry black smoke up in greasy billows. In less than ten minutes not a trace existed of the three intruders. In days to come the prevailing west wind would spread the ashes of the gun and saddle thieves across the big wedge between the Red and Canadian rivers.

Robert and Garcia led the trio's horses back home. It was near sundown when three Spur riders returned from the Canadian's south bank. They had worked hard that day and had collected more than two dozen wild longhorn cattle.

Now, after long hours in the saddle, the cowboys were ready for their supper of antelope stew, fried apples and, as always, the strong pot of Arbuckle's. The three were silent at first. They took large wooden bowls of the steaming soup ladled out by Garcia.

The men bit off large mouthfuls of corn meal tortilla and chewed the firm antelope flesh in stony silence. The stew was well flavored with salt and good red pepper. A rare cinnamon stick had been crumbled into the apples. Hungry as the riders were after their long day of labor, the fare was delicious.

The men showed their approval of the meal with nodding heads and laudatory grunts of satisfaction. Robert and Garcia said nothing. Instead they ladled out seconds and poured the rich black coffee into the enameled cups. At last, Little Joe Coulter broke the silence.

"We saw three riders down by the river this morning," he said.

"Is that correct?" asked Garcia.

"Yep," responded Little Joe. "One of 'em was a big, fat man. Had his se'f a head o' blonde hair, I think; rode a dun mare. Matter of fact that dun looked just like the one out there in the yard pen right now."

"That is strange," said Garcia.

"Me'n the boys saw some smoke up here on the knoll today, too. Real black smoke, it was. You could see it for four or five miles. Garcia, you must have had yer'sef a pretty good cook fire a' goin' up on the knoll, huh?"

"Pretty good," said Garcia, ladling a healthy serving of antelope stew onto Coulter's tin plate. A grin spread slowly over little Joe's freckled face.

"If I find one Goddamn yeller hair in this stew, Garcia, I'm kickin' your Mexican ass." Garcia locked eyes with Robert. Then together, in silence, eyes narrowed into slits of suspicion, they peered intently into the faces of Little Joe Coulter and his two companions. Coulter was still smiling, but his grin was starting to fade a bit. Coulter had started to fear he had said more that he should have. To challenge Garcia, even in jest, might have been the wrong thing to do. Tension electrified the air for what seemed very long moments.

Then Garcia's stony stare began to soften into a faint smile. Coulter looked to Robert who was also showing the birth of a grin. Now the other two riders broke into a noisy chortle. The grins, smiles and chuckles were infectious. In a moment all five men were laughing– lightly at first., then the chuckles gave over to loud guffaws. The laughter became uproarious and uncontrollable. The five laughed until their sides ached, until tears spilled from their eyes. The extravagant mirth though, somehow, seemed built far more on nerves than humor. Robert Trav alone felt remorse at laughing over the death of even a determined bandit.

The Adoption

It was in late summer on the very morning that Robert and Garcia had tried to figure out if the year was 1850 or 1851. The sun was already high the morning sky when the Indian trader, Josey Cotton rode onto the Spur land. He'd been here before and Garcia hated him. Josey Cotton was obviously a made-up name. The trader was, without question, an Indian; maybe one of those strange range colts called "half breed." It wasn't his lineage Garcia and Robert distrusted; it was the man himself. He was as dirty and vile as any human the two friends had ever seen. There was evil about him, too.

He always showed up with strange wares to sell. Things such as slightly worn boots. Maybe a gold watch or a guitar. Once, he had a small, cloth bag with four gold teeth in it. Robert nor Garcia would consider dealing with him. Each time he had appeared, they had rudely dismissed him. Yet he rode in from time to time looking for barter.

When Robert saw him he always thought of Hubert Baker. He could still hear his trapper friend and how he, in disgust, would talk of "trail niggers." Josey Cotton surely qualified. After every visit, even though they sent him on his way quickly, something always turned up missing. A saddle, a bridle, halter; once a bullet mold for thr old Hawken. Something inevitably disappeared.

This morning he had something to sell more shocking than usual. He was riding a bedraggled pinto and leading a bay pack horse in one of the middle stages of starvation. Attached to the pack horse was an Indian style drag called a travois. The affair was made up of two lodge pole pines with a couple of cross braces. The frame was then covered by a blanket or two, laced into place and dragged trailer-style behind a horse. Seated on the drag this morning were two starving, bruised and battered children. The girl was maybe. thirteen or fourteen. A frail child, she was wrapped in a dirty cloak.

Her bare feet protruded and Robert could see they were bruised and bleeding. He knew she had walked barefoot, a long way. Her blonde hair was stringy and filthy, but more appalling was her spirit. She stared at the ground with vacant and empty eyes. She made no sound at all, nor looked up, nor responded to anything around her. Robert had never seen the very soul so taken from any animal.

There was something else about her that Robert was sensing now. The girl was ill. He caught the shiver of her shoulders and realized that fever was, at least partly responsible for her subdued demeanor. The boy looked somewhat sturdier, but he too was covered in filthy rags. Maybe eight or nine years old, his straw-colored hair stood away from his head in dirty clumps. One of his eyes had been blackened, and he sat silent, holding the girl's hand. Robert and Garcia looked each to the other and shared feelings of revulsion. The Indian trader was speaking to them in a broken language, somewhere between Comanche, Mexican and English.

"I sell you these here fine servants, I will, Mister Robert. Why, a man of property like you needs some servants, I'd expect." Robert could hardly stand the sound of Cotton's voice.

"This here boy's a real good worker, he is. Saddles up for me and all that. Make you a real good hand, I'd reckon, and I sells him to you cheap. Just as cheap as anythin'. Take forty dollars for him, I will. Now you take you a look this here girl. She's a might trail dirty right now, but you washes her up and she sure is somethin'. Right purty little thing, she is, when she's proper scrubbed and all. She's real good at funnin', too, you know. I 'spec you know what I mean. She's right smart o' fun when you gets her in your bed at nights. Why, you'd just be the grandest man around here if you got yourself some servants such as these two."

Garcia was watching the face of the trader closely when he saw Josey Cotton's eyes suddenly widen in alarm. Glancing to his right he saw that Robert had, without a word, raised his rifle. He looked back at the face of Cotton and saw the widened eyes were now reflections of terror. The Indian trader knew what was coming. Garcia counted the three, distinct and audible clicks the Hawken's hammer made as it was cocked into firing position. Without a word Robert pressed the trigger. The big rifle exploded so suddenly and so close that Garcia leapt in surprise.

The big .50-caliber lead ball struck the still mounted man about an inch under his right eye. The force was such that the bullet drove the trader from his saddle and some feet beyond. He was dying when he hit the ground. Headshot as he was, his body flopped about in the yard in uncontrollable spasms. It was over in a few moments, and Josey Cotton lay still in death. The two youngsters grasped at each other. Terrified by the exploding rifle charge, they clutched each other.... but still they uttered not a sound. After a moment Garcia reflected,

"He's dead I think, Robert."

"I had an old Uncle back in Scotland that I loved a lot Garcia. Just before I came to America, he told me sometime I might sometime meet a man that ain't fit to live."

"Your Uncle was right." Garcia said. "We meet him here today."

Garcia led a saddled horse from the yard pen and flipping a lariat around the feet of the dead man, he unceremoniously dragged him off. A mile or so away, he dumped the body in a deep arroyo. When he returned he found Robert had the two children in the adobe feeding them the cowboy's antelope supper.

The boy was silent, but he ate ravenously. It was now that Garcia and Robert saw just how ill the girl was. Late that night Robert could hear coyotes quarreling down in the arroyo. He was able to guess where Garcia had taken Josey Cottons remains. The girl grew more ill by the hour....

The two men cared for her the best they could. The lesions of her lower body told them something was terribly wrong. Garcia laid her on his low bed wrapped in his only blanket. At first, she resisted their attempts to aid her. Robert thought her wide eyes reflected the most frightened human he had ever seen. She pulled away from each attempt they made and cried out in fear if they touched her. At last though she just became too weak to resist. She drew herself up into a tiny ball in the center of Garcia's bed and seemingly resigned herself to death. They bathed her with cool water when her fever was racking. They fed her broth and did all that their feeble knowledge allowed.

On the fourth day she died. Even if they had known the name of her illness there was no treatment available for syphilis in its advanced stage. The finest doctors would've lost her too. Robert and Garcia buried her on the grassy knoll above the Canadian still wrapped in the precious blanket. Hers was the first grave in the little cemetery of Broken Spur. Robert took great pains in preparing it.

He made the resting place as perfect for her as he was able. For the next few days the boy remained silent. Robert had him cleaned up now and had shorn his hair. From a Mexican village, Garcia had obtained for the boy clean blue trousers and shirt and a pair of sturdy shoes. The boy ate and slept but only spoke a little, and that only to answer a question or to ask for food or drink.

Then one evening, as Robert sat on the little bench in front of the adobe watching sunset, the boy approached him. He stood watching Robert for a long time. Robert sat motionless and wondering. Then the boy slowly advanced. Suspicious acting at first, he seemed ready to run away at any sudden movement.

He held his arms chest high during his approach; as if he might need to ward off a blow or a punch. But he kept coming. Wide eyed and with a look of fear he drew near, began to climb up on the chair and placed himself on Robert's lap. He put his small, thin face against Robert's chest and then the tears just came. Robert held the boy close and let him cry. They stayed like this for a long time when Robert suddenly sensed another's presence. Turning his head he saw Garcia watching them intently. Now Robert spoke to the boy.

"Son," he said. "What is your name?" He had asked this question several times in the preceding days but to no response,

"I don't have no name I think," the boy stammered. Robert had no way of knowing if the boy knew who he was or not. It occurred to him that maybe the boy knew his past but chose not to remember. From his own past he understood that all too well.

Robert said, "I know a good name. In Scotland, there is a good man who had a son like you, but they lost each other somewhere. That man's name was Colin. Would you like this good name? Should Garcia and I call you Colin?"

The boy nodded. A great "Hah," of approval exploded now from Garcia.

"A birthday," Garcia shouted. "We have a new hand for the Ranchero with a new name. That is all the same as a birthday. I must find a birthday gift for our new Colin." Garcia's face was split by a great smile. His even white teeth glowed against his olive complexion.

"A gift? For me?" The boy was at once thrilled, yet suspicious, wary. "I've never had no gift before," he finally managed.

Now Garcia pressed the object he had been holding into the boy's hand.

"Senor Colin," he bowed regally. "I present you with this fine and royal gift from the Presidente of all Mexico and Texas for your new birthday."

The boy's face was alight now. Robert saw that though his grin was wide indeed, a big full tear had welled in one of his eyes. The boy looked down into his hand and discovered a bright silver harmonica. He looked at it for a long time. Never had he held such a treasure as this. The tear swelled now and, when it could contain its fullness no longer, rolled down the boy's cheek, leaving a shiny trail. Now the three looked each to the other. Their eyes locked in meaningful stares for a long time. There were bridges to cross in these gazes. Wrongs to right. Old trails to close. New paths to open.

At last, the trio burst into peals of raucous laughter punctuated by a lot of dancing about and hugging. Robert later reflected to himself that, though some good things had certainly been happening lately, this was the first real joy that had come to the Broken Spur.

"Senor Robert," Garcia said. "You may never have a wife, but it would seem you have a son.

"Yes," Robert answered. "So it seems."

Part Three: The Big House

Chapter Twenty-four

The Big House
1888

Juan Garcia had been worrying over the wire from Henry Brooker for the better part of an hour now. In brief telegraph language Brooker had sent as many of the details as he knew. The wire sounded somewhat urgent as Brooker felt Colin and his travelers band might need protection.

"How in the world," Garcia wondered, had Colin ever gotten himself involved with a bandit like Amos Younger? What manner of horses were these that would prompt men to kill in order to own them? Most of all, who could this Pamela Carstin be? A man who loved simplicity in his life, Garcia's head was beginning to swim. At last, when he could no longer think, he stuffed the yellow paper telegram into a breast pocket and strode to the bunk house.

"Five riders," he called. "I need five riders now. We ride toward Dodge City to find Senor Colin. He may have troubles." Without a word the eight men lolling about in their bunks began to come to life and reach for pants, boots and hats.

"Only five," Garcia barked. "Jim, you and Rafe and Long John stay here and look to the Spur. Long John, you go and get the Indiana buckboard for Old Robert. He'll want to come too this time." The men were collectively aghast.

"Old Robert trippin'?" The rail thin cowboy called Long John had never known the owner of the Spur to leave. At least, not since he had become a Spur hand.

"I think so. Colin may be in trouble. At least Henry Brooker thinks he might be. Old Robert puts a lot of faith in Brooker. Move your ass now and fetch up the buckboard. You know he won't ride a horse."

"Can't do it, Mister Garcia. Colin took the Studebaker with him on the last drive. It's in Dodge City, I'd reckon."

"If you don't want a .50-caliber Hawken bullet shot in your ass, you'd better make tracks and get Old Robert somethin' to ride in."

"How about a Sunday buggy?" Long John wanted to know. I'll get out the church buggy and a couple of good driving horses. Think that'll do him, Mister Garcia?"

"It'll do... And put a shotgun in the buggy for him, too. I'm sure he'll take the Hawken, but the double- barreled Greener might be needed, too. Rafe, you get over to the cook shack and tell Walter to give you mucho supplies for a trip. Maybe three, maybe four days. Enough to get us up the trail a ways. If we need more supplies, we'll gather them along the way. I don't know exactly when this wire was sent and so I don't know how far we got to go to meet up with Colin. Maybe two or three days, maybe more. Let's move it now. I want us on the trail in an hour... No more time, amigos, vamoose."

Old Robert stirred himself and moved from the little adobe out towards the main bunkhouse. This thing with Colin had him gravely concerned. Henry Brooker wasn't a man to unduly alarm anyone. If he thought a party might do well to head down the trail and meet Colin, then it probably was a good idea. Robert moved by the small cemetery now waiting for the rider he'd sent into the tiny settlement of Travis. He wanted the wires checked to see if any new information had been sent along. Once they mounted the trail to Dodge there would be scant intelligence available.

The rider he had selected was little Bobby Baxter. A diminutive and delicate little fellow who could ride like the wind. Bobby was so small most horses were nearly unaware of his scanty weight, and any horse could make good time under little Bobby. A good horse could fairly fly. Robert now reached the tack shed near the barn and saw that Long John and Rafe were pulling the covered Sunday buggy from its resting place under the shed roof.

"Here now, Long John... What're you boys about with that buggy?"

"Were gettin' it ready for you, Mister Robert." Long John was as thin as a blacksnake, but Old Robert had to admit he was as wiry and as tough as they came. He'd rather be sided in a fight by Long John Petticord than any other man he knew. Except for Juan Garcia of course.

"I ain't ridin' in that Church-goin' preacher wagon. Where the hell's my Studebaker?"

"Mister Colin took the Studebaker to Dodge, Mister Robert. He was usin' that buckboard to haul extra saddles and tackin' stuffs."

"Who the hell told him he could take my bloody wagon?... Here I buy myself a wagon with hard rubber tires on it so's I can ride about like a genl'man, and some wild assed cowboy takes it away on a cattle drive. Great God, it's downright indecent to drive a fine rig like the Studebaker on a cattle drive. Like throwin' pearls afore the swines... That's what it is... Pearls and swines. Damnation anyhow!"

Old Robert was carrying on as though he were totally upset, but every man on the Spur knew he would never be angry with Colin. Not even if his stepson had burned the cherished Studebaker It was now Old Robert saw the small dust cloud to the east at the top of the ridge that was the announcement of a rider coming in.

"See who is that rider, Rafe." Old Robert said.

"I can tell from here, Mister Robert; that's little Bobby. He's ridin' Old Rocket. Them two can raise the dust to a faretheewell." Rafe removed his hat and mopped at his sparse grey hair with a reasonably clean bandana. Using the neckerchief to dry his hat band he went on.

"I thinks little Bobby... He ought to be a race horse rider... Jockey they calls 'em. He don't never find no horses he cain't ride. I sure reckon that's him that's raisin' the powder." The three men stood in silence and watched the rider approach from this notable distance. He was low on the horse's neck.

Bobby Baxter kept his hands low too, near the tree of the saddle. Even at this excessive range, it was plain that his toes were well stirruped and turned into the horse's body. A dressage rider would've perhaps criticized the body posture somewhat, but a Comanche warrior would've called it perfect. The horse was a big blue roan gelding that old Robert had allowed to reach the age of nearly six before castrating.

"Let a good one like Rocket come to full growth and musculature," he had told his critics who believed in gelding stallions at a much earlier age. "He might be a little rough to handle, but he'll be the strongest mount on the Spur."

Old Robert had turned out to be only partially right. Rocket was the strongest horse on the Spur. He was also the rankest. He was far more than a little rough to handle. He was a pent-up hurricane. Letting him go so long before emasculation, Rocket had retained all the riotous behavior of a full stud horse. When an estrogen-laden mare approached, dependability was not in Rocket's nature. Let another male horse appear, and a rollicking fight was inevitable. He knew no peers when it came to kicking, biting, rearing or running away with his rider.

Every Spur cowboy had taken a turn to saddle break the Rocket. The horse had accounted for chipped teeth, bloody noses and even a few broken bones in nearly every encounter. A few, had held him so that one might ride peacefully for five or ten apprehensive minutes, but on

Rocket's best day he was far too unreliable to use as a working cow horse. After much disillusionment, it was discovered that Old Blue Rocket and Little Bobby Baxter had discovered they were kindred souls. No other cowboy on the Spur could get very much out of Rocket, but to Bobby he was a kitten.

"I'd like to buy the Rocket, Mister Trav," Bobby had told old Robert one morning. "I ain't got no money, but I'll work for no wages until you think I've paid you what he's worth. Would you sell him to me on those terms, Mister Trav?" A drifting orphan, who like so many others had found refuge and even new lives at the Spur; Bobby Baxter was as poor as any church mouse had ever dared to be. It was a bold move for this impoverished cowboy to proposition the wealthy owner of the ranch that employed him. He needed his job badly. But he also needed the Rocket. He had, after all, never owned a single thing of value in all of his nineteen years.

"Are you sure you want him bad enough to pay what he's truly worth?" Old Robert grunted. Now Bobby gulped a bit of air and realized for the first time that he really had no idea of the value of a fine animal like this one. It suddenly dawned on him that he might have just pledged a year or even more of wage-less work to pay for this horse. Standing up to his commitment though, he shot back,

"Yes sir, I surely do mean it. I'll work for nothin' 'til you say we've hit his worth." Old Robert could see this boy had a deep love for this horse and would not be dissuaded.

"Fair enough, Bobby lad... Ye can start right now... I'll let you know when the horse's value has been reached."

"O.K., Mister Trav, we have a deal," the little cowboy answered. Taking Rocket's bridle in his hand, Bobby began to lead him toward the stable. He was still wondering how long he might have to go without money in his pockets when Old Robert's voice rudely interrupted his thoughts

"Yer done when you reach the door of the barn, Bobby," Old Robert said loudly and a bit rough.

"What's that, sir?" Bobby's first thought was that he had misunderstood Old Robert's intentions and that he was now being fired for some unknown breach. He searched his mind for what he might have done wrong. "What's that, sir?" he repeated his question.

"I said yer finished when you reach that barn door. That's my notion of the worth of the horse... Lead him to the barn and he's all yours... bought and paid for. But mind you, no wages till you hit the door."

Old Robert turned on his heel and strode sternly back to the adobe. Had anyone seen his face they would've discerned just how hard he was working at covering an impish grin. It was indeed a hard smile to disguise.

The story of Blue Rocket and Bobby Baxter was told in every bunkhouse in Texas and at every campfire on the Goodnight Trail. The cowboys of the Broken Spur would never forget how little Bobby Baxter had acquired the fastest horse on the Canadian River.

"There's nothin' new about Mister Colin at the telegraph office," Bobby Baxter reported. He sat astride the large roan horse. Rocket was lightly lathered at the martingale breast strap but not particularly breathing hard; even after such a run.

He is a mighty horse, this Blue Rocket., Old Robert thought.

"But Mister Conley told me to tell you that Mister Brooker must have been makin' a mistake. He allowed Brooker was in err' when he was thinkin' that outlaw, Amos Younger, must be after Mister Colin. Amos Younger's dead, Mister Robert."

"Dead?" Old Robert queried.

"Yes, sir. Mister Conley said I should tell you some territory marshals found Younger and a wealthy rancher name of Starrett dead. Them and one of Starrett's cowhands was all shot up and dead over in the Nation just below the panhandle. Sounds to me like it must be somewhere northeast of Caney Creek. Mister Conley said to tell you there was a lot of shootin'."

"They got any ideas as to who did all this shootin'?" Old Robert asked.

"No, sir... Just that they think it may have been horse thieves. The trackers found a passel o' hoof prints about... Not enough for a herd... A string maybe. Probably a shootin' over a fallin' out amongst horse thieves."

"Any thin' else to tell me, Bobby?" Old Robert inquired.

"No, Sir. That was all the news they had down in Travis."

"Go put Rocket away, Bobby, and then stop up to the cook shack. Walter's got some peach cobbler up there I told him to hold for you." Bobby Baxter smiled at the mention of peach cobbler. He thanked Old Robert and led his fabled horse away. By now, Juan Garcia had arrived and spoke thoughtfully.

"So it is not Amos Younger that stalks our Colin. Another, we do not know, hunts the head of our son." Garcia's voice was cold and dangerous.

"Hold on now, Johnny," Robert said. Maybe nobody's after him at all. Brooker thought maybe Younger was after those horses but if Younger's dead, then maybe nobody's after Colin at all."

"If Brooker say's someone is trailing Colin, then I believe it." Juan Garcia was stern now. "When Brooker says Colin may face danger, then I believe it... Senor Robert, you know Henry Brooker... He is a Ranger. He's an honorable man. We have always trusted Henry Brooker."

"Well, I guess your right of course, amigo. The thing to do is go and see if Colin needs help. The only thing we know for sure is Amos Younger is dead so Colin don't need no protection against him."

"That is right, Senor Robert," Juan Garcia replied. He pushed his hat back on his head and looked earnestly at Old Robert now. "I wish it was Amos we were going to find. We know him pretty well. He's a thief it is true. He steals many things; but he is no killer. I'm afraid we're riding out to meet the man who has killed old Amos. Far more dangerous, Senor Robert. This killer of Amos Younger is no horse thief... He is a bad man, I think, Senor Robert. He is a shooter. The vaqueros have your buggy ready now," Garcia went on.

"I had them tuck a shotgun under the seat for you, the short-barreled Greener. I'll go up to the adobe now and get some whiskey for you to carry along."

"Just be sure we have extra shells for that shotgun, Garcia. Tell Bobby Baxter to rest his horse a few hours and then catch up with us on the trail." Old Robert wanted this gritty young man and his tough horse along. "No whiskey Johnny. No whiskey this time. We may have some mortal work ahead."

Chapter Twenty-five

Beaver's Raid

Beaver and his two confederates had done a masterful job of imprisoning their quarry. When Abraham Primble had built his little house he had deliberately cleared all the brush and trees from around it so that it stood with more than fifty yards of bare ground on each of its four sides. This. he reasoned. made it impossible for an enemy to approach the cabin unseen. What had been designed as security for those inside now worked in reverse: The bare ground surrounding the cabin had become Colin's chief torment.

The house was surrounded by low hills so that it sat tucked in low and out of the wind. Another of Primble's excellent ideas. The three riflemen. however, had triangulated themselves on the high ground. With no cover around the cabin, their deadly rifle fire held the four inhabitants within the lodge in a tight and deadly grip. All night, Colin had pondered on ways he might slip out of the house and flank his adversaries, or even simply confront them out in the open. But each time Colin appeared near a window or door, no matter how briefly, deadly rifle fire fell upon him like a withering hail storm. He had thought he could have moved out last night under the cover of darkness. A bright September moon had illuminated the cabin's spacious yard until any hope of slipping under the guns seemed foolhardy. It was morning now, and the little band huddled together. They shared a bit of their precious water in a dejected silence and then moved back to their respective guard positions.

"It's not fair," Pamela said to Colin. "It's not fair to the boy. First his father is murdered and now this." Colin saw at once, that Pamela was not afraid; rather, she was angry. Her son had been endangered enough and now, like a wild mare of the plains, she was ready to defend her foal with an unsurpassed rage.

Colin left the window he was guarding briefly and went to comfort her. As he lightly squeezed her arm she turned at once and kissed him hard on the mouth. Openly she kissed him now for the first time in front of Chinagirl and the boy. When they drew apart they saw the boy, Justin, was smiling approvingly. Chinagirl, too, displayed a face bright with the joy she shared with her dearest friends.

"We'll work this out," Colin said. "Just stay low and don't give them a chance to hurt one of us. Don't forget we've still got Chester out there somewhere and we're pretty well armed in here. We'll be all right." Colin's encouragement cheered them a bit, but each knew full well that this would have to end soon. The water wouldn't last much longer, and the growing pangs of hunger were just beginning to make all feel uneasy and nervous. Beaver Parker, usually addled and confused, was handling the siege with the polish of an experienced field soldier. All he had to do was hold things the way they were and make no mistakes. Simply stay under cover, for to sustain a wound now would surely be a fatal error. Fire at the cabin's inhabitants often enough to be a worry to them and let time do the rest.

Beaver knew he had to remain intently cautious. It was true there was only one man down there in the house– a cowboy with two women and a boy– but this particular man was a formidable one. So far, he had made no errors in judgment and his return rifle fire was swift and accurate. Beaver felt he was destined to victory in this conflict but understood the situation would not forgive bad judgment. It fell to Charley Stone to make the first mistake. Charley's error really had its beginning the day before when the trio had raided the Primble home.

Charley had carried out his portion of the grisly duties of this bloody raid without a hitch. As the three were cleaning the cabin of food and water, though, Charley had discovered a bottle of Abraham Primble's finest distilled spirits. Without a word to the others, Charley had secreted the bottle under his shirt and vest and now, as he lay in ambush on the hillside, he sampled his prize from time to time. Both Beaver and Willy had wondered, if only slightly, at the extreme quiet that emanated from Charley's hiding place.

Charley was usually complaining of a back ache or a head ache or a stomach ache or some other ache. Being given to fidgeting, as he was, he found it virtually impossible to be still and quiet for very long. Now, however, he lay on the hillside motionless and as still as death. Beaver was impressed with what he believed was Charley's soldierly change in demeanor. In truth, Charley was passed out; dead drunk.

It was the startling noise of Willy firing his rifle at the rear window that tricked Charley. Willy had thrown four wild shots at the opening when he thought he had seen a flicker of movement. Chinagirl and Colin returned fire simultaneously. The resulting swiftly fired salvo of loud, explosive shots so startled Charley that he was partially awakened. Completely disoriented by the incredible roar of four high-powered rifle shots fired almost at once, the drunken gunman stirred in his stupor. The loudness of the rifle fire confused and jolted Charley greatly. In his alcoholic fog he forgot for a fraction of a moment where he was. Groggy and bewildered, seeking to re-orient himself to his surroundings, he propped himself high up on his elbows to look about. He was promptly shot through the lower jaw with a bullet from Justin Carstin's rifle.

The boy was simply looking precisely in the right direction when Charley exposed himself. Without waiting for a command from either Colin or his mother, Justin swiftly drew a bead on the part of the outlaw he could see. Then, just as Colin had taught him, the boy squeezed the trigger. The heavy rifle exploded against his cheek and its overwhelming pop, so unexpected in the tight confines of the cabin, frightened and startled everyone within the walls into momentarily witlessness.

Once the initial trauma of the shot was past, Colin, his ears still ringing from the deafening roar of the .44-40, composed himself enough to see that it was the boy who had fired. He had pushed his rifle barrel through the open window on the far side of the room and touched of the big shell. Now, he huddled low, taking cover against the wall.

"I hit him, Colin! I think I hit that man on the hill. He was in the grass but I could see him pretty good and he jumped when I shot. Do you think I hit him, Colin?" As if to answer the boy, Charley Stone, who had just now discovered he had been shot, let out a fearful call. It was a mixture of groan and scream. The cry reflected, at once, total dismay and unbridled pain. Colin thought the boy looked a bit dazed. Pamela was swiftly moving to her son's side.

"I think he's hit pretty good, Justin. Keep watch now... If he's wounded light, he'll be bad to handle."

"Keep alert now," Colin called out, fearful that Pamela's' concern for her son might cause her to lapse in her caution. "That shot may bring on the fight."

In dreadful pain now, Charley Stone wailed and lamented his terrible wounds in loud and soulful crying.

"Oh, help me, Beaver," Charley thought he was saying. With his ruined mouth and teeth, however, the sounds he made were only a loud series of croaks and grunts. Colin saw that at each cry the boy, Justin, winced. At last, Colin saw that the boy was crying.

"Come here, Justin. Keep low and come to me."

Pamela freed her grip on her son's arm begrudgingly, and the boy dutifully obeyed. Crawling on their hands and knees, Colin took him to the side of the sheet-covered Annie Primble.

"Look to this, son," Colin said, drawing back the sheet. He saw the boy recoil at the terrible sight of Annie's bloody face and slashed body. His ashen face was a frozen mask of revulsion and terror.

"The man you shot did this, Justin. This was a good woman. If you were to let him in here with us, he'd do it again... Only to your Momma this time. It's hard, Justin, but you have to understand: There are just some men who ain't fit to live."

The boy looked a long time at the pitiful thing that had been Annie Primble. Colin could see that this revelation was making an impact, for Justin began to straighten visibly. Gradually his thin shoulders squared and his tears began to dry and disappear.

"I hope the sum' bitch dies on fire." The boy said, looking Colin directly in the eye. "I hope he dies burnin' on fire."

Pamela looked at Colin with resigned tears welling in her grey eyes. It was a hard thing, but she was beginning to understand. Her son, who had been a frightened boy, was being transformed. Sheer necessity and a primitive survival instinct was changing her boy before her very eyes. Yesterday's boy was today an angry and aggressively defensive man.

Moved by these happenings and in need of support, Pamela was about to reach for Colin's hand when a fusillade of rifle fire shattered the remaining glass from the window nearest her and the glistening shards flew into the room. From Chinagirl came a sharp gasp followed by a low moan. When Colin could look her way, he saw she was lying on her back with her left arm under her in an altogether unnatural angle. Blood was seeping from several glass cuts about her face and scalp. Colin noticed quickly the more serious spreading billow of red, high above her left breast.

·There was no mistaking this injury. It was a bullet hole. And it was a bad one. The question Colin asked himself was whether it was a high chest or a low shoulder wound. Chinagirl's survival might depend on the answer. Colin saw, from the corner of his eye, that Pamela was hurrying to the aid of Chinagirl. freeing him to turn his attention back to their tormentors.

"No more talk," Colin fairly shouted. "Shoot back... Any movement, shoot it."

Stealing a glance, he shot his gaze back to Chinagirl. She now lay in Pamela's' arms but Colin could not help but notice that she was as still as death. A porcelain figurine, pale and still. And quiet.

Chapter Twenty-six

Gunfight

At the moment, it seemed to Colin the situation might be changing for the better. Misfortune and hard luck had seemingly become the prevailing circumstance currently plaguing the little cabin's defenders. Yet now several hours had passed since the bullet had found Chinagirl without any further outbreaks of gunfire. Still, with Chinagirl so harshly wounded, Colin was forced to asses their situation as a poor one. The girl's wounds were indeed serious. The bullet had sped though her upper shoulder but had struck bone and left her left arm dangling and useless from the shoulder down.

Blood was pouring in an unbelievable volume from the gaping exit wound the bullet had left in the rear of her shoulder. Pamela had worked dutifully to staunch the incredible flow with what had been Annie Primble's cherished lace table wear. Colin could see that Chinagirl was not unconscious as her silence had led him to believe. Her eyes were open wide. She responded to Pamela's questions. She made no outcry nor did she complain. Trauma was not the cause of her serenity. She was simply bearing up. Shot badly; flying glass leaving her with several painful and bloody slashes, she made no sound.

Pamela admired her courage so and was forced to wonder if she could display the same demeanor as Chinagirl if she were forced into this situation. To make matters even more pressing, Colin had believed Justin had incapacitated one of the ambushers. Now he wasn't so sure. While it was true Charley Stone had committed a great amount of wailing and lamenting of his grievous injuries, he had somehow found the strength to fire his rifle again. His shots were inaccurate and sporadic but, nonetheless Charley managed to send a rifle bullet crashing in through the window from time to time....

A swift examination by Colin revealed the water supply was dangerously low, especially now that they had sorely wounded Chinagirl to care for. At least some small amount of water was needed to tend her, and it was becoming too precious to spare. The ammunition supply was still in reasonable shape, but another day of this extensive firing and that hard ordinance would start to dwindle like the water. Food was another problem. There simply was none. Colin was as hungry as he ever remembered being, and he could not but wonder how the boy was holding up. It was obvious the raiders of the Primble cabin had cleaned it of all food and drink. It was as if they knew this siege would come and they had readied for it.

Brave little cowboy, Colin said to himself in an effort to dismiss the food problem, at least temporarily.

A single round from the barrage of rifle fire that had injured Chinagirl had struck the receiver portion of the Winchester rifle she was using. The bolt and receiver were smashed and bent from the bullet strike. The weapon was rendered useless. Anyway you look at it we're one rifle short, Colin thought nearly aloud.

The day wore on in heat and silence. Pamela rested from her nursing chores when Chinagirl seemed asleep. From far back in the room, for safety dictated no one should show his head above the window sills, she peered out over the sash of the front window to the dusty lane. Another bright hot September afternoon had brought the shimmering heat waves out to dance above the surface of the lane. From far away she could hear the faint cry of a jay, but the afternoon heat had stopped all other bird activity. Insects monotonously droned on and on. It surprised Pamela how loudly these tiny creatures could sing their non-melodious tunes. But then, she had never had all of her senses as acutely aware and alert as they were at this very moment. She had never listened so intently before. She had never watched as keenly as she did now.

She saw that her son had lowered his head to his knees, and she wondered if he slept. Glancing at Colin she saw that he was intently watching, first the rear window and then the front, on his side of the door. That left one rear window not too well guarded. Still, it could be seen by peering through the kitchen. It had been the window guarded by Chinagirl. If the truth were known, Pamela would have been forced to admit that it was Chinagirl's courage and strength that was keeping her going. She was tired and thirsty and, oh so hungry. She was also terrified of the shooters that lurked outside.

Even her dedication to the thought that Colin would, somehow, invent the strategy that would ultimately rescue them all was becoming suspect. Those images and her confidence in Colin had not yet failed her, but her own courage was beginning to lag. She believed in Colin Trav with all her heart, but these odds might prove too much for anyone. Whoever these enemies were, they had indeed laid out a fine and deadly trap. In short, Pamela Carstin was near to becoming desperate. She felt herself approaching panic. Additionally, she was reliving many of the thoughts she had suffered when Alex had been killed.

It's this country, she thought. It's all death and killing... It's all guns and... stupid killing... dying for nothing." Her sobbing came almost silently at first. Then for some reason she couldn't explain, Pamela, normally a relatively brave and resolute woman, felt herself slipping deeper into the blank darkness of despair. Her sobs increased until they were highly audible. Her shoulders shook uncontrollably. It was this display of despondency that brought Colin from his post by the front window. Sliding along the floor he reached her side and took her gently into his arms. Neither spoke but as he stroked her hair, her crying subsided.

In his embrace, she found the sustaining comfort she needed. Her strength returned in the gentle caress of this hard man. The boy, Justin, looked at the embracing pair. He wished to add his comforting support to his mother's dejection as well. He sensed though, that it was Colin that she needed most right now. The boy moved closer to his window and cracked the lever of his Winchester a bit in order to see the brass head of the shell lying in wait under the rifle's hammer. As Pamela began to calm, Colin noticed the sun was beginning to set. He was afraid they were in for a lot of moonlight again and a night escape would be impossible.

Aware of battle techniques, he thought he knew what might be coming next, and he faced that possibility with dread. He was reasonably sure that with the dawn would come the fire. The ambushers wouldn't attempt to burn at night. There would be too great a chance of someone slipping away in the confusion of fire and darkness together. They would instead, wait until the sun was well up he thought. They had the moon to help them sentry all night; and when the sun was high, Colin feared, they would fire the little house. Attempted escape from the burning building under the waiting rifles would be disastrous.

There was one salvation that might come about when the shooters tried to ignite the dwelling. They would have to come close to light their fires. That could bring them into clear rifle range for a split second. Colin needed that second very badly. All this time they had been pinned under their assailants' rifles, and not once had he had an unobstructed shot at anyone. Indians, he knew, would have used fire arrows and stayed completely under cover while burning the cabin to the ground. He doubted that these white men though would be able to bring about such an assault. Colin hated his position. All he could do was to wait and hope for that one clear shot; or pray that an unexpected rain or a heavily clouded sky might appear and enshroud the anticipated bright September moon. Recent days had been bright hot and dry. The prospects for rain were not good.

The night was a long one as Colin had expected. About once or twice an hour one of the shooters let off a round at window openings. The bullets would spatter into the house to keep the inhabitants terrified. The idea was to keep them ducking bullets in order to prevent an attempted escape into the night. Colin suffered the lustrous moonlight impatiently. He believed that he could have read a newspaper by the moon's brilliance if he had one. He knew when moonset came, the shooting would increase; but the light would fade a lot, too. Moonset came and gave way to the grey of false dawn, and not once did Colin trust the darkness enough to step out into it....

When the sun was at last full up into the sky, Colin saw exactly what he had feared. From the top of the hill directly in front of the house, he saw a faint wisp of smoke. Looking to the high bank on his right another grey curl spiraled in the windless morning sky. There was no sign of life from the shooter in the rear.

This was the one that Justin had fired at and probably wounded badly. Maybe killed. It looked as though the rear was safe from invasion. At least, for a while. But the other two were making their fires, and the torches would come next. Colin checked the chamber of his rifle for the tenth time, and he now placed Henry Brooker's Smith and Wesson pistol on the floor beside him. He was as ready as he could ever be. He heard a low moan from the front bedroom where Pamela was comforting Chinagirl.

Hell of a mess, he reflected. *Things are going to be hard here in a while*, he thought almost aloud.

"They're lighting their fires, aren't they?" Pamela had crept into the room and was now kneeling alongside him. "What can we do about that?"

"They'll have to come closer to throw the torches on the roof. We'll get some shooting then." He hoped he was right. Somehow, he just couldn't see these men using torches and coming in that close, perhaps presenting an open target. So far they had made very few mistakes. The boy, Justin called out at that moment in an excited voice.

"Look Colin! Look to the wagon!" Now, for the first time, Colin saw that the wagon containing the dead body of Abraham Primble was missing from the spot where it had stood from the moment they had approached the cabin. Hurriedly he slipped from window to window desperately trying to spot the missing wagon. When he got to the window Justin was peering out of, his worst fears were recognized.

There was the wagon all right. In the night, because it stood so far away from the house, the wagon had been invisible in the darkness, moonlight or not. The outlaws had slipped down the hill and fastened ropes to the double tree and had hauled it frontward up the steep slope. It poised there now. Its massive tail gate directed down the steep precipice. Colin saw that they had piled it high with brush and even some heavy fireplace logs. Now he understood the plan perfectly. The ambushers intended to start a fire in the heavy wagon and set it rolling down the hill to crash into the little house. ....

Colin knew they would stoke the flames until the fire was a raging inferno before they let it go. He further knew there would be no stopping the flaming juggernaut once it started its down hill flight. This was a freight wagon, built of heavy oak and with great iron-bound oaken wheels. Colin believed it probably weighed, loaded as it was, six or seven hundred pounds or more. He calculated that it would easily crash right through the house's rear wall and into the kitchen. He further discovered they had pulled the wagon alongside a large oak tree so that they could, by standing behind the oak, light their rolling pyre without exposing even a scant inch of themselves to Colin's rifle. Sadly, Colin assumed the lifeless body of Abe Primble was under the fiery brush pile in the wagon.

He saw pure panic now in the eyes of Pamela Carstin. Somehow, she reminded him of a doe deer who is too mesmerized by the hunter's appearance to flee; and so she stands, wide eyed and helpless, awaiting the killing shot. It infuriated Colin to see this woman he had come to love so intimidated. In rage, he swore a bitter and vulgar oath. It was a thing he had not done in her presence before. She drew back in surprise and a little fright at his vile remark. She clutched the boy to her breast.

"Let me go, Mom." The boy exclaimed. "Colin needs me and this rifle now." He tore himself from her. "Where should I stand, Colin?" The boy asked. "There's only two of them... Well, maybe three... Maybe we can kill them all."

Colin was about to try to answer the boy when his eye was taken by a flicker of movement on the high hill to the front and left of the house.

"Look," he said to Pamela. "Look on that hill. Can you see that rider?" Pamela looked and indeed there was a man on horseback on the hillock's highest crest. Then she looked again. Was it a man or a boy? The rider was that small. The horse seemed incredibly large even at this distance. She could see it was a powerful roan, the color of polished steel.

"I know that horse," Colin said. He could not help but grin. "That's Old Rocket. That's Bobby Baxter on Blue Rocket. They belong to the Spur." The wagon was fully blazing now. Colin looked away from the welcome sight of Bobby Baxter and his big horse just in time to see the wagon seemingly launch itself in a fiery streak down the sharp incline. It sped directly toward the rear of the cabin.

"Look out," he called. "Fire comin' in!"

Running swiftly behind the wagon, Colin saw two men. One seemed to have a shotgun. Probably that's Abe's shotgun, Colin thought in a flash. The other man was running full tilt with a large revolver in each hand. Colin grabbed Pamela and Justin both in his arms and ran with them to the front of the house. His intent was to carry them as far from the crashing fire as he could.

Colin was far too busy to look now. If he could have, he would've seen that Bobby Baxter had been joined by two more riders. The big man in rough clothing astride the chestnut was Chester Crawford. The thin rider of the crisp and stylish black stallion was Juan Garcia. Together the three horsemen from the Broken Spur charged their mounts directly at the unaware outlaws. The bandits were running wildly, still following the burning wagon down hill. Abraham Primble's freight wagon burst into his little home with a loud and fiery crash.

The wagon struck the cabin with the force of an explosion. The collision destroyed house and wagon alike. The trio of Colin, Pamela and Justin were racing just ahead of the flaming wagon. The fiery burden was nearly upon them when Colin, gripping the two hard in his arms, leaped at the doorway with an effort that tested his body's every fiber. The three slipped through the protective front door frame of the house. They escaped the burning collision by scant inches. No sooner had the wagon been slowed to a stop by the cabin walls and door frames than Colin was instantly back among the raging flames. He had to find Chinagirl.

Clawing his way through the flame and blinding smoke, he at last found that the impact had rolled Chinagirl a few feet from where he had assessed he would find her. Scooping her up into his arms, he caused her to scream in pain as he offended the shoulder wound. The door he had just passed through was an inferno now, totally blocked by fire.

The cabin was old and dry. Roof and floors alike were exploding into hot blue flame. Colin saw instantly that his situation was a bad one. It would require some desperate action on his part. Holding Chinagirl tightly in his arms, disregarding the fact that he was hurting her shoulder wound, he ran forward as hard and as fast as he could— harder than he had ever run before. Now, with a crashing leap, he catapulted himself full forward. Colin and Chinagirl crashed through what glass was still present in the left front window. He and Chinagirl, still in his arms, landed with a dull thud on the narrow porch. Still clinging to the nearly unconscious girl, he began to roll over and over with her until at last they were clear of the blistering heat.

Colin looked up just in time to see the raider he had spotted with the shot gun was advancing upon him. Colin's own rifle had been lost in the fiery melee, and he cast his eyes about everywhere now for any one of the guns. He slapped his hand to his waist band to retrieve the Brooker Smith and Wesson and discovered it was missing too. He saw the pistol now. It was lying in the dust near the porch. He had lost it when he and Chinagirl had rolled clear of the fire. Never once in his life had Colin Trav felt so defenseless. He saw a thin man with a weasel's face raise the shotgun to his shoulder.

Colin found himself staring down the twin .12-gauge tubes less than ten feet from his face. He realized he was facing his death and that he had no way to fight back. Helpless, he braced himself now and turned his face away, only a bit, preparing for the deadly blast to come. A single thought raced through his mind now. It was a feeling of deep regret that he would be leaving Pamela and the boy behind. It had taken him so long to find them. Pamela saw what was happening to Colin, and she stood rooted in fear, her fist clenched against her teeth. Like Colin, she braced herself for the shotgun's deadly explosion.

No shot came. Instead Colin was stunned to hear a sharp gasp of rushing air followed by a low and pleading moan. Snapping back now, he saw the rat-faced man had dropped the shotgun. An angular rider on a coal black horse, brandishing a Spanish sword, had ridden nearly over him.

In one swift and deadly movement the rider had impaled Willy Parker. The blade had coursed into Willy's body directly from the center of his back. What Colin saw, jutting down and forward from the front of the man's chest, was two feet of bloody Spanish steel.

The Toledo blade had done its job so very well. Entering the center of the back, it had severed the spine as a cleaver. Running through the man's body in a downward direction, the keen double edges had sliced through heart and lungs alike. The wound was a mortal one from which there would be no recovery.

The dying man, now backlighted by the raging cabin fire, staggered about in the little yard. His eyes were enormous and vacant. He appeared terrified of the death he knew was coming. He stared at the protruding blade, baffled and unable to grasp its full meaning, to discern its origin. He attempted a few times to speak, but his lower jaw swung aimlessly and formed no lucid words. In a moment, Willy Parker dropped to his knees and then fell forward. The extending blade spilled him slightly to one side as it touched the earth.

The old vaquero stepped down gracefully from his ebony mount. He retrieved his sword from the dead man's body with a stiff, jerking pull. Without a word Garcia commenced to cleanse the gleaming blade with a clean white kerchief from his rear pocket.

"Juan Garcia, at your service Senor Colin Trav," he spoke regally. A smile played at his lips.

"Bout time you got here, Garcia... I was afraid I'd have to handle this without you."

Both men laughed aloud at Colin's attempt to appear nonchalant and flippant. Garcia's laughter nearly betrayed the panic he felt inside. He knew he had barely been in time. The threat to Colin's life had been too real; too close.

Colin laughed nervously; it was because he had been cut a new deal at the very moment his death had seemed so certain. Relief flooded Pamela's heart, and she ran to be at Colin's side. Their embrace was a vigorous one. The way they hugged now reflected all of their pent-up emotions. Those feelings that come of having thought all was lost, then the sudden unexpected rescue. The regaining of everything believed lost in the twinkling of an eye. Even Juan Garcia's cheeks were streaked. He cried tears of welcome relief and unbridled joy.

The young man with the two pistols and the dirty blonde hair witnessed the fate of his kinsman on the rapier point. At the sight of so many Spur riders he had thrown down his guns and began to run frantically. Chester Crawford, still mounted on the chestnut, was in the process of running him down. Colin was seeing to Pamela and Justin and they, in turn, were seeing to Chinagirl.

Colin breathed his first easy breath in a long while when he saw that they were well. It had been a long time since Colin Trav had even thought about God, much less prayed to him. In this moment of grateful relief he muttered, "Thank you, dear God." He said it loudly enough for Pamela to hear. Throwing her arms around his neck, she kissed him hard on the mouth and buried her face in the hollow of his shoulder. Now other Spur riders began to converge on the little yard. When Colin looked up the hill in the rear of the flaming cabin he simply couldn't believe his eyes.

Coming down the slope was the Broken Spur's church buggy and driving it was Old Robert himself. Behind him came two of the Spur horsemen holding something suspended between their two mounts. As they drew nearer Colin could see they were carrying a man. Each had the man under his arms, and they brought him along swiftly behind the buggy. As they approached, Colin could see the man they carried had been shot in the face. His jaw appeared ruined; his face was covered in blood. He appeared to be in very poor shape. His moans of pain, actually near screams, left little doubt, however, he was very much alive.

Colin reasoned that this was the outlaw wounded by Justin the day before. When the riders reached the yard they dropped the bloody bundle in a heap. Old Robert stopped the buggy and stepped out of his seat and stood squarely in front of his stepson. It was at that moment the fired cabin collapsed and fell in on itself sending an enormous shower of sparks and flame skyward.

Colin had never been so glad to see anyone in his life and he realized at this moment how very much he loved this old man.

"What brings you here to these parts, old timer?" Colin said displaying a wide grin..

"I've come to fetch my wagon. Where the hell's my red-wheeled Studebaker?"

Chapter Tweny-seven

Beaver's Run

Pamela looked at the position of the sun and estimated the time of day to be near noon. She guessed that the fire attack on the Primble house must have started at around good day light; perhaps seven thirty or eight o'clock. The melee had been over for several hours now, and the Spur riders were just cleaning up the aftermath. First, the riders had broken out their water; and the three near-victims drank thirstily. Next came hard tack biscuits, cold smoked ham and thick slabs of pale yellow cheese. Pamela thought she had never tasted anything quite so delicious. There were some raisins, dried apples and rock hard corn dodgers too. A stone gallon jug of sweet cider rounded out the refreshments. To Colin's bunch, it was a fine feast.

It was during this meal that Colin told Old Robert and Garcia the story of the cabin's siege. He spoke in broken sentences between mouthfuls and had never before realized that cheese could be quite so delicious. Even Chinagirl found the strength to eat a bit. It was hard for her to eat though, mostly because Chester Crawford would not turn loose of her long enough for her to try. He held her in his arms and covered her small face with kisses and tears. He was at once laughing and crying, and his joy at recovering his Chinagirl was beyond measure.

"We found this Senor Crawford about two-and-a-half days ago," Garcia told Colin. "He led us straight to you. We stopped only to rest the horses when they were dropping. These men have been in the saddle many hours. Henry Brooker, too. He wired the Spur that Amos younger was after you all."

"I think we'll make a camp here," Old Robert announced. "A little rest and we can move out in a lot better shape."

"Please, Mister Robert…" The plea came from Pamela. "Please, let's not stay here. If we could only move down the trail a little ways… I just can't stay here." Old Robert looked thoughtful for a moment.

"I think that's the most sensible suggestion I've heard in a long time. Of course we shan't stay here. Garcia, bring the men to life. We'll move as soon as we can. First, there's work to do here." Colin knew what was coming next, and he moved to Pamela's side to comfort her. Old Robert began now to give the grisly orders that must accompany such an ordeal.

"Pull the cabin fire apart so's it can cool," he said. "There's four good people in those ashes, boys. We got to find what we can and bury 'em proper, respectful. As friends." Pamela recoiled when she realized she had forgotten the Primbles in the ensuing excitement. It was true, she hadn't known them. But she knew they were a family. She knew they were friends to the man she cared about with all her heart. She felt hot tears pool in her eyes as she reflected on the flaming wagon becoming the instrument that would reunite the separated family, if only in death.

"Long John, come over here and drop a loop on this feller's foot." Old Robert was gesturing toward the fallen Willy Parker. "Drag him off in the brush somewhere and leave him." Robert saw Pamela wince at this. Looking her directly in the eye he said, "Colin just now told me about what happened to the Primble girls and to Annie. I think this feller had a really rough time planned for you, Miss Pamela. I wouldn't worry about not burying him. His type don't hardly never get buried. Coyotes and wolves got to eat, too, you know. Take him out of here, Alvin. Get this rat-faced little skunk out of my sight."

The lanky cowboy with the full moustache and brown hat was mounted on a little sorrel mare. With no effort at all he flipped a loop of his lariat over the foot of Willy Parker and dragged him from the cabin yard.

"What about this here livin' one?" Garcia wanted to know. "He's shot real bad but he's much alive." He was pointing at Charley Stone who sat with his back against the stone side of the well. His body was shaking out of control and he was wracked with fear and crying.

"Buster, you and Johnson come over here." The two Broken Spur cowboys touched their horses' flanks lightly with their heels and rode over to where Old Robert stood. The three looked down on the sniveling and bloody-faced Charley Stone.

"Take this... this raggedy-assed thing down the road a ways. Get him out of the sight of these women and that boy. Find yourselves a good tall tree and hang this foul bastard." Charley's eyes widened at this and through his ruined mouth he tried to protest or to plead. No one was quite sure which– his garbled words were muddled and unintelligible. Once again, the wounded outlaw found himself held under the arms between two horsemen and carried away. This time, attempting to scream out his fear and outrage.

"There's some men just ain't fit to live," Robert said to no one in particular. "We can't have folks here'bouts worryin' over the likes of trash like that one. Now you there– Crawford.. Chester Crawford. What happened to the other one you were tryin' to ride down?" Chester gently lay Chinagirl down on a blanket he had spread on the ground for her and came near to Robert so she wouldn't hear his report.

"He got away, Mister Trav. I don't know how but he found a couple of ditches out there somewhere. I reckon he crawled in a hole or somethin'. I rode them ditch banks for near on to an hour and couldn't see hide nor hair."

"Well, it's too bad he slipped you," Robert said. "Maybe the local law can haul him in later. Or we might find him yet." Colin spoke up now.

"What I want to know is where the hell is Amos Younger. I thought Brooker told you this was his gang. I've seen wanted posters on Younger. But I didn't see anyone in this fight I thought might be him."

"Senor Younger is dead, Collie," Garcia said. "Younger and a rancher named Starrett; and some cowboy, killed up in the Nations. Not too far from here. Since these three had the Senora's horses, it would be a good wager that they are the killers of Amos Younger and Starrett."

"I want to get Pam and the boy away from here," Colin said to Robert, accepting the fact now that he would never know the complete story. The truth could not be extracted when so many were dead.

"Take the Sunday buggy, Col. Get the woman and the boy and head up the road a piece. We'll catch up when we finish here. You got horses and oxen scattered all over the county, these boys'll have 'em back in a few hours. We'll bring the big wagon and the horses along." Old Robert thought for a second and then added,

"Better we bring Chester and that Chinese girl too. We can bed her down in the Studebaker. She looks pretty shot up. Crawford doesn't look like he'd leave her without a fight anyway." Colin swiftly shepherded Pamela and Justin into Old Robert's fine buggy. He was about to drive off when Garcia stopped him.

"Senor Crawford let the one bandito escape him, Collie." He handed Colin Abraham Primble's shotgun he had just taken from the lifeless hands of Willy Parker. "Take your Senora and the boy, Colin, but keep the gun handy... The yellow-haired boy is a bad gringo, I think. Just go up the road a little ways. Don't go too far. We'll be along pretty soon."

Colin nodded to Garcia, fully understanding Garcia's implications. He clucked to the horses and drove the two people he had come to love so very much away from the terrible scene of blood and fire. The boy sat in the rear of the buggy with his feet dangling and his back rested against the seat back. Filled with ham and corn dodgers and fresh cider, he now felt the tiredness rush through his body as a warm flood. Pamela sat close to Colin in the buggy seat, their thighs and shoulders touching.

She, too, had begun to accept the fact that the ordeal had ended at last and that the three of them were safe. The afternoon sun was warm and gentle on their faces, and Pamela knew that the unforgiving heat of September was beginning to wane. It had been more than a half year since she and Alex and the boy had left Illinois. It was impossible for her to calculate all the things that had changed in her life in those few and fleeting months of 1893. She allowed herself to reminisce briefly of Alex. He had been such a good man.

Looking sideways at Colin she thought that she had been very lucky in her life. At least, in the area of knowing good men. It was true, she'd never felt the same way towards Alex as she now felt with Colin, but there was no question Alex was a good man…. a good father.

"Collie," she suddenly blurted, "If Alex had ever met you, I think he would have liked you a lot."

"Henry Brooker said the same thing," Colin answered. "I get the feeling Alex was a real fine Vaquero." She thought Colin's acceptance of Alex, demonstrated by calling him Vaquero, would have pleased her former husband no end.

They allowed the nearly spent horses to select their own pace, and it was a slow one. The little buggy moved lazily along the dusty road in the afternoon sun. The boy in the rear was sitting upright, but he was dozing. The man and the woman sharing the buggy seat were lost in thought and the comfort of being near to each other.

The entire scene was a tranquil one but it did not go unobserved. From a nearby hilltop, burrowed under heavy grass and huddling near to a cottonwood trunk for cover, the narrow eyes of Beaver Parker assessed the peaceful scene on the road. The buggy was in clear view, three hundred yards below him.

He watched its riders with such hate and anger that it actually churned his stomach. Still near exhaustion from the run for his life in front of the big man on the sorrel horse, Beaver Parker had lost all control. He had wet himself again. It was the first time that had happened in a very long while. Not since he had declared himself gang leader had this humiliation occurred. He was, at once weeping and furious. Now, seeing the serene picture that was unfolding right in front of his eyes, his hate was so mighty that his body shook in an uncontrollable spasm.

"You dirty sum' bitches," he said to himself in a whisper. "I'm killin' all of you. You just wait and see… I'm killin' all of you if I got to walk across Texas. I'm gonna kill you all. I'm gonna do ever' thin' I want to you, woman. Then when I'm through, I'm killin' you. That boy, too. Reckon he's your son. I'm killin' him right in front of you. Then I'm gonna kill you. Real slow. Really slow. And it's gonna hurt a lot. And I'm fixin' to kill that greaser with the big knife, too. You're gonna see this ain't over. No, this ain't over... this ain't over by a long shot."

It was only now that Beaver discovered another great personal humiliation had taken place. During the noise and confusion of the melee at the Primble place he now realized he had lost the Leonard Peach pistol.

Chapter Twenty-eight

Justin Carstin and Pecos Bill

The next days on the trail, as the newly established caravan wound its way to the Canadian River country, were the best that Pamela Carstin had known in a long while. The Spur cowboys handled nearly all the work; and she, for the most part, rode in the Studebaker on the seat beside Old Robert. He drove the buckboard carefully and slowly, because the wounded Chinagirl was bedded in the rear, and he and Pamela talked for hours on end.

She told Old Robert all about Illinois, her father's hardware business and about her mother. He, in turn, told her about the cattle industry, the Rocky Mountains and Hawken rifles, carefully avoiding any mention of Iron Woman. He tried to describe for her a few of the faint memories he had of Scotland. It was when he told her, to the best of his recollection, how one went about making the Scottish traditional dish of haggis that she squealed in protest.

"May I ask how you feel about Colin?" Old Robert asked one morning as they drifted along in the Studebaker.

"You may ask. But then I might not answer you." Her grin was a sly one.

"Well, I suppose a father needs to ask." Her answer had, somewhat befuddled him

"Oh, I was just funning with you, Mister Trav," she said. "Of course I love Colin. Love him with all my heart; and so does Justin. He's just the most special man I've ever met."

"I believe Collie to be a good man. I think I can correctly judge you to be a good person, too, Pam. It's not just goodness that I think about…." Robert groped for the right words.

"What then?" Pamela wanted to know. "Are you asking me if I intend to trifle with his affections?" Her mischievous grin was a wide one. She genuinely enjoyed being with Old Robert.

"Well… "he began slowly and she sensed a more serious tone. "Have you given much thought to the difference in your ages."

"Now, Mister Trav, you just stop right there. Of course I've thought about it. There's nothing that I know about Colin that I haven't given thought to." She paused, breathed deeply and continued:

"Quite obviously I've come to terms with that age question. And... with a lot of other things, too. To be blunt, Mister Trav, the difference in our ages is really between Colin and me. No one else. Besides, age is not much of a problem. I get the feeling that you're older than Colin," she teased. "And just look how pretty you are."

"I am right dashing, aren't I?" He slapped his knee and laughed aloud.

"Another thing for you to think about, Mister Trav, is the fact that all you men from the Broken Spur have some much greater problems than just age."

"And just what other problems do we have, Missy?" he queried.

"Well to begin with you Spur riders call full grown women names like 'Missy'. Back at the Primble place you called me 'little lady'. Take a look, Mister Trav... Take a real good look. I stand five-foot-six in my socks and weigh a hundred and twenty-four pounds. Most of the time.

"My teeth are all my own, and an eye doctor from Chicago said I wouldn't need glasses for about a decade yet." Old Robert started to speak, but Pamela kept right on. "Matter of fact he told me that most eagles just wish they could see as well as I can. I can shoe a horse, butcher a hog and bake a cake. I give birth to fine looking and intelligent youngsters like my son, Justin. I ain't little, and I ain't no lady. I was a lady before I met the men from the Broken Spur, but I sure ain't no more. And I, for certain, ain't nobody's 'Missy'."

Colin, riding some thirty yards ahead, turned in his saddle and looked back at the buckboard to see what could have evoked such raucous peals of laughter from Old Robert.

Later that night she and Colin slipped away from the camp and found each other in a dark glade; lit only by a thousand stars.

"Your step-father was inquiring as to the honor of my intentions towards you today," Pamela teased Colin.

"And just what are those intentions?" Colin pulled her close and nuzzled her neck.

"Not very honorable, I'm afraid," she sighed. "...at least not right now."

The danger past, all the travelers became comfortable and complacent. If Pamela took readily to riding and talking with Old Robert, no one found more relaxation and enjoyment on the long ride home than the boy, Justin. He took to the cowboys of the Spur right away, and they heartily reciprocated. Justin formed a special bond with the young Bobby Baxter.

Never had he seen anyone who could ride as wild and uninhibited as the young hero from the Broken Spur.

Whereas Justin had followed only Colin about before, he began now to divide his time to include Baxter. He further enjoyed his visits with the colorful frontiersman that was Old Robert. Of course, deep down, Justin fully understood that his Mother knew more about horses than any of these cowhands. He further knew that the dressage style of riding she was so sternly in favor of was, indeed, the correct way to handle a horse. Compared though to the flashy riding of Bobby Baxter, who could rear his horse on command or execute double vaults to the saddle at full gallop, dressage-style riding was decidedly boring stuff. As young as he was, Bobby Baxter had mastered another very coveted cowboy talent:

He had become a master spinner of tall tales. Many of the drovers had special gifts for bronco busting, fancy roping or trick riding but no ability was more respected and admired on the Broken Spur than the ability to thrill, tickle or scare the wits from fellow cow men with the wild tales of the plains. Bobby was the best of the Spur bunch at spinning the most impossible yarns. That no one believed them made no matter. It was in the listening that hard-bitten men became children.

The thing Justin found he liked most about the cowboys was to listen to their swaggering talk around the campfire at evening. They separated themselves from Colin because he was their boss, and from the presence of Old Robert and the ladies so they could boast more profanely. Their bawdy campfire tales thrilled Justin, and he hurried his supper with his mother each evening so that he might be off to hear the wondrous tall tales of the cowboy. The seeing of the elephant. He especially loved the stories of Pecos Bill Williams

Nearly every cowboy story was of the daring deeds of Pecos Bill. who, without a doubt, was the most famous cowboy of all. Even if he was only a myth. The stories never changed very much although the name, Pecos Bill, was changed from time to time to give the story a new, if familiar, slant. Sometimes Pecos would become Wild Bill Lewis or perhaps O.D. Cleaver. Sour dough Calihan or Lightnin' Bill Carson. Then of course, there was the most famous yarn of all. The tale of Lemuel Sweet, the Texas cowhand whose life story would be forever entwined with the famous wild mustang, Peaches.

"Ever hear the story of the horse called Peaches?" Baxter asked Justin one night after a hearty meal of antelope chops and black eyed peas.

"Peaches seems a real sweet name for a horse," Justin answered.

"They only gave him that name as a joke, son. Why, just one look at this evil brute and you could tell he'd rather kill a man than eat a oat. Big black boy, he was. Had a clear and glassy right eye and couldn't move his ears."

"Couldn't move his ears?" Justin was puzzled and amazed.

"Well maybe he could move 'em, but no one ever saw his ears but one way– laid straight back." Justin understood the joke. He knew that when a horse held his ears back and against his head it signified extreme anger, and wild behavior was destined to follow. He mentally pictured the horse with the laid-back ears and stifled a laugh.

"Well, any how," Bobby continued, "I was bossin' a four man brandin' gang for old Pecos Bill Williams that spring way up high on the Rio. One of my hands was this here feller called Lemuel Sweet. Now Lem, he's a top hand but he ain't too bright. He spots this big black horse standin' out in the corral. He wants to know why somebody ain't saddling' a good looking beast like him. I tells him the horse is a bad 'un and for him to get back to brandin' mavericks and not be worryin' about Mister Bill's horses."

"What did he do then?" Justin's eyes were widening now with anticipation. A Bobby Baxter story was never a dull one.

"Well I get to noticin' Lem is leavin' the supper table early every night, which ain't normal for him. See, he truly loves his victuals, and generally he's still at the table when we're down to just bread and salt. Then one night, he says he wants us to all come down to the barn to see what he's done."

Baxter paused and sipped steaming coffee from a hot tin cup with the caution of a bird approaching a rattler.

"What was it, Bobby?" Justin wanted to know. "What was it he'd done?"

"Seems he'd been goin' out at night alone and workin' that black horse to the saddle. He says, "Look here boys... I done tamed your big, bad widowmaker... Sure enough, there old Peaches stands in the middle of the barn. He's all gussied up with saddle and bridle and he looks tamer'n a housecat. Comes to horses, boys, Lemuel Sweet ain't got no peers," he says. "Why I can tame a cyclone," he brags. "And the horse ain't been born I cain't converse with on a first name friendship." It was now I see he's gettin' ready to step into the stirrup. I said "Wait a minute, Lem. You ain't fixin' to mount inside this here barn, are you?"

"Never fear for me," says old Lemuel, and he swings right up."

"My Momma told me never to mount any horse inside a barn, Bobby," Justin said. "Lead the horse outside before you mount, she always says."

"And that's the right advice, son... Cowboys who mount up inside buildin's ain't likely to come in to supper every night. Anyhow, Old Lem ain't too bright as I already related. But this horse is standin' there as pretty as you please, and me and the boys are just about to think, maybe, Lem is smarter than we thought...." But that's when the badger comes out."

"The badger?" Justin asked.

"Yeah. Just an old badger. Been diggin' under the barn a long time. Pecos said we was to shoot the critter when we could cause he's diggin' up the foundation of the barn. Them things can sure dig. I 'spect if a mole was as big as a bull, he'd be a badger. Anyhow, Lem sees this badger by the barn door while he's sittin' on his new trained horse. He reaches back into his saddle bag and takes out a brand new 41-Colt he's been savin' up wages for and finally bought. He sticks this pistol right between old Peaches' ears and cuts a shot at the badger.

Now, a .41-caliber is loud enough for anybody out of doors. All cooped up in the barn like we was though, the sound of that gun like to deef-uned all of us." Another slow sip of coffee heightened the suspense.

"What did Peaches do?" the boy asked intently. The other hands, too, had drawn nearer for the relating of this somewhat predictable saga. They had heard the tale before, but the excitement was still electricity in the air. And who could say? Maybe Bobby Baxter had a new ending this round...

"First thing he did was to jump straight up in the air with all four feet. Jumped so high he drove old Lem's head right into the barn ceiling... or loft floor, whatever you care to call it. Mashed his hat down over his eyes so's Lem couldn't see a thing, and then starts jumpin' for the door. Three more times he hits the ceiling with the head of Lemuel Sweet, and then he makes it out the barn door. Now he begins to sunfish and crow-hop all over the barn lot. Me and the boys are tryin' to grab the bridle and give Lem a hand, and then I start to thinkin': He's probably dead anyway and just ain't fell out of the saddle yet.

Now Missus Williams— Pecos Bill's wife ya' know— big stout lady she is and just as purty as a roan colt. Anyways she got her a chicken pen made out of slats and wire. This big horse runs right through it and scatters fifty layin' hens in ever direction— that is 'cept for two that Peaches stepped on and kilt outright." The listeners were beginning to replace chuckles now with genuine laughter. Baxter, seeing his audience well in hand, went on:

"Now the blamedest thing happened... seemed Lemuel revived enough he started trying to get a hold on the saddle horn. Problem was he still had the gun in his hand; and just when Peaches started to settle a bit, the damn gun went off again. Now the buckin' started all over again. But that ain't the worst. When the pistol went off this time, the bullet just missed old Pecos Bill who was runnin' to us to see what the ruckus was about."

Justin gasped. He hated guns and bullets. But then this was a mighty funny story.

"Anyhow the bullet missed Bill just barely but it went wild and killed a big fat hog we had put up by the corn crib for winter meat. Now old Bill was fit to be tied. He jerked out his own gun and began to shoot at Peaches' feet. We thought we'd seen some buckin' before but now, with this new gunfire old Peaches commenced to put on his very best show ever.

We had a privy ditch we'd dug near the barn to drain off the privy and all the manure drainage from the barn as well. It was about three or four feet of the awfullest, stinkinest mess you ever smelled. Just pure old liquid shit runnin' off into a gulley. Well that old ditch had fell in some, so me and the boys had dropped about three or four wagon loads of flint chip into it, you know. Now old Peaches spies that ditch and runs at it full bore and jumps the blamed thing. Jus' soon as his feet hit the other side he wheels and jumps back across the t'other way."

The laughter was now so loud that Pamela and Colin, some distance away, wondered at the cause of all this merriment. Rubbing his hands together, Bobby Baxter went on with his story.

"Anyhow the horse makes the jump, but he leaves old Lemuel up there in the air. Now the ditch is 'bout four-foot deep and the horse makes a six-foot jump. So Lems' got to fall near ten, maybe twelve feet into that mess and all that scratchy flint. We walk up on him, and he's just sittin' in all that manure run off. Finally, he pries his hat up, and we can see his nose is bloody and he's bit hisself clean through his lower lip. He's all scratched up and bloody from them flint chips... and o' course he smells like a prairie rose. Now the boss yells at him. 'What in the hell's the matter with you, Lemuel?'

"Now Lemuel ain't thinkin' too clear right now, and he holds up his new Colt pistol and we see that, somehow in the fall, the barrel's been bent right off of the gun and the hammer's missin' too. Lem says, 'Looka' here, Mister Williams... Your horse done broke my brand-new handgun.'

"'You sure my horse broke that gun, Lemuel?' Pecos asks.

"'Right as rain,' says Lemuel. 'Cost eleven dollars, too.' That's when Mister Williams turned to me.

"'Bobby,' he said. 'You stop over to the pay master and tell him to charge "old badger shooter" here for two leghorn hens and a fat butcher hog.' Then he hollers, 'Hold up that gun again, Lem.' Well old Lem he thinks he might have to buy a hog and a chicken or two, but at least Pecos's gonna have his gun fixed up for him."

'You sure that my horse busted that pistol, are you, Lem?'

"'Yes sir, I sure am sure.' says Lem. 'Old Peaches clean ruint this here brand new Colt.' Pecos turns to me and says, 'Bobby, while you're at the pay master tells him I said to give that Peaches horse two days off and a three-dollar pay raise.'"

Peals of laughter rang out now from the cowboys' campfire as one of the oldest yarns of all was once again, successfully spun. This time by Bobby Baxter. It would be told many times over and by many yarn spinners each adding his own flavorful adaptatation to the eternal saga of Lemuel Sweet and Peaches, the coal colored widowmaker.

Colin could see the laughing trail hands quite well by the firelight. He was delighted to see that loudest laughter came from Justin who, only days ago, had been such a sad little boy.

"Do you think they're talking about things over there that Justin ought to hear, Colin?" Pamela asked.

"I think whatever it is, it's just the thing he needs to hear, Pammy. I also think it's none of our business.

The telling of the outrageous sagas had long been a staple of life at the Broken Spur. But now Justin Carstin had added an entirely new dimension. With just a little coaxing, he would produce the silver harmonica he had been given by Colin, the same harp Juan Garcia gifted to Colin so many years ago. With only a bit of encouragement from the Spur hands he would play some of the campfire tunes he had learned.

It seemed that though Colin had tried so futilely for years to play the little harp, Justin was able to coax real music from it. He had not learned a lot of tunes yet, but the ranch hands were deeply moved and even saddened when he played "Little Joe, the Wrangler." As he mournfully worked his way through "When the Work's All Done This Fall," hot tears streamed uncontrollably down the weathered face of Long John Embry.

No one would have dared to hurrah Long John about it though, for he was a man no one cared to anger. Neither would anyone mention that late at night after these sad songs were played, he was often heard crying softly in his bed roll. As hardened as he was, Long John's heart broke when something stirred the memories of the two old folks he had left so long ago in the little shack on the Arkansas.

It seemed everyone enjoyed the campfire humor and the harmonica music immensely except Juan Garcia. He was deeply troubled by an uneasy feeling. It was like a dark mantle that seemed to warn him that all the troubles were not over. He was, more than a little, disturbed by the fact one of the murdering rapists had escaped.

He had known men like these in the past. He knew they were dirty, dangerous and totally unpredictable. He refused to let down his guard for an instant, even for an O.D. Cleaver or Pecos Bill tale. The story of Peaches was one of his favorites, but for now he vowed to keep alert. His sword and pistols would be kept at his side and ready.

It was nearly a five-day journey back to the Spur. At the end of the third day, Colin felt he should have a talk with Pamela about the land claim Henry Brooker had shown him. He was sure she and her father had been duped. Old Robert would never part with a piece of the Broken Spur.

"He'd die first." Colin pondered. Colin was pretty sure he knew how Old Robert might react, and he felt he should warn Pamela. He had staunchly avoided telling her that the map she carried revealed her claim to truly be the choice southeast corner of the Broken Spur, two-and-one-half sections of high quality grass land– sixteen hundred prime acres– located right on the north bank of the Canadian.

This sixteen-hundred-acre parcel was rather insignificant when the eight-hundred thousand acres that made up the Spur were considered. But then Old Robert had threatened to kill men for the encroachment of a foot. Of course, Colin knew that wouldn't happen; but still, when it came to land, Old Robert was almost certain to be a stone.

It was in a dry camp at the top of a big bluff after the evening meal had been disposed of, that Colin summoned Pamela away from the others.

"Pamela, I just wanted to tell you... well... "Colin was having a hard time with this proposition. "Well, Henry Brooker showed me a map of the land claim you're headed for... "When he spoke of her land, her eyes fairly shone.

"Oh, Colin, I'm so anxious to see it. Mister Brooker said it's so near the Broken Spur. Isn't that a lucky coincidence, Colin.? We can live on my place...well it's our place, yours and mine of course. Anyway, we can live right there; and the Spur and your people will all be right there, too. I think it's just going to be wonderful."

"Listen, Pam. I've got to say this to you... that land of yours– If that map is right– that land you've bought is an encroachment on a corner of the Spur." Pamela seemed about to say something else, but when the realization of what Colin had just said fully sunk, in she was thunderstruck. Her previous effervescence was instantly replaced by a dark and cloudy mood Colin had not seen before. Her normally wide and trusting eyes now narrowed into slits of cold suspicion.

"What are you saying to me, Colin? That land is mine... my father bought that land from a broker in Chicago. I remember him. He came to our house, he brought papers, things to sign. He was a short stocky man named Aaron something... Aaron Markley, that's it.

"His name was Aaron Markley. Alex and I didn't have enough money for the land and the horses, too My father, Colin... my daddy gave this to me."

All through this Colin was trying to talk with her. Her thoughts came now like a pent-up flood, and Colin could scarcely get in a word. Further, he sensed she was becoming panicky.

"Now, calm down, Pammy... It'll all work out. Maybe Old Robert'll buy it from you. For that matter, I can buy it back. Don't worry about it... It'll be all right.

"It'll be all right?... It'll be all right?" She was becoming shrill. "I'm supposed to lose sixteen hundred acres, and you tell me it'll be all right? You'll buy it back? Who said I'd sell it? Don't worry?... I'm about to cross swords with a man who kills to keep land. What'll they call it, Colin?... The Canadian River range war?"

"Please Pam... Please, just calm down. I'll talk to him in the morning. I'd do it now but he's already asleep for the night. Just don't worry. You know I love you, and It'll be all right. I'll speak to him first light in the morning."

"No," Pamela snapped. "You'll not speak to him of this matter. This is my land, and it's my problem... No wait. It's my land and it's his problem! Anyway, it's not your problem. Not a word, Colin. I'll take it from here. By the way, thanks for telling me. Thanks for sleeping with me and then telling me."

Colin, stunned, mumbled something that sounded like "That's all right" and moved off into the dark.

Late that night, Pamela lay rolled in her blankets. She was tired, but sleep was not easily coming this evening. She was angry, too. And she felt betrayed. She thought about Colin in his own blankets just a hundred yards away from the camp. She knew he had moved that far away thinking she would slip out of camp in the darkness and join him. In fact, she ached for him. But she would not go to him this night. It wasn't that he did anything wrong in the land discussion. It was more that he didn't do anything right.

Colin had told her that he loved her, and she believed him. Now she was wondering if he might not love the old man and the Broken Spur more. She realized now that she was the one who was assuming they would always be together. Colin had not mentioned marriage or where they would live or any of those things that men

who are making commitments talk about. She would not go to him this night. She began to wonder if she might have been a fool. It was good that she didn't leave the main camp that night.

In a gully, near her sleeping place, Beaver Parker lay in deadly wait... He was less than fifty feet from her. When she finally went to sleep, he thought he could actually hear her soft breathing in the night stillness. Beaver tested the edge of his bowie knife on the ball of his thumb. It was as sharp as any barber's razor. A dozen times he started to crawl to her side; knife in hand. There were just too many guards. Garcia had them walking about everywhere near the camp. When one guard stepped into the leftover light of the cook fire, Beaver saw these men were armed with shotguns, the night fighter's favorite weapon.

He knew the thin man with the sword was out there in the night, but he wasn't exactly sure where. He decided not to go after the man. It was just too chancy. Besides, he wanted the woman. The sentries never let up. They walked their posts all night long without a break. At last, with only an hour before dawn, Beaver gave up his vigil and quietly crawled away in the darkness.

Another time, you bitch, he thought. They can't watch you and guard you forever. There'll be another time....

Chapter Twenty-nine

Lands of the Spur

Pamela decided to say nothing to Old Robert concerning the two and one-half section parcel of land. Not just yet.

I'll wait until we get there, she thought. I want to look at the land, and I want to look at it with Robert standing beside me. Her reasoning was she could better evaluate the measures she must take if she first knew how Robert felt about the land itself. She didn't want him to just 'tell' her how he felt. She wanted to see for herself. The next days, she still rode alongside him in the Studebaker, but the conversation was far more limited than it had been in the previous days of travel.

"Why did you ever stop trapping fur?" she asked one morning, trying hard to open a conversation. He thought for a long time, his gaze straight ahead. It was as though she had not spoken at all. Just when Pamela decided he wasn't going to answer, his voice came low and measured.

"Just so much hurt in the world," he began slowly; thinking out each word carefully before he spoke it. Pamela saw right away that she had accidentally touched on a very sensitive subject.

"I just couldn't add to it anymore. The hurt, that is. One morning I had this little coon in a steel. He was so little that his hide weren't worth nothin'. He'd chewed all night on his leg tryin' to get free. When I saw that pitiful thing, I thought. what have I gone and done here? See Pam, his little pelt wasn't worth nothing'. But maybe his life was. I killed that little old coon for nothin'. I didn't like that feelin' at all. Then I thought, even if the pelt had been worth good money, what did I care that some fat-bellied lawyer could walk around Evansville or Saint Lou with a coonskin collar on his coat?" He paused now, his eyes clouding as if he were remembering some great wrong of long ago.

"Evansville?" she asked.

"It's a town I know about. Evil place back on the Ohio River. Well the river front is. A few good people live there, too, I 'spect; but I didn't meet none of them. I shouldn't talk that way of any place. There's good and bad where ever we venture. I was careless in Evansville. I went among rabid dogs looking for good men. That has often been my nature. It was my good fortune that one good man did find me before the dogs feasted." He reflected a moment and went on.

"Seemed like there was so much killin' goin' on for nothing'. Too much killin' and for no good reason. There was a passel of other things happenin' in my life at that time, too. Hard things full of pain. things I ain't never 'llowed myself to think about no more. I left trappin' and the Rockies at the same time. I ain't never goin' back." There was no way that he could bring himself to tell her about Iron Woman and Bloody Shirt. He couldn't find the words, nor the courage, to talk to her about the friendship he'd shared with Hubert Baker. His past was closed now; even too him.

They rode for a long time in a reflective silence. At this moment, Pamela felt closer to Robert than ever. She loved this old man when he talked like this. She wanted to throw her arms around his neck and tell him that she had felt the same way, too. There was indeed too much hurt in the world. Too much needless hurt. But she held back. There was the land issue to clear up. It was creating an abyss, an impassible void between them. The feeling was a low and distressful one; Pamela hated it. It was late the next day when Justin reined his pony up to the Studebaker and asked,

"Mister Robert, sir, when are we going to be there? How long until we get to the Broken Spur?"

"You're on it now, Little Buck," Old Robert answered. "Been on the Spur for a day and a half now. If your askin' when we'll get to the bunks, like most cowboys wants to know, we'll be there a little after dark."

Pamela was at once relieved and distressed by this news. For her, it meant the end to a long and perilous journey, but it also meant the land confrontation would have to be dealt with very soon. She decided not to put it off longer.

"Mister Trav?" she asked. "Could you rein up here for a minute? I need to see to my bags for a moment."

Robert halted the team and Pamela climbed down from the high spring seat. After rummaging through a battered suitcase that was shiny and new seven months ago, she came out with a folded square of paper. She climbed back into the seat beside Old Robert and carefully unfolded the survey map out on her lap. With a firm pointing of her finger, she tapped the two and one-half sections of land that lay on the north bank of the Canadian River.

"I want you to please take me here. I need to see this parcel outlined by the red mark. It's mine, you know. I'd like you to show me how to get there."

Old Robert was silent and reflective. He looked at the map in her hands carefully but made no move to touch it.

"That's a far piece," he said slowly. "We can't get there yet today. Tomorrow…tomorrow at noon., we'll hook up a couple of fresh horses, and I'll drive you out there." He sat, head lowered and silent. Pamela could see he would talk no more of the matter. Just at that moment Colin rode up alongside them on a dappled gelding that was completely exhausted.

"Were makin' the Spur just in time." he said to Old Robert. "Horse's givin' out. Men, too. I sure hope Walter's been cookin'."

"Mister Trav is going to drive me out to my land tomorrow," Pamela said matter-of-factly. Colin looked from Pamela to Old Robert and back to Pamela again. Neither face betrayed any emotion whatsoever.

"I'm coming, too," Colin spoke. "It's a piece of land I'm interested in seeing."

"You've seen it before," the old man said. Colin could detect no emotion at all in his voice.

"I'd like to see it again," Colin replied. I'd like to see it with you. And with Pamela."

"Then bring the boy, too. I'd like to ride out with the boy," Old Robert said. "Bring Little Buck along."

They did not ride to the Carstin lands the next day as planned. Part of the reason for delaying the trip was a down pouring rain. Another part was sheer exhaustion. The travelers reached the headquarters of the Broken Spur long after dark as Old Robert had promised. The rain had already started and their arrival was during a drizzle. Bobby Baxter had ridden ahead and had reached the ranch base site a little more than two hours ahead of the caravan. He and Walter Payne, the head cook of the Spur, had hot food and gallons of sweetened coffee ready when the wet and wearied travelers arrived.

Pamela and Chinagirl were assigned to sleeping quarters in a neat little bunk house that only found use during round ups, or sometimes during calf croppings when the Spur took on extra hands.

A rider was dispatched in the middle of the night through the now heavy rainfall to the settlement of Travis to fetch back the only real doctor within miles, Doctor Ralph Westfall. Chinagirl was showing a lot of improvement and indeed, had a lot of her old sense of humor back. But

Chester Crawford insisted she needed a doctor. Chester was all ready to ride to Travis himself when he was stopped by Juan Garcia.

"It is near fifteen miles to Travis and Doc Westfall," Juan said. "I think that you are so tired, Senor Crawford, that you cannot make such a ride. I think you will go asleep and fall from your horse. If you land face up, you will drown in the rain. If you land face down, you will drown in the mud. Get some coffee and some bacon and apples. Those apples have real cinnamon, very good. Eat, and go to sleep. I will send Long John, and a doctor will come very soon. And you will not drown."

It seemed to take forever to eat and get dry and roll into clean dry bedrolls, but at last it happened. Bone tired and with the relief of reaching safety at last, the little band of travelers just gave it up. They slept long and deep, and they felt that, for the first time in many nights, their slumber was a safe one. The rain continued to hammer on the tin roofs of the Spur buildings all night long and well after noon the next day. There was no trip for anyone that day. Pamela and Justin slept till after three in the afternoon. Chester Crawford was still sleeping an hour after they were up and around. Famished again, Justin and Bobby Baxter went down to the cook shack and began bothering Walter about food.

Colin had slept in, too. Still, he rose around eight in the morning when Long John brought the Travis doctor to see Chinagirl. When Doctor Ralph discovered his patient was to be a Chinese, he suddenly became aloof and somewhat distant.

"Are you sure I'm to be paid for treating this Coolie?" he asked snidely. Colin slowly burned and then grew visibly furious. He was glad that Chester Crawford was still asleep and not able to hear that remark.

"May I remind you, Doctor Westfall, that you are on the Broken Spur? It was Juan Garcia who gave you the money to open your office in Travis. You agreed to treat Mexicans all to quickly when it hung in the balance as to whether you'd get Juan's dinero or not. If we call you out to the Spur to treat a skunk for a bellyache, you'll be paid if you comply. You'll have your ass kicked out of Travis if you don't. It's as simple as that. This lady is my guest, and she is in need. I advise you to get busy. And things could look real bad for you if you're not gentle and accurate." The sputtering Doctor opened his traditional black bag and, without another word, bent to his work.

It was three days later when Colin, Pamela, Justin and Old Robert finally drove the Studebaker to a high place overlooking the Canadian. Each tried to appear jovial, but the most casual of witness could sense the air was filled with tension.

"There it is, Pamela Carstin," Old Robert said. "There's the land that you have outlined in red on the map that you carry."

"It's beautiful," she said "It's breathtaking."

And indeed, it was. From where they sat, the river uncoiled far below them like a silver ribbon in the wind. It curled and swerved ever so gracefully across the prairie; at last ending it's flow somewhere in the horizon. The waving Buffalo grass was greasy green in the new October sun. Brushy thickets of oak and cottonwood were scattered about the panorama, their turning leaves of gold and red creating highlights that scattered across the prairie like butterflies. Cattle stood here and there, belly deep in the rich Granna, and a small herd of twenty or so antelope browsed along the river bank.

"Pamela," Old Robert said. "I been hearin' so much about these horses you went to such a labor to fetch along. I just was wonderin' if you could let me in on the pay off? What's goin' to happen with these horses that's made you pay such a price? Garcia knows about Kentucky horses. I guess some o' them Mexican generals been usin' 'em for years. He says their fastern lightning' in a bottle but over-all ain't much good for nothin'. Garcia says if you was to rob a bank and needed a get away mount they'd be fine but not for much else. I can't rightly picture you hittin' a bank Pamela." She laughed and shook out her hair.

"No...No bank robbery for me Mr. Robert. But I can tell you something about horses you may not have heard. Mr. Robert...Have you ever heard of a quarter horse?"

"I'd hope the Spur didn't have no horses' worth only a quarter."

"No...Not money...Distance. It's like this," She started. Colin's attention was intent as she spoke.

"Over in England where most of these blooded horses came from in the first place...Most all the race tracks there are one mile around. Well it turns out that these English sports are more interested on betting on a faster race...Just a fourth of the track. A quarter of a mile. That sport has been going on right here in America too. For a long time. Matter of fact George Washington and Thomas Jefferson were really involved in quarter horse track races in Virginia even before the revolution." She had the interest of Robert and Colin completely now.

"Garcia's right to tell you these blooded mounts are difficult for any work other than racing. They are bred so high in spirit all they can do is let off that energy by hard running. They're born to be competitive, so much so they can't hardly stand to have another horse pass them. They always have told me that all a trainer of race horses can accomplish is teach them to run fast and turn left.

Anyway Alex, my husband, had a different picture of what could be…Or what he thought could be. He thought by cross breeding we could get a different horse all together. He wanted to keep the keen head and neck of the purebred but do away with the spindly legs. He thought we'd look for cross breed stock with big rump muscles so the horse could leap off the starting line like an explosion.

Mostly though Alex wanted a more intelligent animal. One that could use that speed and strength to herd cattle or use as a roper. A horse with a more manageable temperament. A stronger more compact body …Like the Texas mustang but with the speed and heart to be cattleman's working horse and companion too. That's the dream for those horses we brought all the way out here. To establish a different kind of a quarter horse. An American Quarter horse.

Colin and old Robert looked one to the other. It was a worthwhile dream to be sure. Colin felt that at last he understood the passion that had brought this lovely woman so far from home and among such different surroundings. He wasn't sure it was possible to cross breed horses the same way a carpenter creates a building or a tailor makes a suit but he agreed the vision was worth while. It seemed to him that her eyes shone with a new exuberance as she explained the ambition.

They sat and thought a long while about the advantage of a horse such as Pamela had described. To have a mount that was lightning fast and strong enough to work cattle all day and still be controllable and docile and smart was indeed a favorable aspiration. Old Robert knew though that if it were possible at all it would take a long time. The thought of Pamela being around for a long time was a pleasant one to him. It was now that Old Robert spoke.

"That lower two hundred acres along the river floods anew every spring," Old Robert was saying. "Every spring, the flood brings in new soil and replenishes that two-hundred-acre piece with the richest soil on the Spur. It's a place to grow hay I think. Maybe corn. It's been left fallow too long. I guess me and Garcia have been feedin' mule deer and antelope long enough.

See my stone marker over on that ridge?" He pointed to a distant place near the river, and Pamela nodded. "Garcia and I put that one in about 1875 I think. That was when Ulysses Grant was our president, you know. I liked him better than this Grover Cleveland fellow we have now. I'd guess Grant drank a lot of whiskey, so they say. But somehow, he seems like a hero to me. Stopped all that sufferin' in the war don't you know? I thinks maybe the whiskey was to help him forget all the bad he'd done and seen."

Robert continued talking slowly, reflectively of the land he loved with all his heart. "I have to admit though Old Grover been 'lected three times. Ain't no body else ever done that. Me and Garcia bought a Hereford bull that last 'lection year. Brought him all the way from England. He wasn't much. Pretty thing to look at, but I don't think he liked cows all that much.

There's a couple o' shorthorn bulls a-roamin' about these parts too. Their home was Scotland. They stay off to them selves mostly. Some Scotty Laird brought 'em over but lost his ranch in the big blizzard. Garcia bought his bulls. Hardly ever sees 'em but them little roan calves come showin' up ever spring."

"I had forgotten this spot," Colin remarked. "It is the most beautiful place on the Spur." Now Colin slowed his speech. His words were coming plain now, and his tone was a serous one filled with sincerity.

"I want you to know Robert that Pam came by this piece fair and square." At the mention of her name Pamela listened more intently.

"I think she wants to keep it. I know, Robert, how you feel about gettin' land and keepin' it. But if I have any part of the Spur comin' to me ever, I'll give it up if you'll honor this sale." Pamela felt her heart swell. If she had ever needed to hear from Colin, it was right now. Right at this very, precise moment. He had been there for her when the chips were down. The doubts she had harbored for Colin simply melted away. He had said exactly the right thing at exactly the right time; She knew she would love him forever for it.

"'Tis kind of a pretty spot, don't you think, Pammy?" Old Robert's voice was cool and steady.

"It's breathtaking. Just breathtaking," Pamela repeated herself.

"Yes, it is," said Old Robert, slapping his knee for emphasis. "That's just the reason I picked it out and just the reason I sold it."

"You sold it?" Pamela asked, not understanding this turn of events at all.

"Well, I didn't sell it. My real estate broker sold it for me." Colin was stunned.

"Your real estate broker? When the hell did you get a real estate broker? Why would you decide to sell a piece of land after all these years?"

"I can't really say, Colin. I just woke up one morning and looked around and didn't like what I saw. Just look at us, Colin— three old men just gettin' older. That's all right for me and Garcia. We're nearin' trails end anyway. But, I just wanted more for you than that, Collie.

I wanted you just to get more out of livin' than Juan and I found time to take. It just seemed like nothin' was changin'. We were forever hearin' 'bout changes in the outside world, but it was like the Spur was locked up in 1862. Nothing ever seemed to change. You were either on the trail or hangin' around with me and Juan. Hell, Collie, you were startin' to look like us. I just decided one morning what the Spur needed was some new blood. Some kind of a change. Hell, any kind of a change.

I thought if I sold off a piece of land, it might bring a new family here. It might bring somebody for you, Collie, somebody or something. And it has. It wasn't supposed to work out the way it did. I mean Alex Carstin was a big loss to us all. I never actually met him of course, but I know a good man when I hear about one. Outlaws just were not a part of the plan. Other than that…Well, maybe it'll still work out.

"How did you arrange all this? I mean the sale and all. How did you know Pam's father?" Colin wanted to know.

"I didn't. I never heard of Oswego, Illinois, nor Carstin Hardware Company, neither. I got it done through Trent Markley."

"Trent?" Colin was dumbfounded. "Our commission cattle dealer in Dodge City? How does Trent fit into this?"

"Not Trent, Collie, his brother. Trent Markley has a brother what lives in Chicago. He's a real estate dealer. Sells land and houses and such 'stead o' cattle. Brother's name is Aaron, I think. Good man. Just like Trent. Anyhow this Aaron sends me a letter and says he knows a family in Illinois wants to bring a herd of special horses to Texas. He says they're lookin' to buy a piece and would I sell some to 'em. I tells him to go ahead…I didn't know about Pamela or Alex or Little Buck. Sure didn't know someone would get killed in a fracas. That's just the way it went. Henry Brooker didn't know 'bout it either. Just me and Garcia and Aaron Markley."

"I remember him," Pamela cried. "He's the one I told you about Colin. Aaron Markley. He's the one who sold my Daddy this property."

"Why didn't Trent tell me about this, Robert?… I was just with him in the Dodge House. We got a little drunk together, but he didn't say anything about this."

"Told him not to. Nobody else knowed about it 'cept Garcia. He was all for it, too. We didn't want you to end up like us, Colin. It's all right to love the land, but a man needs somethin' else to love, too. Somethin' like Little Buck here… He glanced at the boy. "He's worth lovin' a lot." Justin Carstin flushed a deep crimson.

"Oh, Colin," Pamela cried. "This is like a dream. I can't think of what to say. We can live here, and you can be close to the Spur and……."

"Don't decide where you're to live just yet," Old Robert interrupted her. "Let's head back to the ranch and we'll talk some more tomorrow on that.

"Mister Trav... Since this ranch is really mine can I give it a name?" Pamela asked.

"Every rancher needs to name his... er, her... spread and pick out a brand."

"It was the great thouroughbred horses of Kentucky that brought me and Justin... that is, me and Little Buck here," she said. "I want to name this place for those horses. And Colin, if you don't mind, I'd like to give it a name that Alex would have liked." Colin saw her brush back a tear.

"A name that Alex would like would be just fine with me, Pam," Colin replied.

"Then we'll call it Tall Horse Ranch." she said. "When anybody asks where we're from, we'll tell them, I'm from Tall Horse Ranch of Travis, Texas."

Old Robert gave a Comanche war whoop and sent his hat flying into the air. He wheeled the Studebaker and gave the team their heads. As they raced pell-mell back to the Spur Old Robert, Pamela Carstin and Colin Trav all felt it was one of their best days.

Chapter Thirty

The Big House

"You understand, Pammy, that me and Garcia knew all along we could never keep all this land together. It's just too much for anyone. Hoot, mon! I can tell ya now the Kiowa or Commanch could've taken over anytime they wanted to."

"Then why didn't they?" Pamela asked.

"Cause havin' us here made their lives easier. Our remuda is big enough so that they can steal a horse or two now and then when they need one. A cow or calf makes good eatin'for 'em when the buffalo roam too far north. Garcia nor I never take a buffalo 'cause that's their property...or at least that's the way they see it. And when old Juan and I would drive off white settlers and land grabbers...why that's just what they'd do themselves anyhow. No, Pammy, we always knew that something would change all of this. Lawyers would come around sometime...storekeepers...schools and churches. It'll be a while before all that happens I'd reckon, but just keep it in mind. It'll happen.

"Just be sure if we ever lose the Spur and we don't give up the Tall Horse ranch." Pamela weighed these thoughts in her mind, and old Robert, who was in the mood to talk, went on.

"Let me tell you some things I've learned about houses," Old Robert said to Pamela. They were sitting on the stone garden bench that rested squarely in front of the main elevation of the big house.

"When I was gettin' ready to build this place, I realized right off I surely didn't know much about what I was doin'. I read this book that come from Chicago. Had a story in it about the man who built the Westminster Abbey over in London. Once when I was a lad I saw a cathedral. It was in a place called Glasgow. An old Uncle showed it to me. I never forgot that big church. So I thought a man who could build somethin' like that was who I wanted to talk to. Well, I sent to Chicago to get hold of this man– Sir Charles Barry was his name as I recall– Well that didn't work. Turned out old Sir Charles had died back in 1860..." Old Robert used a Barlow pocket knife to scrape at a thick thumbnail.

"So then I tried to get to talkin' to another builder name of Hotep. I. M. Hotep... Well I was real surprised to find he was dead, too. Now I really got a surprise when I found out, not only was he dead but he'd been dead for 'bout three thousand or maybe four thousand years." Pamela laughed aloud at this. She recalled from boarding school history classes that Hotep was the master Egyptian builder. He was the one in fact who had built the greatest of the three pyramids on the plain at Ghiza.

"Anyway," Old Robert continued, "...This banker fellow, also from Chicago, who is handling some cattle money for us, tells me that I ought to see a man named Henry Hobson Richardson if I really want to build a good house. He says that Henry Hobson Richardson ain't very well known just yet, and we can probably get him to come to Texas on account of he ain't workin' too steady. He says not to worry though, 'cause this Henry Hobson is a real smart fellow and he's sure to be pretty famous some of these days."

"I know the name Richardson. There was a story in the Post about him," Pamela said. "He builds churches and railroad stations. I recall that because I thought, when I read about it, that it was such a strange combination."

"Well, he was a strange little feller now that you mention it. We brought him here in a wagon, and he like to have died on the trip. He a nice little man, but you could see right off he spent too much time indoors. At first I think he's a preacher or a doctor 'cause he keeps talkin' about revivin' somethin'. He's goin' on about revivin' this and revivin' that. Finally, I understands what he means. He's talkin' about rebuildin' old historical things. You know, old buildin's what's been around since Moses and Abe Lincoln and the like. He calls it "design acceptance". He tells me that if it has already lived a hundred or a thousand years, then it's got to be good. He says that me and him ought to 'revive' it."

"Is that how this house came to look the way it does?" Pamela asked.

"That's about the truth. Those columns with all the leaves around the top? He said they was Corinthian Revival. See the big curly wooden brackets in the cornice? You know, cornice?... Where the roof meets the upright wall? Well those big brackets are Italianate Revival he says. All that scrolled stuff over the doorway and the windows is called Broken Scrolled Pediment I think. I believe that's where we revived some old dead Greeks if I remember 'krectly."

"It's wonderful," Pamela said. "I've taken some peeks through the windows. I hope you're not angry with me for that... the furnishings and the draperies... everything is just magnificent. It must have taken a few Spur cattle to pay for all that"

"That and some old Scottish gold I had layin' around. Well, Henry Hobson helps me out on that, too. I tells him I want some nice things— spinets and sofas and sideboards and Queen Anne chairs. High boys and secretaries and the like. Well, turns out, Henry Hobson Richardson has a friend, in Chicago of course, who knows just about where to buy everything. This friend's name is Field. Well, Henry writes this Mister Field, and pretty soon everything we needed was here. Some of it came from France and some from England. Believe it or not, a lot of it came from that town I told you about... Evansville, out there in Indiana." Pamela was listening intently and Robert was enjoying spinning his yarn.

"They got a passel of furniture makers there in Evansville I reckon. Well, after that Henry Hobson goes back to Chicago. A few years later I hear he builds a huge store for Mister Field. Takes him two years to build it, and they get it finished in 1887. Just about the same time the folks in New York puts up the Statue of Liberty. I swear the newspapers just didn't know what to do. Question is, which is the importantist: The statue or the store? Marshall Field they calls that store. Now I never did know whether Marshall was Mister Field's first name or whether he got himself a partner named Marshall. Most impossible thing I ever heard though, they claimed eight thousand fellers worked in that store. Seems the biggest lies I hear always comes from Chicago. Course, later on when Richardson is a sight more famous he denies he's ever been to Texas at all. Never did know just why he did that, but I think it had somethin' to do with the more important work he was gettin' into. Maybe it didn't seem proper for a cathedral builder to have built a ranch house on the Canadian River. Anyway, that's the story."

"I don't think that's the story, Robert," Pamela said quite seriously. "I don't think that's the whole story by a long shot."

"I don't know what you mean, Pam."

"You've told me a charming tale about why the house looks the way it looks, Robert. As a matter of fact, all your stories are charming and funny and delightful. But I don't think the real story is why this house looks the way it does. I think the real story lies in why it's here at all. Why did you build it Robert? And why have you kept it empty all these years? What is it, Robert? What is the secret? What does the presence of this house really mean?"

"Couldn't you guess?" the old man asked.

"I've tried already," she said. "Did you build it for the woman that was in your life at one time? Is it a house you built for her?"

"Not at all." he chose his words carefully now. "The woman I loved would never have consented to live in a house. Not any house at all. Her roof was the sky, and she had to have a house that she could roll up and carry on her back when the buffalo moved. No, I built this house for you, Pamela."

"For me? But, Robert, you didn't even know me. How on earth…" Pamela was incredulous.

"No, I didn't know you. But I hoped I would. I hoped someday Colin would bring you, or someone like you, here. Someone that he felt a big true in his heart for."

"A big true?"

"Sorry, that's Crow talk. I still slip into it now and again. See, Pammy, Colin's all the family I've got. Nothin' ever worked out for me in that part of my life. Nothin' other than findin' Collie and makin' him my son. This is his house, Pammy. His and yours. Always has been. I'm just hopin' Colin hasn't waited too long."

"Too long?" she asked. "Too long for what?"

"Why grandbabies, that's what. Me and Garcia are lookin' to you to bring some grandbabies around here. This has been the ranch of old, witherin' men long enough."

Pamela's grin lit up her pretty face. Her sunny expression just delighted Old Robert.

"Knowing you men the way I do, I'd suppose you're goin' to want boys," she teased.

"Boys and girls both," he said. "What I want is for 'em to be fat and pink and look like their Mamma. And be strong and straight like their daddy." Now he withdrew a great iron key, nearly eight inches long, from his jacket pocket and handed it over to Pamela. The key was old and shiny with pocket wear.

"The house is yours, Pammy. I hope you'll move in it today, you and Little Buck that is. I hope you'll always stay here on the Spur. At least as long as Garcia and I are here. Raise your colts out at the Tall Horse, but raise your babies here with people that'll always love you. Just give us a chance… Colin and me and Garcia'll do all we can to make you as happy as your makin' us." When he raised his eyes to hers he saw that she was crying.

"I'll get my things together and open the house yet today. I guess… Old Robert… that we have a deal. I'll move into the house, but what about Colin?"

"He can move in after you're a married lady. Married to him, that is." She laughed uproariously.

"That's not what I meant. Does Colin know about this? Does he know about the big house?"

"You better tell him, Pammy. I never told anybody about my reasonin' for buildin' it before. But you'd better be the one what tells Colin about it. I don't think I can get through the story of Henry Hobart Richardson again anyhow." They were still laughing when Old Robert saw Walter the ranch top cook approaching

"Look, Pam. Here comes Walter. Now you'll see what runnin' a ranch is really all about."

"How do you mean?" Pam asked.

"Oh Walter always has some little something eatin' at him. I swear he can take the littlest problem in the world and turn it into a gun fight. But that's mostly what runnin' the Spur is about, makin' the people who work here feel their problems are important and that they are important. And of course, they really are. I'd hate for Walter to get so upset that he couldn't make a cobbler or fry a steak. He's a good cook, best we ever had at the Spur. There was a time when Garcia thought he could cook. Lord, that was sad! All them Mexican peppers he was feedin' us had the cowboy's drinkin' out of the waterin' troughs right alongside the horses."

They were both enjoying the humor of this visage when Walter approached. He was a heavy man, given to enjoying his own cooking. Pamela could see that his arms were corded with hard muscle from the continual wrangling of firewood. She knew that it was the constant demand for this cooking fuel that caused most ranch cooks to leave their jobs. To replace a man like Walter would, indeed, be hard.

"Excuse me, Mister Robert, Miss Pamela. Could I just have a word, Mister Robert?"

"Sure enough, Walter. What's the problem?"

"Well you know, Mister Robert, that I ain't one to complain. I just never complain. But all of a sudden there's stealin' goin' on at the cook shack and... Well, I don't like it at all. I just cain't abide workin' with fully growed men who goes slippin' around stealin' vittles like little children." Old Robert and Pamela were still enjoying their laughter, and Walter only commanded a bit of their attention.

Old Robert asked. "What is it bein' stole, Walter?"

"Well, it's like I say. They actin' like children. Mostly sweet stuff keeps turnin' up short or missin' Some maple sugar is gone and a jar of honey. I made eight loaves of bread last Saturday and two of them's gone. Bread and honey you know?

"I baked four sweet potato pies, and one of them's gone now, too. I hate to say it, but I think it may be that Bobby Baxter. He's a fool for sugar. He eats it with a spoon if I don't catch him. And I seen him feed that Rocket horse of his sweets, too."

"Damn Walter. I thought I'd heard some good funny stuff today. But I think a blue roan horse eatin' a sweet potato pie's got to be the funniest thing I ever heard of." Old Robert and Pamela were given over to peals of laughter. Walter saw he was getting nowhere.

"Well, all right, Mister Robert. I told you about it. If you don't care, I guess I don't neither." Walter was pouting now. Old Robert composed himself and said,

"Let me talk to Garcia about it, Walter. Don't worry about it. We'll look into it right away. And Walter, thanks for tellin' me."

It was later that day when Old Robert met with Juan Garcia.

"Juan, could you do a couple of things for me?"

"Si, Senor Robert. What can I do?"

"Well, have a little talk with the boys about stealin' pie and sugar down to the cook shack. They're just funnin' around I guess, but Walter's hotter'n hell about it. I'd hate to lose Walter. He's a pretty good cook."

"I'll see about it," Garcia said.

"And, Juan, I want you to gather up all the whiskey on the Spur and lock it in the store room."

"All right, Rob," Garcia agreed. "I'll just hold enough back for your toddy at night."

"Don't hold none back. Store it all. We've got a fine young woman here on the Spur now. And a nice young boy, too. It's time we stopped actin' like a couple of old curly wolves and started tryin' to make a family. No whiskey, Garcia. And ask the boys to clean up their talk, too. 'Specially, when Pammy's about." Garcia grinned widely.

"The Spur... She is changing, eh' Compadre?"

"Yeah. I guess it is." Old Robert looked toward the barn to identify the sounds he was hearing. It was the boy, Justin playing his harmonica. Giving an impromptu concert for a corral filled with longhorn cows. They stared balefully at the boy as he played. The longhorns rolled their huge soulful eyes and lowed mournfully at the strange sounds. Seeing the boy at play with the cattle brought a strange tug to the old man's heart.

"Yeah. It's a changin'. 'Bout time, too."

Chapter Thirty-one

The Deadly Stowaway

It was late that same evening that Colin sat wide-eyed and astonished as Pamela told him the secret of the big house. Colin had lived in the shadow of its walls for years, and not once had it occurred to him that Old Robert had really built it in the hopes that his only step-son would one day fill it with family.

"Why didn't he ever tell me about this?" Colin asked, very bewildered.

"Because he knew you would hurry out to please him, Colin." Pamela took her time answering, and her words were thoughtful. "He wanted the best for you, but he didn't want to order you to go out and find it. He also didn't want you to feel you had to find it to please him. He loves you very much, Collie. He loves us all."

"So, we're to move into the big house?" Colin asked Pamela.

"Well, I am," she said. "You, too, if you can be a good boy at the wedding and get all the words right." She gave Colin a sly smile that was more than a little suggestive.

"Well, how do you feel about it, Pammy? What about your plans for the Tall Horse?"

"The Tall Horse is young, Collie. It has a long time to live and grow. Old Robert and Garcia are not young. They've looked forward to this a long time. I'm not going to be the one who disappoints them. We'll live here for now, right in Old Robert's big house. It may be, Colin, that our children will be the ones who live on the Tall Horse."

"Little Buck," he said.

"Little Buck.... or one of our other children."

Colin looked at her somewhat surprised.

"You don't really think you can get out of giving me a couple of babies do you, Colin Trav?" she asked smiling. "You have a husbandly duty waiting for your full attention. I don't intend that you should get out of any of it. Not one minute."

For the next three days the big house was the scene of near frantic activity. Pamela had employed the services of Long John, Bobby Baxter and a roper called Alvin Twill to help her and Justin get the house in shape for living. There were windows to wash that carried the dust of decades. Carpets were beaten and freshened; linens and tableware were cleaned and made ready for service.

In some cases a few of the furnishings and trappings had been sitting idle too long to be salvaged. They were removed and carefully catalogued for reordering and replacing. Pamela had feared greatly for the tapestries and draperies, but it was revealed to her that they were of such high quality that they had amazing resilience.

They were dusty perhaps, but underneath there was the strong integrity of good materials that somehow seemed to reflect the very essence of the Spur. The spinet needed tuning badly, Pamela thought. After Long John removed the kangaroo rats' nest from its entrails, however, the old piano sounded surprisingly worthy. Pamela was taken completely by surprise by the old elegance displayed within the big house. Outside the mansion had an ungainly appearance. Mostly because it stood so alone and in such startling contrast with the flat emptiness of the surrounding prairie.

Now, as she stood in the foyer behind the great walnut double front doors, she felt her imagination being swept along by the medley of line and form that was the benchmark of master designers. She tried to imagine what Henry Hobart Richardson had felt as he married the rich chestnut paneling to the highly polished oaken floors. He had conceived the use of crystal prisms in the ceiling fixtures. They were delicately outlined by wonderfully ornate crown moldings. The sweeping staircase with its gentle curving turn and double-width treads was simply breath taking. Now for the first-time Pamela noticed the windows.

Each was carefully crafted with the perfectly round romanesque arch as its crown. Delicately fitted leaded glass acted as filters of light at their crests. She saw for the first time now that some window was always in tune with the orientation of the sun's prescribed arc across the Texas sky. Every hour of the day one window or another filled some part of the house with the beauty, swirl and texture that leaded and beveled glass is truly intended to provide. The entire scene was so mysterious and somehow so deeply moving, Pamela could not help but wonder, as she stood in this magnificent foyer, if perhaps some of the vision Richardson would use later in more important works might not have been born here.

All of this architectural symphony was highlighted by splendid wall-mounted sconces that would one day illuminate the mansion by gas light. That is to say when, and if, gas was to become available on the Spur. For now the sconces held fine beeswax candles scented with sandalwood. She decided the place had stood alone and silent far too long. Though it existed in the center of a wild and desolate prairie, here was beauty to be shared and celebrated. She didn't know how yet, but Pamela decided never again to lock up the big house.

Rather, she vowed to offer its unlikely and isolated beauty as a gift to friends and family and to those who would come to do commerce with the Broken Spur. It was the evening of the fourth day when Pamela and Justin moved, finally, into the legendary Trav mansion. Old Robert and Juan Garcia had planned a house warming party; and at eight o'clock Colin led in all the ladies and gentlemen from the Spur and nearby Travis.

There was Earl Halet's string band and Hattie Soames to sing in her lilting soprano for the evening's entertainment. Walter had outdone himself providing platters of barbecued beef, hominy and fried okra. He supplied stone crocks of fine beverages made by hand— birch beer, sassafrass tea and the tart pink tea made from the crimson seed pods of the red sumac. Of course, Walter's celebrated peach and apple cobblers were present as expected.

Old Robert permitted Garcia to bring a few bottles of the remaining Primble whiskey from the store house as well as some fine homemade Mexican wine manufactured from the wild scuppernong grape to aid the festivities. The prairie was ablaze with the spilt light of dozens of oil lamps and bee's wax candles illuminating, at last, the mysterious house. The music and laughter echoed through the night, and the revelry could be heard far down the Canadian.

"I wish Henry Hobart Richardson could see his house tonight, Garcia," Old Robert said loudly over the din of the party.

"I think he's dead," Garcia answered.

"Well, by God, the Spur ain't dead!" Old Robert roared in delight. "Just look, Garcia... Just look at all the life."

In truth, the Broken Spur had sprung to life this very evening. It had for decades been the home of men and horses and cattle and business. Tonight, the Spur was a laughing beautiful woman dancing along the banks of the Canadian River. She was bright and gay and filled with music. The appearance of the Spur this night gave pleasure to all who saw her. All save one....

From the hay loft of the barn on the west side of the house just fifty yards from all the gaiety, the narrow eyes of Beaver Parker observed the goings on in the house below him. Indeed, he had watched the house now for more than six days. He had very often seen Pamela in the company of the old man or Garcia whom hw called the "greaser." Once her son had actually come into the barn searching out a bridle. Beaver had nearly killed him right then, but he had held himself in check. It just wasn't time yet. And besides, he wanted the woman first. He might only be able to kill one. It had to be her.

He scooped away the little pile of garbage from his path so he could move closer to the high window. There were the remains of several loaves of bread mixed in with empty honey pots and pie pans. Beaver had eaten well of stolen delicacies while he reconnoitered his target. As he stared from the darkness now at the lighted house so filled with joy, his eyes became narrow slits of hate. For six days he had lain in wait, his lust and hate festering as an angry boil.

When will they ever leave her alone? he wanted to know. He wondered how long it would be after this party before she would be alone. He sensed this would at last be the night. His body ached terribly for her.

"The minute they leave you alone, you bitch, I'm gonna have you," he whispered to himself. "I'm gonna have you. It's been a long chase…But it won't be long now."

The lamplight spilling from the big house glinted on the knife blade he held in front of him. He turned the knife over in his hand, letting the blade catch the light as though he were showing it to Pamela Carstin. The hunting knife, razor keen, and with it's eight-inch curved blade made him feel all powerful. His confidence, though, was more than bolstered by the weight of the solid object tucked tightly into his waistband at the small of his back.

On a day when all the Spur hands had been away at work, Beaver had crept from the barn and slipped deftly into the bunkhouse he knew Colin occupied. After a few minutes of searching he found the little cache chest Colin used to store special and private items.

He found a silver pen knife, one of the new-fangled watches that you could strap to a wrist, and a pair of fancy dress spurs. Then he saw it– the one particular article that caused his eyes to gleam with delight. Afraid of detection should he linger, he grabbed it quickly and tucked it under his shirt. He swiftly pushed the chest back into its original position. Now in a low crouch, he moved rapidly back to the cover of the barn. He could hardly wait to examine his prize more closely. In addition to his hunting knife, Beaver Parker was now in possession of Henry Brooker's Smith and Wesson, 44-caliber American model pistol. The Rangerin' gun.

Chapter Thirty-two

Beaver's Return

The party had ended and Pamela was gloriously tired. Alone now in her bedroom high in the front of the big house, she stood in front of the tall double windows and looked out at the night. She felt warm. She had danced with Colin and talked to all his friends. She had eaten and laughed with Old Robert and danced some more with Juan Garcia. She felt as if she were still lightly perspiring. She blew out the lamp and stepped back from the window and began to remove her clothing. Completely undressed now, she moved to the nightstand, navigating herself by the faint starlight that fell into the room.

From a ceramic Delft pitcher, she poured water into a matching basin. Dipping a washcloth in the basin, she began to sponge herself. The cool water along with the light zephyr from the window began to cool her at once, and she felt dreamy and comfortable. The house was quiet, and she was alone. Even Justin had gone back to the bunkhouse with the Spur riders he had become so attached too. She welcomed the solitude. It had been days since she had enjoyed a single moment to herself.

Standing well back and to the side of the window so that her nudity could not be seen, she stretched her limbs luxuriously. She enjoyed the gentle songs of a thousand crickets wafting through the open panes. The coolness of the night air on her body was fine and sensual. She found herself longing for Colin. It had been quite a night. First was the food. Everyone had agreed that Walter was the king of ranch cooks, and this left Walter beaming. The music was the wonderful, simplistic cowboy melodies of the plains and trail drives mixed lightly with Irish shanty and Scottish dirge.

One of the highlights of the evening was when her son, Justin, had stood in front of the little band and played Red River Valley on the silver harmonica he had been given by Colin. Nothing though had been quite as exciting as Colin moving about the room and telling his friends that he and Pamela were to be married just as soon as it could be arranged. It seemed impossible that she could ever love anyone with the intensity she felt for her old cowboy. She reminded herself not to think of Colin as old, and at the same time a little pang of guilt struck her. She felt badly that she should be so happy and poor Alex was dead. She quickly dismissed the thought.

It was a useless and futile one. Things had happened that no one could have foreseen nor avoided. Alex was dead and she was here. That was fate and not her doings. She allowed fine thoughts of Colin to invade her mind and drive out any unpleasantness. Dancing with her earlier, Colin had whispered in her ear that after the last guest had departed that he would gladly slip out of the bunk house and come back here to be alone with her. She ached for him so. It had been a long while since they had enjoyed any privacy.

She knew they both missed immensely that wonderful and sensual intimacy they had discovered in the wooded grove along the trail. Pamela very much would have liked to be alone with Colin this special night. She whispered back to him though that they could not. Old Robert, she felt, wanted them to be married before sharing this house in that special way. It would be only a little longer she reasoned, and so she discouraged a disappointed Colin even though she wanted him every bit as badly. They had, she realized, never been together in a real bed but had only shared those unique moments in bedrolls along the trail.

Now she heard a faint noise that jarred her from her thoughts. She recognized the sound at once. While moving herself into the big house she discovered the third step on the main stair had a fearful squeak. She had vowed to make its repair one of her first maintenance duties. It was this loud creak that she heard now.

It's Colin, she thought. He's decided to come to be with me anyway. She smiled to herself and was really rather pleased with this turn of events. She had to admit she missed him terribly this evening, and if he had decided to try a little harder to see her, well, that was really pretty romantic. And very nice. She grabbed up a light robe from the chifforobe and prepared to make him welcome in the dark room.

Beaver cursed softly when the stair under his foot made the atrocious noise. It at once startled and angered him. He could not afford to be discovered this close to his target. He had gone through a living hell to bring himself to this position, and he could not stand the thought of a mistake He had barely survived the walk from the Primble farm to the Broken Spur. He might never have made it had he not been so fueled by the Primble killings. It was this bloodletting and the shootings of Pamela's husband and those at the Starrett meeting. that kept him forging ahead. He had indeed paid a price to be here, and now the woman was nearly in his grip.

"God damn sum'bitch stair," he muttered under his breath.

When Pamela spoke from the darkness, it startled him again. This time more severely, and he nearly wet himself again.

"Colin? Is that you?" Pamela said softly.

Beaver's eyes had been fixed on the squeaking stair though he couldn't see it in the darkness. Now at her voice, he jerked his head up and saw her silhouetted at the top of the stair. The mixture of moon and starlight from the window behind her outlined her body through the nearly transparent robe. Her appearance of near nakedness took Beaver's breath away.

"Is that you, Collie?" she repeated. Beaver Parker moaned a low indistinguishable sound as an answer.

"Mmmm, Hmmm," he managed.

"Oh, Colin," she said. "You're being a terribly naughty boy."

Beaver could sense that she was smiling. Through the faint glow of starlight, he saw her move from the stair back to an open doorway. A bit of light illuminated her body framed in the door ever so slightly. The shape of her, back lighted like this, made him lick his lips. He dug his nails into his palms, and beads of perspiration dotted his upper lip.

"Well, come on up if you must. Be quiet, though," she said. Beaver silently began to ascend the stair toward her. He held the knife low at his side and tested its edge against the ball of his thumb. The knife was ready and so was he.

Colin Trav turned over in his bunk for the fifth time in less than twenty minutes. He was visualizing Pamela alone in the big house. He pictured her warm and sleepy in the big four-poster bed.

How fine it would be to be with her there, he thought nearly aloud. The bunkhouse was filled with the soft snores of his riding buddies, and somewhere in the darkness a cowboy coughed softly. Colin thought about Pam with every breath. He was remembering those few nights on the trail when they had shared his, or her, bedroll. The most disconcerting thing about these thoughts for Colin was the single fact that he had never once felt this way about another woman. Not ever. At last, unable to put it off any longer, he slipped from his bunk, slid into his trousers and a shirt. He moved quietly on bare feet to the door of the bunkhouse.

"Goin' out, Colin?" A voice from the dark side of the bunkhouse startled him.

"Privy," he muttered, trying to compose himself after so rudely being discovered.

"Remember where the outhouse is?" The voice in the dark asked. A little sly laughter was scattered about the bunkhouse. Not answering, Colin stepped through the bunk house door and barefoot into the night.

To hell with them, he thought; but he didn't mean it. Those cowboys were the very best friends he had in the world. It was just that they knew him pretty well.

They sure know what's on my mind, he thought. Easing up he chuckled a little and moved off through the night towards the big house. And, hopefully, Pamela.

Beaver had now reached the top of the stair. He walked the few steps to the open door and peered into the dim bedroom. Pamela stood in front of the tall windows and star light from behind her accentuated every line of her form. Beaver began now to move nearer her.

Pamela said, "I'll light a match so you can see." Before Beaver could protest, she had struck the big blue tip against the lamp scratcher. Its yellow flare probed the darkness. Although Beaver's face was still somewhat in the shadows, she saw at once that it was not Colin.

Stunned, her thoughts began to race uncontrollably. The match glow continued from her frozen hand, and Beaver walked a step closer now. She saw his face plainly. The blonde hair hung in oily ropes into his eyes. The acne had made his face red and angry. He grinned evilly, showing large teeth the color of late summer grass.

My God, she thought. It's the boy that was with Amos Younger... It's the boy that shot Alex.

She gasped when she realized, for the first time, that it was not Amos younger who had done the actual shooting. Rather, it was this boy right in front if her. She saw it clearly now.

Here was the shooter and now she knew it. She had hidden her face that night it was true, but thoughts came flooding back now. She remembered it was the gunfire that had frightened her and made her look away. Amos Younger had not killed Alex. Here was the killer. So, close she could smell his foul breath.

He reached for her, and she screamed as loudly as she could, though her throat was nearly closed in fright. She spun away and leaped onto the bed. Making one bounce, she propelled herself off the other side of the bed and ran headlong for the still opened door.

"Colin! Colin!" she cried as she raced for the stairs. Beaver was startled by her sudden movements. She had reacted far faster that he had imagined she could. She was at the door before he recovered from his surprise, but now he raced after her; hoping to grab her before she reached the stair. He was a second too late.

Terrified now, Pamela ran faster than she ever dreamed she could. She was half way down the stair now. She felt she could outrun her attacker to the front door. Then her bare foot hit a smooth place on the stair and she was suddenly floating through the air. The events happening to her seemed dreamlike. It seemed as if she was in the air a long time.

Then she fell on the stair with a numbing thud. Dazed and groggy now, she was just lucid enough to realize she was lying on her back. She was head down on the stair, and the boy with the dirty blonde hair had her by the ankle. She was watching with her head hanging upside down, as Colin burst through the front door. She heard him cry out in anguish as he saw that she was being attacked.

Dazed and disoriented, with her head in this upside-down position, she saw that Colin was racing headlong without care to her aid. She almost felt safe for a moment, but then she heard the roar of the pistol.

The sound was deafening and terrifying. She saw the bright flash from its muzzle streak scant inches over her face. Still watching, with her head hanging back and down, she saw the big .44 slug smack into Colin's belly.

The weight of the heavy bullet threw him backwards like a rag doll. He went down, end over end, falling down the three or four stairs he had managed to climb. She screamed again, now realizing that Colin had been shot. And now Beaver had her. He sat astride her waist brandishing the knife. She could see it so plainly she could identify the curved blade... The edge of the stairs cut deeply into her back and that pain was fearful. The man sitting on her ripped away the front of the light robe and touched her bare breast with the needle point of the knife.

"You, bitch," she heard the face say. "You aint caused me nothin' 'cept trouble and I'm killin' you right now." Pamela looked on in horror as the boy raised the knife above his head. She tried to brace herself for what was to come. She squinted her eyes, preparing for the pain. She thought of Colin and her son, Justin....Then came the big boom. An explosion so profound that she could feel the stairs vibrate under her body. A bright stream of fire plowed into the boy's face with such force that it threw him backwards and up the stairs two or three steps. Pamela felt small hot grains of something falling from the air and on to her face and bared chest.

The acrid smell of old black gunpowder smoke was overwhelming in the close stairwell. With the weight of the boy off her, she swung her feet around and came to a sitting position on the stair. She saw that she was facing Old Robert. His eyes were intent and narrowed; his ancient smoking Hawken Rifle in hand.

"Help, Collie," she said. "Help, Colin." And a merciful blackness enfolded her into a velvet fog.

Chapter Thirty-three

===

Pamela's Letter
1889

Pamela Trav
Broken Spur Ranch
Travis Texas

October 5th 1889

Henry and Mattie Brooker
General Delivery
Murphy Flats Kansas

Dear Henry and Mattie:

I'm sorry I have been so remiss in writing you. You were such good friends when I was stranded at Murphy Flats and I can certainly never repay you for all your kindness.

I wanted to tell you that I am now a married lady again, this time to Colin Trav. Colin had a bad time recently and was shot by an intruder. He has at last recovered completely and is his old self. It's still to hard for me to talk much about that night, and I promise I'll tell you all the details soon. To ease your minds for now just let me say that we are well and healthy.

It could have been a disastrous night except for the fact that old frontiersmen and Indian fighters are notoriously light sleepers. Old Robert heard our commotions and our plight. He came at once with his buffalo rifle and settled it. Robert may be showing his age somewhat, but I can tell you for sure that he is still the watchful eagle of the Canadian River.

I can't imagine what makes some men as evil as they are. When I asked Old Robert about that, he told me that there are some men who are just not fit to live. I promise to tell you more of this encounter when I am better able.

I hope you won't think too ill of me for marrying so soon after the death of my husband, Alex. Sometimes I feel badly about it myself; but to tell you the truth, it just seems like everything here in the west moves so much faster. It is as if the land knows it has been asleep too long and is trying to wake up all at once. When I said that to Old Robert, he smiled and said it was a "Big True". Whatever that means.

Chester Crawford and Chinagirl are building a house on the Tall Horse Ranch, which is the name of the horse ranch we are establishing with the stallions and mares that Alex and I brought from Kentucky. You'll be pleased to know that three of my mares are now in foal, all bred to the best wild range stallions from the Broken Spur. I must say our tall horses look exciting and handsome as they walk about in the pastures next to the Texas mustangs. The colts from these two fine breeds just might change the looks of Texas horses for a long time to come.

Old Robert and Little Buck (a new name for my son, Justin, and the same name Colin calls his favorite horse.) are the best of friends and spend most days riding about the ranch in the Studebaker. We are bringing a tutor to the ranch for Little Buck and hope in the spring to start a school in Travis.

Little Buck has learned to play the spinet piano with no teacher. He sure is inclined musically. About every evening Old Robert comes to sit with us, and he always has Justin play for him. Justin always plays Red River Valley and Blue Bells of Scotland, and Old Robert always cries.

Sometimes I wish Old Robert would run for President of the country. I'll tell you, folks, I would sure vote for him. To tell the truth I think it would be a better world if we just all did as Robert said and quit thinking for ourselves anyway. He is so wise and so honest. When I suggested that to him recently, he just laughed and said that he doubted that anybody else felt that way. Then he asked if I had been drinking the scuppernong...

Mattie, it'll be Christmas soon; and I think I've got my present early this year. It's a little early to be sure, but I think that I am with child. Colin and I have agreed that, if it's a boy, we'll name him Robert Henry, after two very good men that we know. Robert Trav and Henry Brooker. We intend to use the name Juan Garcia, too, just as soon as we can.

I wanted to tell you that Colin had asked Justin if he'd like Colin to formally adopt him. I remember a long time ago when Justin was alone and afraid he had asked Colin to become his father. I was so proud of my son when he told Colin he'd always love him but he wanted to keep the name Carstin out of respect for Alex. I'll tell you true, Mattie, I was moved to tears. I was so proud of him, and Colin was, too. If we ever get around to obtaining a proper deed to the Tall Horse, it will be a partnership of Trav and Carstin. Alex would have liked that a lot.

Well, I'd better close this letter now. Colin and I send our love. Please don't forget your Texas friends, and let's plan a visit soon. Kiss your children for me, and my Father said to tell you "hello." He and Momma are still in Illinois, but he has admitted that the pull of Texas is starting to give him an itch. We'll see

Sincerely,
Pamela Trav

Chapter Thirty-four

Colin's Letter
1889

Colin Trav
Broken Spur Ranch
Travis Texas

Nov.4th 1889

Mister Trent Markley
Markley Cattle Company
Union Stockyards
Dodge City Kansas

Dear Trent:

This letter introduces Bobby Baxter, our new trail boss. I wont be trailing cattle to Dodge any more, Trent. It's because I have a wife and a son now and another child on the way. I've been on the trail too long now, and so I'm putting our herds into the capable hands of this young man.

Baxter has never been in a big town before, and so I hope you'll see to him. Maybe you can keep him away from Squirrel Tooth Alice and the Birdcage, but I doubt it. I've warned him about packing a gun in Dodge, but maybe you ought to caution him, too. We know where that can lead.

Baxter is fully authorized to buy and sell for the Spur, and his signature is as good as mine. I hope you and he can get along as well as you and I have over the years.

Though I am very much against it, I expect you will see Justin, too. He and Baxter are inseparable. I believe he's too young for the trail, but then I started even younger than he will be by next round up. Watch them both for me, Trent. They are important people here at the Spur.

Trent, I'd be obliged if you would send a man or two down to the Primble place on Caney Creek and see that all there is in order. Check on the graves and just generally tidy up. It's been a long while now and the

350

law men should be all through with their investigations. Although I can't imagine anyone did very much investigating considering the victims were a white woman married to a man of color and two mulatto children. They were dear to those of us at the Spur, but I expect they amounted to very little elsewhere. Juan Garcia was the only one who saw trouble ahead for Abe and Annie. The rest of us missed it completely. I can only wish we had done better in protecting them. They needed us a lot more than we knew.

You can put any expenses you incur on the Spur accounts. Maybe just sell everything that's fit to sell or see if you can find the rightful heirs. Might be that Henry Brooker can help you out on this. If you can't find anyone– and I don't think you will– I think you ought to use the money to help some church or school. I think Abe and Annie would like that. I'll always miss those fine and gentle people.

I don't know how long we'll drive cattle to Dodge as they are talking about bringing the rail head all the way down here to Travis. If they do, Trent, we hope you'll move down here, too. We could certainly use a man who knows the cattle business the way you do. By the way, Trent, do you know what they call a single set of railroad tracks brought into a new area? They call it a spur. Isn't that something?

Old Robert and Garcia send their best. Try to help Baxter get good prices and low shrink.

Your Friend
Colin Trav.

Chapter Thirty-five

The Broken Spur
1891

"Pam," Colin said. He was sitting on the edge of their big four poster bed watching her sit at the mirror and brush out the sun-colored hair he liked so much.

"Today I was looking through the nightstand drawer and found this."

She turned and saw he was holding Henry Brooker's pistol, the .44 that Beaver Parker had shot him in the belly with on the night Parker had been killed.

"One of these days I've got to get this gun back to Henry. It's his old Rangerin' gun you know." He turned it thoughtfully in his hands. It's once gleaming nickel finish now displayed the soft luster of hard service. Its ivory grips were checked and yellowed with age.

"It's guns like this one that has made Texas, Pam. Hawken rifles... these kinds of guns... and men like Old Robert, Garcia, and Henry Brooker."

"Henry's contributing a lot more to the west right now than he ever has before, Colin." Pamela said.

"Lord, Pam..." Colin was perplexed and confused at Pamela's statement. "Henry used to be a Ranger. He chased the Kiowa and Quanah Parker... made Texas safe from the outlaw gangs. He ain't a Ranger no more. Hell, he's just a storekeep now."

"That's right, Collie. He's just a storekeeper... And a husband... And a father... And a good man. And he's doing the one thing Texas and the whole west needs more than anything else in the world, Colin."

"What are you talkin' about, Pam? Just what's Henry doin' that's so all-fired special? So danged important?" Colin wanted to know.

"Well," Pamela started, "I got a letter from Mattie yesterday, and she's just about ready have another new baby. I'll tell you what Henry Brooker's doing that's so important, Colin: He's minding the store."

About the Author

Born and raised in Southern Indiana, Gary Harmon's' young life was filled with daily handling of horses and cattle. His family operated a large stockyard where the trading, buying and selling of livestock were his earliest memories. After being discharged from the U.S. Army, he was employed as a buyer of hogs, cattle, and occasionally sheep for one of the nation's major meat packing companies of that time. A second career in real estate brought about a love for historic houses and the classic architecture of eons long gone.

It was while working on the great central livestock markets though as well as the diminutive buying stations and open outcry auction markets of Kansas, Indiana, Ohio, Illinois, and Kentucky that Gary first began to appreciate the multitude of stories, legends, folktales and bald faced lies that were to be heard being swapped back and forth between the old-time traders that made up the livestock industries cadre. These were men who had spent decades listening to and retelling tales of adventure. These colorful folktales came from breeders, farmers and cowboys, from hard working truckers and no account drunks. The author simply could not get enough of this colorful repartee nor could he wait to repeat it.

These hardy outdoorsmen and their colorful tales have contributed mightily to the tales of *The Broken Spur*. While exploring the fable of the Spur the reader would do well to remember the story was assembled and pieced together from factual and not so factual tales told in scale houses, feed lots, auction barns, trucking yards and bawdy stockyard taverns. Sharp eyed traders, drovers, and truck drivers all have contributed mightily in creating *The Broken Spur*, a yarn of truth and fiction.